THE RAINBOW VIRUS

YOUNG ADULT EDITION

THE RAINBOW VIRUS

YOUNG ADULT EDITION

DENNIS MEREDITH

Glyphus

To Meredith

PROLOGUE

Infection of the first victim began with a sharp stab of metal against flesh. The hypodermic needle plunged into his arm, its razor-sharp point slicing into the outer skin and through the living tissue below. The steel cylinder thrust downward, leaving a trail of torn and punctured cells. It sliced through the layer of fat, rupturing glistening fat cells. It slashed through thin webs of capillaries and nicked spidery nerve cells, launching electrical alarms of pain toward the victim's brain.

Finally, the needle reached the pliant surface of the arm's major blood vessel and lanced through its rubbery membrane into the pulsing blood flow. The metal invader's tip then delivered a gush of liquid into the vessel.

That injection launched billions of viruses—precisely engineered microscopic spheres—into the victim's bloodstream. Those viruses carried a cargo of pirate genes, programmed to hijack normal cells, transforming the cells' biological function and forcing them to reproduce more of the mutant virus to relentlessly spread the infection.

These viruses did not randomly attack. Biological missiles, they were programmed to target only specific cells. Their surface was festooned with the spikes of homing molecules that would link them to only one kind of cell—like a key that fits only one lock.

As the viruses coursed throughout the bloodstream and into narrow capillaries, they began to find those targets—pigmented brownish cells near the skin surface. The viruses' targeting molecules clutched the brown cells, fusing with them and injecting the viruses' genetic cargo. Those pirate genes slithered quickly into the cell nucleus, commandeering its genetic machinery, launching their biological occupation of the unsuspecting man's body.

CHAPTER 1

The emergency room triage nurse had no inkling that the first victim would abruptly shatter the early morning quiet. She paused in filling out routine forms and sighed, letting the soft fog of drowsiness envelop her for the moment. She was deeply fatigued after a hectic night. Besides the steady stream of sick and injured, she'd had to handle two particularly nerve-wracking cases: A little boy fell out of an upper bunk and gashed open his forehead. Both child and mother had come in screaming maniacally. She'd almost had to have the mother restrained. The ER doc used a dab of superglue to close the wound of the frantic, bleeding boy, and the mother took a Valium to calm herself down. Just after that a drunken, cursing man burst through the door dragging a bleeding foot and brandishing a shotgun. He'd tried to shoot a barking dog but tripped in the dark and blasted his own foot. She had been trapped behind the desk while the security guard persuaded him to give up the gun. The doc had picked birdshot out of the bellowing man for an hour.

Now thankfully, the ER had settled into a quiet lull. The overnight trauma emergencies had ceased, and the early-morning heart attacks hadn't begun yet. The nurse's hands still hovered over the computer keyboard, but they settled in slow-motion toward the desk. As her eyes slowly closed, her head nodded forward and her chubby neck sank slightly into the collar of her pink smock, enlarging the soft folds of flesh that draped beneath her chin. Her breath came in steady somnolent puffs.

The metallic clang of a dropped instrument tray shattered the silence, startling her to woozy alertness. She managed to focus on a middle-aged man who had rushed up to her desk. His pear-shaped body was barely covered by a thin, worn plaid bathrobe. His sparse, disheveled hair stuck crazily up from his bulbous head. His jowly unshaven face sagged with sleep and age.

And that face was blue! A solid, bright blue that brought an involuntary grunt of utter surprise from the nurse.

His chest, belly and legs showed the same unrelenting blue as his face and hands.

He stared at her wide-eyed, pleadingly. His mouth opened twice, as if to say something. He released the robe, holding his palms up, but then dropped them to his sides. Then his eyes rolled back in his head, and he collapsed with an alarming thud, his skinny blue legs splayed out on the floor.

The nurse recovered enough to bark, "Patient in acute distress!" to the emergency room staff. She scurried around the desk to find the man's eyes opening as she knelt down. "Sir, are you having trouble breathing? Are you having chest pains?"

"No, uhhhh, I'm . . ." But before he could finish, a doctor and another nurse rushed up. They took one surprised look at the man, and one puzzled glance at each other. Then the doctor crouched at his side. The nurse, a sturdy middle-aged woman in a uniform slightly limp from the night's labors, paused to shout back for a gurney, which an orderly brought immediately. The triage nurse stood back, marveling at the blueness of the man. She was now thoroughly awake.

With brisk efficiency, the doctor, the sturdy nurse, and the emergency tech hoisted the man onto the gurney.

"Sir, can you breathe?" asked the doctor as he placed his stethoscope on the hairy blue chest, listening to the man's heart as they rushed the gurney through the fluorescent-lit emergency department and swerved it into the last treatment cubicle on the left. The open cubicle contained a bed and a full complement of emergency paraphernalia—heart monitor, blood pressure monitor, oxygen source and glass-fronted cabinets filled with medical supplies. They lifted the man onto the bed and wheeled the gurney away.

"Well, yeah, I'm okay," the man answered groggily. "I'm just—"

"Are you having chest pains?"

"No, I . . . just woke up and I was blue." His brown eyes showed rising fear. A sheen of sweat formed on his blue upper lip.

"You just woke up? You were asleep, or did you faint?"

"I was asleep. I fainted just now. I'm scared."

"Well, sir, you just relax. We'll find out what's wrong."

"What's wrong is I'm *blue*," he mumbled. "Am I okay?"

The doctor, a slim man in his thirties wearing baggy light green scrubs, issued orders to the sturdy nurse, as another short dark-haired nurse joined them. Again, he placed his stethoscope on the man's chest and listened intently as the sturdy nurse tore the paper covers off adhesive electrodes and fastened them to the man's chest. Shortly, the heart monitor added its reassuring metronomic beep to the bustle of the room.

"Heart sounds okay. Lungs are clear," said the doctor quietly. He stared at the monitor screen, its luminescent dot tracing a reassuringly regular pattern of peaks and valleys across the small screen. "Heart looks okay." He opened the man's mouth.

"Lug, I'g jus' glue," gurgled the man past the doctor's tongue depressor, as he checked the man's airway for obstruction. Satisfied that the way was clear, he stood back.

"Sir, we've got to do these tests to find out. Just relax," said the doctor, as the sturdy nurse slipped an oxygen tube under his nose.

The dark-haired nurse deftly slid the needle of an IV catheter into the back of his hand, knitting her dark brows at the difficulty of finding the blue vein against the blue skin. Her brows relaxed as she satisfied herself that she hit the vein and taped the catheter into place.

Inserting another needle into his arm, the dark-haired nurse drew vials of rich dark-red blood and handed them out the door for testing.

The team was cool, efficient . . . and increasingly puzzled.

"Stick on a pulsox," said the doctor, but the dark-haired nurse was already slipping the plastic pincer of a pulsoximeter over the man's fingertip and scrutinizing the readings from a small box to which it was attached.

"Blood oxygen is okay," she said.

The doctor continued to stare at the cardiac monitor, as if his concentration would force the tan box to give up secrets to the man's condition. He transferred the intense gaze to the patient, who looked back, trying to read something in the thin face besides a practiced impassiveness.

The doctor picked up the patient's hand and examined it closely, front and back. He scrutinized the face and neck, and worked his way down to the chest, stopping at moles, wrinkles, and the many interesting hair follicles. Then he proceeded to the bony middle-aged legs and the wide ungainly feet.

"Yup, sir, you are definitely blue all over," he announced. "Y'know, this doesn't look like a cyanotic pattern to me. His face is blue, his chest is blue." The doctor looked toward the man's waist. "He's all blue. If he was cyanotic, just his extremities would be blue. And look at this." The sturdy nurse stepped dutifully forward, and the dark-haired nurse craned to look over her shoulder. "The bottoms of the feet are lighter. And up here . . ." he took one of the man's hands, ". . . the palms are lighter. Maybe this is some kind of pigment disorder. Now, you're sure blood gases are okay?"

"Yeah, and the arterial blood's nice and red," said the dark-haired nurse, a lilt of puzzlement in her voice.

"Also, look at the blue," he instructed the nurses. They did so. "Something interesting here. This isn't a cyanotic *shade* of blue, either. This isn't a blue from lack of oxygen. This is another blue."

"Yeah, yeah, now that you mention it . . ." said the dark-haired nurse. Indeed, the blue was a pure blue, a rich simple blue that needed no description other than blue. It was a little darker than bluebonnets, a little lighter than blue jeans. But blue was a sufficient descriptor.

"What's your name?" asked the doctor.

"Malcolm Harding."

"Mr. Harding, I'm Doctor Lesser. You breathing okay?"

"Yeah, doc. What do I got? Why'm I blue?"

"Well we don't know, but we're sure going to find out. How old are you?"

"Forty-five."

"What's today?"

"Tuesday. I don't know the date."

"It's the fourteenth," said Lesser.

"The fifteenth," corrected the sturdy nurse.

"Oh. Right," said Lesser. Lesser went on to quiz Harding about the president and the town he was in. He concluded that Harding was lucid, or at least as lucid as a man could be who had just changed color.

"Tell me how did this come on?" asked Lesser. He directed Harding to sit up and tapped his blue knees and elbows with a little rubber hammer, eliciting the appropriate subtle twitches that revealed healthy reflexes.

"Well, last night when I went to bed, I looked kind of funny. Y'know maybe a little bluish. But I thought it was the light or something. I was tired. Then I got up this mornin', I was blue . . . all over!"

A knowing smile dawned on the doctor's face. "Mr. Harding, what drugs are you on?"

"Well, Tylenol, vitamins, that's about it."

"No colloidal silver? For a rash, maybe? You know, that turns skin blue." He looked up triumphantly at the nurse.

"Gee, no, nothing like that. Tylenol and vitamins. One-a-Day. Could vitamins do it?"

The doctor's triumphant smile faded back into impassive seriousness. "Hmm. No. Well, Mr. Harding, it looks to me like you don't have anything immediately dangerous. You fainted because you were scared, right?"

"Yeah, my dad died when he was my age. Heart attack. Wouldn't you be?"

"Sure would," smiled Lesser. "But your heart sounds perfectly normal. As far as we can tell, it's just your skin. So let's see if we can settle your mind by finding out what's going on."

"Yeah, sure, thanks." The steady beep on the heart monitor began to slow slightly, as Harding relaxed.

"Let's do a chest x-ray while we're waiting for the blood tests. Get Mr. Harding to give us a urine sample, and tell 'em to do a drug screen," he told the sturdy nurse.

"What do we call this?" asked the sturdy nurse, scanning the coding sheet. "You know the x-ray techs. Got to have a good reason for the chest film."

"Well, fiddle . . ." The doctor scratched his head. "I guess we call it 'pigmentation dermatopathia of unknown origin.' Colored skin. But also add 'possible pulmonary involvement.' That ought to keep them happy."

"Yeah, that'll do," said the sturdy nurse. She helped a shaky Harding to the bathroom, where he dutifully delivered a stream of normally colored urine into a clear plastic cup. Feeling reassured by the outcome, he sat gratefully down in a wheelchair brought by an orderly, who took him out for a chest x-ray, past the nursing station. The sturdy nurse was intently filling out the forms, and the dark-haired nurse was edging toward a nearby ward to tell her friends what she'd seen. By the time he arrived back in the treatment room, Dr. Lesser was leaning against the door jamb, leafing through papers on a clipboard.

"Blood chemistry's okay," he said, pursing his lips in concentration. "Liver's okay, kidneys look okay . . . white blood count's up just a bit. But not much, really. No drugs, no methanol in the urine." He paused and looked up. "Mr. Harding, are you sure you're not taking any other medication?"

"No, I just take Tylenol. And I got allergies."

"Oh. You take allergy shots?"

"Yeah, one about a week ago."

"Oh." Lesser was disappointed. An allergic reaction to a shot would have come much quicker. But it was something at least, and he noted it on the chart.

"Well, sir, let's admit you to the hospital so we can get to the bottom of this. I think it's time we get some specialists in here." Lesser paged chief of staff, Lori Meadows. This was big enough to get her involved. After fifteen minutes, a kind of tension came rolling down the hall like a psychic wave. Such tension always heralded the approach of Lori Meadows. Doctors, nurses, orderlies, and even patients always seemed to snap to some form of attention, whether sitting, standing, leaning or prone on stretchers. The petite, middle-aged woman strode into view wearing an ever-crisp lab coat, light brown hair efficiently wrapped into a tight bun and an utter refusal to tolerate the presence of any disease whatsoever in her patients. Disease represented disorder, chaos in the elegant perfection that she demanded of the functioning human body. Rumor had it that she had once cured a vicious case of pneumonia by bullying the germs out of her patient.

As Lesser braced himself, he knew she would be extremely displeased at this unknown pathological interloper in her hospital. She cocked her head suspiciously at Lesser as he gave his briefing in the hall, prepared to pounce on the slightest clue to solve the hated mystery.

Then she entered Harding's room, peering at him as if dissecting him with her eyes. But she was surprisingly gentle as she examined him, questioned him, and studied his chart. Every patient of hers was an innocent victim of whatever demon had visited itself upon him. Satisfied that all possible information had been taken in, she and Lesser stepped into the hallway of the emergency department.

"Okay, now," she said, wrinkling her brow in irate puzzlement and reciting the results out loud to help her reveal the villain. "His examination's normal. EKG normal, chest x-ray normal . . . blood gases, hematocrit, prothrombin time, blood urea nitrogen, calcium, phosphorus, creatinine, bilirubin . . . all normal. His blood pH is okay?" Lesser nodded. "But white cell count's up, eh?"

"Yeah, a little, but not much."

"Soooooo, we've got no congestive heart failure, no congenital heart disease, no Raynaud's disease, no polyarteritis nodosa, no Buerger's disease, no scleroderma, no dermatomyositis, no systemic lupus erythematosus, no arteriosclerosis, no polycythemia, no obliterative vascular disease, no syringomyelia, no arteriovenus aneurysm, no myxedema, and no poisoning." She stared at Lesser, challenging him to think of another possibility.

"Doesn't look like it," admitted Lesser. "And he promised us he didn't dye himself blue. Didn't take colloidal silver."

"So, like you first said, we've got pigmentation dermatopathia of unknown origin. That's nada." She shook her head at the enigma and stalked off to plunder the medical library, ordering that Harding be admitted.

By nine the next morning, Harding's small room in La Vista Community Hospital was crowded with specialists and their egos, summoned by Meadows. Each had arrived smiling, confident. Each had interviewed Harding, taken notes, consulted memories, checked reference works. The smiles slowly faded, replaced by wrinkled brows, distracted peering at the ceiling in puzzlement. Harding was at first stoic, a little embarrassed. As the morning wore on, he lay stolidly in his bed, his stomach growling, becoming more frustrated. Besides the endless blood and urine samples he'd given, he grew weary of the repeated questions about his work as a lumber salesman (no exposure to chemicals), his travels (to Los Angeles recently), his medicines (Tylenol, vitamins, allergy shot). He was also wheeled down the hall for an MRI scan and a CAT scan, spending uncomfortable periods lying alone in coldly sterile rooms, while beige multi-ton, humming machines enveloped his body.

He also assured the doctors emphatically over and over that he'd not dipped himself in dye, ink, paint, food coloring, or any other substance. To make sure the blue was fully skin deep, the dermatologist was called in—a thin, young man with magnificently bushy hair flowing out either side of his scalp, but with only a few scraggly strands on top. He used a tiny needle-like probe to extract a plug of skin from his arm and sent it off for study at the pathology lab. That microscopic examination done, the dermatologist proceeded to a minute examination of Harding's skin, every inch of it, much to Harding's discomfiture. The results of that scrutiny convinced the dermatologist that a lecture to his colleagues was in order, if the cause of this strange malady were to be traced. He glanced at Meadows, who nodded her stern consent.

"If you'll excuse me, Mr. Harding, I would like to show my colleagues some important aspects of your . . . uh . . . situation. May I undrape you?" asked the dermatologist. He peered through large horn-rimmed glasses expectantly at Harding.

"What for?" Harding was beginning to blush, an arresting sight, as his facial color transformed subtly from a pure blue to a purplish blue, as the flush of red blood spread across his skin. The doctors watched with fascination.

"I'd like to show the nature of the color distribution."

"Well, yeah, okay."

"You're sure, now? If you're a bit shy about it, we'll understand."

"Well, uh, no. If it'll help you get rid of this thing . . ." He laid back, determined to endure the indignity for the sake of being cured. The dermatologist drew a curtain around the bed and pulled away the sheet. The blush continued to spread, like the purple haze over a mountain at sunset. He lay in his bed, looking mostly at the ceiling, but occasionally at the doctors.

"Notice that he is not a uniform blue," began the dermatologist, extending a silver telescoping pointer to aid his lecture. He tapped his subject's shoulder, stomach, knee. "His skin has all the shadings of naturally colored skin, except that the color is in different values of blue, not brown." The dermatologist took Harding's hand. "You will see that the palms are lighter, as are the soles of the feet," he said, laying the pointer on Harding's feet, causing Harding's blue toes to twitch nervously. "The freckles are darker here . . . here . . . and here." The dermatologist tapped forearm, forehead, and chest with the pointer.

The physicians left Harding alone to recover from his embarrassment, except for a psychiatrist named Ephraim Goldstein, a spare, wrinkled gnome of a man. Goldstein stayed behind, attempting gently to make sure that Harding wasn't so depressed over his plight that he might try something drastic. Harding assured the intense little man that he was only blue on the outside, and Goldstein promised to return.

As the crowd of doctors gathered outside his room, some still amused, some discussing the case, an intensely serious, rail-thin nurse called Meadows from down the hall. Meadows stepped away to talk briefly on the nurses' station phone, and returned toward the group, a mysteriously puckish look on her face.

"Doctors, I think we should proceed to room three oh four," she said with a hint of the southern accent that led some to theorize she had descended from a Confederate general of the same name. The group followed her to the room, where, fully occupying the bed, tears streaming down her face, lay Joy Chambers, a huge woman with great jowls and small close-set eyes. She blew her nose, saw the doctors, and let out a miserable sob that shook the entire bed. She was bright red. The red of a stop sign. The red of the American flag.

By that afternoon, the La Vista, California Community Hospital held five unusually colored patients. A pretty, tearful teenager named Ellen Lucius was blue like Harding. A muscular construction worker named John Lance was red like the now-hysterical Joy Chambers. But a secretary named Ada Frye was a bright yellow, which was particularly distressing to her, because the black woman's skin had once been a lovely rich dark caramel. By that afternoon, word had reached the puzzled La Vista doctors that County Medical Center ten miles away had one blue, one red, and two yellows. But Central Presbyterian Hospital only had a blue.

The doctors again conducted thorough investigations, and at five p.m. they gathered in the ward to compare notes. By now they had begun to refer to the patients by color "sort of like M&M's," said Lesser, an impish twinkle in his eyes.

"Except there aren't any blue M&M's," asserted a rotund toxicologist. "It's not a good simile."

"Boy are you out of touch," teased Lesser. "There've been blue ones for a long time." A brief argument ensued, resulting in the dispatching of the rail-thin nurse to the candy machine next to the cafeteria. She returned and spread the candy buttons on a tray on the nursing station counter, arranging them meticulously by color. The group intently scrutinized the candies, their obsession stemming, no doubt, from the fact that they couldn't solve the real problem—the strange malady afflicting their patients.

"See, blue ones," said Lesser triumphantly. "They ditched the tan ones."

"Yeah, well, the red ones cause cancer," warned the nurse darkly.

"Ladies, gentlemen," said Meadows. "Enough with the M&M's. Let us address the cases at hand."

The doctors and nurses began munching the experimental candies and continued their discussion. First, they decided to gather the affected La Vista patients in an isolation ward, since they represented the possibility of some sort of communicable disease. The two men were wheeled into one room, and the three women in another. Harding and Lance began to compare notes, as nurses swathed in isolation gowns, masks and surgical gloves bustled in and out of the room, bringing food and taking vital signs.

"Hey, man, what if this is permanent?" asked Lance, vigorously rubbing the back of his arm, and checking his fingers for residue, although it would have been hard to see against the red of the fingers.

In the women's ward, the yellow Ada Frye was also half-heartedly comforting Joy Chambers, who still hiccupped an occasional sob, her bulk making the action an almost seismic event.

"I'm gonna die!" she mourned. "I'm inflamed. I'm gonna jus' bleeeeeed and die!" The tranquilizer she'd received had begun to slur her speech, and her sobs weren't shaking the bed anymore.

"Hey, yeah, this is bad, that's true," said Ada Frye. "But we gonna get over this. We not gonna be colored like this for good. The doctors will find something. It's food or something. Or the smog, or some drug."

"I look like a cartoon!" sobbed Ellen Lucius, minutely examining her perfect-but-blue teenaged face with a hand mirror. "Like, it looks real permanent. This would absolutely ruin my chances for cheerleader! Everybody'll stare! It would be the absolute end of my life!"

"Maybe it's an allergy," said Ada Frye. "I got allergies."

"Yeah, me too," snuffled Joy Chambers, sinking into the pleasant fog of the tranquilizer. "I take shots."

"You take shots? Like, I take shots!" exclaimed Ellen Lucius.

"Dr. Clayton?" asked Ada Frye.

"Yeah, I think. Yeah, that's him! Next to the Domino's Pizza!" exclaimed Ellen Lucius, putting down her mirror in teenaged amazement.

"Yeah, Clayton," agreed Joy Chambers.

"That little scum!" screamed Ada Frye.

Had the women not fallen into an angry clucking of denunciation, they might have heard the bellowed conclusion of a similar conversation in the next room as John Lance shouted "THAT LITTLE JERK! HE DID THIS!"

As the patients raged on, a young man pushing a meal cart down the hall paused outside their door. If anybody had noticed him, they would have seen that he stopped just a little too long at each doorway, peering in just a little too intently at the patients. He pushed his horn-rimmed glasses up on his nose, seemingly a nervous habit, because the glasses were staying put quite nicely. He went on to deliver the meal cart to its proper place on the ward and retreated to a quiet corner. There, he took out a gray, bound notebook and spent fifteen minutes assiduously writing notes.

Had anybody paid any attention to him, they would have noted his remarkably round face, his dark little eyes, his dark eyebrows, and his small, straight nose. His little bow-mouth seemed to be set into his pale face like the parts to a Mr. Potato Head stuck into a cantaloupe. His ears were intricate fleshy shells, also seeming to be stuck into the sides of the round head. The ears were accentuated by his short crewcut, which he rubbed occasionally, seeming to relish the tactility of the brushy hair.

Closing the notebook, he slipped away, unnoticed by the busy doctors and nurses, who paid little attention to people such as him.

CHAPTER 2

Bobby Loudon slumped forward in his chair, slid out a lower desk drawer, sagged back and propped his feet on it. He poked at a tablet computer to bring up the home page of the *San Diego Union-Tribune* and held it up in front of his face to obscure from his vision his desk piled with paperwork, and his computer screen glowing expectantly. He scanned the tablet screen absentmindedly, his thoughts on lunch and the bracingly ice-cold, smoky tang of the scotch-rocks it would bring. Lunchtime was still two hours away, and as the time neared, he increased the tally of planned drinks he deemed necessary to support him through the afternoon.

His dark tie hung crookedly loosened about his wrinkled collar. The sleeves on his white shirt were rolled haphazardly up, and his gray suit coat was draped sloppily over the back of the chair. His boyish face had reached the very limits of youth, perhaps a bit jowly, but still with knowing blue-gray eyes only slightly dimmed by drink, and a full head of tousled light-brown hair.

Loudon promised himself to get back to work soon. He had an office inspection in a week, and he was trying to bring his case files up to date. Typing reports into the computer was tedious, but he didn't want the headquarters goons writing up substandards on him. He was in enough trouble as it was.

"Okay, Bobby," he heard from the desk pushed against his on the other side. "You're awake now. What was her name, eh?"

"I know her name, Walter," grumped Loudon, not looking up from his tablet screen, but lowering it to his lap.

"I'm sure you do, Bobby, so tell me." Walter Philips sat down with his brown-stained coffee cup in his hand, wedged his ample middle-age paunch tight against his desk and leaned his elbows expectantly on a pile of papers. His squinty little brown eyes gleamed impishly over the top of his great fleshy bulb of a nose. He sipped his coffee expectantly.

The phone rang, and Loudon reached for the receiver, but at his desk Walter was faster.

"Good morning, FBI Temecula," he said in a slightly overdramatic baritone, listened for a moment and gestured at Loudon.

"It's for you. First, what was her name?"

"Uh . . . Cindy," said Loudon, then immediately thought better of it. ". . . Candy!"

"Sandy!" Walter corrected triumphantly, grinning and raising his wildly bushy gray eyebrows in delight.

"Loudon," said Robert Hayward Loudon into the phone.

"Please hold for Mr. Bowers," said a secretary. Loudon silently mouthed the word "Bowers!" Was it ADC Bowers in Los Angeles?

"Agent Loudon?" he heard. It *was* Bowers. Loudon easily recognized the voice of the Assistant Director in Charge of LA—the ADC. It seemed to flow from the phone like liquid floor polish. He remembered the last time he'd heard it. The confident voice then had been smugly triumphant; the voice of someone who knew he couldn't be touched; the voice of someone who had neatly rid himself of an annoyance—Special Agent Bobby Loudon.

"What can I do for you?"

"How are you, Robert?"

"Fine," said Loudon tersely. Across the desk, Walter picked up the intonation, slurped his coffee and watched Loudon's face for clues, avoiding the pile of paperwork on his own desk.

"Good," said Bowers. "Now, I've just received a case out near you

I want you to handle. Seems like a routine missing person, but they called up here first. I took the call, and I thought I'd pass it on directly."

"Sure, fine," said Loudon. It was a bit strange that the Assistant Director in Charge and not his assistant would call him. The assistant had been his contact before. Something didn't smell right here, but he didn't know what.

"Are you current on your case load, Robert?"

"Sure. But, uh, why me?"

"Robert, look, I know we've had our problems." Loudon could almost see Bowers eloquently waving his well-manicured hand. "But I've decided to begin giving you a chance to work yourself out of that."

Was the guy being straight, or just playing with him? He grabbed one of the reports on his desk and turned it over to the blank side. He shuffled through the pile for a pen, pitching papers on the floor until he found one.

"An employee of a company in La Vista is missing. It's a biotech company named ArchiBiologics."

"Yeah, I think I know it. Big place, I think. Went public a few years ago."

"Missing guy's name is Arthur Lupo. He's been gone a few days. Contact there is his supervisor, named Sam Gupta. They've called the local police, but they wanted us involved, too." Philips gave him the phone number and address.

"Why are we coming in? Doesn't seem like there's any evidence of kidnapping yet."

"Well, they do DOD work. So, there's a federal angle there. I want us to be in early, just in case. Look, I'm giving you this chance to be the point agent. A chance to start working your way back after . . . well . . . your problem. So, go out there, see what's going on. Keep me appraised . . . a report tomorrow, if you would please. I'll have the assignment paperwork emailed down."

"Sure," said Loudon, modulating the word to carry both agreement and sarcasm. Bowers was probably just playing with him, calling him with a rotten assignment just to twist the knife one more time. But maybe Bowers really was trying to reestablish some link.

"Thanks, so much, Robert. 'Bye now."

"Yes, goodbye . . ." Loudon hung up the phone but continued talking to the dead receiver ". . . you jerk."

"So, whaddaya got, Bobby?" asked Walter.

"Missing person."

"Was that Bowers?"

"Yeah," said Loudon, excavating the pile on the desk for his notebook to record the scribbled information from the back of the report. "Kind of strange. These people in La Vista have a simple missing person, just a few days gone, and they want us. So, ADC called here himself."

"Sometimes they think of the little folks in the boonies, eh?" chuckled Walter, as Loudon called ArchiBiologics and arranged for an interview. He'd do it just after lunch, which meant he'd have to drink vodka-tonics with his sandwich so his breath didn't smell.

"You be at the bar tonight?" asked Walter.

"Yeah, ain't I every night?"

"Maybe you'll see Cindy, eh?"

"I know it's Sandy, Walter." Loudon was emerging from his morning funk. But he knew there'd be another hard night in the Gaslamp Quarter, another night letting the jovial noise and music surround him, and letting the drinks lay a boozy fog on the evening. He would circulate among likely spots—Stingaree, Hard Rock Hotel, Whiskey Girl, settling on one depending on the crowd. The doormen all welcomed him. He'd slipped all of them his card, and they appreciated having the law around, especially somebody who could get them out of whatever personal scrapes they might encounter.

Returning from his pleasant reverie, he bent back to his work, filling out forms. He had to finish reports on a routine security clearance case and on some legwork he'd done checking a shipping company that might have been smuggling cheap knockoff watches from Tijuana. He hurried through the work. The security checks especially galled him. They were the work given agents on the outs. Then there was the stupid detail he had drawn of watching over a visiting ambassador coming to town next week from some little Baltic republic. He had to check on security. These were all the usual kinds of assignments that came to Resident Agencies, the little two- or three-man FBI offices away from the big cities. He wondered whether he was more disgusted with his situation or grateful to get out of the mess in LA alive. When he'd drawn his gun on Bowers, the ADC could well have prosecuted him, much less thrown him out of the Bureau, he knew.

By eleven-fifteen a.m., Walter had grown tired of Loudon's antsiness and told him to get out to lunch, so he straightened his tie and unrolled his sleeves, donned the coat and smoothed it down, grabbed his nine-millimeter Glock from the gun safe beside the door and slipped the light, deadly black pistol into his shoulder holster. With a salute to a grinning Walter, he left the small office in the glass tower downtown. He went to one of his usual bars for lunch, a dark place in the basement in the Vallejo Hotel where cops and DEA agents hung out. He knew the bartender and a couple of the other customers, and he sat at the bar with them and had a corned beef sandwich and a few drinks. The alcohol took some of the edge off the afternoon, but left him functional. Maybe even be alert enough to figure out whether Bowers had laid some kind of trap for him in the assignment.

At one p.m., he started for La Vista in his regulation FBI blue Ford Taurus. The town was twenty-five minutes down the sun-drenched freeway, one of the well-manicured, impersonal suburbs that had sprawled their way across the dry, brown hills outside San Diego. He found the exit and drove down the wide boulevard and into the long entry road with the granite-and-metal ArchiBiologics sign out front. The company's symbol was an arty collection of circles and curves that looked biological, he guessed.

He reached the low complex of concrete-and-glass buildings and walked out of the dry desert warmth and into the cool three-story glass-walled atrium lobby lit by sunlight filtered through blue-tinted windows. It was like walking in an aquarium with no water. He flipped his leather holder open to show his picture ID to one of the guards, who escorted him back into the offices. On his way past the guard's desk, he caught a glimpse of the security console. Big time equipment, he thought. From the outside, the building looked like any other mild-mannered biotech company, but the console told him that anybody who even spit on one of the sealed windows from the outside would set off an alarm. That is, if they could get close enough, given the proximity detectors, the infrared cameras, and the pressure and motion sensors probably buried on the grounds outside. Such elaborate electronic protection probably meant serious firepower somewhere in the building to respond to any threat, he surmised.

But figuring out the reason for such heavy security wasn't his business today. He was just supposed to find some poor lost employee who was probably taking an unannounced vacation. He still had a satisfactory buzz from his lunchtime drinks, so he figured he could make it comfortably to the cocktail hour.

The guard handed him off to a slim and swarthy Indian—dot not feather—with dark, slicked-down hair and little black caterpillar-eyebrows, wearing a neat white laboratory coat. He was most certainly Loudon's contact, the missing guy's supervisor.

"How do you do, I am Sam Gupta," he said with a tongue-rolling Indian accent. "Thank you for coming so quickly. Here is my card. That's the best way to give you my full name." Indeed, his full name was Samramananantha K. Gupta. Loudon decided not to ask about the K.

"I'm Special Agent Robert Loudon." Loudon found a business card in his coat and handed it to Gupta.

"We are so worried, Mr. Loudon. We hope you can help us."

"Sure. The Bureau is happy to do what it can."

They passed along a light-gray corridor along the outside of the building, reaching an anonymous wooden door. Gupta held a plastic card to a magnetic panel beside the door and opened it to reveal a spacious office piled with papers. The back wall of the office held another door and a wall that was glass from the waist up. Through the glass, Loudon could see out into a large laboratory with several dozen white-coated researchers scattered about. Some bent over their laboratory benches manipulating pipettes and racks of small vials. Others operated the controls of machines vaguely resembling clothes dryers, microwave ovens, or stacks of DVD players. Even dulled by drink, Loudon could sense a tension in the place, an almost paranoid discipline of privacy, beyond even the usual tight corporate culture. The discoveries made here would not be trumpeted in the morning papers, he thought. The faintest tang of suspicion wafted itself into Loudon's comfortable afternoon alcoholic fog.

"Please have a seat. Will you have tea or coffee?" asked Gupta, sitting behind his desk and carefully moving aside a stack of papers to give himself a better view of Loudon.

"Coffee, thanks. Black," said Loudon, settling into a simple metal and cloth chair. He had just gotten out his notebook and was fishing for a pen when the outer door opened and a young woman appeared with a china cup and saucer with fresh hot coffee, as well as tea for Gupta. Loudon gave her a puzzled look.

"Oh, I just leave the intercom on," explained Gupta, "and my assistant simply listens to what I am saying. I am afraid that unless she did I would forget many things. I am terrible that way."

"Yeah, I can understand. So, tell me about this missing employee . . ." Loudon glanced at his notebook ". . . Arthur Lupo."

"Yes, Arthur. We are very puzzled, very worried. He just stopped coming in three days ago. We have called his apartment, and the security director from the company went by. His car is missing. We are most worried."

A brisk triple-rap on the door prompted Gupta to press a button on the desk, causing the sharp click of the lock unlocking. A well-coiffed male head poked itself in. The face, clear-eyed and with small waspish features, smiled a toothy smile.

"Sam, is this the gentleman from the FBI?" asked the man.

"Yes, it is. Please come in."

The head was followed by a dark gray pinstripe suit, with a carefully knotted striped silk tie.

"Hello, I'm Brad Riker," he said smoothly. He had a rich sailboat tan and a slim tennis build. "I'm the Vice President for Public and Community Affairs. We're ready for you now."

"Ah yes, ah yes," chirped Gupta. "They are waiting for us in the conference room. They thought you might like to talk to them as well."

"Who?"

"Oh, I am sorry," answered Riker, smiling apologetically. "Sam didn't tell you? The president and the security director."

Now, Loudon's suspicions rose into a stiff breeze that blew away the comfortable fog. Big-time executives wouldn't take such an interest in a low-level employee who had only been missing a short time. He took a last healthy gulp of his coffee to perk himself up, and followed Riker out of the office, tracing a path past white-coated researchers and well-dressed executives, through a glass-walled passageway to a connecting administration building. An elevator carried them to the third floor, and as they entered the executive suite, the lower floors' functional dark gray carpeting and light gray walls changed to a rich burgundy carpeting inlaid at intervals with a sculpted representation of the company logo. The walls became paneled, and the furniture changed from corporate efficient to mahogany arm chairs sitting magnificently across from the large polished desk of the slim, attractive receptionist. And the air became quiet and heavy with corporate authority and the scent of healthy profits.

They walked into a large paneled conference room, where, waiting at the head of a long walnut table was a compact balding man, slim and dapper in a blue pinstripe suit. He wore old-fashioned wire-rimmed glasses, and he stood up ramrod straight and smiled warmly as Loudon entered. Although he was slight, he carried a sense of intellectual substance about him. Loudon knew not only how to read people, but when he wasn't preoccupied with alcohol, he was a pretty fair judge of how well those people read *other* people. And this little man regarded him with a solid shrewdness hidden behind that mild exterior, showing perhaps the faintest hint of disapproval at Loudon's rumpled suit and bleary air.

"This is Charles Platt, president of ArchiBiologics," said Riker, and Loudon shook hands with the man. He gave a firm, pretend-cordial handshake.

"Thank you, Agent Loudon, for coming."

"And this . . ." Riker turned smoothly to his right ". . . is James Houston, our chief of security." Houston stepped from beside the door. He was a burly black man of imposing size, made to look even more so by the dark brown double-breasted suit he wore. It was large enough to conceal whatever weapon was necessary. Houston's hair was cropped closely to his round head, and he stood solidly with his hands clasped in front of him, like a policeman on a beat. He also rested easily on his heels, and his unsmiling eyes darted from person to person, coolly assessing them. He had obviously walked patrol at one time.

Loudon shook hands with Houston, feeling his powerful grip, carefully calibrated to communicate the man's strength, but not to overpower.

Houston knew the subtleties of establishing authority. Houston had probably been a very effective cop. Loudon returned the message with his own grip.

The compact Platt sat at the head of the table and Loudon sat to his right in an armchair across from a tinted glass wall overlooking an inner courtyard. It had clipped green lawns and tall trees. Across the courtyard were tables with umbrellas outside an employee lunchroom. At two tables, white-coated people sat comfortably having afternoon coffee.

Gupta sat to Loudon's right, his white lab coat contrasting with the suits and the dark surroundings. Riker and Houston sat across from Loudon interfering with a full view of the courtyard. Houston set a large leather portfolio on the table in front of him. He was clearly keeper of the records, the others far too exalted to bother with paperwork.

They all stared at him expectantly. Loudon felt the fog of his lunchtime drinks fade completely, replaced with a caffeine-aided buzz about what this assignment would bring. He took out his notebook and opened it, looking from person to person, letting a silence settle over the room. In his early days with the Bureau, he would have come barreling into a situation like this with an attitude, firing questions, establishing his authority as an agent to intimidate subjects into giving him information he wanted—even seemingly cooperative subjects like these. But lately he'd become more of a spectator, easing in, listening to the subjects establish their stories, waiting for the cracks. Maybe it was age, maybe it was wisdom. Maybe it was because most of the time he didn't much care.

"Now, Mr. Gupta tells me that Arthur Lupo has been gone three days. I'm not sure you need the FBI at this point. Perhaps the police, or maybe a PI—private investigator. Three days is really not much."

"Oh, for Arthur it is," said Gupta. "He has been here five years, since he got out of college. For five years, he worked six days a week, often seven . . . from before most of us arrived in the morning till after we had left. He loved his work." Gupta's voice lowered a step. "I don't think he really had anything else."

"What did he work on?"

"Oh chromophores. The genetics of chromophores."

"And they are . . ."

"Colored substances. Pigments in plants and animals. He was developing ways to use them as genetic markers to indicate the incorporation into a gene from a vector into a target genome—"

"Whoa, you lost me," interrupted Loudon scribbling a few key words in his notebook. "Bottom line, any commercial value to his work? Something a competitor might be interested in buying from him? Or maybe he might be interested in selling?" This healthy-looking corporation didn't get that way pricing its services cheap, thought Loudon.

"No, not at all," said Platt with a dismissive wave of his small hand. "Well, maybe it might be useful for some narrow technical purposes, but there wouldn't be a big market for it. As Dr. Gupta will tell you, Arthur was working on a very narrowly useful system, a biological indicator that would be used in other experiments."

"We're moving quickly on Arthur's disappearance because we're a small company," said Riker smoothly, smiling and clasping his hands on the table in front of him, as if in prayer. "We are all very close. Artie was like family to us. We are concerned about him."

"Did he have any close friends here at the company, anybody I could talk to?" Loudon directed the question at the genial Riker. Riker shrugged slightly and looked at Gupta, who raised his eyebrows in uncertainty. Some family, Loudon hmphed to himself. Didn't even know about their employees' social lives at work.

"I will introduce you in his lab after we finish here," said Gupta.

"I should also say that we're asking you in early because ArchiBiologics works under a number of government contracts," said Platt. "We're especially sensitive to any personnel problems because the government—most understandably I might add—wants to be sure that their contracts are being properly handled. We want to be able to tell them that when an employee becomes . . . absent . . . we're doing everything to locate him."

"What does ArchiBiologics work on? Without the technical jargon."

"Oh, basic research, cell biology, molecular biology, genetics."

"Secret?"

"Yes, some, but not Arthur's."

Gupta shook his head. "No, not Arthur's."

"Well, I'd like a complete file on him."

Houston reached into his portfolio and pulled out a file. His big, brown cop hand with a scar on the knuckle slid it across the rich wood-grain surface to Loudon. Loudon opened it to find a small picture of a round-faced scraggly-bearded, shaggy-haired young man with glasses. The glasses were slightly cockeyed, perhaps from holding the mop of dark, straight hair out of the eyes. The eyelids were partly closed, as if in the act of blinking. Loudon flipped through the papers.

"Is this his complete personnel file?"

Houston shot a sideways glance at Platt, the whites of his dark eyes flashing. He paused for an instant before answering. It had been an unexpected question, and Loudon's powers of observation had managed to clear themselves of alcohol enough to see that it was an uncomfortable question.

"No, that's most of it though . . . just about all of it," said Houston.

"I want to see his *complete* personnel file."

"Certainly," said Platt, waving his small hand in friendly agreement. "We'll have it delivered to you, though. We want to make copies of everything. I would imagine it's a pretty large file." He looked at Gupta and back at Riker. "We will give you copies of everything."

"And you said you drove past his house?" Loudon asked Houston. The big man, ironically, was the weakest link in the chain of lies this bunch was trying to maintain.

"Yeah, I did myself," said Houston. His silhouette looming large against the large window showed him shifting uncomfortably. "He has an apartment about three miles from here. I knocked, checked the exterior premises, looked through the windows. No sign of the subject. The car was gone. Interviewed the manager; he didn't know anything. I didn't feel I should go into the apartment; that you or the police should."

"Did you call his cell?" It was an intended insult by Loudon, to see how Houston would respond. The former cop did show a trace of irritation.

"Yeah, of course. Went to voicemail."

"And you did call the police?"

"Yeah, here in La Vista." Houston's face remained impassive, but his stare at Loudon was more pointed. "They took a report after twenty-four hours, but they said they wanted to wait a week before they sent out a detective."

"Anything else?"

"Yes. I interviewed the employees he worked with. And he has no family; parents are dead. And no evidence that he planned any trip."

For the next half hour, Loudon continued to quiz them on Lupo and his habits. As he had hoped, he succeeded in needling Houston even more. Needled people make mistakes. Platt was becoming more impatient, too, and he ended the meeting by abruptly standing up, triggering everyone else to stand. Loudon decided he had aggravated them enough and had enough information, so he stood, too. Loudon also decided that his suspicions had been tweaked, and not only by the corporate mentality. For one thing, the company did DOD work. True, he'd seen no indication at all that Lupo was anything but temporarily AWOL. After five years of such a daily grind, maybe the guy found some girl, or had gone across the Mexican border to wallow in the nightlife in Tijuana.

They said their goodbyes and Gupta led him out of the plush executive suite and back to the laboratory building, to Lupo's office. They entered a small cubbyhole just off the large laboratory behind Gupta's office. Outside the office sat the lab benches crowded with chemicals and lab glassware, where Lupo did his work. As Gupta introduced them, Loudon interviewed the people who did their arcane scientific work near Lupo. They showed him the machines that Lupo used—the ones that Loudon had thought looked like clothes dryers or stacks of DVD players. They were actually ultracentrifuges, DNA sequencers, and DNA synthesizers.

"What's this?" asked Loudon, pointing to a machine that looked like a microwave oven.

"A microwave oven," said Gupta.

"Oh."

Loudon then quizzed the coworkers, a collection of young, intense lab-coated people, who seemed eager to help. But they confessed they knew little of Lupo's personal life. Lupo seldom said anything about what he did outside work; never went out for a beer or saw a movie with any of them. One of the co-workers, however, seemed to have something on her mind. Jeany Moody was a lab technician, in her twenties, with milk-smooth skin and dimples and long brown hair. She was a pretty girl even with no makeup and dressed in a stained labcoat and old sneakers. As she talked about Lupo in front of Gupta, she stood uneasily, shifting from foot to foot. When he'd finished his questions, she walked with him toward the door to Gupta's office and asked in a whisper if she could speak to him alone. So, as they reached the end of the bench and stopped, Loudon asked Gupta if he could catch up with him back at his office. Gupta hesitated, but under Loudon's pointed stare, he finally smiled uneasily, showing white teeth against his dusky skin and disappeared through the door to his office.

"Well, he . . . I don't know how to put this," she began, screwing up her cute face in indecision. "It's probably not anything."

"Miss Moody, Arthur is missing. You should tell me anything, even if you don't think it's important."

"Well, he kissed me."

"And?"

"That's all."

"Is it? What else?"

"Well, no. Arthur was . . . I think he kind of had a crush on me. He asked me to go have coffee with him a couple of times. Tried to make it look casual, y'know. But he was kinda strange. I really didn't want to hurt him, but he was kinda strange. I'd see him sorta staring at me. He knew I had a boyfriend, so he really didn't try to ask me out. I wouldn't have gone, anyway. Y'know, he was . . . well . . . he was strange."

"We've established strange. So what about the kiss?"

"Well the day before his last day, he walked up to me when I was pipetting and just kissed me on the cheek. He said he was sorry."

"For kissing you?"

"No, I don't think so. It was like . . . like . . . he was apologizing for something he did. Or maybe was gonna do. I was kinda freaked for a minute. I thought he was maybe gonna do something to me."

"But he didn't?"

"No, he went back in his lab and didn't say anything to me the rest of the day."

"He'd never done it before?"

"Oh no, not Arthur. He was strange."

Loudon thanked her and decided to inspect Lupo's lab bench and office, to see what a strange scientist would leave sitting around. Gupta immediately appeared to watch him. The lab bench was covered with carefully taped blue absorbent paper and held racks of plastic vials, beakers, and pipettes that Loudon had seen before on other such cases. The bottled chemicals on the shelves above the bench didn't ring any bells. There weren't any components that could be used to make drugs. He moved into the small office to find a built-in desk in the corner holding a few books, a computer terminal and some assorted papers. No personal objects to speak of, except for some small plastic animals and some magazine pictures plastered on the walls. The colored pictures were of birds, butterflies, lizards, snakes, lobsters, daffodils, squash, and tomatoes. Loudon puzzled over the odd collection, as he shuffled through the papers, alert for anything out of the ordinary—say a receipt for a plane ticket or a travel brochure. Nothing.

He took down a gray-bound lab notebook from a shelf above the desk and flipped through it. The cover was labeled with Lupo's name and the start date, as was the notebook's spine. There was space for a completion date on the cover and spine. This notebook had been started only about a week before, and held only a few written pages. Loudon knew something about lab notebooks from a case he'd run in which a drug dealer kidnapped a kid who was making drugs at a university. This one seemed in order, and he snapped it shut.

"Any other place that he used?" he asked Gupta.

"Oh, yes, he had space in the animal room," said Gupta. "He kept some animals that he isolated pigment genes from."

Gupta led the way out of the office and down the hall to a room with a locked door. Gupta opened the door and Loudon's nose was assaulted with the cloying funky odor of animals. A rack of cages along one wall held assorted mice, rats, and birds including a canary and a cardinal. On the other wall, a rack of aquariums held fish, crabs and a couple of snakes. Loudon inspected the cages and the aquariums, finding several with the initials AL in black marker on attached tags and tapes.

"These were Lupo's?" he asked pointing some of them out.

"Yes, the ones with his initials."

Loudon went from cage to cage, aquarium to aquarium, examining them carefully. He came to an empty one, with a tape that said "al. *Homarus vulgaris.*" A gray substance swirled along the bottom, but otherwise it was empty.

"What was in this?"

Gupta inspected the tag. "Oh, his lobster."

"What happened to it?"

"Oh, I don't know. It may have died, or he might have used it in an experiment. Or maybe he just ate it."

Loudon nodded, and quickly stepped out of the room, away from the smell. They walked back to Gupta's office, Loudon jotting notes as they went. For a reason he couldn't fathom, an ache of suspicion had returned, and it demanded that he keep gathering pieces to some puzzle that might not even exist. He suddenly became thirsty. A few scotches would sure help him put this all into perspective. Finally, they stood outside the door to Gupta's office, and Loudon reviewed his notes. A corner of his mind, however, pictured the bars in the Gaslamp Quarter. But he forced himself to take a minute to gather his thoughts, to see if some puzzle piece from the afternoon's events might fit with others. What else? What else did he need to know? His mind went back to Lupo's lab. He mentally scanned the room. His mental image finally found itself focusing on the notebook.

"Lupo's lab notebook was just started. Where do you keep the old ones?"

"Oh, locked in my office," said Gupta. "It's standard practice that each time a researcher finishes a notebook, he turns it into me. I certify it and lock it away. It's to protect patent rights and the company's rights to the data and such. We do both electronic and paper."

"Yeah, I know, I've had cases like that. Can I see Lupo's notebooks?"

Gupta hesitated, and Loudon watched him steadily. Perhaps he was weighing whether proprietary information would be revealed. He finally decided. "Oh, certainly," he said, and they entered Gupta's office. He pulled out a key chain and opened a large locked bookcase. Inside were shelves holding perhaps hundreds of lab notebooks, each labeled on the spine with a name and a time period. Gupta pointed out Lupo's shelf, and Loudon scanned the line of carefully labeled notebooks, reading the dates. He stared at the shelf, letting the sight sink in. Something didn't sit right, and it took a while for his powers of observation, now slightly duller than they used to be, to sort out what it was. He reached up and ran his fingers lightly along the scores of notebooks, back and forth several times. He looked over the entire case full of notebooks and returned his gaze to Lupo's shelf. Gupta backed up and sat on the edge of his desk and folded his arms, fidgeting a bit.

"They are all the standard notebooks that we use," he finally said, as if to prompt Loudon to finish his scrutiny. Loudon still didn't say anything, but a mental "Aha!" suddenly popped in his brain like a small firecracker. Once more, he ran his fingers along the line of notebooks, this time stopping to pull several out slightly as he went. They stood like volunteers that had stepped forward from a military rank. He examined those more closely. There were eight, including three near the right-hand end, where the most recent books were kept.

Abruptly, he snatched one after another of the eight notebooks off the shelf, piling them in one arm. He turned around and set them on Gupta's desk in a small clear spot.

"Check those," he said, watching Gupta's face. Gupta looked puzzled. He picked up the first notebook and opened it. His eyebrows went up in surprise. The pages he'd opened to were blank. He riffled through the pages. All blank.

"Oh, dear," he said, as much to himself as to Loudon. Now his caterpillar-brows drew closer to one another, furrowed with concern. He picked up the next notebook and the next, riffling through all eight. They were all blank. "Oh, my goodness."

"They were new," said Loudon, studying Gupta's reaction. "Their spines weren't creased like the others. Notebooks that sit open on a bench get creased. They get soiled. These weren't."

"This is very strange. This is serious."

"Yeah," said Loudon simply, taking out his own small notebook and gesturing for Gupta to sit down. Loudon wouldn't see a bar for a while.

CHAPTER 3

La Vista Hospital looked positively sterile from the outside. Its aggressively geometric angles, with corners that appeared sharper than ninety degrees, seemed to dare germs to invade. The building's horizontal expanse of polished, dark-tinted windows set in pristine light gray concrete made it look aggressively hostile toward the outside world plagued by pestilence and multifarious microbes. The sleek hospital surrounded itself with weedless broad lawns forced to eternal greenness by sprinklers that regularly popped from the ground to make little rainbows in the sun as they misted the air. The last bank of sprinklers was just finishing its work in the low morning sun.

This Wednesday, the curbs beside the hospital had been invaded by bulky white television vans. Some sprouted death-ray antennas aimed toward their stations in downtown San Diego. Atop others, large parabolic dishes were cocked expectantly toward the low sky, waiting to transmit images to satellites of the now-famous strangely colored patients. A crowd of television cameras and reporters with notebooks milled impatiently in the front lobby, drinking cafeteria coffee and trying to worm information out of the harried PR officer, a flustered young woman normally used to giving out routine condition reports on local victims of traffic accidents involving fast, expensive cars, and heart attacks on golf courses.

Inside the seminar room in the blue wing on the third floor, a gathering of doctors was still puzzling over what to feed the reporters and the cameras. Many had visited the coffee urn at the back of the room and sipped hot coffee gingerly from styrofoam cups. The physicians in their white clinic jackets sat in the chairs with foldaway desktops studying their notes or scanning scientific papers. Some, fresh from rounds or the operating room, wore green surgical scrub suits and paper booties. A few interns who had seen the patients stood leaning against the back wall, waiting to hear what their all-knowing mentors would say. This was the most excitement since Kevin Costner had fallen off a horse on a nearby trail and been brought in for treatment.

Internist Lori Meadows stepped up behind the lectern wearing her usual crisp white jacket, with her name tag centered exactly on the right breast pocket and her stethoscope folded in her side pocket. She precisely placed her neatly typed notes in the middle of the lectern, adjusted her glasses and jerked the microphone down to suit her petite stature. She stared sternly out over the group of physicians whose confidence had lately been shaken by the appearance of the strange patients.

"Doctors," she said tersely, "after careful consideration of all the data, patient histories, and test results, a thorough review of the literature, and reports from specialists in endocrinology, dermatology, infectious diseases, internal medicine and epidemiology . . ." She paused while the room quieted and attention riveted even more on her. ". . . I can't figure out what is going on here." Embarrassed chuckles and a murmur of assent rose from the audience. "We now have a total of twelve patients that have turned red, yellow, or blue. We've got another yellow referred from a local physician late yesterday, and County got another blue. All the same shades, no different. As we expected, the patients' families have notified the media, so as you well know, we've got more and more reporters gathering at our doorstep. We'd better make sure we have our facts straight before I talk to them."

After Meadows outlined the basic medical findings on the La Vista patients, the other hospitals' chiefs of staff presented similar results. The patients all appeared healthy, except for their color, and a slight elevation in white blood count. A young physician from County Medical Center also reported on a gallium scan on its patients. He explained that the scan involved injecting mildly radioactive gallium into the patient, and then using a nuclear scanner to follow its distribution in the body. Since gallium tended to concentrate at sites of infection, it would pinpoint problem areas. The gallium had distributed evenly, he said, with a slightly disappointed shake of his head.

Meadows then introduced a resident who had spent the previous night doing a computer search of the medical literature. The somewhat haggard resident leaned on the lectern and scratched his scalp with the tip of a pen as he spoke.

"Well, as you know there's all kinds of diseases that affect the skin. Thyroid dysfunction gives a deep tan color. Congenital heart diseases and some poisons gives a blue cyanosis. Hemochromatosis makes the skin bronze, and jaundice makes it yellow." He absentmindedly scratched an itch around his nose with the pen, leaving a long blue mark. "And there are inflammations that leave a red blush on the skin. But there are no known diseases that yield patients in the glorious technicolor that we have here. The closest we could come . . ." he flipped through pages of printout ". . . were cases where people ate lots of carrots, and the carrot color turned them orange. I called a dermatologist who handled one, and he says it's a real nice, bright orange." He looked up and winced guiltily at the lack of data.

Meadows returned to the podium, giving the resident a slightly annoyed look. "Well, maybe that gives us some chemical basis, but we've clearly got some disease process here." She introduced the dermatologist who had examined the patients' skin tissue. The lights dimmed and onto the screen came a slide showing large cells peppered with small dark spots.

"These are normal melanocytes. They put out these little dark melanin granules that spread to other cells and color the skin. Now . . ." he said with a touch of drama, clicking on the next slide. "Look at this guy." Another cell appeared, but the dark spots were lighter, yellowish. "This is from our, uh, African-American patient, who is now yellow, poor woman. Look at the color of the melanin granules!" He clicked on slides of the blue and red patients from all the hospitals. Indeed, their spots looked bluish and reddish on the screen. The dermatologist clicked back to the normal melanocytes.

"Now, what happens with melanocytes is that they keep pumping out this pigment until they die. But it looks to us like even the new melanocytes are beginning to put out colored chromophores. So this thing looks genetic. We're going to have to culture these cells and do all sorts of toxicology work to figure out what this stuff is." He paused, looked back at the slide and smiled. "To quote the estimable Doctor Meadows, we don't know what is going on, either!" To appreciative chuckles, Meadows took the lectern again.

"Now, normally, I might say we just had a bad night with some weird coincidences," she said knitting her brow in puzzlement. "But we do have a commonality. All the patients say they've gotten shots of various kinds at Russ Clayton's office. Doctor Clayton, on the advice of his lawyer, is not here at the moment."

"Yeah, and on the advice of his bodyguard!" quipped one doctor to a chorus of chuckles.

"He's closed his office and sealed it, and we've asked the local police to post a guard until investigators can show up," said Meadows.

"From where?" came a voice from the audience.

"Centers for Disease Control and Prevention. The state health department epidemiologist, Joe McMann, has asked that we send our patients' blood, urine and tissue samples directly to the CDC, and we've done so. He's formally asked them into the case, which we all think is best, since this looks like something really exotic, and it just feels like some kind of microorganism. Any other questions?"

"What are we calling this thing?"

"Well, pigmentation dermatopathia of unknown origin. PD for short. We've been talking to the insurance and HMO people. They're willing to go along. And, it gets us off the hook on a cause."

"Yeah, and makes us sound like we know what we're talking about," said the dermatologist to appreciative nods.

"More important, who's gonna be first author on the paper on this?" asked Lesser to the loudest laughter and applause yet.

"I am. Next question," said Meadows and not one voice was raised in objection, not even from Lesser, who had the distinction of having the first case walk into his emergency room. They both knew that scientific publication of the cases would bring instant fame, and likely fortune, to its authors. "We've already contacted *JAMA*. Don't worry. You'll all get representation."

"Yes, we will!" grumped the chief of staff of County Medical Center. They then fell into a genteel argument—later turning viciously backstabbing—over the authorship of the scientific papers. The La Vista group would argue that they had more patients. County Medical would argue that they did the most sophisticated pathology work. And Central Presbyterian would argue that their name came first in the alphabet.

The group did decide that the patients should remain in quarantine until the CDC had done its work. They also agreed that representatives of the three hospitals would lead the press conference.

The press conference, held half an hour later in the seminar room, was a loud confusion of lights, shouted questions, furious scribbling, and a crowd of cameras and microphones. The physicians answered the questions as best they could, but one answer brought shouts and groans from the reporters. There would be no visuals, because none of the patients had consented to being filmed.

"Look, they're trying to adjust to a pretty traumatic experience," Meadows snapped. "And, more importantly, since we don't know what this is, they're in strict quarantine."

"But the public has a right to know!" shouted a television reporter from the front row.

"You'll have your film when they're ready; not before." Meadows left the podium as the reporters muttered their protests, and the camera crews trooped outside to film the featureless, tinted windows of the patients' rooms, the hospital sign, anything colored on the grounds, and each other. Some stayed to whisper to any staff member they could corner that they would pay big money for first footage of the patients.

• • •

Ephraim Goldstein had to shake Joy Chambers awake, because she was so pumped full of tranquilizers that she had settled into a large, torpid mound of red flesh. Once he'd managed to bring Chambers to reasonable consciousness, the spare, elderly psychiatrist settled down in a chair in the center aisle on the ward and crossed his legs, looking from one patient to another.

"So, how about we all talk? You should talk, you know. If you have any problems with this color thing, you should talk about them. That's what I'm here for." He had to enunciate clearly, for the surgical mask muffled his words.

"Well, Doc, first of all, you gotta pretty well understand that we don't wanna be these colors," said Ada Frye. "When we gonna get this stuff off and go home?" Frye held up her yellow arm indignantly, and glared at it as if it offended her by merely being attached to her body.

"I wish I knew. Doctor Meadows has told you everything she knows. They want to keep you a few more days."

"Few more days! And why am I yellow? Look like a dang daisy, or whatever. Nobody'd want to be yellow. First I'm black and dang, everybody gives black people trouble . . . and now I'm yellow!"

"Well, it's a nice yellow," offered Chambers sleepily. "You wanna be red, instead?"

"Naw, I guess not." Frye contemplated her arm with somewhat more charity for a long moment. "Well, I guess a flower color ain't real bad."

"We were on the radio," said Ellen Lucius, holding her mirror in her lap. "Ada and me talked on the phone. Was that okay? They called before the switchboard started stopping the calls so we wouldn't be disturbed."

"Sure, of course it was okay," said Goldstein. "You can talk to whomever you wish."

"I told them I was blue and about my high school, and, like, how I wanted to be a cheerleader. Y'know, like, maybe it's even kinda cool, I think. Blue, y'know. Like, I could go to Puente Hills High. Blue's a school color there. I'd have to get new clothes, though."

"Clothes, I never thought of that," said Frye. "Insurance pay for that? New clothes? Everything I got goes with brown." She looked at the yellow arm with renewed contempt.

"Well, I don't think so," said Goldstein, jotting something in a small notebook. "But they will pay for counseling, if this doesn't go away. I'm here to help you cope with this, just in case."

They continued their talk for another hour, ranging over the difficulties of looking different. Really different. Joy Chambers finally fell into an unrousable sleep and Goldstein moved to the next room, where the colored men had other concerns.

"I called the lumber yard," volunteered Harding. "My boss said he wants me to come in as quick as possible. We'd get a load of business. People would come in to see me, if I'm not contagious. Am I contagious?"

"We're not sure, but you don't seem to be."

From the bed nearest the window came the voice of a new patient.

"Heck, Malcolm, this is an opportunity!" exclaimed Eddie Chandler, waving his skinny yellow arms. With long, lank hair and a small goatee, Chandler looked like a rock musician, which he was when not stuffing burritos at the local Taco Bell. After he'd arrived the previous day, he'd spent some time recovering from the shock of the transformation. He'd spent the rest of the post-recovery time in furious scheming and fevered phone conversations with his fellow band members. "You know what we got here?" He displayed his yellow palms, his eyes wide and bright with the promise his hands represented.

"What?" asked Harding.

"We got a movie of the week, man! We got bucks! I got this agent, man. Name's Benny. He's up in Hollywood, man. Y'know, Benny could get us all together. Get the women to sign on, and go as a group. Maybe we even got a . . . watchamacallit . . . a feature film!"

Harding was dubious. "You think so?"

"Sure, maybe Tom Cruise'll play me, and . . . whatsisname . . . the guy in that movie . . . anyway, I'll think of it. He'll play you!"

"Really?"

"Doc, am I right?"

"Well, I'm sure such arrangements might be possible." Goldstein made a note to call his brother, who also knew a Hollywood agent. He mused over his place in this story. It could be central. The wise psychiatrist, seeing all, understanding all. Maybe the narrator.

The men continued talking of women, work, and agents; and Goldstein finished his session with the men and left to confer with Lori Meadows. He found the chief of staff in her office, poring over a textbook on skin disorders.

He settled into the chair across from her desk, watching her scowl at the book. He reported, "Well, the patients are dealing with it okay here in the hospital. But they haven't really realized what's going to happen to them outside . . . if this is permanent. We've got to do some preparation." Meadows distractedly agreed, opening another reference book to resume her scowl at it, and Goldstein went into the waiting area for the families, flipping through his notebook as he went.

As Goldstein sat on the couch and reassured the worried families, he took no notice of the pudgy young man with the horn-rimmed glasses sitting in the corner. The young man wore the blue work uniform of the hospital staff, so even the hospital security guards, on edge because of the crowds and the possibly infectious patients, didn't bother him.

When the little man saw that Goldstein had finished counseling the families, he casually wandered over to ask him how the patients were doing. He told Goldstein he was on his lunch break, and Goldstein answered generally—limiting his remarks because of doctor-patient confidentiality and the possibility of a movie deal. The man might be a Hollywood writer or a reporter. But the round-faced young man didn't press too hard; just thanked him and went back to the couch.

He also chatted with the other relatives of the patients and intently watched the news as it came on the television in the waiting room. Between each chat, though, he would go back again and sit on the couch in the corner and write in his gray notebook.

CHAPTER 4

"**J**ust exactly what did Bowers tell you?" asked Walter, hitching his pants up over his belly and stuffing his shirt in at the front. He followed Loudon down the sidewalk amidst the maze of condominiums, looking for the manager's office. Arthur Lupo's condo was in a typical southern California complex, with narrow twisting paths through a lush, shady landscape of birds-of-paradise, ferns, and ivy, and with oddball addresses on the buildings. They were looking for the manager to let them into Lupo's unit at 10435 Camino de la Azalea.

"He said just to keep on with the investigation at this local level," said Loudon. "He said I could get you to help, since it looks like there's a couple of complications."

"Like the missing notebooks?"

"Yeah, and also that Lupo could have taken them. The research guy, Gupta, said that Lupo had gone in to check one out the day before he left. He was alone with the notebooks, so he had time to switch them."

"Or this guy Gupta could have switched them any time he wanted," observed Walter.

They came to a dead end on the path—and doubled back to find the last sign pointing to the manager's office.

Walter was beginning to perspire. Field work made him do that, which was why he didn't like field work. "But the company guys told you the stuff he was working on wasn't secret, or valuable, or anything."

"That's what they said. I'll get his file today. I'll get somebody who knows about this stuff to look at the scientific papers and tell me . . . Well . . . something!"

They had taken the wrong path again. They were on Gusano de la Madre Real, and it had ended at a small swimming pool with a metal fence around it.

"So what're you gonna do? You got a plan?"

"Well, we're gonna look at his apartment, and I'll look at his file and make a bunch of calls. With luck, we'll get enough information to convince the La Vista cops that there's a missing person case. They'll want jurisdiction. And they can have it, since there's no evidence of kidnapping, and since the company doesn't think his work compromised national security."

"Well, this is better than the routine stuff." Walter tugged at a fern, inadvertently yanking a chunk of it out of the ground.

"Yeah, well, I came down here for the routine stuff."

"I know. I know." Walter remembered their long boozy talks. He knew Loudon had left LA after his wife had left him. And he knew why she'd left him.

After yet another false trail, they found the manager's unit. They rang the doorbell, and the door opened to a harried mother with two kids squabbling in the background. It was the manager's wife, and they flashed their IDs and a search warrant. She scrunched her face into a mildly irritated "now-what" expression, separated the kids, plopped them in front of the TV, and led the agents to Lupo's apartment. As she thwap-thwapped along in front of them in red flip-flops and baggy shorts, she told them that Arthur was a renter, not an owner, so not part of their friendly neighborhood. Loudon tried to keep track of the turns, so he could find his way back. They passed the pool and made their way down a short sidewalk off the main path. Lupo's building was identical to the others, a vaguely Spanish-style white stucco structure with dark brown wood trim. Standing at the apartment door, Loudon could see over a fence into a small patio off the living room. The patio was bare, except for a very dead plant of an undetermined species.

The manager's wife rang the doorbell, and after a wait with no answer, let them in. She hung around the door, peering expectantly in at the agents. Loudon emphatically thanked her, telling her that they could manage. Getting the message that she should leave, she thwap-thwapped disappointedly back to her apartment.

Standing in the foyer looking into the living room, Loudon sensed that some aspects of the apartment didn't fit the usual decor for a young bachelor. For example, the living room held an old-fashioned, overstuffed chair with a rather feminine flower pattern on the uphol-stery. More appropriate was the sloppy stack of magazines and science journals on either side of the chair. An expensive floor lamp sat on one side of the chair, and a slightly rusty folding TV table sat on the other. In the opposite corner of the living room sat a table with a small LCD television, and a DVD player on the floor underneath. The living room held nothing else. Nothing on the walls, no sofa, no coffee table, no bric-a-brac. Lupo sat in this chair and read journals and watched TV, and that was about it.

Loudon sat in the chair and began shuffling through the magazines, which consisted of copies of *Scientific American*, *BioScience* and *Science*, as well as the *Journal of Biological Chemistry*, the *Journal of Genetics*, and a reference book on *Secondary Plant Compounds*. Walter motioned that he'd explore the dining room and kitchen at the back of the apartment.

After satisfying himself that the magazines held no information, Loudon thought for a second, then pulled out his cell phone and dialed Lupo's cell number. A voice answered.

"Yeah."

"Who's this?"

"Well, who's this?"

"Bobby?"

"Walter? Where are you?"

"Kitchen. He left his cell phone here on the table."

"Interesting. Bag it." Loudon headed for the kitchen to find Walter with his head in the refrigerator.

"This boy ain't no gourmet," he said, opening the door wider to reveal a near empty bottle of milk, an opened can of Coke, and some chemicals in brown bottles. The cupboards held a few mismatched dishes and seven glasses from McDonalds with pictures of cartoon characters on them. One cupboard held boxes of Cap'n Crunch and Froot Loops, and a jar of peanut butter with marshmallow creme.

Loudon checked the garbage and found wrappers from some snack cakes. They weren't a national brand—Tastykakes.

In the bedroom, they found a double bed with a worn wooden headboard and a rumpled quilt that matched the chair in the living room. Beside the bed was a matching nightstand with a small reading lamp. Again, piles of magazines and journals overflowed the night stand onto the floor.

"I bet he got this furniture at somebody's house sale. Like some old folks," said Loudon.

"Or maybe Grandma or Mama gave it to him."

The clothes in the closet were similarly undistinguished. "Stuff missing," Walter concluded. "See the empty hangers? And no suitcase." Walter pulled out and pitched aside what was left —a pair of old sneakers, a pair of dress shoes, ratty sport shirts, faded slacks, a few striped ties, and a suit with dust on the shoulders. The chest of drawers held a few pair of underwear and undershirts.

Loudon sat on the bed and considered what they'd seen. The living areas seemed barren, the casually kept shelter of a loner with few emotional connections. He smiled wryly to himself. The place reminded him of his own apartment.

He headed for the second bedroom, which Lupo had made into an office. "Now we'll really see what we see." The room held a large work table and an old metal desk. The work table was bare, except for a desktop computer.

"Great," said Walter. "We'll dump his hard drive."

But when Loudon looked closer, he saw that the computer's cover was loose. He slid it off to reveal the computer's welter of components.

"Not likely. The hard drive is gone. This is getting more interesting." Loudon then bent down so that the light from the window would reflect off the table. "Look at the dust pattern. About the size of notebooks or papers. He had a pile of stuff here that's gone now."

"If you say so, Sherlock," said Walter, plumping down into the old desk chair and stretching out. He looked bored, but Loudon knew he was very busy. Walter's practiced eyes were scanning the room, and he periodically turned the chair about ten degrees to look at another section. Knowing Walter, if somebody asked him weeks later what was in that room, Walter would be able to tell him in remarkable detail. Walter was lazy but he was also very sharp.

Loudon began going through the desk drawers, pulling out files stuffed full of scientific papers. But rifling through them he found no letters, memos, or other handwritten materials that might be immediately interesting. Loudon extracted a file marked "Money" and found some old bank statements.

"Hm. Pretty rich guy. He had six-figure balances in savings, and some CDs." He set aside the files, knowing that he now had an easy way to track Lupo's finances. He bent to his favorite rummaging place for agents, the wastebasket, but it was empty except for another Tastykake wrapper.

The bookshelves over the desk held college textbooks and numerous reference works of biology and biochemistry. There were some science fiction books, several laboratory equipment catalogs, a book on personal finance, and the memoirs of a couple of famous financial swindlers.

There was also a ten-year-old yearbook from the Illinois Institute of Math and Science. Loudon recalled hearing of the high school for brilliant kids. He sat on the edge of the desk and flipped through the yearbook. The index listed Arthur Lupo, along with his activities—science club, math club, biology club, and a string of academic honors. The index also listed the pages on which Lupo's picture appeared. Nerdy-looking kid, as usual. But there was something about the expression that didn't sit right. He wasn't smiling, which might be expected. But there was a grim look to the kid. He set the book on the desk to take with him, along with the other books and papers.

By now, Walter had turned the chair toward the bookshelf, and he abruptly got up and snatched up the phone directory. He grabbed a pad of yellow Post-it notes from the desk drawer and slid the chair over to the work table.

"He's got a print directory, and even geek-types will use one. Lemme show you a trick I learned watching CSI," he said, carefully opening the telephone book and gently turning through the pages, minutely scrutinizing the upper corners. "This guy lived alone, so he was the only one who used this book. If you're reeeeaaaalll careful . . . hah! . . ." Walter stuck a Post-it note between two of the pages and moved on ". . . you can tell where these pages are wrinkled from being used a lot. Lots of times they turn 'em down, too. You keep on what you're doin', and I'll have this for you in a bit."

While Walter leafed through the book, tagging a few more pages, Loudon decided to try a trick of his own. With a heave, he pulled the desk out from the wall and peered down into the dark space. He made out a pencil and a paper clip, but the space also held scraps of paper, as well as a couple of whole sheets. He stretched his arm down and fished them all out, spreading them on the desk.

There was a Domino's pizza menu, a credit card receipt, a receipt from Walmart, a couple of old Post-it notes, and a small wadded-up piece of paper that had apparently bounced off the side of the wastebasket and landed behind the desk.

The credit card receipt was for some books; the Walmart receipt was for some socks. And the Post-it notes showed only indecipherable scribbles. He unfolded the wadded-up paper. It contained a list of some kind of codes:

EZV422

AV9900

DF205

HV330

mH660

Beside each was a check mark. Maybe they were license plate numbers, or radio call signs. Loudon fished a plastic baggy out of his pocket, put the paper into it, and marked it. He'd have it examined by an expert.

"Okay, look here," said Walter, finishing his study of the phone book. "Here's where our boy let his fingers do the walking." With a smug smile tightening his jowly face, he carefully opened the book to the first yellow Post-it. The heading was "Automobile Dealers - Used Cars."

The second was "Computers - Dealers." No surprises so far. The third Post-it note marked a page headed "Laboratory Equipment & Supplies."

"That could be something," said Loudon. "You can check out these last places, and see if our boy was making a lab."

Walter flipped to the next markers "Office Supplies - Retail" and "Pizza - Retail."

"Yeah, pizza. Of course," said Loudon. "What else?"

"Hold on, buddy, the best is yet to come, eh?" Walter flipped the pages to "Trucking - Motor Freight."

"Okay, now," said Loudon appreciatively. "Mr. Lupo is looking to ship some stuff. We should find out what. Besides the lab supply houses, check out the shippers and see if Arthur is moving something interesting."

"Oh, great. More routine stuff to do." Walter slapped the phone book shut.

"I knew you'd like this case."

They found their way back to their car, pulled out some boxes, and returned to the apartment where they loaded the papers and other materials for removal. However, Loudon kept the bank statements and the envelope containing the checkmarked list.

The carport behind the apartment was empty. Loudon had already checked the state motor vehicles department that morning and found out Lupo was driving a dark blue 1994 Ford van. They hadn't put out a bulletin on it though. They weren't even sure he was really missing. He still might have decided on a little vacation. Although the presence of the cell phone and the missing hard drive was raising suspicions.

They stopped at the manager's apartment and told his wife that Lupo's place shouldn't be entered, and asked her to call if she saw any visitors.

"Looks like he's kind of a sad little guy," said Walter as they climbed into the car.

"I don't know if sad is the word. Something tells me that there are other words besides sad."

After negotiating the traffic-clogged freeways, they arrived back at their office. There, the security guard handed Loudon a thick manila envelope delivered from ArchiBiologics. In it, Loudon found Lupo's personnel file and a collection of scientific papers with Lupo's name as author or co-author. Walter decided the morning's work rated a trip out for a sandwich, after which he'd check Lupo's bank accounts and get his phone records. Loudon settled in behind his paper-piled desk to look over the scientific papers first. Later, he would reward himself with a hot lunch and an appropriately generous measure of cold liquor.

Lupo had published seven scientific papers in five years. Loudon didn't know whether that was good or not. He flipped through the papers, comprehending little but the page numbers.

On a hunch, he decided to find out just how much Lupo had been involved in secret work. After some fiddling around with the computer to get into the FBI network, he managed to call up Lupo's security status. There was none. Lupo had no security clearance, although his prints were on file from a summer college job at a drug company. Maybe it was odd, considering that he'd been working in a company that did classified work. But maybe they hadn't gotten around to it, since Lupo didn't do any classified research himself.

It was getting closer to lunch, but Loudon was actually intrigued enough to postpone his break. He was a little pleased with himself that he had at least kept a vestigial trace of the eagerness to pursue paper trails he'd had when he'd first joined the Bureau. He began with Lupo's personnel file. Lupo's high school was listed as the Illinois Institute of Math and Science. Then he had gone on to Caltech, where he got a degree in biology, an achievement that rated a sardonic grunt from Loudon at his memories of that notorious institution. The Caltech students were brilliant, of course, but they were also well known for pranks. When he was in LA, the Bureau had several mild run-ins with techies, in which they'd broken into federal computers, thwarted sophisticated federal building security systems, and so forth. Fortunately, the ASD LA would have to deal with the students this time. He'd ask the ASD to send an agent out to Caltech when he called in to report on his progress. It was time to begin making calls.

Lupo's file said his parents were both deceased, but maybe there was still some local connection that could help. So, he called the Chicago office and briefed the ASAC there, Rick Wayne, asking if a field agent could go out and check family friends and neighbors. The Assistant Special Agent in Charge, whom Loudon knew well from his time in Chicago, agreed to have an agent do a bit of legwork—in return for a bottle of liquor to be specified later. Loudon agreed, as long as it was cheap booze, thanked the ASAC and hung up.

He continued to look through Lupo's personnel file, which contained many more documents than the company had originally given him. There were medical reports, performance reports, and a project assignment history. He scanned through them. Nothing unusual. He couldn't really understand the assignments; they were too technical. But it did appear that Lupo was doing a lot of stuff. He cleared all the previous mounds of papers off his desk, revealing for the first time in a year the desktop's wood grain, and spread out the reports on a clean surface. Walter, with his trick with the phone book, had started Loudon thinking about what the pages looked like.

The assignment history drew his particular attention. There was one page, with a simple list of project names, the last of which began about a year ago. But all Lupo's previous assignments had come at intervals of six months or so. So, maybe Lupo had gotten a new assignment six months ago. The assignment sheet was filled in to within a few lines of the bottom, and the assignments took a few lines to describe. Maybe the latest assignment had started on a second page. Loudon examined the page, and then smiled to himself in triumph. Walter would be proud.

"The dummies! Who'd they think they were trying to fool?" Now he had them.

The Xeroxed assignment page had a couple of faint spots in the upper left-hand corner. The spots marked where the original had been stapled, obviously to a second page. But there was no second page anywhere in the file. Lupo's latest assignment had been left off. Now Loudon would go back to ArchiBiologics, but with a scientist; somebody who could interpret what was going on. Now, he'd go in kicking butt.

He leafed through the other papers, finding that, for one thing, Lupo had a pretty simple medical history, except for some allergies. He'd been seeing an allergist, a guy named Clayton. Loudon remembered that people who saw allergists had to go in pretty often for shots; maybe Lupo had made some arrangements with his allergist. Loudon looked up the allergist's phone number and punched it into the phone. The phone rang seven times before it was answered.

"Dr. Clayton's office."

"Yes, this is Special Agent Robert Loudon of the FBI calling. Can I talk to Dr. Clayton?"

There was a pause, long enough to be significant. "Well, he's not in now. The office is closed. I'm not in the office. I moved out to the answering service office. Are you calling about the infections?"

"What infections?"

"Oh . . . you know . . . the people who turned color. You're not calling about that?"

Loudon remembered seeing a TV news report at the bar about some weird disease out in La Vista. "No, I need some information about one of Doctor Clayton's patients."

"Oh, well, maybe you can reach him at home. You say you're FBI?"

"Yeah. But tell me about these infections."

The receptionist hemmed and hawed in reluctance, so Loudon lowered his voice to his best official-sounding baritone and vaguely threatened to bring her in for questioning. The threat worked, and the receptionist proceeded to spill all she knew about the strange disease, and what she'd heard from the hospital. Her voice tight with strain, she also told him that all the people who'd come down with the disease had been Dr. Clayton's patients. And, they'd all had shots in his office a week before.

"So, they shut up the office," said the receptionist, eager to end the conversation. "And I hear some health people are coming in to investigate. They want to find out how those things . . . they called them . . . uh . . . chromophores . . . got into the patients."

"Chromophores?" Loudon shuffled through Lupo's records spread on the desk, pitching some on the floor, until he found the word in Lupo's assignment list. And he remembered it in his notes. He went back to the receptionist. "Well, miss, looks like the health people aren't the only ones who're going to come in there," he said. Satisfied that he'd done well, Loudon was ready to reward himself with a liquid prize in the darkened bar in the basement of the hotel.

CHAPTER 5

Kathleen Shinohara strode through La Vista Hospital's automatic doors, which barely managed to swing open before her long-limbed, full-throttled gait would have carried her right through the glass. She hefted a thick briefcase in her right hand and had a camera bag slung over her left shoulder, leaning forward to propel the load. Several of the lounging reporters looked up from their chairs to admire the tall, striking young woman whose skin was the color of coffee with a touch of cream. She swept past them in her sunglasses, wearing a long-sleeved green cotton shirt, sand-colored jeans and sturdy hiking boots. A smartphone rested in a holster attached to her wide belt. She plopped both pieces of luggage down in front of the reception desk and turned to look behind her, taking off her sunglasses and brushing back a few strands of her gloriously rambunctious mane of curly black hair. Her smooth movements portrayed a strong, svelte body that had undergone vigorous training to its owner's specifications and was required to perform as such.

Lips pursed, she was staring impatiently at an old man tramping in after her, wearing a red plaid flannel shirt, a multi-pocketed bush jacket, and khaki work pants, and wheeling a larger case. He was thin and wiry, and his dark-tanned skin had the texture of cow hide from being in the sun. His rheumy blue eyes darted around the room, taking in the reporters and cameras with a look of crusty disdain. His long, sparse white hair was a confederation of individual tufts that had agreed to occupy the same head, but with each determined to emerge from his scalp in any direction it saw fit. The old man waved at her impatiently to go ahead, while he hauled the case into place. She turned to face the receptionist.

She had almond eyes so ebony dark that her forthright stare disconcerted many. The eyes, set beneath expressive dark eyebrows, seemed fathomless, hungry for image, open to information. The geometry of her oval face was as striking. Her slim nose curved the slightest bit upward, ending with fine nostrils. Her mouth was wide and expressive, the lips turning up at the corners, inviting a contemplation of the aesthetics of their curves.

"We're from the CDC," she said quietly to the receptionist. "We're here to see Doctor Meadows." The receptionist called to check with Meadows.

"Kathleen, I want a drink," declared the old man. "You want a drink? A fruit juice?"

"No, Doc," she said briskly. "Let's get in first. Let's see what we've got to do."

"I'm getting a drink," grumped the old man. "And I'm getting you one, too. I'm getting you a juice. Maybe a bagel. You didn't eat, Kathleen. Again you didn't eat, Kathleen."

"Okay, Doc, okay." She turned back to the receptionist, her expression demanding action.

"Tell 'em to wait," the old man said over his shoulder as he wandered off to find the snack bar.

The receptionist confirmed the appointment and nodded to the security guard, giving Shinohara directions to Lori Meadows' office. Shinohara told the receptionist to pass them on to the old man, picked up the luggage and hiked away. The old man reappeared shortly with two cartons of orange juice and a bagel, got directions, grabbed his case and rolled it away after her.

They reached Lori Meadows's office within a minute of each other, entered together and introduced themselves. Meadows invited them to sit down, and the old man immediately thrust the carton at Shinohara, scowling at her until she opened it and proceeded to drink. He held the bagel at the ready, preparing to thrust it at her to demand that it be consumed. He then opened his own juice.

"So, you have some people that have turned colors?" began Shinohara, quickly finishing her juice and pulling out a notebook. She pointedly ignored the bagel.

"I gotta tell ya, you've sure got Atlanta interested," said Doc between sips of juice. "They sent us out here because we've sort of specialized in these weird kinds of cases. We've worked on hantavirus, meningitis, Legionnaire's disease . . . all kinds of bugs. Anyway, they're beginning to culture the cells you sent. The melanocytes. Don't exactly know what the cells are doin' yet, but the morphologies are real weird. They said this clearly ain't a chemical thing."

Meadows shook her head in puzzlement and briefed them on the medical histories of the patients at La Vista and the other hospitals. She also briefed them on the fact that all the patients had seen the allergist, Russell Clayton.

"Well, we haven't seen any final results on the cause," said Shinohara. "But I talked to Atlanta this morning, and they said it's very possible it's a virus. Maybe even likely. We're with the National Center for Emerging and Zoonotic Infectious Diseases, and they're doing a regular workup on the putative virus. Innoculating mice, rats, monkeys. Some monoclonal antibody work to see if it's like something we know. If it is a virus of some kind, we need to know how it got started."

"Then you'll be interested in a call I got from the FBI yesterday," said Meadows. "They're looking for a patient of Doctor Clayton's who's missing, and the agent said he wanted to talk to you, and to go into Clayton's office when you did." She held out a slip of paper neatly inscribed with Loudon's name and phone number on it, and Doc took it.

"I'll call the guy. I've worked with 'em before. They can be a pain sometimes."

"So, shall we go see the patients?" asked Shinohara, standing up quickly, betraying her eagerness. "We'll do some re-interviewing and take another set of samples to send to Atlanta. Okay with you, Doc?"

51

"Yup, I'll call the FBI after we're done." He resignedly stuffed the uneaten bagel in a pocket in his jacket.

They donned green scrub suits, blue paper booties, surgical masks, caps, and gloves, and entered the women's ward. Lying in bed with her knees up, the teenager Ellen Lucius held a small digital recorder to her pretty blue lips and mumbled into it. So did Ada Frye, who also had earphones on listening to the television. Joy Chambers, however, was peering at herself in the mirror, lifting one of her chins to see underneath. Her skin was no longer red, but a reddish beige, a caked slather of makeup revealing an attempt at disguising her color.

"They are colored all right!" exclaimed Doc. Shinohara nudged him and shushed him, the shush puffing out her mask.

"Ladies, I'd like you to meet two field epidemiologists from the Centers for Disease Control and Prevention—Doctor Smith and Doctor Shinohara. They're here to help us figure out what you have."

"Epidemiologists? You mean we got an epidemic?" asked Ada Frye, taking off the earphones to hear better.

"Well, not necessarily. We think it may be a virus, though," said Shinohara. With that information, Ada Frye and Ellen Lucius both held the recorders to their mouths and mumbled portentously into them.

"They have this Hollywood agent," explained Meadows, "and he told them that they should record everything that happens . . . for the movie script." Doc snorted, and Shinohara smiled, her dark eyes narrowing to amused ebony slits above the mask.

"And how about the lady in the corner?" asked Doc. "She doesn't look too colored."

"Joy, show them," suggested Meadows, and Joy Chambers laboriously reached over to her side table and held up a large jar of theatrical makeup. She grinned, and the shifting folds of flesh revealed lines where the makeup had collected.

"Joy wasn't too comfortable being red, so she thought she might try a little makeup."

Doc snorted, again, and Shinohara shot him a warning look.

"So, ladies, any new developments since I saw you last?" asked Meadows.

"Oh yeah!" said Ellen. "This is cool! At least I think so. Ada don't much like it!" She put down her recorder and pulled her long brown hair apart to reveal her scalp. "See! See! The roots are turning blue! I'm gonna have blue hair!" Shinohara leaned in to look. Sure enough, the hair at the roots had turned the same blue as the skin, a preview of the hair to come. "Ada, show 'em yours," said the teenager. "It's even cooler!"

"Cooler my behind. Look at this!" spat Ada, parting her short hair to reveal the beginnings of bright yellow roots on the shiny black hair. "I'm gonna look like a haystack in a few months! Or one of them Raggedy Ann dolls. Some white doll."

With that, Meadows excused herself to tend to other duties, and Doc and Shinohara set to work. They interviewed each patient at length, going over their medical histories and their habits. The women all quickly volunteered that they had each visited the allergist Russell Clayton. Joy Chambers became teary eyed, Ellen Lucius sputtered with adolescent indignation, and Ada Frye described graphically and physiologically what she planned to do to Clayton once she caught him. Her plans involved some pretty serious bodily harm.

The two CDC doctors quizzed each of the women in detail about the treatment they had undergone in the doctor's office. Then the doctors opened their cases, pulling out instruments and containers to take samples of blood, skin, hair, and urine from each woman. After the samplings, each woman mumbled at length into her recorder.

After two hours, they moved into the men's isolation ward and performed the same routine of interviewing and sample-taking. The men were cooperative, with the two young men being particularly cooperative with Shinohara, wondering just what kind of face lay beneath her mask to go with the striking dark eyes. They were slightly embarrassed at having to go into the bathrooms to deliver urine samples, but Shinohara's no-nonsense manner allowed no modesty.

"Okay, you're a woman . . ." Lance began his hypothetical scenario.

"Observant," said Shinohara. "Your point?"

"You think the red's a turn-off? Y'know, to women?"

She smiled, and above the mask her eyes again became amused, dark slits. "No, actually I think it's kind of macho," she answered with a sarcasm that was lost on Lance. The answer pleased Lance no end.

"Hey, you got an agent?" asked the skinny, goateed Eddie Chandler.

Shinohara shook her head. "Look, here's my agent's card. Benny. Call him. Get set up. There's big bucks in this."

After the men had finished giving their interviews and samples, they, too, clicked on their digital recorders and began recording.

That afternoon Doc and Shinohara repeated the process at the other hospitals, finally finishing up in the evening. Shinohara, driving the rented black Ford suv, headed for the airport to ship their samples to the CDC laboratories in Atlanta, while Doc called the FBI office on his cell phone.

He got Loudon's voice mail and announced, "We're startin' early; about seven. We're not gonna wait, so if you want to be in on this, be there."

• • •

About ten a.m. the next morning, a yawning Loudon pulled into the parking lot outside Russell Clayton's office. The California sun had long ago warmed away the night's desert chill, and the asphalt was beginning to bake under the dry heat. After showing his FBI credentials to get through a police line holding back a small crowd of reporters, TV cameras, and onlookers, he found a black SUV already parked in front of Clayton's office. A large patrolman sat on a borrowed office chair a safe distance from the office door, drinking coffee. Loudon flashed his credentials again.

"Nobody's supposed to go in. Not even you," said the patrolman rising to a height well above Loudon's.

"It's okay," said Loudon. "We're all federal." Before the cop could figure out what that meant, Loudon had slipped past him into the waiting room. On the coffee table, he found a small cardboard drum like an ice cream container marked with the three ominous red pincers that was the international trefoil symbol for a biohazard. The drum was full of screw-top vials, as well as plastic bags full of other vials that looked as if they had come from the doctor's office. He poked through them with a pen, wiped it off on his pants, and stuck it in his shirt pocket. He then wandered back into the examining rooms, still yawning and opening his eyes wide in an effort to wake up. In one of the rooms, he found a small man in latex gloves, surgical cap, and booties and a large disposable isolation suit. A respirator covered his head and face, its hose connected to a small, whining air filter strapped to his waist. He used small cotton swabs to dab samples from the surfaces of the examining room, dropping them into the screw-top vials and labeling them. He glanced up.

"You the FBI guy? Get out of here!" he commanded without pausing from his work, over the noise of the filter, his voice muffled by the respirator. He bent over a sink, poked a swab down the drain, and dropped it into a plastic bag, which he labeled.

Loudon waited until he looked up and shouted. "Yeah, fine, but I need to see about getting something with fingerprints on it."

Doc shook his head and waved him off. "I don't care what you want. Get back outside. We don't know what we've got here, and you ain't got a suit on."

Loudon folded his arms and leaned against the doorway. "Well, then how about if I go out there and take that whole box with me?"

From behind him, Loudon heard, "You do, and we'll have you quarantined along with the other patients." He turned to see another isolation-suited person standing in the hall, an orange bag of vials in her latex-gloved hand. It was a woman. He could tell by the curves even beneath the baggy suit, the voice, the flashing dark eyes through the full-face respirator, and by the bulbous surgical cap confining a mass of hair. He could also tell that she was serious about challenging him by the aggressive tilt of her head and the forward angle of her body.

"Look, I've got to do my job, miss. I'm looking for this guy. He could be important to both of us."

"I hope you got your gun with ya, Mr. Agent," said Doc wryly, crouching down to peer under the sink. "You're gonna have to shoot that woman, you want to take those samples."

"Am I going to have to shoot you?" Loudon smiled his best smile.

"It's been tried," she said, her eyes still serious from within the mask. "Look, go outside, and we'll come out and talk in a minute. Don't touch anything on the way out. Don't put your hands to your mouth." She watched Loudon leave. "And quit yawning."

Loudon went outside, leaned against the wall and talked to the cop. The minute stretched to thirty, and Loudon was considering whether to try talking the cop out of his coffee when the two suited figures emerged into the sunshine, each carrying a cardboard drum. The woman motioned Loudon back. They walked out into the parking lot, put the cardboard drums into the back of the SUV and began to strip off the isolation suits.

As the woman began to remove the equipment, the cop abruptly stood up, keenly interested in the process. She stripped off the respirator to reveal a beautiful dark-eyed face, creased only by the temporary marks pressed into it by the mask's seals. And she emerged from the baggy suit like an exotic butterfly emerging from a homely pupa, to uncover a lithe, brown t-shirted body that had seen the benefit of much exercise. Loudon joined the rapt audience of two. The woman ended the disrobing process by stripping the booties off her tennis shoes and pulling off the cap and gloves. She bent over at the waist and shook her head vigorously, fluffing out a mane of dark hair and flipping it back.

"Interestin' people, these scientists," said the cop, not taking his eyes from the woman.

"Yeah," agreed Loudon. "I always did like science."

The old man also stripped off his suit, except that he wore a red plaid flannel shirt and khaki work pants. And he left his white hair plastered against his head in an unruly mess. The two carefully stuffed the isolation clothing into an orange plastic bag marked with the biohazard symbol. They then proceeded to rinse their arms, hands, faces and necks with a blue solution from a squirt bottle in the trunk of the car. It dribbled off their bodies, making a large puddle on the asphalt that immediately began to evaporate in the warm sun. After drying off with towels, they approached Loudon, carrying with them the smell of disinfectant. The woman held out a squirt bottle of the blue liquid.

"Did you touch anything?"

"Well, maybe the doorknob. I'm not sure."

"Put out your hands." Loudon obediently did so and received a rinsing with the pungent liquid. The old man gave him a towel to dry off.

"You're lucky we didn't make you strip and bathe in the stuff," said the old man. "We can't take chances. I'm Doc Smith," he said, shaking Loudon's now-smelly hand. "This is Dr. Kathleen Shinohara. We're from the CDC." Loudon nodded to her. So the name was Shinohara. He thought he'd detected a hint of the orient in those eyes.

"I'm Robert Loudon, Doc. Call me Bobby." He turned to the woman. "Call you Kathy?"

"Kathleen," she said folding her arms and looking dourly at him.

"Then call me Robert," he said flashing a smile.

"Right, Robert, you say you need some fingerprints?" asked Shinohara.

"Yes, I'm looking into the disappearance of a patient of Doctor Clayton's. A few days ago. It's an interesting coincidence that he's a biologist, and he was working on, uh, chromophores."

"Coincidences like that can break open cases," said Doc. "What else you got?"

"Well, first, we've got to settle this business of the fingerprints. I need any bottles that he might have handled." Loudon knew he had their interest; now, they'd be more willing to cooperate.

"Of course, you know that if he planted any infected bottles in that office, they'd probably be long gone. They'd be in the medical waste stream and may well have been destroyed. We're going to try to track them later today. There's a company in San Diego that handles the stuff. But those would be contaminated, too. So, you can't have any of it."

"Look, let's not get all uptight about it," said Loudon. "How about we let Atlanta deal with it? When you send stuff to Atlanta, just tell your folks there not to handle the bottles so that it would destroy the prints. And when they decide the bottles are noninfectious, the Atlanta FBI office can pick them up and do the latents. I'll tell my supervisor in LA."

"Right, okay, that takes care of that," said Doc. "Let's go to the hotel, get cleaned up, get breakfast and talk about this guy you're looking for."

"You did all this before breakfast?"

"Yeah, we're pretty tough that way." Doc smirked at Loudon's obvious bleariness.

Loudon followed them in his car to a nearby Ramada Inn, where he went to the coffee shop while the CDC doctors showered and changed. Sitting in a booth with a view of a nearby golf course, he called Walter's cell phone to get an update. He had also downed two mugs of coffee, which had stopped his yawning, when they arrived, smelling better than they had before. Doc wore a fresh red plaid flannel shirt, bush jacket, and khaki work pants. Loudon wondered whether the old man had multiple copies of the same outfit. Shinohara had on brown jeans and a sleeveless blouse, with her damp hair tied back in a loose ponytail. Her face was moist and glowing.

Over omelets and toast, he briefed them on his investigation of Arthur Lupo and ArchiBiologics. As Shinohara took careful notes in a notebook beside her neglected plate, he told them that his partner, Walter, had found an odd pattern in Lupo's bank accounts. Over the last year, he had been drawing several thousand a month out in cash and cashing out CDs. Overall, he'd depleted accounts worth about $850,000 down to about $40,000. However, Walter was still trying to trace the original source of all the money. And Loudon hadn't found anything unusual when he spent the previous day poring over the files from Lupo's apartment. He told them about the trip to ArchiBiologics and the missing notebooks, and that the Chicago agent was going to interview family, friends and neighbors.

"The cops grilled the allergist Clayton," he said spreading jam on his toast. "I downloaded their video and phone-interviewed him. He said Lupo was just another patient. He gave Lupo shots for a pollen allergy. He's scared of being sued by the colored people. He'd be delighted if Lupo was responsible."

"You figured out where his lab is?" asked Doc, tapping Shinohara's plate with his fork and staring at her pointedly until she gave him a look of mock exasperation, put down her pen and began to eat. It seemed an unspoken joke between them.

"You means besides his lab at work?"

"Yeah. If he's working on some kind of virus, I don't think he could have done this at work. People would've known. At some point, we need to see his lab at work; then we'll know for sure."

"When we looked at his apartment, Walter figured out he'd been looking to buy lab equipment. Walter's already checking into that. And there's evidence that he was looking for somebody to truck something somewhere, so Walter's checking that."

"Walter's a busy guy," said Doc, sipping his coffee.

"Ball of fire," said Loudon. "You'll like Walter."

"Look, we need to get into his apartment, too," said Shinohara. "We've got to do the same . . ." she stopped to pull her vibrating cell phone from her belt. She answered, listened for a moment, and then said, "It's Atlanta. You keep talking, I'll be back." She pushed out the chair and walked outside the restaurant, where she paced up and down, talking animatedly. Loudon watched her movement with great interest.

"You'll show us his apartment?" asked Doc, loud enough to regain his attention. He returned reluctantly to the old man.

"Sure. Think there's any danger that my partner and me were exposed to anything?"

"We don't rule that out," said Doc.

Loudon felt a chill skitter up the back of his neck. He reminded himself to look more closely at his face in the mirror. "Those people really turned colors?"

"Yeah . . . red, yellow, blue . . . bright like Crayolas. We don't know what is going on here."

"Yeah, well, neither do I. Listen, could you two do me a favor and look over Lupo's scientific papers? I don't understand them. But there may be something there that indicates why those notebooks are missing."

"Yeah, we can do even better." He signaled the passing waitress for more coffee, and thanked her gallantly. "We can find out what else he's published and do a rundown on ArchiBiologics. We've got to do it anyway. There's some answers here somewhere."

Loudon gave him the address of Lupo's apartment, which Doc scribbled in Shinohara's notebook, and they planned to meet there later that day. Loudon was about to raise the subject of Shinohara's social life when she returned, a look of deep worry on her face.

"Doc, Atlanta has managed to do enough with the monoclonal antibodies to figure out a little about the virus. It looks a lot like vaccinia." She sat down, taking a sip of her tea, her brow knitted in thought.

"Vaccinia's harmless," Doc explained to Loudon. "It's used as the basis for smallpox vaccine."

"Well, then it's okay?"

"No, it's *not* okay," said Shinohara. "Vaccinia's also used as a test virus in gene insertion experiments. Atlanta says this virus has been genetically engineered. They've got to do a lot more work. They're going to isolate the genes and get their structure. But it looks like somebody, maybe Lupo, managed to stick the genetic blueprints for chromophores into it. It's man-made. Atlanta hasn't come close to figuring it all out yet. They say the virus particles appear to be built like Swiss watches. They're masterpieces of biotechnology."

"Well, if it's just color, it can't hurt, can it?" asked Loudon.

"That's not the point," said Shinohara. "This looks like it was just a test . . . an indicator. Atlanta thinks somebody's trying to build viruses that can infect the body without triggering the immune system. That means there's no defense against them." She slowly closed her notebook and sat back in the booth, looking at Doc, then at Loudon, worry clouding her face. "Somebody released this one as a test on humans. Or maybe a warning. We don't know. But it worked, and the virus carried the chromophore genes into the human cells, and they turned on. They started pumping out pigments . . . chromophores . . . and the people turned color. Whoever did it could sneak *any* genes in there! Doc, I told you. Didn't I tell you?"

"Yes ma'am, you did. You surely did."

"Told him what?"

"I told him that genetic engineering techniques were getting so powerful we'd have a case like this soon."

"A case of what?"

"Well, the traditional biological weapons were horrible enough, but at least we kew what we were dealing with. Anthrax, hemorrhagic fevers, smallpox. We could detect them, and we could track their production. And before, it took an industrial-sized plant to make enough to be widely dangerous. But no more. The equipment is cheaper and easier to use. And there's more information out there about how these bugs work. So now we've got our first bioterrorist who could have the equipment and the knowledge to build something science, or nature, has never seen before. These bugs could be the genetic equivalent of nuclear bombs!"

CHAPTER 6

Arthur Lupo always got a sort of existential, sensual pleasure out of the act of pipetting. Precisely transferring a minute amount of liquid from one container to another was an art, and he was good at it. Like a musician wielding a fine instrument, he raised the automatic pipette to eye level, peering slightly cross-eyed at its plastic tip. His little mouth pursed slightly, and his brow wrinkled as he concentrated.

"Okay, okay," he breathed to himself. "Just enough. Just precisely enough." He'd gotten into the habit of talking to himself during the long stretches alone in his lab. He liked what he said. He was a good coach, a good advisor, a good cheerleader.

He pressed his thumb down on the pipette's plunger, lowered its tip precisely into the bottle of clear liquid, and released his thumb. The act drew a microliter, the merest speck of liquid into the pipette's translucent tip. He inserted the tip into a tiny plastic vial, held in the same hand as the bottle, and pressed down on the plunger, depositing the glistening, infinitesimal droplet in the vial's pointed bottom.

"There you are, safe and sound."

Again and again, he deftly repeated the procedure with other vials, adding a single perfect droplet to vial after vial. He loved all the technical steps in his experiments. He loved the way each movement, each perfectly planned step, combined to form a well-wrought experiment—like individual molecules joining and interlocking to form a crystal. And he loved the way each experiment, intricate and beautiful, combined to build a theory, like crystals combining themselves to form a beautiful glittering crystalline flower—the kind of mineral flowers he once saw sprouting from walls in the dark, moist depths of a cave in northern California. This vision of perfection helped him to overcome the failures, the many experiments that went wrong through bedeviling, insidious error, or foul, dark, uncontrollable fate.

But his last experiment had gone brilliantly, and his newest experiment promised to go just as well. He remembered the sense of achievement he felt at sitting in the hospital waiting room carefully recording the results in the gray lab notebook. The virus had performed just as he predicted. The infected people were adding useful data to his beautiful flower of scientific achievement, one that would grow and grow until it burst open, shaking the world like an earthquake.

So, he stood with satisfaction at the lab bench, preparing the rack of samples, concentrating completely on the technical ballet of action. Like a dancer or a concert pianist caught up in the flow of a performance, he moved swiftly and gracefully through his complicated experimental process.

"Now you . . . and now you . . . and now you," he told the little vials as he deposited a drop of liquid in each.

Between steps, he glanced over at the desk at one end of his small laboratory, concentrating on the brown cardboard box sitting on it.

"Hello there," he told the box. "I'll take care of you guys in a minute. Just you wait." He'd received a new shipment from Philadelphia, and he stood looking at it in delicious anticipation. He'd open it soon. It would be his reward for an experiment well done.

His small laboratory, built with his own hands, was his world most of the time. The whole complex was fifty feet long and ten feet wide. At one end was a door to a small bedroom and bath, both of which he regarded as places to be used as little as possible, since the activities there interrupted his experiments. At the other end was the door to the outside, his new motorcycle parked there beside his small desk.

Beside the desk sat his computer, his pride and joy. He had used it to invent a massive mathematical computer model that allowed him to construct simulated viruses in the computer before building them in the laboratory. Using that computer, he'd hatched his plan for the Lupo viruses. The plan had worked like clockwork so far. He also used the computer to store massive amounts of data on the DNA genes of viruses, to tap into GenBank, the government's repository of gene sequences, and to play his special version of StarStation Death. He had altered the famed blast-the-aliens game to replace the standard monsters with images of various people he didn't like, which he exploded into bloody pulps with shotgun, machine pistol and chainsaw, as he skulked through a setting he'd reprogrammed from a space station into the laboratories of ArchiBiologics.

Over the desk hung pictures—mostly images of viruses, and one of Jeany Moody he'd taken through a telephoto lens. She was sitting at a table outside the company cafeteria, the sun lighting her pretty face, her white lab coat open to show her legs in a short skirt.

But most significant of all was the photo of the smiling middle-aged couple that were his inspiration, his motivation. He always lingered on that image before returning determinedly to his work.

He finished his pipetting and checked his separatory electrophoresis gel. It was a thin slab of glistening clear gelatin poured between closely-spaced squares of glass and enclosed in a clear plastic box with electrodes attached to either end. He had injected samples of protein mixture into the gel at one end, and a tickle of electricity was drawing them along the length of the gel. The electric current would separate the many components of the protein mixture, with some being drawn through the gel faster than others.

"Hey, how you little proteins doing?" he asked. "Hurry up, now, let's see who gets there first?" When the proteins were separated, he would stain the gel to see them. Then, he would have the last answer he needed for his next experiment. Previously, he had extracted the mix of proteins from human cells infected with the new virus. They were his soldiers. They were the gorgeous little molecular machines that his virus made in the human cell. In turn, they did the work of churning out the chromophores he wanted the infected cells to make. It was a daring new experiment, another step toward his goal. This experiment would tell him if his new virus, his latest pride and joy, was taking control of human cells and making them produce just the right proteins.

He had some time until the gel was finished. He hungrily eyed the cardboard box with the Philadelphia return address. He decided he deserved it.

"Okay, you guys just keep on," he told the proteins on the gel. "I've got to see these guys over here." He took off his lab coat, washed his hands in the little sink at the end of the lab bench and stepped over to the box.

"You want out? You want out of there? I'll let you out of there." He slit the box neatly with a pair of scissors and carefully opened the top. There they were, sealed safely in their little cellophane packages.

Tastykakes!

His round face lit up and his mouth watered as he carefully lifted the packages one by one to admire them in the light.

"Hi, guys," he said as he took them out and lined them up on the desk. "Welcome. Glad to have you here." He lined up Jelly Krimpets, Strawberry Krimpets, Koffee Kakes, Chocolate Cup Cakes, Lemon Pies, Honey Buns, Chocolate Kandy Kakes, Peanut Butter Kandy Kakes, Dunkin Stix, Pecan Twirls, Coconut Juniors, Soft & Chewy Chocolate Chip Cookies, Tasty Klair Pies, Vanilla Sugar Wafers, Pastry Pockets, and Frosted Mini Donuts.

"Okay, we'll have you and you, and you," he incanted as his eager pudgy fingers sorted through the box. He chose a Blueberry Pie to begin, a Chocolate Iced Creme-Filled Chocolate Kupcake for the middle, and a Vanilla Sugar Wafer to climax the meal. He washed each down with sips of an ice-cold Coke Classic from the small refrigerator beneath the desk.

After he finished the meal, he carefully replaced the Tastykakes in the box and stored it in the cupboard above the desk. He returned to his work, first greeting and checking on the electrophoresis gel. It was ready. He carefully opened the box, separated the glass plates, and peeled the gel gently off one of them and stained it. He smiled at the clean procession of little blue smudges along the glistening gel.

All the proteins were right where they should be. The line of smudges in the gel that told him the new virus was working as expected. He examined the smudges to determine what proteins were present, and inscribed the information meticulously in his lab notebook.

Now, he had to check his results with his computer simulation. He stepped to the computer and addressed it.

"Hello, computer," he said.

"Hello," the computer replied. It was Jeany Moody's girlish voice, sounding stilted and mechanical because the computer was stitching together her words. He'd secretly recorded her in the lab, in meetings, or giving talks. And he'd digitally taken apart syllables and fed them into the computer. The computer reassembled them as it needed to respond. "What is the password?" asked the electronic Jeany Moody.

"Sweetheart," said Arthur.

"Thank you, Arthur," said the computer with a digital coquettishness. "May I have the virus program?"

In response, a colorful pattern of viruses swirled onto the screen. It was an artwork he'd developed to open his program. He tapped in a few keyboard commands to call up his mathematical virus simulation, and shortly floating before him was a computer picture, the familiar spiked surface of his new vaccinia virus, Lupo390. He fed the new protein data in, and the virus abruptly sprouted a have-a-nice-day smiley face. The smiley face was the computer's signal that the virus would infect as planned.

"Thank you, computer. That will be all," said Arthur.

"You're welcome, Arthur," said the computer and turned its screen off, its cooling fan still whirring quietly.

Now was the time to work with the viruses themselves. He was always excited when he worked with the viruses. He moved to the sealed isolation chamber at the far end of the lab. It was a large clear lucite chamber, with a pair of arm-length black rubber gloves sealed to its side, waiting for him to insert his hands, to alter and control the tiny living organisms in the screw-top flasks within. Beside the gloves was an airlock for disinfecting things to be transferred in and out of the box. Sitting just outside the isolation chamber was an aquarium, its bottom covered with sand. Nestled in one corner was a large lobster, it's antenna lazily wafting back and forth.

"It's going very well," Lupo whispered to the lobster. "Very, very well."

He thrust his hands into the gloves, flexing his stubby fingers to check for leaks and peering through the lucite at the virus cultures in the little plastic flasks. First he checked his ongoing cultures in a rack along one wall of the chamber. They were all there and all looked healthy. Each flask had a thin film of human cells coating the bottom. Inside those cells, the viruses grew, parasitically drawing their needs from the living human cells.

"Are you happy, guys? You look happy? Is the food good? I'll get you more later." He scanned the labels: VACA, VAC304, EZV422, AV9900, DF205, HV330, MH660. He paused at the last one, considering what the vial held—a masterpiece of genetic engineering.

But now he turned his attention to his own viruses, his babies, his creations. They were even more amazing. He greeted Lupo313, regarding it with pride, because it had already done its work. But now there was Lupo390.

"Ah. You look fine. Pretty fine," he told Lupo390, lifting the little plastic flask and unscrewing the top. His heavy breathing fogged the plastic wall of the chamber. He set down the flask and picked up one of a small pile of hypodermic syringes. Beside the pile was another pile of the cellophane bags they'd come in. He uncapped the needle and drew an infinitesimal drop of virus into the syringe, replaced its protective cap and set it aside. He repeated the procedure with two dozen more syringes, drawing the tiniest bit of live virus into each. He resealed each in its cellophane bag with a dab of glue. The result was a stack of syringes that looked unused, but each of which harbored a drop of his new virus.

He carefully recapped the virus culture, placed the bagged syringes in a plastic rack and pressed a red button to wash down the entire chamber with a fine mist of diluted bleach, followed with another button to wash the chamber with distilled water. Still another button sent a blast of warm, drying air through the chamber.

Then, he reached over, opened the inner door of the airlock and slid the rack into the chamber. He withdrew his hands from the black gloves and pressed buttons spraying the inside of the airlock with formaldehyde and bleach, followed by water. He somewhat disliked the disinfecting procedure. He knew it was necessary to kill any errant viruses that might escape, but it seemed such a shame. They were such exquisite, coolly efficient little creatures. After drying the airlock with a blast of warm air, he opened the outer airlock door and withdrew the rack of syringes, a faint smell of formaldehyde and bleach still clinging to them. He put his face close to the syringes.

"You guys okay in there? You guys okay? Ready to go? Okay, then."

He transferred the syringes one by one to a plastic Ziploc bag, inspecting each to see that the bag was sealed such that it didn't appear to have been tampered with. He rejected a couple. The seals didn't look pristine. Maybe a little glue clung to the outside, or the seal was a little crooked. Not that his latest test subjects to be infected by the new virus would notice, he thought. Those kind of people didn't notice much of anything in their drug-induced fog.

He placed the plastic bag into a backpack and went to the door.

"Computer?"

"Yes, Arthur?"

"Is there any movement outside?"

"No, Arthur. No signals from the motion sensors."

"Show me the cameras." Onto the computer screen came images from the four small low-light video cameras mounted outside the laboratory. They showed no intruders.

"Thank you, computer. Activate the security mechanism. Good night."

"You're welcome, Arthur." He loved it when the Jeany-Moody computer voice said his name. "Security mechanism activated. Good night, Arthur." The computer screen went blank.

He unlocked and opened the door and peered outside, left and right several times. It was quiet at one a.m. and pitch black. He slung the backpack over his shoulder, put on his big new red helmet and pushed the motorcycle out the door. He climbed on, started the motorcycle, and revved it a few times. Satisfied with the sound of its rumbling engine, he slipped it into gear and accelerated into the night to launch his next experiment.

CHAPTER 7

Loudon always hoped that his daughter Lindy would answer the phone, her lilting little voice boding well for the conversations that would ensue. However, it was Rochelle's refined "hello" that followed the click of the receiver lifting.

"Hi, this is Bobby," he said, trying to sound cheerful. "My weekly call, as usual. Lindy around?"

"Sure, Bob." Her voice lowered a half-step, a tension creeping in. Rochelle forced herself to be always polite, always correct. "Of course. First, though, we have to have a little talk." Loudon winced. She hadn't even tried to make small talk. This would be serious. The pieces of their broken marriage seemed like shards of a shattered bottle scattered on a beach. They lurked unseen, still sharp, still capable of suddenly rising to pierce, to wound.

"Bob, are you still wanting her to go out there after school's out?"

"Sure, of course. That's what we planned. Maybe the summer—"

"Listen, I hear you still don't have it all together. I hear you're drinking."

One of Rochelle's so-very-helpful friends must have seen him. "Well, I go to a bar now and then. But when Lindy comes out, that doesn't happen. Listen, you know that was never a problem."

"No, that was never a problem . . . to you. It was a problem to me, a symptom to me, but not to you. Bob, they sent you down to Temecula to figure things out. Have you settled down, got your priorities straight?"

"Yes."

"Really? I have a right to know. She's my daughter."

"Well, she's mine too . . ." Loudon stopped himself. They were about to step on one of the dangerous shards. He took a breath. "Rochelle, I promise it will be just fine. Lindy always comes first, you know that. Are you okay?" The question caught Rochelle off guard. She wasn't prepared for his concern for her.

"Sure, fine."

"You got anybody? I know it's not my business, but . . ."

"Well, I have a friend I'm seeing. I'm okay."

"Good."

"And you, Bob?" Her question was more than ex-wifely concern.

"Well, sure. I'm seeing a couple of people."

"A couple. Well, I hope they're both nice."

"Sure Rochelle, of course. Listen, it would be great for Lindy here. I know some couples who have daughters her age."

"Sure." She knew Loudon was lying, but she also knew he'd find some twelve-year-old friends for Lindy if she came out. "Look, I'll go get Lindy. But we'll have to have a longer talk before I let her come out there." There was a pause, and then the inexpressibly sweet voice of his daughter came on the phone.

"Hi, Daddy."

"Hi, sweetie. You doing okay? How's orchestra?"

"Oh, fine. Well, like, I've got this problem with this piece we're doing . . ." She went on to tell him about orchestra, school and the ups and downs of her pre-teen social life. He tried to stay one step ahead of the conversation; always trying to think up something else to talk about, to keep her on the phone. It didn't matter much to him what they talked about, but that she was there at the other end of the phone. His little girl. He began to tell her about the Lupo case and the strange colored people, trying to make it interesting, but keeping the information general, maintaining security. She was impressed that he was involved in the famous case she'd seen on TV, and that made him happy.

They talked for half an hour, and then said goodbye. When she hung up, he held the phone for a moment, reluctant to put it down, feeling the familiar ache of loneliness rise within him. He had mostly stopped missing Rochelle, realizing that the marriage was over. Perhaps it had never really begun. Maybe it had been merely a duty for him to marry the daughter of one of their social set in Chicago. But missing his daughter was different. He felt a deep void without Lindy that he managed to cover temporarily with alcohol and the company of women, but which was always with him. Maybe having Lindy more in his life was a reason for him to get serious about somebody, not just a "couple" of people. He shook his head at the stupid answer he'd given. That comment had been a big mistake, he realized. He'd have to be more careful with Rochelle, making sure to present a stable image.

He sat for a moment in the office, the slight achy hangover of the morning reasserting itself, adding to his ache at missing Lindy. At least he had time to recover from the hangover, since it was Saturday, and he was the only one there. It was too early for him to be up on a Saturday, but Rochelle insisted on an early call so Lindy could go about her weekend. And there was the meeting with the CDC doctors. For some reason, he wanted to impress them, too, proving he wasn't the slacker they seemed to think.

Last night in the bar, he'd told Walter not to bother coming in for the meeting. Besides, Walter had spent the last two days tracing Lupo's activities—phoning and slogging around the area checking out the laboratory supplies and trucking companies. So Loudon understood when Walter wanted to play a little golf in the morning and sit in his back yard and drink beer in the afternoon. Loudon busied himself going over Walter's reports on the computer. One of the lab supply places looked promising, but none of the freight companies had heard of Arthur Lupo or recognized his picture from the ArchiBiologics file.

He decided to try asking the Chicago agent who was checking up on Lupo's Chicago background. He knew he'd better have a full report for ADC Bowers in LA. Constantly haunting Loudon was the distinct possibility that Bowers had given him this case as a way of testing him, looking for a loophole to kick him out.

He wished he'd made sure he'd gathered all the facts on the nasty business he knew Bowers was up to. Instead, he'd only had enough to convince himself—enough to stupidly pull a gun on Bowers, which gave him the excuse to send him on the bricks to Temecula. And it sure wasn't enough certain information so that he could let anybody know the real story of that LA shootout with the drug gang, to let them understand how the result had devastated him. He hadn't even told Walter, although the veteran agent probably guessed there was more to the story he told about his assignment to Temecula.

The Chicago agent, Ron Clark, answered the phone. He sounded young. He hadn't been in Chicago when Loudon was there.

"Ron? Sorry to bother you at home on Saturday. It's Bobby Loudon in the Temecula RA."

"Oh, yeah." Clark's voice took on an edge. He knew of Loudon's reputation; the agent who had pulled a gun on his boss. The drunk in LA. "I thought I'd get back to you on Monday."

"Well, I need it now. What've you got?"

"Why don't I just email you a report?" Clark clearly wanted to stay as far from Loudon's case as he could. An email put distance between them. And it was a concrete record of their communication, meaning Clark's short performance record couldn't be sullied when this rogue agent maybe accused him of some vague transgression he couldn't even think of now.

"Look, Ron, can't you just give me the basics over the phone? I really need it now."

Clark paused for a long time, and the silence became a contest to see whether Loudon would retract his request or Loudon would relent. Clark gave in. "Well, you knew both parents are dead. But there's more to it. His mother was one of the people apparently sickened in the 2001 anthrax attack."

Loudon sat up straight in his chair. Any mental haze evaporated. "What?"

"Yeah, she was exposed. She worked in a federal building. She just went downhill for a couple of years. They moved to Chicago to be close to relatives. She eventually died. But Homeland Security and the CDC never did conclude it was from the anthrax. Then there was his father."

"What about the father?"

"Well, according to the neighbors, the mother's illness just devastated him. He had a bad heart, anyway, and he died in 2005. They said the kid just withdrew after that."

Loudon sensed that the parents' deaths would have given Lupo a prime motive. But a motive for what?

"How about friends? I mean Arthur's."

"The neighbors didn't know of any. Not in Chicago. Not anywhere, for that matter."

"Any other contacts?" asked Loudon.

"Oh, yeah. I forgot to say I went out to the school to see what they knew about Lupo. The principal remembered Lupo. He transferred in, so he didn't have any long-time school friends, either. The principal said Lupo was one of the most brilliant students ever. He went on to Caltech. Never did come back to visit."

Loudon remembered the old adage, "Follow the money."

"Say, were Lupo's parents well off?" he asked Clark.

"Oh, yeah, even with the illness and all. They lived out in Oak Park. Fancy big house. I guess the son got it all. Look, I've got to run. I'll send the email."

Loudon hung up and plunged into typing reports, energized by the discovery that Lupo's mother was essentially killed by a bioterrorist, and the father indirectly. At two minutes to ten, he considered whether to straighten his tie and put on his suit coat. But he decided since it was Saturday, he could go casual for his visitors. But he did clear his desk, stuffing piles of papers into a drawer and shoving more onto Walter's desk.

Exactly at ten, the CDC agents buzzed to be let into the cluttered office that was the FBI Temecula Resident Agency. Loudon showed them into the small conference room, with its scratched formica table, six plastic chairs and television cabinet with two of Walter's FBI golf tournament trophies on top. The CDC doctors wore their usual field clothes chosen to take just about any punishment that chasing epidemics could mete out. For Shinohara, it was faded blue jeans, a cotton blouse, and sneakers. Doc wore his usual red plaid flannel shirt, bush jacket, khaki work pants, and work boots. He had apparently made a stab at combing his hair, but failed, and was apparently not terribly concerned about the failure. Shinohara sat down and crossed her legs, two slim ankles showing between the bottom of her jeans and her sneakers.

Loudon bustled around getting coffee for them, hauled in Lupo's file, fished a pen out of one of Walter's golf trophies and settled down to talk.

"Where's your partner, Walter?" asked Doc. "I wanted to ask him about those lab supply places."

"Gave Walter the day off," he explained. "Even a ball of fire gets to rest sometime. I'll get him in touch with you. So, what have you got so far?"

"Well, we sent off the samples from his apartment," said Doc. Loudon remembered standing outside the apartment watching them through the windows. Dressed as before in full-face respirators and isolation suits, they'd gone over Lupo's sparsely furnished apartment with extraordinary thoroughness. The manager and his wife stood outside with him the whole time asking worried questions about a recent flu their kids had come down with. A concerned crowd gathered when the doctors came out to strip off their suits.

"We don't expect results for a while," said Shinohara.

"Yeah, well, I'm waiting with bated breath. So is Walter. It's not much fun thinking you could have been infected."

"We know that," said Doc. "We'll let you know of any exposure as soon as we can. Now for the really interesting stuff," said Doc, hauling a battered briefcase onto the conference table and pulling out a file. "We heard from CDC early this morning. They worked around the clock on this one. They confirmed that the little sucker is a vaccinia, so it's not airborne. So it can only be transmitted by being injected. And it's a masterpiece of genetic engineering. It's got some kind of coat protein that makes it invisible to the immune system. The body doesn't even know it's there, so it can do whatever it wants. It's also got a protein on its surface that binds only to melanocytes. And inside the virus, beside the usual vaccinia genes, it's got these genes that take over the melanocytes to make pigments. Turns off the body's regular brown pigment—melanin—and starts making colored ones. They're isolating genes and doing PCRs to get enough for sequencing."

"PCR?"

"Polymerase chain reaction. It's like a biological Xerox machine for genes. You can have just a single gene from a virus and it makes a zillion copies. Takes a while, but they'll figure out that whole virus eventually. They already got the chromophores identified, they think."

"The color genes?"

"Yeah, this is really something!" chortled Doc, flipping through a yellow pad. He found the page and set the pad down on the table, reading from it. "He apparently built three separate kinds of vaccinia viruses. There's one that infects human cells and makes them produce yellow carotene molecules, like from squash. And there's one that makes lycophene, like the red in tomato."

Loudon, grinning in amazement, said, "This guy is sticking vegetable genes into people? He's making them colored like vegetables?"

"Well, yeah," said Doc. "Guys at universities have already stuck human genes in plants. He just did the opposite. It works, obviously."

Loudon shook his head. "And the blue? There's no blue vegetables."

"Oh, that's clever, too. Some lobsters have a blue carotenoprotein—that's the blue you see up near the top of the legs. I've even seen all blue lobsters. That's the gene he used!"

"Lobster genes? So was all this hard for him to do?"

"Hard! That ain't the half of it!" Doc leaned back in his chair and slapped the table. "It was like building a car from safety pins. This guy put together all the genes for building the proteins that make these chromophores. He stuck them in a virus. He got the virus to target only human melanocytes and infect them. Then, he figured out how to turn off melanin in the human cell and turn these genes on. If this thing weren't so squirrelly, he'd be going to Sweden, pick up his Nobel, nothin' flat. CDC sure doesn't know how he did it!"

"So, he's just doing this vaccinia virus. It's a safe virus."

"No, you don't understand," said Shinohara, uncrossing her legs, leaning forward, shaking her head. "If he can do this, he can do *any-thing*. Let me tell you about viruses." Watching her eyes narrow, Loudon could tell this was her passion, the reason she was so devoted to her work. "Viruses are little parasitic machines. Their only purpose is to take over cells to force the cells to make more viruses. They're relatively simple, and they can be manipulated. They're basically genes wrapped in a protein coat, with maybe a lipid layer on the outside. They're, well, molecules with an attitude . . . a really nasty attitude." She shook her head again, shifting the curly hair back and forth.

"So, he could use these methods on other viruses?"

"Yeah, given enough time."

"What other viruses?"

"How about rabies, polio, encephalitis, smallpox, measles, yellow fever, . . . AIDS?" The names were like darts flung into the air.

"AIDS," sighed Doc sadly. His expression grew dark, distant with the memory of an old nightmare. The nemesis of his profession had been invoked. "That godforsaken bug. We missed that bug. We didn't have enough people, enough resources, enough brains, enough leaders." He looked suddenly tired. "We missed it. And look what's happening; look at the terrible, terrible things." He took a breath and recovered himself. "But we're not going to miss this one."

"Look, those aren't even the worst," said Shinohara. "There are viruses out there—hemorrhagic fevers, Ebola, Marburg, influenza—that are even more dangerous than AIDS. I've seen them work. It's like nothing you could imagine. If this guy knows what I think he knows, he could well be the most dangerous person on the face of the earth."

Loudon decided he'd better bother Bowers at home, once they had everything together. Maybe he couldn't really do this. Maybe it was time to turn some big boys in LA loose on it. Maybe he should ask Bowers to let him turn it over to another case agent. Bowers might stick a bad letter in his file, but he couldn't kick him out. Loudon really didn't know what to do.

"So, what've *you* got?" asked Doc, interrupting Loudon's musing. "Anything new on this guy?"

Loudon knew he had his own bombshell. "Well, if he wanted to spread a bioweapon, I think I know why he might want to do it. Revenge. His mother died as a result of the 2001 anthrax attack, and the government refused to admit it. His dad died probably because of the stress of the mother's death. From the reports I got, he is probably one angry, crazy, smart little punk."

A shroud of silent dread enveloped the room. Each of them looked down at their papers.

"We've got a potential disaster," Doc finally said. "We can't really call a full-on emergency based on what we have now. But we've got to get ready."

Loudon roused himself and rummaged through Lupo's file and pulled out a picture. "Anyway, we know what he might look like." The picture was a series of computer renderings of Lupo in different hairstyles, with different facial hair. "I transmitted his personnel file picture to a guy we have in DC who does computer facial renderings. He took off the hair and beard, put on a mustache, took off the glasses . . . did all kinds of things so we could see what he looks like with different arrangements. I just got them back this morning. We're going to run them all over town. One of our agents took the original around, but nobody recognized it; maybe they'll recognize this. From what you're saying, looks like we ought to run it all over the country."

"Yeah, and right now," mumbled Doc, scrutinizing the pictures.

"And here's his papers," said Loudon, handing a thick folder of scientific papers to Shinohara who began to read through them.

"Also, I wanted to show you this," said Loudon, pulling out the crumpled slip of paper that he'd found behind Lupo's desk. "These mean anything?"

Doc scanned the list, frowned and shook his head, then passed it to Shinohara.

"Maybe library references," she said. "That's what people write on little pieces of paper." She passed it back to Loudon. "Give us a Xerox, and we'll see if anything pops up. We'll read through his papers tonight. I already did a computer library search that pulled up the titles of his published papers. They show him working on what ArchiBiologics said . . . just the chromophore genes. These texts of the papers may give a hint, but we still don't see how he progressed to putting them into vaccinia viruses. There's a gap in his research we don't know about."

"Yeah, I think I got a hint of a gap," said Loudon, showing them the staple mark on the page from Lupo's personnel file. "They didn't give me the whole list of his assignments. At some point, I've got to go back to ArchiBiologics. We should all go."

The two CDC epidemiologists nodded.

"Yeah, Kathleen did a computer search on ArchiBiologics. I never can use those things. Tell 'em what you got, Kathleen."

Shinohara searched through her own leather portfolio and brought out some papers, proceeding to outline the search of ArchiBiologics's scientific work.

"They were doing some basic medical research for the National Institutes of Health on diagnostic tests for diseases. And they did contract work for other companies developing biological and medical products. But the kicker is that the company is apparently doing some classified work for the Army on anti-biological warfare methods . . . defensive stuff like vaccines," said Shinohara.

"I'd say that's a real kicker," said Loudon.

"Yeah, except that it's absolutely strictly defensive, and we don't see Arthur Lupo mentioned anywhere in the material."

"Well, there may be some answers out there," she said. "I haven't got the Bureau's search on ArchiBiologics and its personnel yet, but when I do, we'll have to see what's happening."

They gathered their materials and stood up. Loudon once more took note of Shinohara's slim figure. They left the conference room and went down the hall to the floor's shared copier to photocopy the little slip of paper for them.

The copier finally hummed to life and commenced a glowing scan of the slip. He handed her the photocopied page. As they headed for the elevator, Loudon remembered the hospital patients, the people who had started it all.

"So, since this thing isn't airborne, it's not very contagious. What happens to the . . . uh . . . colored people?"

"We told the hospitals they could release the patients," said Shinohara as the elevator opened.

"Ought to be a circus when that happens," said Loudon. As he rode down with them, he wondered whether it was time to put a move on the dark-eyed woman. She was beautiful. She was intelligent. She had a name that was easy to remember. But something about her put him off his rhythm. He was holding back, and he couldn't figure out why.

"Next thing, we really need to get into the medical waste facility," said Shinohara as the elevator door opened. "The vials we just got from the allergist's office were almost certainly not the containers that held the virus. They're long gone, in the medical waste. I talked to Clayton last night, and he said that the company picks up the stuff every two weeks, and they'd had a pickup a couple of days ago . . . one bag. And the disposal company guy I talked to said they hadn't done a burn in a week. So, we can probably find something. You going to go?"

Loudon took time to answer. On the one hand, there was the attraction of being out there with Shinohara. On the other hand, there was the prospect of wading, slightly hung over, through piles of old hypodermic needles and who-knows-what other biological grunge. Then, of course, there was the job he was supposed to do . . . at least until he decided not to.

"Well, I guess I should be there," he reluctantly concluded. "I may see things you don't."

"You'll have to suit up." Shinohara raised her eyebrows and smiled slightly, a sardonic smile. She had a small gap between her two front teeth, distinguishing her smile, making it more than a routine event. "If you're going into a medical waste facility, even to stand outside, you'll have to suit up."

Oh great, thought Loudon. What joy, being trapped inside a claustrophobic isolation suit amidst lethal biological garbage. "Yeah, well, I'll suit up. Won't be my favorite thing, but I'll suit up."

Chapter 8

"You *sure* you wanna do this?" asked the manager of the medical waste facility, scratching his head of well-oiled hair. "Nobody's ever gone down there." They stood peering by the light of his flashlight through a manhole into the shadowy depths of a large room-sized chamber. The manager had just pressed a large red button to open the sealed cover. The light played over mountains of orange and white plastic bags, most marked with the biohazard symbol. Some had split open, spilling their vile contents. Glittering in the light beam sweeping over the piles were used syringes, vials and bottles—some broken. The light revealed the white and brown blotches of bloody gauze bandages scattered over the soggy bottom of the chamber. A moist organic stench smelling like a mix of decay and disinfectant rose from the manhole. On the other side of the chamber was a large chute where medical waste trucks backed up to unload into the pit.

The manager shook his head slowly.

"Look, we don't even touch that stuff after it's loaded on the truck," he said. "We just dump it down there, and when it gets full, turn on the burners. Burns it to ash, and we open trap doors to let the ash out." Sure enough, Loudon could see large gas burners lining the bottom and sides of the sooty chamber. "There's used needles down there, and infected bandages and razors and all sorts of medical waste that people throw in those bags. They even dump scalpels in there."

"Looks like a cave," said Shinohara, almost to herself. For the first time, Loudon detected something other than absolute confidence in her voice.

"I know it does, Kathleen," said Doc. "You don't have to go." Loudon sensed an unsaid history behind Shinohara's hesitance.

"Well, I do," she said resolutely. "There's a bag down there somewhere that's got bottles in it that have the virus. We'd have a pristine sample. We'd know how it started out." She was talking herself into the descent.

Loudon peered down into the darkened pit. The same bottle might also have a fingerprint on it—the only evidence that would link Lupo to the infection in Clayton's office. Otherwise, Loudon only had a coincidence and a hunch. A print would be the main link in the chain of evidence that would convict Lupo. Otherwise, he might get off. But climbing down in that pit was testing the limits of Loudon's dedication. He hadn't tested those limits since LA. And that ended up with his marriage breakup and the banishment to Temecula. His mind tentatively explored those limits. What would he do for a case now?

"Sure a lotta junk down there," he said philosophically. "Y'know, we could—"

"Let's do it," interrupted Shinohara and headed for the SUV to pull out their equipment. "Full isolation suits," she said over her shoulder. "This is a hot area."

Doc nodded, set his jaw and followed. Loudon stood for a moment, then turned and followed, too. He really didn't know why he was doing it . . . duty to the Bureau, the challenge of the case, the danger to people, the embarrassment of backing out, the woman. But he really didn't know why he did most things these days.

At the SUV, Shinohara was already pulling out pressurized suits. They were heavier duty than the suits and respirators used before. They had rubberized fabric helmets with faceplates and backpacks.

"These are Racal suits," said Shinohara. "They're pretty tough, but they can be punctured. They carry an air pump that filters the incoming air. We always bring four suits, so there's one for you.

"Great," said Loudon. "My size, I take it?"

"Strip down as much as possible. You may have to dispose of your clothes afterward." She handed Loudon a suit, a flashlight, and a large spray canister with "Envirochem" marked on the side.

"This is for decontamination afterward," said Shinohara briskly. Doc also carried a large, black case. They followed the manager to the facility's locker rooms, leaving the canisters and the case beside the manhole on the way. Shinohara went into the women's room, and Loudon and Doc went into the men's room. In the men's room, they both stripped down to their shorts and put on the suits. Each suit had heavy puncture-proof shoes. Doc zipped Loudon into the suit and pulled the helmet over his head. He zipped it down, and closed a Ziploc-type seal around it. The moisture from Loudon's breath began to cloud the faceplate. Loudon wondered fleetingly if he could unzip for a quick drink. But then Doc flipped a switch on the backpack. A small pump whined to life, and the hiss of fresh air inflated the suit, clearing away the condensation. Doc went over the suit meticulously looking for leaks, and checking the exhaust valve. He took Loudon by both shoulders and looked into his face.

"You're not claustrophobic, are you?" he asked, his blue eyes searching Loudon's.

"Only in confined spaces," said Loudon, smiling grimly through the plastic faceplate. Doc's eyes were set amidst a deeply wrinkled face, but they still showed a twinkle. Loudon hoped he was as keen at that age.

"Ahh, you're okay," snorted Doc, giving him a pat on both shoulders, but Loudon knew it was a form of encouragement, rather than a statement. "You've got about two hours on the batteries. When you hear a beeping start up, it means you've got half an hour left," he said. "It's enough to get back out of the pit and get decontaminated." He put on his own suit, zipped himself in, and reached around to switch on his air supply. He carefully checked his own suit for leaks. The suits were light, but still cumbersome, and they clumped out of the locker room to find Shinohara already in her suit at the edge of the pit with the manager.

"Okay, there's rungs set into the side goin' down," he said pointing to the side of the pit. "Be careful, it's kinda slick at the bottom and the burners stick up. We stopped deliveries scheduled today, so there won't be anything comin' down. To find your bag, look for a white tag with the name on it. Clayton's the name?" Shinohara nodded, but the bulky suit reduced it to a mere shift of the helmet.

"Now, sir, you can't come anywhere near us when we come out," warned Doc. "We'll be covered with who-knows-what kinda germs. Wait till we've covered ourselves with this stuff in these spray cans."

The manager nodded, agreeing thoroughly. "Anyway, I'll stick around and keep a watch," he shouted, as Doc switched on his own flashlight dangling from a strap around his wrist, stepped nimbly to the ladder, grabbed the metal handhold sticking up from the floor, swung around and disappeared through the dark manhole. The light beam from his flashlight grew dimmer as he disappeared into the chamber's depths. Loudon felt his hands start to perspire, and a knot of nerves form in the pit of his stomach. He'd always hated heights, not to mention deadly diseases. Some FBI agent he was. His knees were a little weak, too. He tried not to think what would happen if his gloved hand slipped off the steel rung, or if his legs gave out. He realized how out of shape he'd let himself become. His heart rose to a pounding thud, and his breathing became heavier. Deep down, he knew that the problem really wasn't the ladder or the pit or the medical waste. It was the first time he'd faced any kind of dangerous situation since LA.

"Look at the wall, not down," said Shinohara, perhaps sensing his case of nerves. Her voice was muffled, but she was shouting, so he could understand her. "You can't see down anyway with the helmet, but don't try. Take it slow so you don't run into me. Just one rung at a time." With that, she switched on her flashlight, took an agile step onto the ladder, swung around and was gone. Loudon risked a glance through the manhole at the swinging lights marking the two descending, and drew back.

"Whoa," he said, the word amplified within the helmet. He took a breath, thought about a nice cold scotch-rocks, grabbed the metal railing, switched on his light, swung around and searched for the first rung with his foot. He missed once, but found it. Then, both feet were on the ladder and he slowly lowered himself, rung by rung. He concentrated on the sooty concrete wall, inches from his face, taking one rung at a time. As he descended rung after rung, the light from above dimmed. But he could still see well enough by the flashlight dangling from his wrist. He glanced up occasionally trying to see the top receding, but his helmet obscured the view. Finally, he felt a tap on his leg, and knew with relief that he was nearing the bottom. He took three more steps down and at last felt concrete floor instead of steel rung. He turned around to find himself face-to-face with Shinohara.

"Careful. It's wet and slippery," she said through the faceplate.

They shone their lights around, revealing that the floor of the pit near the ladder was clear, except for a few bags that had tumbled away from the main pile. A couple were split open, and had leaked liquid. But nearest the loading dock was a precarious two-story pile of the orange bags, with occasional white bags scattered among them. There seemed to be hundreds rising before him into the shadows at the top of the chamber. It seemed an impossible task to find one bag from one physician. The air from the whining pump brought no smells into the suit, so he felt comfortable that the filter was working.

Doc had already waded carefully into the foothills of the mountain of bags, shining his light to and fro. He would carefully lift a bag, examine the identification tag in the light and carry it over to deposit it in the empty space. He stepped deliberately, keeping his feet beneath him, as if walking on ice. Shinohara and Loudon did the same, stepping into the pile.

"Look at the dates, not just the names!" shouted Doc. "The dates on these are recent. Last week or so! I think we're in the ballpark!"

For twenty minutes, they picked at the mountain of medical waste, their lights playing about the inside of the dark chamber, whose blackened walls seemed to swallow the beams. Loudon was beginning to sweat, both from the exertion and from nerves. A couple of times, he reached for a bag and stopped short when he noticed the gleam of something that had pierced the plastic—maybe a needle or razor blade. It was difficult to examine the bags through the faceplate, but he tried. One bag fell open as he picked it up, dumping white surgical dressings over his legs. They were brown with old blood. Occasionally, he would feel a crunch beneath his foot that told him he'd stepped on an old hypodermic needle or a glass vial.

"So, you get hazardous duty pay for this kind of thing?" he shouted to Shinohara as they picked through the mound of bags surrounded by darkness.

"It's all hazardous," said Shinohara tersely. She looked at him seriously, then turned back to the mound. She was in no mood for chatter. He shrugged and bent to his work.

After a while, Doc grabbed them by the shoulders.

"Keep a very close watch above!" he warned. "We're undermining the bottom of the pile. At some point, it's going to come over. Be ready to get away when it does!" They both nodded, looked up, and bent back to work. It was too bad the pile was too far down the wall for the manager to start a controlled avalanche from above. Loudon looked back at the pile of examined bags they'd created. It was impressive. He continued to take bags carefully away from the old pile. It was like a kid's game he remembered, where you try to take blocks away from a stack without toppling it.

"Look out!" he heard the manager yell from above, and shined his light up in time to see an avalanche begin. He scrambled out of the way, tripping on a burner and slamming forward onto his stomach, smashing his flashlight onto the floor as the bags fell onto him. He stayed still, his back and legs covered with the bags. One felt heavy above him. It must have contained bottles of liquid. Some medical facility was throwing hazardous wastes away in the bags, not just empty containers. He felt cold on his legs. The liquid was leaking!

"Don't move!" he heard Doc say above him. He felt the bags shift, as Shinohara and Doc removed them.

"Yeah, I thought I'd just lay here a while under all this garbage," said Loudon.

"Okay, stand up very carefully. You hurt?" asked Doc.

He shook his head and stood up and checked his light. It was still working. Shinohara and Doc brought their faceplates close to his body, playing their flashlights over him, poking, pulling and prodding his suit to look for leaks and tears.

"All right," said Doc finally. "You're fine. Let's get this done."

The avalanche had leveled the left side of the pile, but the right still towered precariously above them, even worse now that it wasn't supported from the side. There were scores of bags left, so they bent to their work.

"We're in the right time frame!" shouted Shinohara from the right side, a bag in each hand. "These dates are right on!" She was standing next to an almost vertical wall of bags reaching into the darkness, shifting them in place, one by one, until she could see the identifying tags.

"Awright!" she shouted, holding the tag on one bag, "I've got—"

The manager's warning shout from above interrupted her. But before she could react, the towering right side shifted and collapsed over her, and she disappeared in the falling orange cascade. Loudon heard the sounds of glass striking glass, as bottles within the bags slammed against one another. More ominous, he also heard the shattering of glass.

He heard a scream from the depths of the falling mountain.

"Don't move!" Doc shouted, wading forward through the still falling bags. One bounded toward him and he slammed it out of the way. Loudon came in from the side, dodging a bag that burst open, spilling scores of half-filled urine sample bottles.

"I'm cut!" shouted Shinohara, her voice barely audible from beneath the pile. "I'm cut in the—" the words were drowned out by a beeping in his ear. His battery was running out. He had half an hour to find her, get her out of the pit and decontaminated. The beeping continued, and he could hear a faint beeping from Doc's suit as well. The two sounds syncopated with one another, as if the two suits were communicating. Was there no way to turn the noise off?

He waded beside Doc into the bags, heaving them out of the way.

"Keep talking!" yelled Doc, and they heard a faint response that made them veer to the left. They thought they could hear a third beeping. After several minutes, they saw the glow from her flashlight, and Loudon lifted a bag to see a booted foot. Doc saw it, too, and they quickly had Shinohara uncovered. Doc reached down and cleared away the bags around her, pulling her to her feet by her shoulder. His hand came away bloody in the dim light.

"You really took one, didn't you?"

"Felt like a scalpel," she said, her voice shaking slightly. "I fell against it. Went in deep." Her face looked pale and doll-like behind the faceplate. Her eyes were open wide and dark. She clutched a small orange bag tightly in her left hand.

"Not as bad as the bats," Doc reassured her, taking the bag and setting it aside.

"No, not as bad as the bats," she smiled faintly. Doc turned her around, and shined the light on her to reveal a slash down her back on the right shoulder blade from which blood flowed freely.

"Scalpel cuts bleed the worst," he muttered, helping her toward the ladder. He put his helmet next to Loudon's. "She may have a muscle cut, and she's losing blood with a little shock setting in," he said. "She may not be able to take the ladder. Loudon, you're bigger than me. She goes up first, you go right behind her. And hold onto the ladder around her so she doesn't fall!"

Loudon nodded and as they got to the ladder, moved behind Shinohara. She reached for the first rung with her right hand. It was trembling. She grabbed the rung determinedly, put her foot on the bottom rung and hauled herself up. Then she did the same with the left. Once she was up one rung, Loudon pulled himself up behind her, her body causing him to lean out. If he lost his grip, he knew he would fall, but at this point he didn't care.

"Okay, Kathleen, I'm gonna tailgate you all the way up," he said. "I gotcha, sweetheart. Go ahead." He felt the right side of her body haul itself up another rung, and he followed, feeling with his right foot for the rung her foot had just vacated.

"Don't even think about me. Just climb as you need to," he said. His face was against her back, so he could dimly see her blood continuing to flow, coating his faceplate. The beeping continued in his ears. How long had it gone on? He felt fierce determination in the muscles of her body, as she painfully pulled herself, rung by rung, up the ladder. He had no idea how high they were; he didn't want to know. He concentrated on coordinating his steps with hers—his right step after her right, his left after her left.

Suddenly, she faltered back, slumping against him with her full weight. He tightened his grip on the rungs to support them both, feeling his fingers growing numb. He knew they were high enough now that a fall might mean serious injury. Or death.

"Just take your time," he said. "But I got an appointment in an hour." After a moment she recovered and once more pulled herself up.

He realized suddenly that the whine of the pump motor had lowered in pitch. The battery didn't give out all at once, but gradually lost power. The air flow through the suit was lessening, and he could feel himself beginning to pant for breath. He could also feel through his chest that Shinohara was gasping, too. A faint mist began to form on his face plate, the flowing air not quite wafting away his breath.

He was beginning to feel woozy when, after another several minutes of climbing, her weight against him suddenly lifted, and the light from above spilled into his helmet through the blood-smeared faceplate. She had made it all the way up. He found the edge of the manhole with his hands and pulled himself up the last rungs and over the edge. Shinohara was half-lying on the pavement beside the manhole, breathing hard, and the manager stood several yards away in anguish.

"What do I do!" he shouted. "I can't touch you!"

"Call 911! And start spraying!" gasped Shinohara, dragging herself away from the manhole, her wound still bleeding profusely. "Take one of these canisters and soak us down. Use it all!"

As the manager made the call, Loudon grabbed a canister, and began to spray Shinohara. She slumped tiredly in the suit. He felt the force of the spray on his own suit, as the manager began to decontaminate him. Then through his dizziness from lack of air, he saw Doc beside him, an orange bag in his hand. Doc had waited until they were all the way up the ladder, probably poised to break their fall, if necessary. Then, he had retrieved the bag Shinohara had found and scrambled up himself.

He pitched the bag aside and took over spraying Shinohara, and when he was satisfied that it was sufficient, grabbed the cut edges of the suit and with a knife from his black case, ripped it open, revealing her back. He held the wound closed with his hand, motioning toward the case. Loudon understood and found a first-aid kit. He yanked it out and brought it to Doc. Shinohara's faceplate was fogged, and so were his and Doc's. They had to get out of the suits fast, or risk suffocation. He continued to pant, but he had to keep going. Doc took Loudon's hand and pressed it onto the wound. Doc snatched a QuikClot pad out of the first aid kit, ripped open the package and slapped it firmly onto the wound. The chemically treated pad immediately began to do its work, and the bleeding slowed.

"You're decontaminated. Get your suit off, and take hers off, then put pressure back on!" said Doc. Loudon did so, fumbling with the seals and the zippers of his suit. He ripped off the helmet and gulped in fresh air mixed with a strong smell of disinfectant that made him hack uncontrollably for what seemed like minutes.

He turned to Shinohara and quickly removed her helmet. She emerged pasty-faced and gasping, her mane of dark hair plastered down and dripping wet with perspiration. While Doc still held the clotting pad, he helped her up, unzipped her suit and peeled it from her body. She wore panties and a bra, and her caramel skin was dripping with perspiration and condensation from her breath inside the suit. She sat down hard on the concrete. Doc passed the duty of holding the clotting pad back to him, while the old man decontaminated himself.

"I'm okay, just hold that pad on," she said firmly, filling her lungs with air. "It's not an artery. It's okay." He held the pad hard against her back, bracing it by placing his other hand on her sweating chest. Her heart was pounding so hard he could feel it, even on her right side. He also experienced a wave of tenderness for this woman who was willing to risk her life for a case. It made his own reluctance seem utterly petty.

"You're sure you're okay?" he asked, and she nodded, looking back at him with a stoic expression he could not fathom. Those dark eyes.

Doc finished dousing himself with Envirochem and stripped off his suit, his baggy boxer shorts emphasizing his tough stringy body. He drew in a couple of deep breaths and went to work.

"Get some blankets from the car and the black doctor's bag from the back seat!" he shouted to the manager. "We're not hot anymore. You can come close!" He picked up an Envirochem canister. "Kathleen, hold your breath and close your eyes," he said and began to spray her again, the blue liquid cascading off both Loudon and her. He concentrated on her back, and had Loudon lift the clotting pad to douse the wound once more. Shinohara flinched when the liquid hit the wound, mixing with the flowing blood, but said nothing. Doc handed Loudon a fresh pad which he applied with the same determined pressure as before.

As the siren of an ambulance rose in the distance, the manager arrived with the blankets and the bag. Doc changed the clotting pad once more, taped it down, draped Shinohara with one of the blankets, then helped her up. Loudon stood and watched her walk with Doc's arm around her toward the women's locker room, stumbling slightly, her bare feet leaving small wet footprints on the dry concrete.

"Did we get the bag?" Loudon heard Shinohara ask.

"Yes, Kathleen, we got the bag. I wouldn't forget the bag."

"You bet you wouldn't," she mumbled thickly, as they disappeared behind the door.

CHAPTER 9

Loudon finished his second scotch before Doc had finished his first beer. The bracing smoky tang quickly produced a welcoming warm glow in his gut, and he ordered another and leaned back in the booth, enjoying the comfortable noise of the bar. They were in one restaurant of a yuppie chain decorated with funny signs and cute junk. It was about a mile from the Ramada Inn where Doc and Shinohara were staying. He and Doc sat in a booth across from the bar, where the clinking of glasses and the babble of conversation drowned out the sound of the bar's television, leaving only the picture glowing unnoticed.

They'd already discussed the orange bag, which Shinohara insisted be sent off to Atlanta that night. They'd left the bag sealed, but Loudon was assured its contents would be properly treated; that an Atlanta FBI lab tech would be on hand for the analysis; that there would be no fingerprints lost.

Loudon had also called Bowers once the bag was sent off. Bowers said he'd have the LA office coordinate with Atlanta, as before. Loudon thought he'd detected a faint edge of disappointment in Bowers' voice, but he couldn't figure out why. Loudon considered pitching Bowers on having a senior agent in LA take over the case. But he realized that it would give Bowers too much of an opening. The case wasn't really beyond a routine inquiry yet. He didn't have grounds. He took another thankful swallow of icy scotch. And maybe he wouldn't want to be taken off anyway, given the people involved. *The* person, that is. Shinohara.

"Is she in any danger?" he asked, sitting back and taking another sip of his drink to appear nonchalant.

"Don't think so. It bled a lot. The emergency doc agreed that we should dose her with antibiotics for a few days. But she could get hepatitis. Something like that."

"AIDS?" The word hung in the air, seeming to float apart from the noise of the bar.

Doc shook his head. "No. No chance. It's ironic. AIDS is so dangerous. So devious in the body. But it's a fragile bug. It only transmits when people exchange blood or fluids. Or, it can live in the fresh blood of a needle a couple of junkies share. Even if the scalpel that stuck her was used on an AIDS patient, the blood's dried. The virus is dead." He stared into his beer. "If only it were that easy to kill the virus inside humans."

Loudon finished his drink, waved for another and decided to change the subject slightly.

"Well, in any case, I really didn't feel right about leaving Kathleen in the hotel room," he said, his voice rising above a burst of laughter from the bar.

"Yeah, well, the emergency room did say she was okay to release," said Doc. "We can't be sure what was on that scalpel. We should watch her. But leaving her alone was the only way to show her we were worried, so she'd keep still and rest."

"How's that?" Loudon didn't follow the logic. He squinted his eyes at Doc and wondered if the scotches weren't clouding his thinking.

"Okay, it's complicated. Like Kathleen," said Doc, leaning forward and dipping a chip in salsa. "See, if we leave her in the hotel, she knows it's because we're trying *not* to show we're worried. So, she knows that means we really *are* worried." He munched the chip, giving Loudon time to catch up. "Since she knows we're worried, she'll stay there in bed and be quiet like she's supposed to, so she don't pop her stitches."

"And what if we'd stayed with her?" Loudon was still working on the logic of the last sentence.

"Then she'd think we were trying to pretend like we were worried, but that we really weren't very much. And she'd feel since we were there, she had to work on the case. So she'd be up movin' around doin' stuff."

Loudon remembered how they had left her, lying quiet and pale on her side, her curly hair fanned out on the pillow, her legs drawn up, the long slim caftan following the curves of her body. At the shoulder, the caftan bulged with the large bandage and with her right arm strapped to her side. On the bed in front of her was a pile of Lupo's papers. She was holding one in her left hand, trying to read it.

"Sounds complicated, dealing with her."

"Well, I been doin' it for five years. That's the way you got to do it with Kathleen."

"How'd you two start working together?" Loudon's next drink arrived, and he sipped it. He'd have to sip it slowly if he was to follow Doc's torturous logic.

"Well, when we started, she'd been with the CDC about two years in the field, after she got her MD. She just wore out her first three partners. They wanted a life, and she wanted to hunt bugs."

"Bugs?"

"Viruses, bacteria . . . epidemics. It's easy to get too wrapped up in the job. You go in, people are sick, dying. You find the bug wherever it is . . . how it was transmitted . . . you figure out how to stop it." He took a sip of his beer. "Oh yeah, one of her partners wanted to marry her, I guess. Wanted her to stop huntin' bugs for a while. But she didn't want to slow down to get married. And she just wore him out, like she wore the other partners out." He sipped his beer and shook his head. "She decided to tolerate me because I've been doin' this for forty years. She decided I had a lot to teach her. Besides that, my wife took one look at her and decided she was so headstrong, if I didn't partner with her, she'd drown in a swamp or something."

"You've got a wife?"

"Boy, do I! We raised two daughters and a son together. And all the while, she put up with me off huntin' bugs. We got a little ranch, and she raises horses in Colorado Springs. Pistol of a woman." Doc's eyes crinkled with delight.

Their dinners arrived, heaping plates of steaming Mexican food. Doc slathered his with hot salsa and ordered another beer. They both began to eat hungrily, Loudon hoping the food would moderate his drunk. He was also a little uncomfortable, because he didn't have any undershorts on. He had on his white shirt and suit, with no tie, but he'd had to discard his shorts. Since he wore them under the Racal suit, they might be contaminated. Doc, on the other hand, had been able to clean himself up and climb into a fresh red plaid flannel shirt and khaki trousers.

"You got a family?" asked Doc between mouthfuls.

"Well, I'm divorced."

"Oh. That's too bad."

"Yeah. I have a daughter. Lindy. She's twelve. She's a sweetie."

"I'm a nosy old fart, but was it the work? Did it cause the divorce?"

The fourth scotch was working on Loudon, and his tongue was thoroughly loosened. Besides, he liked Doc. The old man reminded him of his grandfather.

"Well . . . yeah. First the job and the marriage together was okay. After I got out of the FBI Academy, I was a First Office Agent in Chicago. It was my OP . . . my office of preference. I had what they call a rabbi in the Bureau . . . a friend of my Dad's. He got me the assignment. So, I went back to Chicago, where I grew up, and Rochelle and I got married. She'd grown up there, too. It was great . . . for me anyway. I was playing cops and robbers, but not really the dangerous stuff. I worked in the White Collar Crimes Section. I had some hot cases, though. Then I got a chance to go to LA. It was a big move. They gave me an undercover assignment."

"Dangerous?" asked Doc.

"Well, wasn't supposed to be. Because I had a degree in accounting and one in law, they put me into this little company that was investing in drugs with the Colombians. I was supposed to be this Princeton guy, which I am anyway, and get into the company and trace the money. That was all, just trace the money."

"And your wife?" Doc waved his empty beer mug over his head, and the waitress nodded back.

"Since I was supposed to be undercover, Rochelle and Lindy stayed in Chicago. Rochelle hated it, but accepted. Well, I was big time out there for a while. Actually got close with the company president. Then things went south. The president apparently cheated the Colombians. Tried to hide profits they were supposed to cut the Columbians in on." Loudon took a stiff drink of his scotch. He'd never really talked about the case before like this, but he was rolling. And the scotch, and Doc, and the dangers they'd shared made him talkative.

"And they went after the president?"

"Yeah, one night at his house. I was there, along with the company officers. The Columbians set up a meeting, but they came in with guns. Well, I had a little .32-caliber in an ankle holster. They were blazing away at everybody. I got caught in front of the bar. This one guy had an Uzi, and I had a crystal decanter filled with single-malt scotch. Glenfiddich. If I'd dropped down for my ankle gun, he would've got me. Well, he aimed the Uzi at me, I aimed the decanter at him. I pitched baseball at Princeton. I got him right between the eyes. He went down, I got the Uzi. I shot a couple of Columbians, the rest took off. That's why I drink scotch. It saved my life."

"A bottle of scotch, eh?"

"Yeah, the guys in the office did up a trophy. They took a baseball pitcher and put a little bottle in his hand."

"You must have been scared."

"Well, not really scared. I started to realize that the bad guys used real bullets. I got one in the arm. It wasn't cops and robbers anymore. Especially during the shooting when I looked this one guy in the face. Young guy. He had a gun . . . so I shot him. I remember his eyes. He was a kid. It rattled me bad." Loudon took a stiff slug of his drink. His hand shook slightly. "The thing was . . ." He stared down at the half-eaten plate of food.

"Yeah?"

"I heard something." Loudon had crossed the line for the first time.

"What do you mean?"

"Well, I was in another room when the Columbians came in. One of them said something in Spanish just before they started shooting. I know some Spanish. Sounded like he said 'Bowers said we've got fifteen minutes.'" Loudon felt suddenly relieved. He'd never told anybody. But at some point he had to. It had been almost a year. And for some unfathomable, hazy reason, Doc seemed the logical choice.

"Bowers? Fifteen minutes? What did that mean?" Doc sat up, staring intently into Loudon's eyes.

"Bowers is the ADC in LA, the Assistant Director in Charge. He's the boss."

"You sure they said that? Sure they meant it?"

"Well, I was sure enough to go after Bowers. After I got out of the hospital, I caught him in his office. He denied it, but I was so crazy-mad, I pulled a gun on him. Some agents came in and disarmed me. I realized I'd better shut up, so I haven't told anybody."

"Nobody? Don't you have people that look into this stuff?"

"Yeah. Office of Professional Responsibility. But I didn't have enough. And I was freaked. And, y'know . . ." He stared into his drink. "I don't really know why I told you."

"Guess I look honest or something."

"You won't let it out?"

"Son, I carry secrets that'd curl your toes."

"Well, thanks."

"So, what happened after?"

"Well, a couple of things. After all the killing, I decided the game was getting too serious. I didn't . . . well . . ." He sipped his drink, thinking how to put it. "I didn't want to be the Man. Maybe the kind Bowers was. I saw myself on the road to becoming a SAC in charge of an office. Of having responsibility for people's lives. I tried talking to some people . . . counselors . . . but it didn't help. I kind of opted out . . . of my job, my life. And Bowers did his part."

"What?"

"He sent me down to Temecula. Easier duty, he said. Time to recover. But I think he wanted me out of the way. And maybe he's got plans for revenge. Y'see, that area is nearer the border. Lots going on down there. I'm watching my back."

"Tough situation," said Doc. They ate in silence for a while.

"And then there was my family," Loudon continued. "I just cut them off. Maybe the marriage was another thing I did that wasn't serious, and

I couldn't handle it. I also worried that the Colombians would go after them. And it would be my fault."

"Well, you might not want an old man's advice. But at some point, you're going to have to act. You can't stay down here hiding."

"Yeah, but not now. Not yet. I've decided to take it easy for a while." He took another drink. "Lindy's coming out after school's out. And I plan to take off a lot. That's another reason I'm staying down here. It's good for kids, and it's quiet . . . the job's pretty routine."

"Well, if this Lupo turns out to be what we think, it won't be routine."

As they began to discuss the case, Loudon was glad to get away from his history. Doc began to quiz him on how he planned to go about his investigation. Loudon was explaining how dull most investigations were, when he glanced over to see a press conference on the television. The screen showed a bright blue girl sitting behind a bank of microphones, parting her hair to show her roots.

"Hey, pal," complained a voice to the bartender. "Color's gone bad on the set. Fix that, willya?"

The bartender peered intently at the picture.

"Nah, that's the right color. She's blue. That's one of those weird colored people."

"Watch your mouth, Jack!" joked a black man at the bar, and everybody laughed.

Meanwhile, the cameras had turned to a large woman with a floppy hat and a veil. She was saying something unintelligible, because of the bar noise.

"Those the people you saw?" asked Loudon.

"Yeah, that's them. Looks like they're famous."

The veiled woman was followed by a bright red young man, wearing a white t-shirt that showed his muscles. Then there was a middle-aged blue man who wore a t-shirt that said "La Vista Lumber." Two yellow people—a woman with curly black hair and a skinny, young long-haired boy—also answered questions. The yellow woman seemed angry, punching the air with her finger.

Finally, the cameras centered on an attractive middle-aged woman in a white coat, who began to take questions from the reporters.

"That's the doctor who treated the ones at La Vista," said Doc. "Lori Meadows. She's probably saying that this thing is permanent."

They watched the news conference for a while as they ate. After they finished, Loudon had another scotch, and they went back to the Ramada Inn. They wanted to look in on Shinohara, but the window of her room was dark, so Loudon waved good night and piloted his car as carefully as an FBI agent over the legal alcohol limit does along the busy freeways back to his apartment. He considered stopping for one more drink, but decided that he'd had enough of about everything that day.

His apartment was one box among an elaborate complex of stucco boxes covering a hillside just off Route 8, near downtown San Diego. It had a big pool in the middle of the complex and was near Balboa Park. When Lindy came, they would spend lots of time in the pool and at the park, with its zoo and museums.

He had climbed laboriously out of his car, the drinks still weighing on him, when he noticed another car with somebody in it near the stairs to his apartment. The car was parked away from the dim lights of the parking area. His instincts alerted, he started up the outside steps to his apartment. He heard the car door open and shut, and steps behind him. The steps stopped on the landing below when he reached his floor. The boozy fog lifted immediately. His training told him when somebody's behavior was out of sync. The darkness, the sounds, some indefinable air of danger, triggered a flashback of the night in LA that enveloped his body. He remembered the cool, quiet desert night; the sound of car doors before the Columbians came in. He drew his pistol, leveled it at the stairs, backing down the hall away from his door, silently retreating into a dark corner by a fire extinguisher. He bent his legs slightly, shook the cobwebs from his brain, and aimed the gun at the entry to the stairs. The muscles in his arms tautened, his hands gripped the pistol with practiced muscle memory, his trigger finger tensed.

A man emerged from the stairs, looking left and right. Loudon couldn't tell in the darkness whether the man's hands were empty.

"I'm FBI, and I've got a gun on you!" he announced. "Step back under the light!" Loudon could tell from the man's deliberate reaction that he was used to such situations. His hands went up, and he slowly backed under the porch lamp. The light showed him to be tall and husky, wearing a polo shirt and sports jacket. He had an erect military bearing, a short haircut and shiny black military shoes. He stood looking steadily in Loudon's direction, his eyes in shadow. The shadow of a bulge in his jacket told Loudon he had a gun in a shoulder holster. His stance told Loudon he was well practiced in instantly drawing the gun and firing.

CHAPTER 10

"It's okay, Mr. Loudon. I'm with Army intelligence, San Diego. Chavez. I just wanted to talk to you." Loudon's trigger finger inched closer to the trigger, as the man slowly opened his jacket, reached in, and brought out an ID case. He flipped it open and a silver badge gleamed in the porch light.

"I'm at the office every weekday, pal. You could talk then."

"Sir, it's not formal. I just needed some information. One federal officer to another."

"I'd feel much better if you'd take that gun out real slow and just lay it down on the floor in front of you."

"Certainly," said Chavez and with two fingers extracted a hefty .45-caliber automatic from the shoulder holster and laid it carefully down.

"Ankle?" asked Loudon, and the man lifted both pants legs to reveal only socks. Loudon holstered his gun and unlocked his door. He turned on his light and looked closer at Chavez's ID. Satisfied, he motioned for Chavez to pick up his gun, and they went in.

"So, what is it? I'm tired." Loudon took off his coat pulled his tie from the pocket, pitching the coat onto the couch next to the week's papers. He hung his tie over a kitchen chair along with the others. He needed a drink of water, so he went into the kitchen searching for one of his four glasses.

"I've been asked to find out how your investigation of Arthur Lupo is going," said Chavez, checking his gun for dust from the floor and holstering it. He spoke with the slight remnant of a Spanish accent. Columbian? Loudon remained on guard.

"Why?"

"My commanding officer knows that he is missing, and he works for a company where the Army funds research."

"So, why don't you look for him? I'd be happy to hand over the case."

"Well, he's not directly involved in Army work, but the Army likes to know if there's anything wrong at their contractors. Even if it doesn't immediately affect our projects."

"Chavez, don't you think there's something just a little hinky here? I mean, this guy who's missing is not supposed to be doing anything connected with your outfit, but here you are. And why the middle of the night at my apartment?" Loudon pried ice cubes from the frozen mass in a bowl in the freezer, dropping them into the glass and filling it with tap water.

"Sir, I was just told to find out and report back. Just a routine inquiry—"

"Hey, listen, routine inquiries come to the office on official memo forms and get answered officially. Try that." Loudon took a long drink of the cool water. It felt good going down. "Or . . . gee . . . how about this bright idea? Why don't you go see those folks that you're paying all that money to. Ask them at ArchiBiologics what they know about where their boy is?"

Chavez dropped the formality. "Look, man, it's my fault, I don't go back with a report."

"Well, then, it's your fault isn't it, Chavez? Have your boss call me Monday. We'll talk. Meantime, I'm really tired."

Somebody was nervous, thought Loudon. Somebody wanted to know what he knew. That made his information valuable, and he never gave away valuables.

Chavez stood for a moment, deciding what to do. He had clearly expected cooperation. Finally, he abruptly turned on his heel and opened the door.

"Awright, man, we'll just see," he muttered on the way out.

Loudon closed the door, locked it, and finished his water while he considered what to do next. He'd have to call Bowers again. He'd get Walter's read on the visit by the Army. He'd also have to check on ArchiBiologics and ask Walter to look harder at the yellow pages leads— the lab equipment dealers and the freight companies.

Finally, he decided the wisest course for the moment. He tiredly kicked his shoes in a corner and hung up the suit in the closet alongside its four nearly identical brethren. He dug a pair of shorts out of a pile of clothes on the floor of the closet, put them on and went to bed.

• • •

Loudon squinted into the low morning sun, driving slowly along the road beside the golf course, until he saw her. He shook his head in wonder. There was Shinohara, jogging along, her hair done up in a bushy ponytail that jounced to and fro as she ran. Stray curls had escaped to dance about her forehead. She wore a large floppy t-shirt over the bulky bandage and her bound-up arm. She ran erect and with easy loping strides despite the handicap, pumping her left arm vigorously to compensate for the immobilized right arm. She wore baggy shorts, and wide, serious jogging shoes. As he neared her, he could see her calf muscles flex with each step, the sheen of sweat on her neck.

He eased the car ahead of her and got out, pulling off his jacket and flipping it into the back seat. Only a few golfers were on the course that early. They were milling around talking, paying little attention to the lone jogger on the cinder path that skirted the green rolling hills of the course. Beyond were the low desert mountains, still in blue-gray shadow with the sun behind them.

She noticed him about half a block away and smiled a perfunctory half-smile, stopping in front of him and continuing to gently bounce.

"Morning," she said only slightly breathlessly.

"Morning. How can you be out here with that thing?" He pointed to his own right shoulder. "You only had Sunday off."

"Yeah, well, that was enough. I get itchy if I don't run. I feel a little like Quasimodo . . . with the hump. But the stitches seem to be holding. How'd you find me?"

"The desk at the hotel said you'd gone out in jogging shorts; that this was where you'd probably be. Doc wasn't around."

"Yeah. He's at the hospital . . . getting final records on the patients."

"Look, we've got to talk. It's important."

"I can't stop now . . . You'll have to run with me."

"Well, I haven't—" before he could finish, she was gone, loping away, the bushy pony tail bouncing as if in impertinent challenge. He shrugged, pulled off his tie and stuffed it in his pocket, and started after her. He sprinted at a higher speed and managed to pull up next to her and match her stride.

"Look, there's been some things . . . about the investigation. Saturday night . . . I got a visit . . . from somebody from the Army."

"Yeah, we did, too. Yesterday."

Loudon paused in surprise, and she jogged ahead. "Why you? How'd he know about you?"

"We don't know. He just said he knew we were working with you . . . and that our case . . . might have something to do with yours."

"What . . ." Loudon was becoming winded. He panted hard, trying to regain his breath. His speech began to come between pants. "What did you tell him?"

"Doc told him we couldn't comment on a case in progress . . . especially one with the FBI. Doc also told him to buzz off. But Doc didn't say 'buzz.'" She smiled wryly at him, showing the little gap in her front teeth.

"Yeah . . . well . . . ." Now he was *really* getting winded. "Look, can we stop now? . . . I've got to find out—"

But she shook her head determinedly. "If you can't keep up, we'll talk later. I want to finish this run." She jogged briskly away, leaving Loudon bent over wheezing, with his hands on his knees. Sweat stains showed on the armpits of his white shirt, and droplets formed on his brow.

• • •

Leaving Loudon behind, Shinohara continued to jog down the trail, rounding a bend near the clubhouse. More golfers were lining up for early tee-offs, standing about under the tall graceful eucalyptus trees practicing their swings. The trees' faint fragrance added deliciously to her deep breaths. Two joggers passed her, glanced curiously at the hump beneath her shirt, and moved on. Her muscles were loose now, and the run felt especially good in the still-cool morning. She experimented with looking back to see what had happened to Loudon, but the bulky bandage and arm brace were too confining. The wound twinged a bit, but she only planned to go a few miles, maybe once around the course. The run felt good after spending yesterday sitting around the hotel reading scientific papers.

She settled back into her own thoughts. Maybe it was too bad he'd stopped. She liked company, even him. He was handsome in an unaffected way. But she knew the type. They'd hit on her before. Twice she'd even let herself enjoy the charms of such a man. But not this one. Not now. Too lackadaisical, too undisciplined. Doc told her Loudon was a drinker. Bad sign. But he'd also told her about their talk at the dinner Saturday night. At least some of it. She knew when Doc wasn't telling her the whole story. He always paused between sentences to think. He was a lousy liar.

Her musing was interrupted by a whining sound behind her. Loudon abruptly appeared on her right driving a golf cart, leaning back, smiling broadly, clearly pleased with himself. She hmphed in amusement in spite of herself.

"Well, I said we had to talk," said Loudon.

"How'd you get that?" She was breathing heavily as she neared the three-mile mark, but she could still manage a conversation.

"Flash an FBI credential, and you can get just about anything. We call it roast-beefing. Look, tell me more about the Army guy."

"Not much to tell. He just tried . . . to get information and left."

"Name was Chavez?" Loudon was concentrating on her and bobbled the cart a bit, but recovered.

"Yeah, but that's not the important thing that happened yesterday."

"What was?"

"I was reading Lupo's papers . . . I found a reference to one that was still in press . . . It was in a genetics journal . . . it should have been published by now. But it wasn't anywhere in the file . . . or in his list of publications. So, I called the journal editor at home yesterday. He remembered it. It was accepted but then suddenly withdrawn. No explanation."

"What was it about?" Loudon was trying to watch both her and the path ahead. He almost hit a middle-aged man who stepped aside just in time and muttered a curse at him.

"Well, I won't go into details . . . but it was about the possibility . . . of sticking those color genes . . . chromophores . . . into viruses as a visual indicator of infection. That's what he was really working on. The Army really *was* supporting his work."

"Why?"

"Well, the editor said . . . the paper suggested sticking the gene into animal viruses . . . and exposing a large population of animals like mice. You could follow the epidemic by watching the color change. It would be very important medically. Nobody really understands how infections spread."

"But why the Army?"

"Well, they want to know how infections propagate. To protect soldiers and citizens from biological warfare. It's pretty basic research. They've been doing test releases of harmless test bacteria out at Dugway Proving Ground near Salt Lake City. For years. It bugs us at the CDC."

"You mean into the air? Bacteria into the air?"

"Sure, even in big cities. Washington, St. Louis, San Francisco. In 1966, even during rush hour in the New York subways."

"What?" The distracted Loudon allowed the cart to drift off the path and suffered several teeth-chattering bounces over large rocks. He swerved back onto the path.

"Yeah, but the big problem was detecting the spread reliably. Lupo's color system would fix that. But like I said, they could only use it with animals."

"Then why didn't ArchiBiologics tell me about it? All they said was something about . . . uh . . . *Victor*." Loudon managed to slow the golf cart and whip behind her to let a jogger pass. Then he returned it to her side. He grinned in self-satisfaction at his ability with the maneuver.

"You mean *vector*?"

"Yeah, that was it."

"Well, then, they *did* tell you about it. You just didn't understand. A genetic vector is usually a virus they engineer to carry genes into a cell."

"Look, it's more important than ever we go to ArchiBiologics now. And it's obvious you and Doc have to be there, too."

"Yeah." She nodded in certain agreement. They were coming back around to where Loudon had parked his car.

"One more thing, and this is important."

"What?"

"Kathleen Shinohara. That's an interesting name. What's your background?"

The man was expressing interest in her personally. She wondered whether this was the beginning of him hitting on her. "You mean nationality? I'm Irish on my mother's side and Japanese on my father's." She gave a quick glance at Loudon for his reaction.

"It's a beautiful combination. Listen, we should get together for dinner. I felt bad that you couldn't join us Saturday night."

"I do thank you for helping me," she said dutifully, with a touch of warning not to assume too much from her gratitude. "I did appreciate it. But we've got more important things to do."

"You want a ride?" he finally asked. She shook her head, and he veered off to return the golf cart. "Okay, see you at the hotel then."

Shinohara winced slightly. The wound was beginning to hurt, so she slowed to a brisk walk to cool down, and crossed the wide street toward the hotel.

• • •

Loudon arrived first back at the hotel, finding Doc in the restaurant going over some papers. He settled into a chair across from him. Doc glanced up, greeted him with a distracted grunt, and went back to the papers.

"I just got back from the golf course," said Loudon. "I found Kathleen jogging." The waitress arrived, delivering coffee.

"Figured she'd try something like that," he grumbled. "That's why I asked the ER doc to double-stitch her." He held up the papers. "They got it."

"What?"

"Atlanta got the virus. They said the first stuff we sent—from the doctor's office and Lupo's apartment—didn't show anything." Loudon blew a sigh of relief. "But the bag we sent yesterday from the waste facility got there, and they went right into it. Found pure vaccinia in twelve empty bottles. And I checked at the hospital. That's the number of patients they got, and the labels on the bottles matched the injections they got."

"And prints?"

"They said your guys took the bottles away to check. They called this morning and told Atlanta that they found latent prints on two bottles. Lupo's. The little punk somehow sneaked into the refrigerator where they keep the allergy stuff and injected virus into a random bunch of bottles. You'd think he'd be more careful about prints."

"That happens," said Loudon, opening a menu. "He either figured the bottles would be long gone by the time the virus showed up. Or he didn't care. Anyway, now we've really got something to hit ArchiBiologics with."

"Put down the menu for a second," instructed Doc. His voice had lowered a notch.

Loudon did so and looked expectantly at the old man. "Yeah?"

"Kathleen said you were frisky with her?"

"Frisky?"

"Yeah, you're expressing a little . . . social . . . interest."

"So?"

"From last night, I saw you're a drunk."

"Well, I wouldn't—"

"And you've got a shady history." Doc leaned toward Loudon, his jaw set. "Look, she doesn't need protection by any stretch. But you should know you're not good enough for her."

"Look, I—"

"That's all I'm sayin'. And if you get too . . . frisky . . . you get in trouble with me. And you don't wanna do that."

Loudon decided to say nothing. He picked up his menu, ordered, then called his office and asked Walter to meet them at the company as soon as possible. He called ArchiBiologics and told them to expect another visit. Shinohara arrived shortly, fresh and showered in clean clothes and was scolded half-heartedly by Doc for jogging. She was clearly unrepentant. They briefed her on the developments, and after Doc spent some time in her room checking her dressing, they drove separately to ArchiBiologics.

When they arrived, Walter was already there, leaning his bearlike bulk against the guard's desk, chatting amiably. Loudon knew he was also pumping the guard for information and checking the security system. Loudon motioned for him to join them away from the guards. He introduced Walter to Doc and Shinohara. With only a slightly raised eyebrow, Walter showed that he fully appreciated Loudon's interest in Shinohara.

"Walter, I get to be the bad guy this time," Loudon whispered to Walter, who grinned and nodded, his large face coming alive. Loudon turned to a puzzled Doc and Shinohara. "Listen, whatever we do, you just go along, okay?" Doc shrugged and grunted in agreement.

"Well, they ain't gonna tell us anything they don't want to," he said.

Loudon and Walter smiled conspiratorially.

They showed their credentials to the guard, and a secretary led them through the corridors to the door of the same plush executive conference room as earlier. Loudon took out his credentials and slipped them into his pocket so the small gold badge showed. Walter grinned and did the same. He enjoyed this kind of thing. They opened the door, and a smiling Brad Riker, still expensively suited, every blond hair in place, rose to meet them. Doctor Platt, the ArchiBiologics president, sat at the head of the table, and Gupta and Houston the security chief were in the same places as before. They expected a replay of the previous meeting.

"Ah, Agent Loudon, we're so pleased that—" But before Riker could finish, Loudon grabbed Houston by his shoulder, spun the burly security man around and slammed him against the wall.

"Slap the wall and spread your legs!" he shouted. He drew his pistol and pointed it skyward, kicking Houston's feet back away from the wall. He deftly reached into Riker's jacket and withdrew a Glock semi-automatic pistol, put it inside his belt, and continued to search, discovering a small silver .32-caliber pistol in an ankle holster.

"Check the suit," he barked to Walter, who drew his pistol and proceeded to frisk Riker. Startled, Doc and Shinohara backed against the wall by the door.

Loudon turned to Platt and Gupta, still holding his pistol up to the ceiling. "Put your hands on the table . . . NOW!" Platt and Gupta, both wide-eyed, obeyed.

"What is this?" demanded Houston. "What do you mean coming in—" Loudon grabbed Houston by the collar and with a heave, launched him toward the table, motioning for him to sit down.

"Now," smiled Loudon walking around the table, holstering his pistol. "We can all have a little talk. We've got lots of evidence that you've been lying to the FBI. That's me, gentlemen, and that's a felony. And I come in here and find concealed weapons. I consider that a threat."

"We will not be subjected to this—" began Platt.

"You *will* be subjected to my questioning, and you *will* give me some answers! These are investigators from the Centers for Disease Control. You will also give *them* straight answers and full access to anything they wish at this company!"

"We demand our lawyers!" said Riker, straightening his coat.

"Fine, okay, as you wish. Walter, you got your book?" Walter looked puzzled for an instant, but reached in his coat pocket and took out a small notebook. "You have the number of the *San Diego Union-Tribune* in there?" Walter nodded. "And you've got the San Diego bureau of the Associated Press and all the TV and radio stations?" Walter nodded again. "Then go call them anonymously, and tell them the FBI is now taking the top executives of ArchiBiologics in for questioning on charges of defense contract fraud. Tell them if they get over here quick enough, they'll get great visuals of the arrests. Later, they can get shots of us bringing the people into our offices."

"Now, wait a minute," said Walter placatingly, playing the good guy. "That'll ruin the company, Bobby. You did that last time, and the people lost their shirts. They lost government contacts, private contracts and—"

"Don't argue with me, Walter, just do it!"

"Wait, wait, wait, Agent Loudon," entreated Platt. "There's no need for all this formal legal business here. Let's talk, let's just—"

"Okay, tell me about the missing notebooks. I don't think I got the full story the first time."

"Well, as I said, that was not our fault, that was—" Gupta started to say.

"But this was your fault," shouted Loudon, slapping a paper before Platt. He looked down at it through his bifocals and passed it around.

"What's the problem? It's Arthur Lupo's assignment record," said Platt.

"Obviously. And it is incomplete. Somebody neglected to notice that there was a staple mark on the front of the Xerox, but no second page."

Platt folded his hands delicately and looked coolly over at Riker, who blushed and looked down.

"Now, the CDC investigators also tell me that there is a missing scientific paper that Lupo wrote," said Loudon. "It was withdrawn from publication." Platt now turned his gaze on Gupta. "And my colleagues have found Lupo's fingerprints on medicine bottles that link him with the infections I'm sure you are aware of."

"What do you want?" asked Platt, grim-faced.

"I want his full assignment sheet. I want that withdrawn paper. I want full access to all your laboratories by these CDC investigators. And I want you all to stop lying to me!"

"Get the papers," said Platt to Gupta, who looked at Loudon for permission to leave. "Agent Loudon, we'll cooperate in any way we can. But as for full access to the labs, the Army—"

"THE ARMY!" shouted Loudon. "Agent Philips, go make your calls!" Walter shook his head in resignation and started out the door, but Platt waved his hands in surrender.

"Look, we'll let you in, but please don't tell the Army. We will cooperate all we can, but please, let's keep things reasonable."

"Look, Platt, the Army already knows more than you think. They already know about this investigation."

"Hmph," said Houston in his deep baritone. Platt sighed, leaned his head back and stared at the ceiling.

"We'll tell you all we know," said Platt. "And you can see whatever you wish." Gupta returned with the papers, which Loudon scanned. Gupta meekly assumed his previous seat.

"I see he had an assignment at Fort Detrick," said Loudon, handing the papers to Shinohara.

"It used to be a place for biological warfare research," she paused, reading the assignment sheets, then handing them to Doc. "Now they do cancer research and defensive biowarfare work." She began to flip through the scientific paper.

"Okay, tell me about Lupo," said Loudon. Platt nodded to Gupta, who folded his hands and began.

"Well, he is a genius," said Gupta in his lilting Indian accent. "He is perhaps the most brilliant young scientist I have ever seen. He isolated the genes for color, for chromophores, that you no doubt know about. Then he made them work in vitro . . . in the test tube . . . then he got them into a viable animal virus. Then, he got the viruses to carry working genes into mice. It was a big breakthrough. Very big."

"And the Army paid for it?"

"Oh, yes. It was incredible basic research. It helped understand epidemics. The Army also wanted it for basic defensive studies."

"So, why did he go to Fort Detrick?" Loudon took out his notebook and began to scribble notes in it.

"Oh, yes. You see, he was asked to go to the US Army Medical Research Institute for Infectious Diseases at Fort Detrick . . . AMRIID. They wanted him to further develop his chromophore gene system. He was gone for six months. Then he came back."

"Do animal viruses infect humans?" Doc and Shinohara shook their heads.

"No, not generally," Doc said. "Cats, dogs, mice can't catch human diseases, for example. Or vice versa. Very different biological systems. It'd be a big step to get those genes going in a human virus."

Loudon tried out his best penetrating stare on Gupta. "So how did he get these genes into human viruses? Did he do it here?"

"That we really don't know." Gupta lowered his head slightly. "When he came back from AMRIID, he just said he got the mouse genes working there and they were studying the effects. He didn't say anything about human viruses."

"Next big question. Why all the secrecy? Why isn't Lupo even listed as having security clearance?"

"Oh, I don't know . . . I can't—" stammered Gupta.

Platt interrupted. "I think Mr. Houston dealt with that." He nodded at Houston, who shifted his large frame in the chair, cleared his throat nervously, and spoke.

"The Army security people came to me before Mr. Lupo was going out there. They said they wanted this all off-the-books. Totally. They said that this was black research. No record. They did their own security check on Mr. Lupo, and they told us to keep minimal records. Look, Loudon, you've got us caught right in the middle. We did what we were told."

"This gets real interesting," said Loudon. "All right, now Mr. Gupta, I want you to take these CDC folks on a full tour of the facilities. I mean full! Agent Philips and I will stay here and have a little more discussion with your bosses."

Gupta looked at Platt who nodded his assent. Then he got up and led Doc and Shinohara out of the room. As they left, Shinohara gave Loudon what might have been a respectful look, and Doc smiled wryly.

Walter stationed himself by the door and Loudon paced the room, peppering the now-compliant men with questions. After an hour, the CDC investigators returned.

"He didn't do it here, that's for sure," said Doc out of earshot of the ArchiBiologics executives.

Now, Loudon was satisfied. Almost. He remembered the list of codes from Lupo's apartment, pulling a copy from his pocket.

"Does this paper mean anything?" he asked, passing the paper to Platt, who again examined it through his bifocals. He passed it around and the men all read it and shook their heads with certainty.

Now, Loudon was fully satisfied. He gathered the slip and the other papers, handed Houston back his guns and left, motioning the others to follow. Still sitting in their chairs dumfounded, the ArchiBiologics executives could hear from down the hall the fading sound of Walter whistling the march from *Bridge on the River Kwai.*

Chapter 11

Loudon sipped his too-small airline drink and made notes on a yellow pad as he shuffled through Lupo's case file stuffed on his lap. The process was not easy. He was shoehorned into the thinly padded sardine-can window seat, jammed against the wall, hemmed in by an avalanche of cotton-covered flesh that was the large woman next to him. The flight attendants had begun serving ridiculously expensive sandwiches, so he'd have to put the file away soon. But before that, he wanted to list the information so far, to give him something to stare at while trying to put together his ideas. Also, he knew he'd have to give a thorough, concise report to the assistant director in Washington, especially if he wanted the AD to back him up when he went boots-first into Fort Detrick. That was US Army territory. He'd better be ready to go. The lists were the way he'd figured out most knotty problems.

And it was still very much his problem, he thought, staring resignedly at the seat in front of him, seven inches from his face. After he'd linked Lupo to the genetically engineered virus, he'd decided to risk suggesting to Bowers that maybe one of the LA office's field superstars should take it over. But Bowers smoothly boomeranged the case right back at him; said he was doing fine getting the case together; said he should "keep up the good work, Bobby." Maybe Bowers was really trying to give him a chance. Maybe he'd misheard the Columbians that night. Maybe the large woman would move her fourteen-pound arm and give him the armrest.

He turned his attention back to the list and began to jot down the current known facts, thanks to two weeks of his and Walter's bulling-through-it routine field work:

No sign of subject, A. Lupo. Covered tracks well. No credit card usage, no banking activity. Huge cash withdrawals. Subj. has big $$$$ to play with. Inheritance from parents. Remember books in his apt. on con artists!!

Guy fitting subj. description bought lots of lab eqpt. over past year for cash. Standard stuff. Hauled it off in van.

Subj. not seen at any freight companies shipping lab eqpt. Maybe lab in San Diego?

Subj. last seen, La Vista Hospital. Admins photo-ID'd him as quiet guy who got a temp job in food service. Asked lots of questions. Took notes in gray lab book.

Yearbook photos: nothing unusual. Shots of groups of kids in clubs.

Travel: Airline records:

— trips San Diego.

— to Washington Natl. to go to Detrick.

— to Denver ???? Then back to SD.

The dinner cart arrived accompanied by a smiling flight attendant with nice blue-gray eyes, an attractive young woman whom Loudon would have normally tried to chat up. But on this flight, he merely smiled back distractedly over the woman-mountain in the next seat, contorted himself to reach his briefcase and stuffed the file into it, leaving out the yellow pad. As he chewed the dry sandwich, moistening it in his mouth with sips of scotch, he stopped to write down the next steps in his investigation:

To do:

Ask CDC about lab eqpt. What special machines, chemicals would AL need? Where would he get it?

Ask CDC about virus? Anything new?

Ask guy in white-collar crimes to update on how Lupo could hide money. Bank account under other name?

Has Chicago RA found any high school friends?

Has LA checked Caltech?

Why was AL in Denver?

He finished the meat-like sandwich and studied the list over its crumbs. He'd noted that CDC should be a prime source, but he hoped it would be in the person of Shinohara. He hoped she'd be at FBI headquarters the next morning for the meeting with the AD. After they'd rousted ArchiBiologics, she and Doc had flown immediately back to Atlanta to monitor the work unraveling the virus. Logically, one of them might stay in Atlanta to follow the virus work, while the other went with him to Detrick.

He decided the list was complete and spent the last hour of the trip into Washington allowing his mind to mull over it. Apparently, the Bureau's directors didn't consider the case important enough yet. Otherwise, he'd get more perks as the case agent. In a macabre mood, he decided that if Lupo turned out to be a mass murderer, maybe they'd at least let him upgrade to business class.

The plane came in for a landing, and after he unkinked his legs and walked into the terminal at Reagan National Airport, he retrieved his bag and moved quickly to the FBI lot and picked up a Bucar. He'd asked the FBI motor pool to have the Bureau car waiting for him. He stayed that night at the Hyatt near FBI headquarters. That evening, he enjoyed a dinner with his rabbi, FBI Assistant Director Henry C. Cleland. The grandfatherly Hank Cleland was a survivor of the Hoover days. He'd been a roommate of Loudon's father at Yale, and they'd remained close friends ever since. Cleland had spent his time "on the bricks" as a field agent. He'd worked his way up to administration, but had shrewdly hid out as a SAC in field offices in cold places where Hoover never visited on his famous inspection/vacations with his friend Clyde Tolson. After Hoover died, Cleland surfaced, working with the new breed of directors to remake the Bureau. Cleland had advised Loudon to join the FBI.

He'd told Loudon, "Son, it's evolved beyond the muck and mire of the antediluvian days when I had to deal with Edgar's lunacy. It's worth the time of a bright young man to pursue."

That evening, they talked over a fine dinner in a quiet bistro in Georgetown. As he allowed the delicate taste of scallops in a light orange sauce to chase away the memory of airline food, Cleland advised him once more.

"I know what you're going through," he said, peering thoughtfully into his glass of claret. "I had some problems deciding early on, same as you. Work your way out of it. Your stats are good out there. I checked. Sure, you got sent down, but now, you've got a good case, and the SAC is giving you your head. You can do it." He smiled encouragingly, the wrinkles around his eyes deepening into a friendly topography of decades of joviality.

Loudon nodded and finished his drink. He was almost convinced.

• • •

The next morning at nine a.m., he strolled down busy Pennsylvania Avenue toward the immense J. Edgar Hoover Building, a tan concrete juggernaut. The formidable building was shaped like a lopsided tetrahedron. Its face was a precise geometry of waffles, pocked with small holes meant to be decorative, but resembling bullet holes. Its unyielding mass, sterile windswept plazas and massive square pillars reminded Loudon of Hoover. It was overpowering, authoritarian. It was an appropriate monument to Hoover.

Loudon saw with private amusement that Freddie was still there. Good. The gaunt, ragged homeless man had taken up residence around the building years ago. He haunted it like a loud-mouthed banshee, railing against the FBI and the building. Loudon fished a five-dollar bill out of his pocket. Freddie was sitting slumped against the building wall in a bit of shade, singing softly to himself. He saw Loudon and wrinkled his brow, trying to squeeze out a memory. Then it dawned on him.

"You. Yeah, I know you. You're . . . uh . . . him."

"Freddie, what do you think of the building?" prompted Loudon, grinning and dropping the bill into Freddie's lap. Freddie examined the bill, marshaled his energies and rose with ruined majesty to his full tattered height.

Firmly grasping the bill in his dirty hand, he shouted, "Abomination!" to the earnest government employees hurrying to work. "An indecent monument to an indecent man!" he yelled, eyes flashing, at the gawking tourists. "An ugly monster of a building! An affront to all that is good and decent in architecture!"

Freddie continued in full throat and Loudon strolled on, quite satisfied with what he had triggered.

He entered through the Pennsylvania Avenue employees' door and showed his creds. He went through the metal detector, signed in and got a building pass, and made his way along the crowded halls into what was called mahogany row, the paneled hallway where FBI executives had their offices. With the CDC and the Army involved, the case needed oversight from Washington, with LA handling the local investigation.

He found the office of the assistant director who had been assigned to the case and pushed his way through the heavy wood door into the reception area. A crisp-looking Shinohara sat on a blue sofa, her legs crossed, her mass of curly hair framing her fine, exotic face. She wore a handsome silk dress and low heels. She smiled politely, and the little tooth-gap was still there. He smiled, too. He looked good, too. He'd worn the newest of his gray suits, newly cleaned. And the tie that Lindy once told him was awesome. He still couldn't figure out, however, how much of his sartorial interest was because of her and how much because of his meeting. It was an important distinction.

"So, Kathleen, you're representing the CDC today?"

"Yes, Robert. Doc's following up on the patients in California. I'm not the only one, though." She introduced a middle-aged balding black man whom Loudon hadn't even noticed. John Craig was a CDC assistant director in Washington. The CDC needed some national-level muscle, too.

"How's the injury?" he asked.

"Fine," she said. Indeed, there was only a small mound of bandage apparent under the dress. "Stitches come out in a week or so."

"No scar, I hope."

She just shrugged and took a look over her shoulder. "I can't see it from here."

After a few minutes, the receptionist invited them into AD Lucas White's office. White, a lanky sandy-haired hawknosed man with a somewhat gaunt face, introduced himself.

"We're going to do this meeting in the SIOC," he said, calling his assistant on the intercom. "Depending on how this case develops, we may run the investigation from there." His assistant, a prim, efficient-looking young lady, joined them in the outer office, and the five of them took the elevator to the Strategic Information Operations Center, a high-security room with a red restricted-access sign outside. White keyed a code into the vaultlike door, turned the lock and opened it. They entered a complex of glass-walled rooms, where technicians sat at consoles with computer terminals, phones, and video screens. The atmosphere was hushed, muffled by the thick blue carpeting. They picked up coffee in a small galley and passed rooms marked OPS1 and OPS2 and entered the conference room. White invited them to sit down at the long conference table. They faced the end of the room with several large-screen monitors and a map of the world. The assistant sat down to his left and took from her briefcase several color-coded briefing books and a pad of note paper.

"So," he began settling back in the large chair. "If you don't mind, I'd like to start with Agent Loudon's update on the situation. We're putting all this in the blue book for the director." Loudon dutifully pulled out his notes, and for half an hour, detailed the current status of the investigation. White listened intently, his fingers making a tent in front of his lips. He occasionally gave a quiet instruction to the assistant, who took copious notes for the blue book that was the director's weekly rundown on major cases.

Once Loudon was finished, Shinohara reported on behalf of the CDC. The CDC's scientists were still amazed at the complexity and sophistication of the virus, she said. And they were extremely worried about what might happen next. Throughout her presentation, Loudon watched her attentively, nodding at the appropriate time. Her lips had an interesting way of pursing when she concentrated on answering a question. And that dress fitted her figure very nicely.

"Now, we've got to talk about this serious media problem here," said Craig. "They're all over the story. They're interviewing the . . . uh . . .

colored people . . ." He smiled fleetingly at the reference. "They're going on talk shows. We've got tapes you can see if you like." He motioned at the video monitors. He leaned toward White, cocking one eyebrow. "Now you FBI people have got us in a corner. You've got to get us out. This story about the virus being a rare skin disease that contaminated Clayton's office . . ." Craig gave a dismissive shrug. "This story just ain't got wings."

"Well, the Bureau still has an element of surprise here," said White. "The Bureau is not going to lose that. You'll just have to live with it."

Shinohara joined in the argument. "Look, we've got field people trying to run this case the right way. They can't get good data if they have to pretend this virus is something it's not."

"The fact remains . . ." said White, his Adam's apple bobbing, his voice thickening with tension, "that Mr. Lupo doesn't know we're look- ing for him."

"Come on, sir," said Craig. "This guy is no dummy. He's built this complicated virus. He's eluded you so far. He's not going to—"

"But he won't elude us for long." Now White's voice clearly showed his anger. "You stick with this story until we—"

"Mr. White, you'd just better understand that this won't hold long," interrupted Craig. "*The New York Times* has their best medical writer on it. He's an MD himself. And so does the Atlanta paper. The independent virologists they're talking to are telling them there's no such rare skin disease. The CDC will simply not be caught in the middle of this."

"What do you think of this?" asked Shinohara, turning to Loudon. "What do you think of this deception?"

Loudon tensed. He was caught in the middle. One way and he ticked off White, who would make sure the whole Bureau would find out he wasn't a team player. The other way he ticked her off. Which one? His job or a beautiful woman?

"Uh . . ." He bought time by shuffling through his notes. "Well . . . the ArchiBiologics people are too scared to say anything. But somebody's going to put together information from the hospital or Lupo's neighbors. Lupo's a smart guy, all right. But he's not streetwise." He decided maybe a way out was to simply recite a series of facts. It didn't work. Craig, Shinohara and White all glared at him.

White's demeanor suddenly changed, as if a switch had been thrown. He smiled, but only with his mouth. Wielding the authority of the Bureau hadn't worked. "Well, I can assure you that the Bureau understands your position," he said, bobbing his head about in agreement. He reminded Loudon of one of those bobble-head dolls he'd seen in the back windows of automobiles. "The Bureau won't try to hold it long. We recognize something's bound to leak soon. As soon as the truth's out, the Bureau will make him an IO fugitive."

"A what?" asked Craig suspiciously.

"There'll be an Identification Order put out on him. Now, he's just a missing person. An IO is one of those wanted posters you see in post offices."

Craig sat back, still dissatisfied. "And you'll absolve the CDC of any participation in this farce," he growled.

Casting another look of annoyance at Loudon, Shinohara leaned forward and gestured emphatically, "Look, the important thing is to move as quickly as possible to get into the labs at Fort Detrick. We need to find out what Lupo did there . . . what they know about him there."

"What about the Army?" asked Loudon.

"Don't worry about the Army," said White smiling again, now confidently. "The Bureau has already finished extensive negotiations for you to go in. The Army said that given the hazards there they'd only allow a couple of people. So, it's you two," he said gesturing at Loudon and Shinohara.

"And it's today?" asked Shinohara.

"Yes, it's today," said White.

"I'll want backup if I need it," said Loudon.

"Call us. Whatever you need."

"Well, let's do it," said Shinohara.

The meeting over, Loudon and Shinohara said goodbye to their respective ADs and walked down the hall together. Loudon tried to be friendly. Shinohara was coolly businesslike.

"Look, Kathleen, about what went on in there. I'm really on your side. Don't confuse me with the Bureau."

"Believe me, I'm not. In fact, I'm not confusing you with much of anything."

In another attempt at amity, he agreed that they should take Shinohara's car for the hour's drive. It was full of equipment they might need.

"You don't mind me driving?" she asked. It was a test.

" 'Course not. Why would I mind?" he grinned, raising his eyebrows.

"Somehow, I thought you might," she said, as they got into her car in the FBI underground garage, and Shinohara maneuvered down Wisconsin Avenue and onto Route 270 toward Frederick. Loudon watched her sitting alert in the driver's seat, her slim body slightly tense with concentration, her smooth right calf muscle tensing and relaxing as it operated the accelerator pedal and the brake.

Shinohara was also acutely aware of him, sitting relaxed beside her in his somewhat gray suit and slightly overdramatic patterned tie. It was a little more carefully than he usually dressed. She realized with some annoyance at herself that she'd dressed a bit too carefully, too. But it was certainly because of the meeting, she decided. He continued to watch her as she drove, and she glanced occasionally over at him as they talked. She felt slightly constrained by the demands of driving. She felt in control, but at the same time under control.

During the trip through town they talked over the case, their theories, Lupo, and Doc. But to Loudon, it was also a chance at more. It was the first time he'd had any time alone with her. Maybe they'd both get past their facades, past the problems he'd just had.

Soon, they were passing through the rolling, thickly wooded hills of Maryland, lush with the full greenery of late spring.

He eased the conversation from discussing the case into their personal lives. She relented slightly, purely in the interest of a cordial working relationship, she told herself.

"My mother is an Irish woman," she said. "She was working with Doctors Without Borders in Bangladesh. And she met this Japanese diplomat and fell in love with him. Watashino-chichi."

"What-a-what?"

"Watashino-chichi. It's a formal Japanese way of saying my father. He's very traditional. He taught me Japanese traditions. He was a government attaché there; or that's what he said. I think he was probably a spy or something. Anyway, they had quite a romance. Mom married him there, then broke the news to the rest of the family in Boston and Ireland. She really put one over on her family. Told them that she thought he was Irish . . . that his name was Shin O'Hara . . . two words!" She laughed, narrowing her eyes, and it was a pleasant sight. "I don't know what he told his family, but they accepted them. Anyway, I was born a few years later. Mom calls me a shamrock samurai. Watashino-chichi is descended from an old samurai clan. They're in Kyoto most of the time."

"Well, my family's not nearly as interesting. My folks are in Chicago. He owns a brokerage. We moved all over establishing the business when I was young. Mom was very patient, setting up house a dozen times. But I got used to moving a lot, making new friends."

"Well, you appear to make friends quickly," she said smiling wryly.

After a significant pause, he said, "Well, I'm glad you decided to come."

"Doc had to be in California, and . . ." she trailed off.

"But you didn't have to come. You did decide to come."

She stiffened again. Her defenses went up again. "Strictly business, Robert. Look, I'm not saying you're not a bad guy—"

"You want to have dinner tonight? It'll be business. We'll have to talk over what happens at Fort Detrick."

"—but there's a problem."

"What problem is that?"

"Frankly, I think you're just too loosely wound for me. Doc told me your story. And all the other things I've seen."

"Doc told me your story, too," he said smiling. "Hey, maybe you're just a little too tightly wound for me.

She thought a moment, turned toward him smiling sweetly. He smiled back.

"Not a chance." He realized that the sweet smile held more than a touch of acid.

"Not even one chance?" His smile broadened into a self-mocking stupid grin.

"Give it up. That's my advice." She stopped smiling and turned back to her driving.

"Tell you what . . ." He decided to try plan B. ". . . Let's just enjoy each other's company. Let's start with lunch. That okay?"

121

"Well, I could eat. You haven't really made me nauseated—"

"Hey, that's something."

"—yet."

They had lunch in a restaurant in Frederick that was appropriate for a business meal. As they talked, he was sure that she enjoyed his company. But she didn't want to admit it. She remained in full control, concentrating on business. She looked at her watch several times, and precisely at the right minute, she stood up and announced that they just had time to make their appointment with Colonel Ned Gaines, head of the Army Medical Research Institute for Infectious Diseases.

They drove out to Fort Detrick passing through thick woods to reach the steel gate. They presented credentials and picked up passes from the guard and received directions to the army institute. As they drove out into an isolated section of the base, the building came into view from behind a screen of trees. Its very form spoke of the biological death it held inside. It was a sprawling low-rise brick building, imposing and solid, and isolated in a huge expanse of field. Few windows pierced the expanse of walls. A steel forest of vents on the roof were the exits for carefully filtered, purified exhaust air. There seemed to be only one entrance.

Loudon and Shinohara each held their own thoughts, as they silently got out of the car and prepared to enter a place that harbored the most dangerous organisms on earth.

CHAPTER 12

Ned Gaines looked like a career army colonel—short, powerful, bull-neck, and a brush haircut that showed no compromise with style or vanity. He was the essence of discipline. He had fought hard against a burgeoning belly of middle age and had largely won. His crisp uniform and jutting jaw gave him an added authority that was probably necessary in a place where one slip could mean death from an invisible, microscopic enemy. He clearly was not happy with the visitors as he stood up ramrod straight behind his desk. The white walls were decorated with citations and photos of men in uniform.

"Good morning, sir, ma'am," he said smartly, as Loudon and Shinohara introduced themselves. They exchanged firm handshakes and sat down. Gaines opened a folder and picked up a pen, making a notation. "We've already worked out the ground rules of this inspection. Do you understand them?"

"Well, we understand that you're allowing two people in . . . us. That's all we understand right now," said Loudon.

"You will have someone with you at all times. And you will ask permission to enter any area and will observe the biohazard safety regulations of that area. We will reserve the right to evacuate you from any area at any time."

"Colonel, that's just fine. But you will give us your cooperation in finding out what Arthur Lupo was doing here." Loudon leaned back, fixing an almost insolent gaze on the colonel. "The guy appears to have developed a possibly extremely dangerous capability. If he obtained any of that capability here, we want to find out about it."

The colonel looked back at him coolly with piercing gray eyes. "We'll do what we can. But I want to make clear that AMRIID only does defensive work. We're trying to protect soldiers against biological agents. We do vaccines, drug therapy, biocontainment. That's it. We do absolutely no offensive work. As you know, that was stopped years ago. All our work is unclassified."

"But not the results, right Colonel?" Shinohara, leaning forward, anger coloring her voice. Still looking hard at Gaines, she spoke to Loudon. "The CDC and the Army have a little difference of opinion about the Army's work. They're still releasing bacteria into the air and not telling us what happens. Right colonel?"

"Defensive work, ma'am." Gaines tapped his pen on the desk for emphasis. "Has to remain secret. Never know when an enemy might attack. Like I said, offensive work was stopped years ago."

"Well, it looks to me like Lupo's decided to start it up again," said Loudon.

"We'll see. I understand that Lupo was here just for a few months and that he was a good worker. Seemed to be a good technician." Again, Gaines tapped the folder on his desk. "Reports were that he stayed within the bounds. But if he didn't, we want to know about it, too."

"Who worked with him?" asked Shinohara. "That's the person we really should be dealing with."

"That would be Lieutenant Colonel Kyle McLaren. He should be waiting outside now. He'll escort you." With that, they exited Gaines's spare office to meet Kyle McLaren, obviously the next participant in a tightly orchestrated tour of the facility.

McLaren, a slim man in his forties, stood outside the door in a white lab coat. He introduced himself with a rather perfunctory handshake and led them down the hall. His pale skin seemed nearly as white as the lab coat. He had close-cropped reddish hair and brown eyes. His stoic expression revealed that he was also not especially happy with the visitors.

"I can show you where Lupo worked," he said. "But there's not much to see. He was just here to get us started on his system. He worked in a BSL-2 lab."

"That's Biosafety Level 2," explained Shinohara to Loudon. "It's for working with organisms that are generally not hazardous." Sure enough, the inscription BSL-2 was emblazoned in large yellow letters along the walls.

They entered a small, bare laboratory. No bottles remained on the shelves, no glassware on the benches. An empty chair was pushed against an empty desk.

"See? It was cleaned out long ago. It's for visiting scientists, and we've got one coming in tomorrow."

"Can I see the records of his work here?" asked Shinohara.

"Records? He had his own notebooks."

"I know that. I want to see the notebooks you kept on the work you did with him."

"Well, I didn't actually work with him directly, but—"

"Then I want to see the notebooks of those who *did* work with him. And I want to see the folder Gaines had on his desk." Loudon smirked. Shinohara was not going to let McLaren slide anything past her.

"Let's see the notebooks, the folder," said Loudon.

"Of course," said McLaren. They went down the hall to his office, and he sorted through a shelf of notebooks, pulling out several. Shinohara sat at his desk and began to scan through them, hooking her hair behind her ears as she bent to her work. McLaren went into the adjacent secretary's office and made a cryptic call to someone, mumbling a few words into the phone. A beige folder arrived shortly. It appeared to be the record that Gaines had referred to. Shinohara took it and, after she finished with the notebooks, began to go through it.

"Where did he stay while he was here?" asked Loudon.

"Oh, BOQ I think. Bachelor's Officers Quarters." Loudon began to quiz McLaren on Lupo's social life while at AMRIID, which seemed to be minimal.

"Did Arthur Lupo ever go into BSL-4?" asked Shinohara abruptly, closing the folder.

"Well, he had no reason—"

"Did he ever go into BSL-4?" asked Shinohara, her voice louder. "I know you've got logs. We have a BSL-4 lab at CDC and we keep scrupulous logs. We could look at them. It would probably take a week to go over several months worth of logs. We would have to have offices here. But we could do that." She fixed her forthright dark-eyed gaze on McLaren, until the faintest blush began to rise on his pale face.

Loudon realized that she knew how to use her alluring power with men when it suited her. "Yeah, and if we found any irregularities, any at all, we'd have to start an investigation," he added.

The prospect of having the two investigators in his hair for a week seemed to convince McLaren. "Actually, I think he did spend some time in there. He wanted to see what it was like . . . get some experience . . . and he was helping with another guy's experiments."

"Then where's the other guy's lab notebooks?" Shinohara was pinning McLaren at every chance.

"I'm sorry. I forgot about those. I can show you those," said McLaren and pulled them down. Shinohara began to go through them.

"By the way, what's BSL-4?" asked Loudon.

"Biosafety Level-4. It's the highest containment level. It's where we keep the lethal organisms for which there is no vaccine, no treatment," said McLaren.

"It's where we want to go," said Shinohara, not looking up from the notebooks.

"Then that's where we're going, okay?" Normally, Loudon would have been satisfied with peeking through the window into such a lab. But Shinohara had his blood up.

"It's highly restricted. We have to get formal permission—"

"Then let's get on that, okay? I'm sure the colonel will understand."

"Sure, fine," said McLaren, his jaw set. He went into the adjacent office to make the calls.

"Why BSL-4?" asked Loudon. "What'll we see by going in there?"

"I don't know. I'm sure we won't see any direct evidence of his being there. But if he's *really* dangerous, that's where he got the capability. I've been in the BSL-4 labs at CDC. I want to see what they're like here." She looked back at the notebooks, continuing to talk. "Besides, if somebody doesn't want me to go somewhere, that's probably where I should go."

"Woman's intuition, eh?" he grinned. He couldn't resist the needle.

She looked up, her forehead wrinkled in a reproving scowl. "No, actually I want to see you squirm. You're going in, too, Robert."

"Sure, sure. Get me in another hot place."

She bent back to the notebooks, and McLaren arrived shortly with permission. Once Shinohara was satisfied that she understood the experiments in which Lupo had been involved, they hiked down the maze of corridors into the depths of the building. They passed lab-coated researchers and peered into rooms where squat washing-machine-like ultracentrifuges and DNA sequencers festooned with indicator lights did their work. They walked down bare corridors whose only decorations were large orange BSL-3 insignia. Finally, they reached the entrance to an area emblazoned with the red biohazard symbol and red BSL-4 signs. McLaren held his identification card to a magnetic reader and the heavy steel outer door unlocked with a click. He pushed the door open, and they walked into a large foyer with a glass wall looking into the laboratory.

They could see workers dressed in bulky blue space suits bent over benches and tables. The workers carried out their tasks with painstaking deliberation, making each movement with methodical care. As they moved about, they pulled along with them coiled yellow air hoses attached to outlets on the ceiling.

In one room of the lab, workers pipetted samples into small flasks. McLaren led Shinohara and Loudon down the glass wall to the other room, where two workers had the carcass of a monkey splayed out on a dissection table, methodically probing its bloody, open chest. Each worker periodically stopped to dip his hands in a pan of disinfectant. They examined each others' gloves carefully each time. They wore latex surgical gloves over the cumbersome blue gloves of their space suits.

"This is it," said McLaren. "Listen, one slip in here, one break in your suit, and you're dead. Period. These are hot agents. You still want to go in?"

Loudon tried to picture what it would be like to be shrouded in the suit, knowing that only a layer of rubberized fabric separated his skin from a roomful of deadly disease. He felt claustrophobic already. He took a deep breath. "They look tight enough for government work," he said. "Well, I guess if she goes, I go."

"Show us the prep room," said Shinohara quietly. The look on her face was grim, as if she were about to face an old nemesis.

They left the observation area and walked down a narrow hallway to the staging area, and McLaren escorted each of them into individual dressing cubicles, asking them each to strip completely and don surgical scrub suits. When they emerged, McLaren had donned one, too, and he proceeded to prepare himself to enter the lab. Shinohara followed, and Loudon mimicked them.

They put on white socks, surgical caps and surgical gloves, which they taped securely to the sleeves of their suits. Loudon felt his hands immediately begin to grow clammy with the trapped sweat from his hands. McLaren motioned for them to follow him into the next room. Again, he pulled his magnetic card across a card reader and a door opened with a faint inrush of air into a BSL-4-level staging area. The space suits hung on pegs, looking dull gray under bright ultraviolet lights. They had soft plastic helmets with large, clear faceplates, and soft rubber-soled feet like those in children's bunny-suit pajamas. The three climbed into their suits, inserted their hands into the gloves and pulled the helmets over their heads. Shinohara expertly zipped her's shut and sealed its Ziploc-type seal over the zipper. Then, she turned to Loudon and did the same for him.

"You'll make sure this is sealed, won't you?" he smiled through the faceplate as it clouded with his breath. She put her hand to her ear, and he had to shout to repeat.

"Don't worry; you're driving home," she shouted back, drawing her fingers across his throat, completing the suit's seal.

They quickly stepped into a large airlock, closed it behind them and opened the other side, stepping through to the BSL-4 lab. Loudon felt his heart rate rise, and through the clouded faceplate, he saw that Shinohara looked perhaps a bit more nervous, too. As they left the airlock, McLaren turned and pulled a chain, and behind them, a shower drenched the inside of the chamber.

They were inside, and Loudon's faceplate was almost completely clouded. He could just see McLaren and Shinohara reach up and plug the air hoses into their helmets. Shinohara did the same for him, and with a loud whoosh, a rush of dry air cleared his faceplate and cooled his body. The air smelled faintly metallic, as if it had been run through an air conditioner.

McLaren handed them thick rubber boots from a stainless steel closet flooded with ultraviolet light, and they put them on. They shuffled slowly, deliberately through the lab, as if they were underwater. McLaren would periodically lean his helmet close to theirs and shout brief explanations. They stepped up to where the two workers were pipetting.

"What's the organism?" McLaren shouted.

"Equine encephalitis," they heard a muffled voice say from one of the suits. The worker did not look away from his task.

They moved into the room where the monkey was being dissected, sliding their hoses on overhead pulleys. The animal lay spread on its back, its chest split open. Its internal organs had dissolved into a pulpy pinkish mass. The stomach, kidneys, lungs, spleen—none of the organs could be distinguished. Dark red blood had clotted over the monkey's gaping mouth and even its open, staring eyes. Its skin had fallen away in places, revealing yellow bone.

"What's the organism?" shouted McLaren.

"Ebola Reston," came the faint reply.

"It's a version of Ebola that infects monkeys," shouted McLaren to Loudon. "We don't understand why."

They stepped briefly into the animal room, where infected animals were kept. Some sat at the front of their cages, staring dully out at the visitors, picking feebly at the cage wire. Others curled into ratty-looking furry balls, breathing fitfully. One convulsed, bloody froth oozing from its mouth, its body twitching uncontrollably. The animals were under death sentence, but people's lives might be saved, thought Loudon.

"Where's the cryo-unit?" shouted Shinohara, over the hiss of air.

"Sure, sure," said McLaren, waving his gloved hand. "The zoo."

They stepped to a large stainless steel cylindrical freezer, and McLaren opened the top. A thick cloud of white vapor curled up and over the edge and swirled downward to their feet.

"What's this?" asked Loudon. His nose was beginning to itch, but to open the helmet to scratch it would have meant death. He decided to let it itch.

"It's where they keep the frozen samples," said Shinohara. "Seventy degrees below zero, but they're alive in blood samples and pieces of tissue." She turned to McLaren. "Could Lupo have taken samples?"

"It would've been impossible," said McLaren resolutely. Despite the helmets and the bulky suits, Loudon could tell by the stiff posture of McLaren's body that the man was reacting to Shinohara's relentless presence. "Well, extremely difficult," he finally admitted.

"Come on. Could he?"

"Well, yeah, if he was good."

"Let's see some of the samples," said Shinohara, even her muffled voice revealing that she would allow no refusal.

McLaren paused, seeming ready to refuse. Then, he slowly put on a mitt, reached into the thick vapor and began to lift vials of frozen tissue from a rack inside the freezer to display them. One vial was labeled LFV204.

"Lassa fever," said McLaren. He picked up another labeled MV143. "Marburg virus." Shinohara suddenly stepped forward and leaned over, reaching deep into the freezer. Loudon couldn't see what she was doing.

She came up with a vial, her eyes wide. She showed McLaren the label. "What's this?"

McLaren paused for a long moment. Shinohara thrust the vial closer to him. "Mutant H5N1 influenza," he finally said, his jaw tightening. She turned the label toward Loudon. It said "mH660." Loudon didn't grasp the meaning at first.

"The list!" she exclaimed in an urgent whisper, and Loudon remembered. That code had been on Lupo's list. The one with the check marks! "Why didn't I think of that!" Shinohara scolded herself. "We've got to get out of here! We've got to talk!" She replaced the vial and moved quickly toward the airlock, yanking her hose behind her.

"So, what's the problem?" asked McLaren, following, but she didn't answer. They slipped off their boots, slid them into the closets and went back through the airlock. McLaren motioned that they had to go individually, to allow thorough decontamination. Shinohara went first, pulling a chain inside the airlock to start the decontamination cycle, which took five minutes. Loudon watched as the outside of her suit was drenched with a succession of three different sprays. She stepped into a pan of the liquid, scrubbing herself with a brush. Then came a final gush of water from the shower, and she was out. Loudon did the same, clumsily cleaning himself, trying to see through the liquid streaming down his faceplate. Then he was through and into the staging area, stripping off his wet suit as quickly as possible. Shinohara was already in the first staging area, ripping off the surgical gloves and the cap.

"What is it, Kathleen?"

She turned, her eyes intense with fury.

"He's got a sample of mutant H5N1. It's a lethal influenza virus engineered to be airborne. It's called bird flu, and it's deadly. But it could only be transmitted by contact between birds and people. That is, until scientists mutated a few of its genes and came up with a new strain. Lupo stole that strain from here, and if he figures out how to use it, he could trigger a flu epidemic like the one in 1918. It killed a hundred million people. And if he figures out how to increase lethality, it could kill everybody!"

McLaren came through the door to be greeted by barked instructions from Shinohara.

"Listen. You set up a meeting with Gaines and your security officer. Now!"

"But look—" McLaren started to say.

"Now," said Loudon coldly into McLaren's face. "You want a hundred FBI agents here? Maybe a load of CDC people? I just have to pick up the phone. You want the Secretary of the Army to get a call from the FBI director? I just have to pick up the phone. Okay?"

"Okay," said an abashed McLaren, stepping to a nearby phone.

"Why didn't I see it before?" Shinohara scolded herself once again.

"What?" asked Loudon.

"Get Lupo's list, I'll show you."

They each showered, scrubbing away the sweat of tension that came with any trip into the hot zone. It was also a symbolic act, an attempt at cleansing away the memory of the lethal organisms. Within twenty minutes, they were dressed and in a small conference room arranged by McLaren. Shinohara had the list in one hand, a blue marker in the other, writing on the white plastic board. Gaines entered, muttering darkly about "having other duties." Behind him was a younger dark-haired man in uniform. Gaines introduced the man as their chief of security. Shinohara finished her writing and stepped back from the board. She had written:

EZV422—Ebola Zaire Virus—Ebola fever

AV9900—Adenovirus—Various Diseases

DF205—Dengue fever

HV330—hantavirus

mH660—mutH5N1

"Is this about right, gentlemen?" she asked. Gaines cast an accusing look at McLaren, who nodded.

"Yeah, but how did you know our internal codes for the strains?" asked McLaren.

Loudon took the list from Shinohara and slapped it down on the conference table in front of them.

"I found this in Lupo's apartment. See the checks by the codes? That means he must have gotten them. I recognize Ebola and influenza. These are all nasty critters, right? And you let him get away with them!"

Gaines now glared at the security chief, who glanced nervously at McLaren, who suddenly became occupied with some papers in front of him.

"In particular, what were you doing with a stock of mutant H5N1?" demanded Shinohara. "Nobody was supposed to make that, much less store a stock.

Now it was Gaines' turn to become occupied with the papers in front of him.

"Well?" demanded Shinohara again.

"I'm about an inch from calling in half the Bureau on this, and I'm sure Miss Shinohara's folks would like to come along," said Loudon. "So, give me some answers. First, about mH660."

Gaines shot both Loudon and Shinohara the kind of cold-blooded look that only a military man could muster. "Well, after the airborne version was first made, there were questions about it we had to answer."

"Like what?" demanded Shinohara.

"Well, that early version wasn't particularly contagious or lethal. We needed to know what the potential biological endpoint might be."

"ENDPOINT! ENDPOINT!" sputtered Shinohara. "You mean you wanted to see how bad you could make it! And that's what mH660 is?"

"Defensive research," said Gaines simply, and Shinohara rolled her eyes in disgust. "We had to know what was possible; what terrorists could do—"

"And so you made this stuff and had such lousy security that it is now in the hands of a terrorist!"

Loudon placed a calming hand on her shoulder, and raised another thorny question. "And why was Lupo off the books on security clearance if he was working on something that was part of your normal mission?"

"Look," Gaines growled. "I want answers, too. You can bet I'm going to get them. And as soon as I get them, you'll get them."

"Do you know a guy named Chavez? Army intelligence?" Loudon asked the group.

"I do not know a Chavez," said Gaines crisply. He looked at the others who shook their heads.

"Does this have anything to do with Plum Island?" asked Shinohara. Loudon looked at her, surprised. She had apparently decided to ambush the three soldiers, and it worked. They looked confused.

After a long pause, Gaines said tersely, "We do not discuss Plum Island. That is classified."

"Gentlemen," said Shinohara. She turned to Loudon. "The CDC has heard rumors about a research lab on Plum Island, just off Long Island in New York. It's supposed to be a place where animal viruses are studied. The Army suddenly evacuated the place a few years ago. There were rumors of a viral release. There were also rumors of platoons of soldiers entering the labs in isolation suits, setting out electric frying pans full of paraformaldehyde. When it's hot, it releases formaldehyde gas."

"We do not discuss Plum Island," said Gaines again.

"Well, then let's discuss these viruses" exploded Shinohara. She pulled a thumb drive out of her bag and inserted it into the room's digital projector. "Let's start with Ebola Zaire. It's the hottest strain of Ebola. It first emerged in 1976 in Africa. Went through fifty-five villages like a wildfire. Kills ninety percent of those it infects in two weeks. AIDS kills a hundred percent, but it takes a decade and it's not nearly as contagious."

She pressed the projector's control button and a slide appeared titled "Deadliest Diseases". Another press and a slide appeared of a man writhing in agony on a hospital bed.

"First symptoms, right?" asked Shinohara. McLaren nodded somberly. She went on. "First thing the victim gets is a monster headache and fever. Then his blood starts throwing clots all over, like a stroke throughout the body. But he still bleeds like crazy internally. The virus crushes the immune system. The patient has no defense."

She brought up another slide. She examined it. Another patient, his face fixed, ghostlike. His skin was blotchy with clotted blood beneath the surface.

"The clots plug arteries," she continued. "The victim's mind goes and there are massive strokes that may paralyze an entire side of the body. The skin develops bruises and begins turning to pulp. Starts to look like tapioca pudding."

Another slide, even more gruesome. The third man's face was a blank death mask, his eyes bloody and open, his blackened blood-filled mouth in a permanent scream. His lip was split and hanging by a flap, revealing teeth caked with clotted blood.

"The intestines fill with blood. The eyeballs bleed. The patient vomits black fluid." Shinohara was furious now. The three men were stunned. They had seen the slides before, but then the images were academic exercises in pathology. Now they knew that a possible psychopath—a brilliant one—had escaped with a sample of this killer. And it was their fault.

"At the end, the patient leaks massive quantities of blood from the nose, mouth, and eyes, and from the tearing skin. This blood has huge quantities of virus particles. After death, the body almost liquefies, because the connective tissue has been dissolved." She switched off the projector, leaving the room in darkness.

"And throughout this disease, the patient is viciously infective," she said in the darkness. "A cough may send clouds of virus particles into the air, and coming near the body, much less touching it, can cause infection."

She clicked on another slide, a black-and-white photo of vast rows of corpses. "Okay, now it gets worse, if you can believe that. The flu bug you cooked up could cause a worldwide pandemic that'll make the influenza pandemic of 1918 look like summer cold season." She turned to Loudon, her voice choked with anger. "In 1918, a hundred million people died. Two billion infected. It spread like wildfire throughout the world. People would sit down to breakfast healthy and be dead by noon. They were carting away corpses in freight wagons."

McLaren flicked on the lights. Shinohara had a haggard look on her face. Loudon stood up and looked from one to the other. The soldiers were still staring at the blank screen, not wanting to look at him or Shinohara.

"We're leaving now. We've got a lot to do. And you have a lot to do," he said. "I'm going to report to headquarters that we have the potential for a world-class disaster. You'd better be prepared to explain how this happened." He picked up his briefcase and followed Shinohara out.

They walked with an urgent stride back to the car. Loudon drove this time; he really didn't think Shinohara could, anyway. She was silent during the ride back through Frederick, her head leaning against the headrest, looking away out the side window. They had passed through Frederick and into the green rolling farmland when she spoke.

"What triggers a little meek guy like him to go off like this?" she asked. "What happened to him?"

"The obvious answer is his mother's death. And his father's. But we need to know how that bomb went off. I'm going to feed everything we've got on him to the behavioral sciences unit at Quantico. They'll do a psych profile that'll tell us enough to try to predict what he'll do next. They'll tell us the key details, like whether it was because he wet the bed when he was a kid."

"Yeah? Good. Good." She wasn't relaxing though. She sat tensely in the seat, now staring ahead into space. He glanced over to see her chest rise and fall, perhaps a bit more than it would for relaxed breathing.

"You okay?"

"Oh, sure. I've dealt with these organisms a long time. I know what they can do. But this one gives me special nightmares." His hand was on the car's console. He reached over patted hers and left it there. It was the first time they had touched. He thought it was magic. Her hand was soft and fine.

"Robert," she scolded absentmindedly, her voice low. He withdrew his hand.

"Can't I even show sympathy?"

"Give it up."

As if to punctuate her declaration, her cell phone tweedled. She reached into her pocket, pulled it out, and began to talk quietly.

"Jeez," she whispered as she hung up. "It was Doc in California. In LA. Lupo's hit again. They're bringing dozens into LA County Hospital. Dozens."

"What? Are they just colored?" Shinohara asked the question into the phone and received the answer.

"Yeah," she breathed. "Just colored . . . so far . . . but it looks like it's just the beginning."

Loudon immediately pulled off the highway and called the AD, Lucas White, in Washington.

"White, he's there at the hospital!" said Loudon. "I know he's right there! Tell Bowers to flood the place with agents and the local cops. It's the best chance we'll have! And I'll need a Bubird, a jet, at National. We'll be there in an hour." He hung up the phone. "We'll get him," he promised Shinohara.

They climbed into the car and sped away, rocketing onto the freeway. They moved so swiftly that the dark green sedan that had followed them at a safe distance almost lost them. But it managed to keep up, settling into the same lane, several cars back. Loudon was so preoccupied that his usual sixth sense didn't detect the tail.

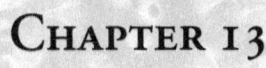

CHAPTER 13

Malcolm Harding sat watching television, a *Cheers* rerun. He enjoyed the camaraderie on the screen, the kind of bluff, hearty friendships he never seemed able to cultivate. And every time he raised his hand to click the remote control, he was reminded how much more difficult any kind of normal socializing would be in the future. Grasping the remote would be this strange blue hand. It seemed almost not his. Before, he always preferred to remain in the background, safe and quiet and watching the scene. It would never be so again.

The doorbell rang. He hoped it wasn't another reporter. He'd left the phone off the hook and told all of them he was tired of talking to them. Last time it had been a German reporter with a camera. But when he opened the door now it was Flo. She tried not to appear to stare, but she failed.

"It's okay," he said. "You can look. Everybody does."

"Oh, I'm sorry. I just came down to see how you were. Can I come in?" She stood uncertainly in the hall in her reticent way. She was round and soft in face and body, with the settled anonymity of middle age. Her short hair was of a determined uniform brown not found in nature.

She wore a nice green dress with a white sweater over her shoulders. She smiled shyly.

"Sure, sure, of course." He stepped back, and she walked in and stood in the foyer, again uncertain what to do. "I'm really glad to see you," he said, standing embarrassed in front of her. "I didn't call or anything because . . . well . . . I didn't really know whether you'd want to get all mixed up in this." He waved his hands at himself.

"Oh, Mal, you know it wouldn't matter. I sort of waited until things settled down to see if you'd come by. You didn't, so I thought I would." She laid one hand tentatively on his shoulder. He put his hands around her waist, then they hugged, each enjoying the warmth and softness of the other.

"Flo, I'm sorry, but I didn't know . . ."

"I know. Have you had dinner?"

"Well, I was going to fix something."

"I've got a casserole upstairs. I could bring it down."

"That would be nice."

She left and he hurried to the kitchen, bringing out his two best matching glasses, some silverware and plates. She liked iced tea, so he quickly mixed up some instant. She returned in a few minutes. She'd obviously had the casserole ready to bring. They sat down, and she spooned some of the steaming chicken and rice onto his plate.

"Has it been hard? I saw you on the news and on those shows. You did really well."

"Well, they asked lots of questions about how it felt. Like I said, I guess it feels okay. I'm not used to people asking me a lot of questions. Except maybe what kind of wood they should buy."

She smiled and nodded. "You're back at work?"

"Yeah, I've been back a few days. There's lots of people." He took a bite of his casserole. The chicken flavor was marvelous. "Good," he said. That was considered high praise between them.

"Thank you. Does it make you nervous? The color? I would be."

"Yeah. Y'know, it's still just me, but people think I'm different. But it's just me. They're going to make me a manager."

"That's great!" She patted his arm.

"Well, I don't know if I like it."

"You mean the responsibility?"

"Well, yeah, but also because they're making a *blue guy* the manager. Not me. A *blue guy* who gets offers from other places."

"Other places?"

"Yeah, this car dealer wanted me to be a salesman. Probably lots more money. But I'm going to stay at the lumber yard."

"Well, if you want to you should."

"Yeah, there's going to be money from the movie or TV show or whatever. So I can stay where I want. But I still don't like the color thing."

She drew herself up in her chair and delicately cleared her throat. She always did that when she was about to say something daring.

"Mal, listen to me. You are very special. The color . . . well . . . that just made them notice you and give you a chance to show it. But you'll be a really good manager because you can do it."

"Well, my wife . . . my ex-wife . . . didn't think I was so special. She thought I was boring."

"She didn't know you."

They ate for a while in silence, each looking down at their plate.

"I'm glad you're here," he finally said quietly.

She smiled and blushed slightly, continuing to eat.

• • •

"Which was better, Ada? C'mon, which was better, *Today* or *Good Morning America?*" pleaded Cheryl.

"Oh, they was both great. *Today* was cool. I dunno. The people at GMA were real nice. I dunno." Ada Frye was tired. The high of being in New York and going on talk shows had faded on the flight back to San Diego. She wondered if, now that she was yellow, she'd show up pale when she was tired. She flipped down the sun visor and looked at her face in the makeup mirror. No, she was still a brilliant yellow. Her yellow roots were more prominent now. She considered dyeing her hair black. A reality was beginning to settle in; a reality of a different life that frightened her.

Cheryl gunned the red Toyota onto the freeway, finally out of the airport traffic. Her long silver earrings jangled as she whipped her head around to check behind her, zipping the car in and out of traffic lanes.

"I know you're tired, honey. I'll get you home."

"Yeah, I really appreciate you picking me up."

"There sure was still a lot of news people there. And people lookin' to see you."

"Well, we're hard to miss, y'know. Blue folk and yellow folk and red folk. You heard anything about that virus? Anything in the papers?"

"No, they still sayin' it was some kind of pollution thing. Maybe you'll get cured. Like a cold virus."

"Sure don't look like it so far. It ain't faded at all."

"You goin' back to work?"

"Well, I got some money from the movie people. And there's a book writer, and that newspaper, the one at the checkout stands. I'll have some money, looks like. But I'm not gonna quit. I just hope I don't . . ." Ada paused and stared out the window.

"What?"

"Well, y'know, since I'm colored. I mean another color. You know. They gonna do somethin' at work?"

"Yeah, well the law says no discrimination on race, creed or color. Don't say what color! And hey, baby, I thought of this, too. If people give you trouble, you tell 'em they don't understand you. You say 'Hey, it's a yella thang, man!'"

Ada laughed and slapped Cheryl on the knee. "Go *on*, girl!"

Cheryl stared comically at her knee. "It really don't come off!" she exclaimed, and they both laughed uproariously, poking playfully at each other. Ada was feeling better now that she was with her best friend. But she grew more wary as the car turned onto her block, where her neat little stucco house stood halfway down, compact and homey and inviting. They pulled up to find a knot of excited neighbors outside, with a "Welcome Home, Ada" banner between the two spindly sweetgum trees in the front yard. The trees had yellow ribbons tied around them. Ada donned a saucy smile when she got out of the car, and the neighbors crowded around, congratulating her on becoming famous and welcoming her home.

"Now, she's just gonna stay a while," shouted Cheryl. "She's had a long day. Just you all say hello and then that's it." She moved away from Ada, scanning the crowd for Aunt May. Aunt May was who Ada needed now. She spotted the old woman, sitting quietly on the front porch of Ada's house. Aunt May knew that she would be needed. She saw Cheryl and nodded meaningfully, pulling her large, comfortable old frame out of the aluminum lawn chair and going into Ada's house. Cheryl tossed her head, jangling her earrings, and waded into the crowd, extricating Ada and taking her into the house. Aunt May sat on the couch. She was the matriarch of the neighborhood. She watched over all the people on the block, advising, hugging, scolding and even backhanding as they needed it. Nobody, but nobody, went against what Aunt May said.

Ada came into the shady coolness of the house and cocked her head in pleasure when she saw Aunt May sitting on the couch. She set her purse down on the table by the door, went over and sat down beside her. Aunt May put a large arm around Ada, and Ada laid her head on Aunt May's shoulder and sighed. Cheryl closed the door and left, shooing the neighbors away.

"Sweetheart, I know you've had it hard," said Aunt May. "Darlin', you just relax now, and we'll talk it out."

"Oh, May, this thing is just such a mess. I don't know who I am, this color thing."

"Baby, you still Ada Frye. You still the same big-hearted, tough-talking woman you always were." She shifted so she could look in Ada's eyes. "Only thing you needed is a hug from Aunt May. Don't I know? Don't I *always* know? Say 'Yes, ma'am'."

"Yes, ma'am," Ada smiled through the slightest glisten of tears. Sitting there in the still house with Aunt May, she could let go. "May, you sure got the touch."

"Sweetheart, forty years as a nurse, I know people. I know you're gonna do fine. Listen, I'm gonna leave you alone. But I'll be home watchin' my stories. You want to come over, you come over. We'll talk a long time." With the effort of her age, she stood up, looking down at Ada smiling. Ada basked in the warmth of her sweet grandmotherly gaze.

"Thanks, May," sighed Ada as Aunt May opened the door, nodded her head at Ada in the certainty of her confidence in the young woman, and left.

Ada got up, still enjoying the comforting glow of May's visit. She reached into her purse and pulled out the small recorder and sat back on the couch. She turned the recorder over in her hand and looked at it tiredly. She clicked it on to record and thought a moment. Then she put the little machine to her lips and thought some more.

"Nah," she finally said into the recorder.

She clicked it off, and went into the kitchen to make herself some soup, when she heard a tapping on the back door. She peeked through the window to see the smiling face of a very handsome man with a neat pencil moustache and a carefully shaped do of shiny black hair. She frowned the deepest frown she knew how.

"You're not supposed to come around here. You go on, now. I don't want to see you."

"Aw, come on, babe," he said, a mock-hurt look on his face. "I wanted to make sure you were okay, I was worried. Let me in."

She was too tired to argue. She unlatched the door, and he came in. He was wearing a sleeveless t-shirt showing his muscular dark brown arms, tight jeans that showed his slim hips, and blinding white sneakers. Ronnie looked good. She reminded herself that he was, however, very bad for her. And that they were divorced. And that last time he came around, he left with a loan that hadn't been repaid. She concentrated on heating the soup.

"I saw you on *The View*. You were fine, woman, talkin' that talk on those shows."

"Yeah, I did okay. I wasn't sure I would, with all those people."

"Yeah, yeah," said Ronnie, looking down the hall to the living room. He went over and opened the refrigerator, peering in. "Got a beer? It was hot waitin' out back there. I didn't want to run into May out front." He found one and popped the top, took a long drink and sat beside her at the table as she ate her beef and barley soup. "You sure be yellow!"

"Yeah, Ronnie, I sure am that." He took a drink of his beer, got up and came around behind her, putting his hands on her shoulders and bending down to whisper into her ear.

"Yeah, but babe, you still look fine to me."

She shrugged her shoulders, but let him keep his hands in place. It had been a long time. Her dating had been sparse.

"Listen, babe, you need to relax. Ronnie can help you relax. We'll do a little relaxin', then we'll talk about you and me. Our future."

"We got no future, Ronnie. Last time was my mistake. I don't make that mistake twice." She held a spoonful of the soup to her lips. It was hot, and she blew carefully on it.

"But baby, I can make us some money. I hear you got some deals goin', I can help you manage them. I can make sure you get everythin' that's comin' to you . . ." He nuzzled her yellow ear. She put down the spoon, stood up slowly and turned toward the stove, and he put his arms around her waist, reaching to kiss her. She twisted to pick up the pot, which still had an inch of hot soup in it and turned back toward him, smiling invitingly.

"Yeah, babe, I bet you look like somethin' fine with no . . ."

She flipped the pot onto his head, dumping the brown liquid onto his slick hairdo. She stepped back, raised the pot high and bonked him as hard as she could. The pot made a terrific metallic clang when it careened off his skull.

"HEY!" he yelled throwing up his arms for protection. "You got my . . ." But she was already on him, punctuating each word with a wild swing of the pot, whacking him on the arms, shoulders and, finally as he made for the door, his butt.

"GET . . . OUT . . . OF . . . MY . . . HOUSE!" she bellowed.

He managed to wrestle the door open under the rain of blows and make it down the steps out of her reach. He turned, wiping the soup from his face, and shouted up at her.

"YOU MEAN, NASTY, FOUL-TEMPERED, YELLOW . . . WHATEVER!"

She looked at him for a moment, then started to giggle, then chortle, then laugh hysterically. He stood at the bottom of the steps with a stupidly indignant look on his face glistening with the soup. She felt liberated. She brandished the pot like a scepter, drawing herself to her full height and with her chin held high in her most regal attitude, declared:

"Baby, I ain't yellow. I am *golden!*"

• • •

John Lance stood up on the rung of the bar stool and shouted down the bar, "YOU SUCKERS WANNA SEE SOMETHIN' AMAZING? YOU REALLY WANNA SEE?"

"Yeah, Johnny, let's take a look! Yeah!" came the return cries. The girls giggled and egged him on, and the men booed and waved their caps at him in hearty mock disgust.

John Lance downed his shot of whiskey, slipped off the bar stool, unbuttoned his shirt, and with his baseball cap still on his head, leaped onto the stool and onto the bar, whipping off the shirt. Drunken shouts and whoops greeted him as he pitched the shirt onto the stool, flexed his bright red muscles and strutted up and down the bar in his tight jeans and work boots. He turned his red back to the crowd and flexed his arms high. Then he turned toward them and flexed them low, showing the rippling red muscles.

"Hey, Johnny, what're the others like?" asked a burly young man in a cowboy hat, leaning over the bar to talk around Honey. "How about that little blue chick I saw? And that fine red woman?"

"Well, that red woman was over at County Hospital. I just saw her in person once when we were doing pictures for a magazine. But the little blue chick, she really looked fine, y'know."

"How 'bout that yellow one?"

"Oh, yeah," Lance's voice lowered conspiratorially. "That was so funny, man. This black gal turnin' yellow. She had that kinky hair, and it was gonna turn yellow on her. She was just real funny lookin'."

They laughed and drank up. Lance continued to regale them with stories of his adventures at the hospital and in LA, where he'd done talk shows.

"Well, we'd best be gettin' on," he said finally.

"Johnny, we gotta talk," she whispered.

"Sure, baby, we will. My place."

"Johnny—" she started to say, but they were already out the door. They sped away in his Camaro, with her sitting silently in the passenger seat, and they soon reached his apartment. He led her into the small living room with the furniture that was worn and cigarette-burned from too many beer parties. He turned and put his arms around her, and tried to kiss her.

"I really want to kiss you," he said. He bent to kiss her, but she pulled away.

"Johnny, I can't."

"Honey, don't be bashful jus' because I been on TV and all. Is that why you won't kiss me?"

"Well, it's that . . . well . . . you're colored."

"What does that mean?"

"You're colored. Y'know. Well, it's different, because you're red."

"Hey, baby, it's like a sunburn. Like a bad sunburn. But don't worry; it don't hurt." He slapped his chest.

"Well, I can't . . . that's all. I keep thinkin' it's like . . . it's maybe yucky . . . The skin and all. It's just different and I don't like it."

"Baby, it's me!"

"Well, I dunno . . . it's not. Look, I just don't want to, okay! I don't wanna see you any more, either!" She whirled and yanked the door open and was gone.

John Lance stood there for a moment, an uncomprehending look on his face.

• • •

The cell phone played a tune, and Ellen Lucius leaped onto the bed, bouncing herself twice onto it and pressed the screen to take the call.

"Hello?" she said pulling her nightshirt down over her slim blue legs.

"Ellie, it's Chrissie."

"Hey! I was hopin' you'd call."

"Ellie, you were so coool, today! You looked so good, kid!"

"Yeah, you think so? Like, the dress was okay?"

"Girl, you looked great! That white was perfect!"

"I was so scared. Like, I just hated my color! I thought I was so ugly! You remember what I said about how scared I was. What'd everybody say?"

"Oh, they just thought you were cool! You shoulda heard Deanna, though. She was so jealous. She goes 'She just looks like a big blueberry.'"

"Oh, did she say that?"

"Yeah, but everybody said for her to shut up. Marcia goes like 'Hey, like she's so brave!' And, they said you were cool and that, like y'know, even though you were famous you weren't stuck up or anything."

"Yeah?"

"Yeah, and I heard that Mrs. Cataloni's gonna postpone the cheer-leader tryouts so you can go."

"Yeah, she told me. That was so cool of her. Also, *Brad* called," said Ellen with a coquettish lilt to her voice. Chrissie squealed and Ellen held the phone away from her ear and screwed up her face. Chrissie was too loud sometimes, but she liked her. Ellen continued. "Like, he said he wanted for us to get together again. He said he was sorry, y'know, that he hadn't called."

"Yeah? Tell me!"

"Oh, it was just . . . well . . . cool, that's all," said Ellen coyly.

"C'mon Ellie, we're best friends. I won't tell. Like, really!"

"Well, he said he thought we should go out on the beach. In his Jeep."

"Yeah, like he said he wanted to kiss me on my cute blueberry lips! That's what he actually called them!"

"Really?" Chrissie screamed. "He is so funny!"

"Listen, listen, listen, we got to go to the mall tomorrow. To The Gap maybe. My mom said I could use some of my money to get new clothes. I wanna look at bathing suits."

"Oh yeah! Girl, you would just look so cool in a little two-piece like maybe Cool Whip white!"

They both giggled.

"Your mom has been sooo cool through this," said Chrissie.

"Yeah, she cried when she saw me in the hospital. But she's okay. My dad's cool, too. He was talkin' about punchin' out Doctor Clayton. But the people, the government disease people, they said it wasn't the doctor's fault."

"And it's not catchin'?"

"Yeah."

"Yeah . . . ummm."

"Yeah, well I gotta go. I gotta do homework. I got way behind in Mr. Fortnam's class."

"Oh, Fart-nam's such a jerk."

"Yeah, a major dweeb. Like, okay, tomorrow after school, the mall."

"Cool . . . okay . . . well . . . g'bye."

"G'bye."

• • •

Waiting for the newly red Joy to come home, Bubba Chambers briefly examined the hole in his undershirt, scratched an itch through it, then picked up the worn TV remote with the tape around it. He flipped through the channels til he found wrestling. He thought it was on then. He shifted his bulbous mass in the butt-sprung easy chair, making it creak. His beer was empty. He considered getting up, but decided to wait until he had to pee. But he heard a rattling at the front door, so he decided he should get up then. He rolled forward, grunting at the effort of bending with his belly, and stood up. He shuffled around the chair, kicking the squeaky rubber dog toy out of the way with his white-socked foot just as Joy came in the door. She wore a large floppy hat and a raincoat with the collar turned up. She put down her brown plastic suitcase and took off the hat and shrugged off the coat, and a chihuahua came yapping up, dancing around her red bulk in celebration. She bent and swooped up the small dog, allowing it to lick her great red jowls.

"Hey," said Bubba. "Yer back."

"Yeah," she said timidly. "They was interviewin' me before I came home. The papers. Remember, I called? I was in a hotel?"

"Yeah, I remember. You didn't go on TV."

"I couldn't. I just couldn't."

"Well, I looked to see you."

She stood by the door for a moment, petting the dog, worry on her large face. "Bubba, now I'm home, first off I gotta ask you."

"What?"

"Well . . . the color . . . the red. Is it okay?"

"Whaddaya mean?"

"Are you gonna, like . . . can we stay married?"

Bubba scratched his belly contemplatively for a long time. "Does it come off on food?"

"No."

"Then how about makin' dinner?" he asked, leaning his weight toward the bathroom to get himself launched in the right direction.

Joy Chambers smiled happily, kissed the chihuahua on the mouth, and waddled toward the kitchen.

• • •

"Okay, we start with the spotlight on me," said the skinny rocker, Eddie Chandler, into the darkness of the empty night club.

"Right," came a bored voice from the darkness.

Chandler turned to the band, swirling his black velvet cape. It covered his body from his shoulders to the floor, contrasting sharply with his bright yellow face.

"Okay, gimme the opening chord when I enter. Let's try it." He flipped the cape dramatically and strode off stage. "Make the announcement, Nate."

"Okay," said the bored voice. "Ladies and gentlemen, presenting Eddie Chandler and Yellow Peril."

An ear-splitting, unearthly wail arose from the instruments, as the band members tortured from them the heavy-metal chord. Chandler swept on stage, and the spotlight struck his black-swathed body. He threw off the cape, raising his skinny arm high into the air. He picked up his guitar and slipped the strap over his head. His hand slammed down against the strings of the black guitar, and it added its own keening twang to the amplified roar.

The group launched into the number, which contained the words "baby," "lovin'," and "slimy," repeated in random order, although they were difficult to discern amidst the wailing instruments and yowling band members. Finally, with a last cacophonous crash of drums, the song finished.

"Yeah, great!" enthused Eddie.

"Words? Who's missin' words? There's just seven. Or six," said the nearly deaf Waco Travis, slouching over the drums and scratching his cheek absentmindedly with a drumstick. Waco had been playing heavy metal the longest, and thus had the most hearing loss.

"Say Eddie, I think your A string's a little sharp," said Cooch, running his fingers over his Fender X43000 bass guitar.

"Yeah, man, okay, the important thing is we're ready for this gig. It's big, guys. We can go pro if this works."

"Yeah, say Eddie, tell me again why you got lead billing?"

"We went over that, Cooch. I'm the attraction, dude. Like, I'm the one they're comin' to see, right?" He stalked to the edge of the stage, swooped down and picked up a magazine. "See, man? Cover of *People*, man! And they even did a color spread inside!"

"Got a bed in time?" asked the puzzled Waco. "Whose bed?" The others ignored him. They'd learned long ago to ignore the deaf Waco's non sequiters.

"Eddie, you're just there in the back row," said Cooch looking at the magazine. "And it just mentions a little bit in there that you're a musician."

"Look, Cooch. I told ya. Any time you want to do what I said to, you can be featured, too."

"Hey, man, I ain't gonna take blood from you, get the virus, or whatever, and turn yellow. That sucks."

"Yeah," said Fungus, lifting his Stratocruiser 29XLZ guitar over his head to take it off and setting it onto the stand to get a smoke. "The band breaks up, we're just some yellow dummies."

"Whatcha mean yellow mummies?" asked the deaf Waco.

"Hey, suit yourself," said Eddie, shaking his head at Fungus. "But until then, it's Eddie Chandler and Yellow Peril. Listen, Benny says he can get us gigs all over since I'm yellow. And for all us colored people, he says we're also talkin' about comic books, action figures, all that merchandise stuff. All us colored people are gonna be big, lemme tell ya! We need to go again."

"Pen? I got a ballpoint," said Waco, fishing in his jeans, nearly missing the beginning of the song. "I wish you guys would lemme know when you're goin' again!"

They launched into their repertoire, and Eddie practiced sweeping off the cape and performing gyrations that would show off his yellow body to its best advantage. He was just trying out a tentative split when the bored voice from the back notified him that he had a phone call. He went to the back, and the band members heard him talking. Then they heard a loud "No? Aw!" Then there was more conversation.

"What's up?" asked Fungus when Eddie returned with a disgusted look on his face.

"That was Benny. Awww man . . . bummer!"

"The gig canceled?" asked Cooch.

"Worse. He said a report came on the news. There's a whole bunch of people got this thing up in LA. They're all different colors, man."

"So?" asked Fungus.

"Man, don't you understand? We ain't exclusive any more. They got colored people up there. Man, they can get agents, form bands. Pretty soon there'll be colored bands all over."

"Yeah . . . wow . . . bummer," said Cooch philosophically, lighting a cigarette.

"Not until summer?" asked Waco.

CHAPTER 14

Shinohara held the cup up to the pumpkin-colored Randy Joe, with a practiced patience.

"Hey, sweetie, I'll pee for ya, no problem. Jus' ask me." Randy Joe grinned a broken-toothed grin, his gaunt pumpkin-colored face showing bleary, impish delight. He lounged back in his hospital bed, putting his needle-marked hands behind his head, and watching the other patients take up the cry.

"Yeah, yeah, gimme a cup," shouted a goldenrod-colored Loco. "But it'll cost by the pint, man!"

"Come on, settle down," said Shinohara, distributing the other cups. "You know you have a virus. It could be dangerous. We need to find out."

"I don't feel like I got no virus," whined Carl, his red bloodshot eyes staring balefully out of a pea green Basset-hound face. "I'm strung, that's all. I need my *friend*. Gimme my money, I'm goin' to get my friend, man."

The others began to shout, whine, and protest. Shinohara looked around the room disapprovingly.

"Shut up!" boomed a deep, resonant voice. It came from Jimmy D. Once a massive black man, he was now a bright blue-green. "You said you'd stay here, give blood, pee . . . whatever," he continued. The noise subsided. Jimmy D. was a man to be listened to, in the hospital or out. "So, do what the lady say. Jus' do what she say, keep yo honky mouths shut."

"But we ain' honkies no more, Jimmy D.," retorted Randy Joe from his bed. "Man, we're all colored people now. You look more honky than us. You blue, man."

"I'm *turquoise*, and don't you forget it!," rumbled Jimmy D. "I been brown all my life, everybody call us black. Now that I'm turquoise, ain't nobody gonna call me blue!"

"Okay, Jimmy D., okay!" Randy Joe raised his pumpkin hands in surrender, and the ten men on the ward lapsed into a spirited discussion of what constituted colored people. As Shinohara finished distributing the cups, she looked up to see Loudon standing at the door. She nodded at him and shook her head in frustration at the men. She walked over to him as they began to file, one by one, into the bathroom off the large ward to produce their samples for a waiting nurse.

"It was a good idea, paying them to come in," said Loudon. "Doc's with another couple in admitting downstairs. They threw one guy out though. Came in with food coloring all over him and tried for the money."

"Well, we didn't know any other way to corral these people. They all seem to be addicts. We've got ten men, three women. Most really didn't care whether they were turning colors, as long as they got their next fix."

"So that's the common thread? They all looked pretty rough."

"Doc's got interviewers talking to them. They've all got needle tracks. We're almost sure Lupo got the virus into them through some injection route. They sure didn't all go to the same allergist. We'll know soon." She scanned the rows of beds. "This is certainly a new wrinkle."

"You mean the colors?"

"Yeah, we haven't found two exactly alike yet. Look at them." She strolled down the row, reading down a list and pointing out the colors. "Pumpkin, goldenrod, chrome yellow, pea green, vermillion, turquoise . . . ."

"That's right!" exclaimed Jimmy D. when she reached him.

Shinohara smiled and continued ". . . avocado, maroon, fuchsia, and strawberry. No two alike. He's mixed the three chromophore genes

152

in the same virus and developed a modulating control system that we really don't understand. We don't understand why yet, either."

As she talked, patients in adjoining beds occasionally held up their arms to compare colors, some of their hands trembling from drug withdrawal.

"How'd you figure the colors?" asked Loudon.

"We had the hospital decorator come in. I don't know what we do if we get more people. The shades may become too subtle to describe."

"Oh, Miss Shinohara, here's my sample," said Squirrel, a frail, wild-eyed young man, maroon in color. He held up the small cup in his bony, shaking hand. Shinohara motioned for the nurse to take it.

"How was the news conference?" she asked.

"Huge. Bowers handled it okay, and Craig was good. You'll be happy to know they released Lupo's picture. The whole thing's out now."

"Good," she said with finality. He sensed that she was on the verge of forgiving him for his earlier waffling.

"They agree that we shouldn't go near any press. Our faces shouldn't be in the media if we're going to move around freely."

"Yeah, one time we had a bad epidemic of salmonella poisoning spread by marijuana that had been cut with manure," she said as they walked toward the door. "It got all kinds of press, but we kept a low profile so we could go in and investigate without attracting a crowd. It's the best thing."

The nurse approached with the tray of urine samples, and Shinohara instructed her on how to ship them back to the CDC in Atlanta.

"Any sign of Lupo?" she asked.

"Nope. I guess I'm not really surprised. He knows his picture's all over. He know's the place is lousy with agents and local cops." He stopped and cocked his head, adjusting the earphone in his ear. "This is Hunter One. Go ahead, Hunter Four," he said into the microphone clipped to his collar. He listened again. "Yeah, I'm in ward three twelve, green wing. Hunter Four, take another run through the basement of the green wing. That's ten-four, Hunter four." He continued to work the radio, contacting other agents in the building. There were several dozen, dressed as orderlies, nurses, doctors and patients, each cruising the halls or sitting in corners watching for Lupo. As he finished, Shinohara had picked up a notebook and started out the door.

"I've got to go begin interviewing the women," she said.

Loudon walked along with her, as the men whooped and whistled their goodbyes behind her.

"Kathleen, it's been three days. You've worked around the clock almost. Take off tonight. Look, this is no hustle or anything. We'll have dinner, go somewhere, talk. Really, I'm not trying anything."

"Right," she said. "And Jimmy D.'s blue. Look, even if I wanted to, I couldn't. I've got far too much to do. One of the patients told us there are others still out there. He gave us an address in LA. Doc and I are going out to find them." She looked at him impishly. "Besides, you've surely got other sources of companionship . . . a guy like you."

He ignored the taunt. "Hey, then I'll go with you. Lupo might be out there observing them. If it's in the neighborhood where these bozos hang out, you should have somebody along anyway. If we find something, we can all go out and celebrate. All of us. You, me, Doc, Walter. Okay?"

"I might go along with that," she said. Her expression was one of mild exasperation, but he thought he detected some secret satisfaction. "Maybe if we find something, and maybe if we all go, and maybe if we eat somewhere close."

Loudon smiled and nodded. She was right. "Okay, close. I'll meet you and Doc in an hour at the west entrance."

"Don't be late, Robert," she instructed him.

Loudon contacted Walter—Hunter Twelve—who'd come up from Temecula. He was sitting in the cafeteria drinking coffee, in case Lupo decided to have lunch. Walter was a good partner to have along. He wouldn't play hot shot. Loudon asked Walter to bring a car around to the west entrance in an hour. Then he began a tour of the huge hospital, pacing through its labyrinth of crowded corridors, briefly touching base with all the agents. Radio contact didn't really give a supervising agent a sense of what was going on.

Finally, with no hint of Lupo's presence, he ended at the waiting room near the west entrance, settled into a soft, plastic-covered chair in the corner and watched the front door, continuing to direct the stakeout by radio from there. Crowds of people streamed steadily in and out, carrying with them the indefinable aura of illness and anxiety. A young couple with a baby; a grizzled old man; a large woman with a little boy; a middle-aged matron with a frail, bent older woman . . . the parade went on and on. He eyed each carefully, but there was no round young man with shaggy hair and a beard. Or even with newly cut hair and a newly shaved beard.

Twice he leaned forward expectantly when a man fitting the description entered. He quietly radioed the agent at the front desk, who stopped each suspect out of sight farther down the hall. The agent asked for identification and examined the men's faces more closely. But so far, the suspects had checked out. After fifteen minutes of watching and periodically contacting the other agents around the building, he pushed out of the chair, stretched languorously, and went to the west entrance.

Walter leaned comfortably against the information desk, affably chatting with the receptionist, waiting.

"This case gonna go on much longer?" he asked. "I wanna get this guy before the weekend. I gotta golf game."

"Yeah, I know, Walt. There are things I'd like to be doing, too."

"I bet," said Walter slyly, as he saw Shinohara approach, followed by Doc.

They climbed into the FBI car at the curb, and Loudon checked in, making sure his radio patch through to the hospital was working. Walter drove through the sunny, spacious slums of LA, past buildings whose walls were scrawled with gang graffiti. They drove beneath the towering multi-level freeway interchanges, along the neglected boulevards, where jaded-looking people lounged in shady porches of crackerbox houses and slouched along the weedy, littered sidewalks.

After searching along a largely deserted La Reina Boulevard, they found the building, an anonymous brick structure, its sterile entrance devoid of any decoration save graffiti, trash, and broken bottles.

"This is the address the guy gave me," said Shinohara. "He said the third floor was a shooting gallery . . . that he thought this was where a lot of the affected people were. He said they probably hadn't found out about the money, or they would have been at the hospital."

"Gosh, Walter, this looks like a place you should go into first," said Loudon brightly.

"Nah, there's glory in there; there's fame in there. You go in there."

But they barely had time to catch up with Shinohara, who had already left the car and entered the building, followed closely by Doc. Inside, the hazy sun gave way to a dry, musty gloom. The metallic tang of LA smog mixed with the odor of human decay. The ground floor was apartments. Two of the doors stood open, revealing garbage-strewn rooms, one holding a television set with a smashed screen, the other a paper bag with liquid leaking from the bottom. Greasy, brown-stained carpeted stairs led to the upper floors. Loudon loosened his pistol in his shoulder holster and went first, taking care not to touch the gray walls, whose dirty peeling paint crumbled at a touch. Voices echoed above; a shout; the hollow bang of a door slam. They reached the second floor, to find more apartments, most seemingly abandoned. A bent man in a tattered sport coat muttered a curse and scurried for one of the doors, a paper bag in his hand, slamming the door behind him. He was flesh-colored, so they moved on.

They reached the third floor, crunching through the grit that covered the old wooden floor where the carpet had been torn away. Loudon motioned Walter to go one way down the hall, while he went another. Doc followed Walter, but Shinohara stopped, listened at one of the doors and then knocked on it.

"Hello? We're offering money for anybody who is colored. We're from the hospital."

Loudon leaped toward her, yanking her to the side of the door.

"You could get a bullet through that door!" he hissed. She looked at him indignantly. Down the hall, Doc was knocking on another door, dutifully standing to one side.

"Hey! We're not after anybody. We're not narcs! We got money."

There was a scratching sound from behind Shinohara's door.

"What you want?" came a faint, hoarse voice from within.

"We understand there are people here who have turned color," said Shinohara. "We want to talk to them. We're willing to pay." They heard the sound of locks being undone, and the door opened slowly. Standing before them was a shirtless young man with long, oily strings of hair hanging in front of dull staring eyes and a slack jaw. He was barefoot in baggy, dirty jeans. His bright chartreuse color made the train of needle tracks down his arms stand out.

"You got money?" he asked dully. "I got some bad dope. Did this to me. Get another score . . . a little white, I be all right."

Loudon pushed open the door, and the man stumbled back and stood silently. The air smelled of human dirt. Behind him, sitting on a grubby torn sofa were two other people—a teal-blue woman and a canary-yellow man. A wine-red man sprawled on a filthy mattress on the floor. At the sight of Loudon, he rolled onto his knees, scattering spoons, plastic vials and syringes off the mattress and staggered up.

"Hey, man, it's heat!"

"No, no!" said Shinohara. "We're here to help."

But he was already scrambling for something under a blanket in the corner. He thrust his hand underneath, but Loudon's foot was there first, slamming onto his hand pinning it. The man screamed, more in anger than pain. Before anybody could react, Loudon leveled his pistol at the man's head, grabbed his arm and flipped him back against the wall. He reached down, tearing away the blanket to reveal a sawed-off shotgun. Loudon then leveled his pistol at the others, picking up the shotgun. It got their attention, and they waved their hands.

"No trouble, man!" said the canary-yellow man.

"Hey man, easy!" said the chartreuse man.

"Like the lady said, we're not busting anybody," said Loudon. "We just want to talk to you." He rousted them up, patting each down for more weapons and doing a quick search of the room. Then he backed away, holstering his pistol, still holding the shotgun.

"Awright, so talk," said the skinny young chartreuse man, sinking onto the sofa, stretching out his dirty feet and contemplating his toes. "You pay?"

"Yeah, you pay like the other guy?" said the teal-blue woman.

"Other guy?" asked Loudon.

"Yeah, down the hall. Little guy. Been here all today. Takin' blood samples. Ten bucks a sample. He gave Mookie—"

"Where?" Loudon demanded.

"Three oh four," she mumbled, wiping her runny nose with her forefinger and trying to focus her eyes.

Loudon thrust the shotgun into Shinohara's hand, motioning for her to stay in the room. He raced into the hall. Doc and Walter stood talking to an old man at the far end, and Loudon waved at Walter. He moved toward the end of the hall they'd not yet explored. Room three oh four was there. Loudon paused in front of the door as Walter reached him.

"FBI! Lupo, it's FBI! Come out!" Without waiting he backed up and kicked in the flimsy door, and it immediately gave, swinging inward and crashing against the wall. He crouched down, aiming his gun into the room, then charged to one side of the door. Walter heaved his bulk around the door frame and leaped into the room in the other direction.

They stopped, holding their guns in both hands, aimed at the ceiling. They heard a sound from a room to the right, and took up positions on either side of the door. Loudon gently tried the knob, turned it, and slammed open the door. They aimed their guns through the doorway, and heard a high scream. A young burnt-umber girl sat on a rickety metal chair beside a card table covered with papers and blood sampling equipment. Her eyes were wide with fright. She began to sob.

"FBI! Where is he?"

"Out there," she cried pointing at the window. "Don't hurt me! Out there!"

Loudon dashed to the window in time to see the top of a dark crewcut head stumble down the bottom fire escape stairs and run down the alleyway toward the street. The man carried a small case.

"Walter, stay up here with Doc and Kathleen and get some descriptions. I'm gonna see if I can get this guy."

"Yeah, go for the glory, Bobby, see if I care," said Walter, as Loudon hauled himself through the window and started down the stairs. As he clattered down the rusty metal steps, he kept his eyes on the street, but saw nothing. He reached the street and peered in both directions. A few cars went by on the nearest cross street, and a green Toyota zoomed past on the street in front of him. He turned the other way in time to glimpse a motorcyclist zoom across the street a block away. The rider wore a red helmet. The traffic continued to flow, but there was no evidence of Lupo. Loudon stood for a while, then turned and went back into the building, climbing back to the third floor.

There he found Shinohara arranging for six more residents to check into the hospital and Walter quizzing them on the little man.

"The woman, the blue one, said that a week ago Mookie was selling kits that had syringes he'd bought from Lupo," said Shinohara. "Then Lupo showed up day before yesterday to talk to them, to examine them."

"And which one is Mookie?"

"The chartreuse one."

"And what color is chartreuse?"

"You don't know your colors? You'd better learn your colors," said Shinohara, her expression dead pan, except for the slight upturn in the curves at the corner of her mouth. "It's green with a little yellow."

"Oh, yeah, of course. I should've known that," said Loudon as he moved to interview the jittery chartreuse Mookie with some intensity. Lupo had, indeed, shaved his face and cut his hair short. A new photo would go out.

The planned dinner that night was cancelled. The new patients and the fleeting appearance of Arthur Lupo spoiled any chance for anything more elaborate for Loudon. However, Loudon campaigned mightily for a future commitment. Shinohara, perhaps a bit more respectful, agreed to a dinner for four at some unspecified future time. Loudon knew from his past persuasions of women that a "yes" to a dinner was strategic progress.

Unfortunately, he would be busy for a while. Mookie had given Loudon a lead on four more colored people in the sprawling slums of LA. He sent CDC/FBI teams out to find them.

That evening, Loudon leaned against the wall outside the hospital entrance, chewing reflectively on an undifferentiated white and beige substance from the hospital cafeteria. The label on the plastic wrapping said it was a chicken salad sandwich. A scotch would have disinfected it nicely. He watched the traffic streaming by. Lupo was around somewhere; would probably come back. He was clever and probably arrogant and who wanted to witness his success. Loudon knew that the little terrorist, not to mention Shinohara, had generated in him the spark of a quality he thought he'd thoroughly extinguished—dedication.

• • •

"Computer?" said Arthur Lupo, but the machine didn't answer. He swallowed the mouthful of Jelly Krimpet and tried again. "Computer?"

"Yes, Arthur?" it asked in the warm-but-stilted voice of Jeany Moody.

"Hospital program, please." Lines of numbers and letters skittered across the screen, as the computer accessed the hospital system. He was pleased. It had taken him weeks to figure out how to tap into the LA County Hospital computer and move around within its complex collection of databases. To do it, he'd stolen an ID badge and wandered through the wards, peeking over the shoulders of record clerks. He'd made off with manuals from empty offices. He'd rummaged through the administration office's garbage. And he'd done some "social engineering," simply calling up offices, pretending to be from IBM, and asking to "verify" passwords. His roommate in Dabney House at Caltech had been a computer science major, and he'd learned the techniques from him. Good old Larry Schwartz.

"Hospital computer accessed," said the computer, and Lupo finished the Tastykake and bent to his work. He'd gotten the name of one of the first patients from the television news. Feeding the name into the hospital computer, he'd figured out the patient's location and doctor. Now, he had information that would easily lead him to the records of the new patients as they came in. Even as the information was fed in by nurses and doctors, he downloaded it, printed it out and taped it into his notebook.

"Hello, Mr. King," he said to the record of one patient, as he downloaded it. "Glad to have you with us, Mr. King . . . uh . . ." he checked the medical record ". . . you green person." Mr. King, better known as Mookie, was a new arrival, the nineteenth. Arthur was pleased. The people chasing him had done their job. Soon they'd have the other four, and he would have recorded a hundred percent infection.

But all the data in the world didn't substitute for first-hand information. A good scientist always personally gathered the data on his own experiments. Arthur had only a partial first-hand sample. He needed to really see how Lupo390 had modulated itself in all the patients, not just the few he'd examined so far. He needed to know so he could proceed with Lupo400, a totally new virus in his series. Only a personal look at the patients' colors would reveal how the control segments of

DNA he'd engineered into the virus had modulated expression of the chromophore genes.

Arthur picked up his cell phone and punched in a number.

"Yes, this is Mr. Dabney. I'm calling about the pickup. I'm confirming it. Mrs. Dabney will be ready. You have the nurse's address, too? Thank you so much."

He hung up the phone and unwrapped a Coconut Junior Tastykake. He rummaged through the plastic trash bag full of the materials he'd need the next morning. He asked the computer if there was any movement outside the lab. The electronic Jeany Moody voice reported none. The computer offered images of the scenes outside the labs. Indeed, all was clear.

"Activate the security mechanism. Goodnight, computer," he said.

"Security mechanism activated. Goodnight, Arthur," it said with mechanical sweetness, shutting off its screen. Lupo glanced at the lobster sitting quietly in the corner of the aquarium. It was sleeping. He wouldn't say goodnight to it.

He moved to the isolation chamber, thrust his hands into its rubber gloves and prepared for another four hours of hard work on Lupo400. He was excited by the prospect. It would be a stunning, massive achievement.

Chapter 15

Loudon signed in at the front desk of the FBI's huge LA field office and stowed his gun in the vault by the door. He made his way past the dozens of desks in the open-area snake pit. Under the efficient brightness of the fluorescent lights, white-shirted agents pecked out reports on computers, hunched over telephones having low, intense conversations, and lounged at paper-strewn desks trading gossip with their neighbors. An intense young woman agent smacked her fist into her hand in emphatic conversation with a scowling middle-aged man. Several agents hovered over a desk, nodding earnestly, while an ASAC scrawled a diagram on a yellow pad. The clicking of computer keys and the flowing chatter of conversation was punctuated often by the insistent electronic trill of the telephones.

Loudon liked the place. Operations were going down. Snitches were giving up secrets. Strategies were being hatched that would carry cars filled with agents to warehouses harboring unsuspecting bad guys.

His progress across the broad, cluttered office was slow. Along the way, agents he knew from his days in the office greeted him, and he stopped to talk and trade insults. The mild embarrassment he'd felt at returning vanished. None of the agents mentioned his being sent down.

"Hey, Love Boat," teased one balding agent, grinning. He referred to the time Loudon had arranged a boat tour of San Diego Harbor when a bunch of agents had come down on a case. The boat had been populated with many of his female friends from the bars.

He smiled, reached the empty desk he was using and took off his coat. He draped it sloppily over the chair and sat down tiredly, loosening his tie.

"Anything on the freak?" asked a young agent three desks away.

Loudon shook his head. "Nah. We've been all over scuzztown. He just vanished. Nothin' from the hospital, either."

He went over reports for a while, then checked his watch. It was almost ten o'clock. Time for his meeting with Bowers. It was the first time they'd seen each other alone since he'd pulled his gun on Bowers. He still felt the same deep anger.

He put on his coat, straightened his tie and went down the short hallway to the ADC's offices and reached Bowers' spacious corner office. It was decorated in muted desert colors, with a sleek rosewood desk and a large overstuffed couch and side chairs. Loudon always thought it looked like a Hollywood producer's office. In fact, it was probably modeled on one. Bowers had paid for the whole thing himself out of money he'd made as a technical adviser to the movies and from playing a few walk-on parts. Bowers loved being in LA. The ADC sat behind the desk shuffling through reports. He stood up, tall and handsome, with the dark vulpine good looks of a Steven Segal.

"Hello, Robert," he said flashing perfect teeth and extending his gold-ringed hand.

"Hello." Loudon said tersely, standing by the desk. He didn't take the hand. Bowers withdrew it amiably and motioned for him to sit down, and he did. Almost in the line of sight between him and Bowers was the usual gold-framed portrait Bowers kept on his desk. It was yet another publicity photo of a stunning Hollywood starlet, signed to Bowers with a feminine flourish. Bowers was considered a prime date in Hollywood, and his picture often appeared in *Hollywood Reporter* escorting one ingénue or another. The agents called him Star Stalker behind his back, but headquarters was very pleased with his visibility, his way with the media. Loudon noticed that the edge of the frame was worn from replacing the photographs.

"Let's get this old business out of the way first," said Bowers. "Perhaps we can discuss it rationally after a year."

"Whatever you say."

"Did you ever consider that maybe you didn't hear what you thought you heard?"

"Maybe."

"Agent Loudon, I was easy on you, and you know it. I could have had you fired, brought up on charges, for pulling a pistol on me."

"And then there would have been a hearing. And maybe some things would have come out."

"Like what? Besides something some drug dealer might have mumbled in Spanish." Bowers leaned back in his chair, seeming to be at ease. But Loudon could sense that the athletic man was coiled like a spring.

"Like how you did, indeed, hold the order for the hostage rescue team for fifteen minutes . . ." Loudon leaned forward, measuring out the next words carefully and emphatically. ". . . even though the surveillance car outside the house sent a shots-fired message."

"And an inquiry would have shown I had good reason. The team wasn't completely assembled. You know Bureau tactics. Go in with full strength. When you're ready. Remember what happened in Florida?"

"Big difference, sir. Big difference." The "sir" was said with measured sarcasm.

Bowers let out a sigh and shook his head. "Agent Loudon, in the end I don't care what you think you heard. And I'm going to bring you back up the ranks. My conscience wouldn't let me do anything else. You'd be a good agent, if you could get that operation out of your craw. I'm giving you this chance. So, what about the case?"

Loudon decided that business was business. Maybe he'd trip Bowers up sometime. Maybe Bowers would get tired of him and send him back to the quiet of Temecula. Whatever.

"Well, first of all, the really bad news. There's evidence he has his hands on Ebola Zaire, Dengue fever, hantavirus, . . ." he paused for a moment, not wanting to say the last name ". . . and airborne H5N1."

"It's time to bring the WMDD in on this. I'll call the AD and transmit the reports."

Loudon nodded. The FBI's Weapons of Mass Destruction Directorate was the Bureau's lead investigative force for such threats. He felt a little more confidence in Bowers' leadership.

"But you're still lead agent. CDC and WMDD know the science, but you know the people. What about finding the target?"

"Well, we've got all the standard things in place. Searches, stake-outs. Nothing yet. We've got people here and in Chicago interviewing everybody that knows him to refine the psych profile. And we're working with CDC as before to find out as much as we can about how he made the virus. They'll work with WMDD now."

"What do you think he'll do next?" Loudon realized that Bowers talked as if he were saying lines in a movie. His speech was clear, his words enunciated and projected. Acting lessons. Was Bowers acting when he'd given the little speech about rehabilitating Loudon?

"The profilers say his personality shows he doesn't give up. CDC doesn't know for sure about what his next scientific step would be. But they said he's working up to something big. The new virus is more sophisticated than the other one. It's still harmless. But they said they think it's like he's launching missiles with dummy warheads to get the system right. Then he goes on to nukes. The H5N1, the Ebola . . . whatever."

"But where's he doing all this?" Bowers leaned forward and jotted something on a yellow pad. His tortoise-shell pen was expensive, gold trimmed, probably a Mont Blanc.

"We don't know. The CDC said the new virus would've required a lot of lab work. We still don't know where his lab could be. What's more, they said he'd need all kinds of machines he couldn't possibly afford." Loudon opened his notebook and took out his own pen, a cheap Bic. "Y'know, machines that build genes, that analyze proteins. They cost a hundred thousand apiece."

"So, any ideas?"

Loudon scanned his notes. "Well, he went to Caltech. We're thinking about checking out there in more depth."

"Well, the agents that went out there before didn't find anything. But that would be a place to look at closer."

"I'll take the CDC agents. They'll know what to look for."

As they talked, Loudon watched Bowers. The ADC was slick, but he was professional. He was very clever. He hadn't gotten where he was just by being a pretty boy. Loudon felt his confidence ebb. He decided to try for an out again.

"Look, now that we know that this case is big . . . now that it's centered in LA . . . you're sure you don't want to put an ASAC here in as case agent? You know, Theopolous would be good. He's worked on scientific cases. Or Lehigh. He's got more experience around here."

"Like I said, you know the people. You're it. *Period.*" Bowers precisely clicked the cover on his pen, laid it down and leaned back in his chair, lacing his well-manicured fingers together, regarding Loudon with a steady stare. He had Loudon exactly where he wanted him. But for what?

"You know, it's unusual to keep a relatively junior agent heading up a major case like this."

"Like I said, Bobby, you are a talented agent, and you can do the job. You can run with it." He opened his hands, gesturing elegantly. "Sure, we've got problems. And this is an important case. The most important we have right now. Certainly the most visible. I've got press conferences every day on it." Bowers didn't seemed displeased with the last responsibility. "But I've got drug cases, bank robberies, kidnap cases, extortion cases, murder cases. We need people to handle those, too, Bobby." He stood up and gave Loudon a measured smile—no doubt a well-practiced one. He was probably going to use the fancy pen to jot down his words after Loudon left, for possible future use in a script. "So, forget trying to get me for a while. Find that little terrorist. I've got enough troubles with this as it is. I've got to go out there in an hour and tell them about your near-miss yesterday."

Bowers leaned over and pressed a button on his intercom, calling in the ASACs and the other key agents on the case. They crowded into the room, occupying the sofa and the comfortable chairs and spent the rest of the hour going over the details of the investigation, including the lab studies of the materials from Lupo's room at the shooting gallery. Loudon relayed the report from the police lab that they'd found Lupo's fingerprints, but no clue to where he might have gone.

When they were done, Loudon pulled his gun from the vault and headed back to the hospital. He had to brief the agents on duty there. And for now, that was the only place where answers might lie.

• • •

Mookie looked cleaner lying in the hospital bed, but no more reputable. The needle tracks still clearly speckled his chartreuse arms, and his greenish-yellow face still held the hollow stare of an addict. And he still gave off an indefinable odor of the streets. It seemed to be infused into his flesh.

"Mookie, that guy Lupo did this to you guys." Loudon pointed down the long rows of beds on either side of the ward, now filled with men of varied hues. Some lay sleeping, while others wandered about talking to their fellow color-tinted junkies. Four sat on a bed playing cards, muttering occasional epithets at one another. The brilliant colors of their ravaged faces and scabrous arms were in sharp contrast with the crisp white of the sheets and gowns. In the next bed, a tile-red man hummed tunelessly, staring at the opposite wall. Mookie grunted indifferently at the group.

"He sold you the syringes that had virus in them." Loudon leaned into Mookie's line of vision. "And you sold them to the others. Pal, they're gonna start blaming you. You tell me what you know about him, and when we find him, we'll see that you're protected."

"Look at 'em," said Mookie, with a dismissive wave of his hand. "Man they don't care what color they are. In fact, long as they're get-tin' paid for it, they're perfectly happy to be colored. Whatsisname . . . Lupo . . . may have done us all a big favor. Man, now we gonna be stars. I saw all them cameras when they brought us in. You can't fool me."

"Problem is, Mookie, we don't know enough about this virus," said Shinohara, arriving at the other side of the bed. "It could mutate . . . change . . . and be dangerous."

"Junkies don't live long, anyhow. Look, you want me to tell you what I know, you give me money. It's that simple."

"How much?" asked Loudon.

"A thousand," said Mookie, smiling, showing the gaps of two miss-ing teeth behind the cracked lips. The rest were stained yellow-brown, clashing with his skin.

"Tell you what. I'll give you five thousand if your information leads to Lupo's capture."

"Thousand now, FBI Agent-Loudon," spat Mookie.

Loudon cursed and stalked away, and Shinohara followed.

"Druggies," he growled.

"Look, I think he'll talk eventually," said Shinohara. "I've interviewed people like that before. I'll get to him."

"Well, maybe." Loudon tried his smile. "I know I'd rather be interviewed by you than me. Coffee? I've got some information."

She shrugged tiredly. "Sure, it was a late night."

Another yes, thought Loudon. More progress. He automatically scanned the people they passed. A young woman helped an older woman down the hall. The old woman wore a black shawl over her head. "I was out late, too. We flooded the area around the shooting gallery. Bowers told me to stay on as case agent."

They passed a nurse, walking with a large man who was attached to a near-empty intravenous bag hung from a rack on wheels.

"You mean you tried to get off the case?" She stepped aside as they passed an orderly pushing an old woman in a wheelchair. Her face was bandaged and she had a magazine in her lap with an Apple computer ad on the back.

"Well, just as head of it. I said I thought one of the LA agents, maybe an assistant director, should lead it. But I said I'd stick around . . . work the streets." They passed a swarthy doctor scanning a clipboard. He had long hair and a bushy moustache and eyebrows.

"That's just like you, isn't it?" asked Shinohara, frowning in annoyance. They passed a plump nurse bending over a patient on a gurney.

"And who are you to say that, Miss Shinohara?" He sensed that her irritation with him wasn't necessarily a bad thing. At least she was interested.

"Well, I just don't like it when somebody doesn't live up to their full potential." They got into the elevator as a portly old man got out, walking with a cane and holding a newspaper. They reached the cafeteria, a spacious light-filled room holding a scattered population of nurses, doctors, patients and visitors having mid-afternoon snacks. They went through the serving line, got their coffee and sat down.

"So, you're interested in my future?"

"Well, you need guidance," she said, sipping her coffee. He thought he detected a microscopic ember of warmth in her voice. He'd fanned much hotter flames from much smaller beginnings.

"Yeah, well maybe we can talk about it tonight. The four of us." He sipped his coffee and studied her face for a reaction.

"Look, I don't want to take social time when we have this case." She had almost snapped at him. "We have to find this guy. We'll just have to postpone your little social trip."

"I meant when we go out to Caltech tonight. Looking for his lab."

"Oh." Shinohara was slightly embarrassed. She'd assumed Loudon was talking about the dinner. Maybe he was more dedicated than she thought. "Well . . . sure . . . of course . . . Caltech."

He had her off balance, and he took the opportunity. "Can I ask a question? I'm just curious; I'm not trying to start anything here. But are you in a relationship now?"

"It's really none of your business, but I'm seeing another doctor in Colorado Springs. Whenever we can." She paused. "You?"

He didn't answer. He was staring at the table, suddenly immersed in thought.

"Robert? Hello?"

"Something," he mumbled. "There was something . . ."

"Something where?"

"Upstairs. Something I saw wasn't right. What was it?" He stared for a moment longer. Suddenly, recognition dawned on his face. He smacked his forehead with the tips of his fingers, jumped up and ran out of the cafeteria, nearly tripping up a nurse carrying a tray of food. He veered to the right out of the cafeteria and down the hall, and dashed into the hospital gift shop. Shinohara followed, arriving to see him shuffling through the magazines, grabbing one, glancing at its back cover, then slapping it back on the rack. The pink-smocked volunteer women who ran the gift shop glared at him with disapproval.

"Hah!" he shouted triumphantly, showing Shinohara an Apple ad on the back of one of the magazines. He turned it over. It was *Scientific American*. "Little old ladies read *Modern Maturity*, or *Good*

Housekeeping! They do not read *Scientific American!*" He clicked on his radio as Shinohara let out a shocked gasp.

"Hunter One to all units. Be on the lookout for an old lady in a wheelchair. With a hospital orderly. Subject may be Lupo. Repeat . . . *may be Lupo*." He and Shinohara ran for the elevator, catching a car as the door was closing. "Take the women's ward on four; I'll take the two men's on the third floor. You know what he looks like." The door opened, and he dashed out, almost tripping over an agent dressed in the light green work garb of an orderly. The agent was holding on desperately to the handles of a wheelchair as a skinny, irate old woman railed at him. She cursed and swung over her shoulder at him with her cane.

"That's not the one," shouted Loudon. "She's got a bandaged face. Nice try, though." He ducked the cane and sprinted down the hall to three twelve, stopping at the door. A nurse stood waiting for him.

"An old lady was pushed in here about five minutes ago," said the nurse. "She said she thought her doctor's office was in this room. The lady's male nurse stopped and talked to me—"

"He wasn't an orderly? He didn't work here? The guy was a nurse?"

"Yeah, private duty. He talked to me while the old lady was parked at the door. The agent is already after them in three twenty four." He hollered the last sentence after Loudon, who had already bolted for the ward holding the other male patients. He skidded around the corner onto the corridor holding room three twenty four in time to find the female agent, dressed as a nurse, quizzing the real nurse on duty.

". . . yeah, the nurse parked her at the door while she tried to figure out the right room. They headed that way," she said pointing down the hall. Loudon barked instructions into the radio as he and the female agent ran down the hall. They met Shinohara coming down the stairs.

"She's . . . uh . . . *he's* upstairs I think," said Shinohara. "They just left the women's ward." Again, Loudon gave instructions to converge on that floor. They bounded up the stairs and into the hall. The nurse down the hall shouted one word:

"ELEVATOR!"

"Watch the elevators!" barked Loudon into the radio. On each floor, agents stationed themselves across from the bank of elevators, guns drawn. "Don't push the buttons!" instructed Loudon into the radio.

"I want them all to come to this floor." He stabbed at the call button, even though it was lit, drew his pistol and backed against the wall. The female agent did the same. Shinohara backed away to be out of the line of fire. There were three elevators in the green wing. The lights over the doors showed one descending from the sixth floor, one ascending from the basement, and one ascending from the first floor. Loudon directed agents to all those floors. The car coming down from the sixth arrived first. As the door opened, Loudon and the female agent crouched, aiming their pistols. A young woman and a little girl in the elevator shrieked and cowered when they saw the guns aimed at them.

"It's okay, we're FBI!" said Loudon. "You see an old lady in a wheel-chair?" The wide-eyed woman shook her head, bolted from the elevator and hurried away down the hall. Loudon slammed his hand onto the call button once more.

The elevator from the basement arrived next. It opened to reveal the male nurse who had accompanied the old woman. He was handcuffed to the wheel chair, struggling to free himself. He looked up, saw the guns and sat hard onto the floor, his non-skid soles sticking through the elevator doors. Beside him on the floor was a gray wig and face bandages.

"I didn't know!" he cried. "I was just hired to bring her in! I just got picked up by the ambulance! I didn't know!"

"What happened?" demanded Loudon.

"We got to the basement and she . . . he . . . jumped up and hand-cuffed me to the chair and ran out! I didn't know!"

"Basement, green wing!" shouted Loudon into the radio and slammed open the exit door, leaping down the bare concrete stairs, followed closely by the female agent and Shinohara. He jammed his pistol into its holster, to have both hands free to grab the hand rails. He was panting when he reached the bottom and burst through the door into the basement.

The steamy smells and hiss of a laundry permeated the basement. Large, wheeled laundry hampers lined the wide hall outside the eleva-tors. He directed the other agent to go to the right, while he went to the left, and he motioned to Shinohara to stay behind him. Another agent jumped out of the elevator, and Loudon directed him to check the hampers. The agent drew his pistol and began to kick one canvas hamper after the other, stopping to drag large bundles of white sheets out of the heavier ones.

Loudon walked briskly down the hall and turned into a room filled with rows of large industrial-sized clothes washers. The light was dim, coming from small fixtures spaced along the rows. He walked from row to row, stopping at each and peering around the corner. He stopped suddenly. He heard a noise. He jumped around the corner to find one of the laundry workers, a large black woman, loading clothes. She yelped in surprise.

"Lord, you scared me! I wish you people would quit runnin' by here like that!"

"What people?"

"Little guy, came up on me just like you. Wearing a dress!"

"Where?"

"Down there he went."

Loudon shouted his position into the microphone and ran to the end of the row. He rounded the corner to see Arthur Lupo at the far end of the room wearing the frumpy dress of the little old lady. His face was caked with makeup. He stood in a doorway through a chain-link enclosure that held large drums of laundry detergent. He had dropped the magazine on the floor but still held the gray notebook that had been inside.

Loudon smiled at Lupo, who looked at him with fathomless black beady eyes. There was no expression on Lupo's round face.

"Arthur," said Loudon quietly. He held his hands out, palms toward Lupo. "I'm Agent Loudon. FBI. I'm not going to hurt you, Arthur. You have to come with me quietly. You have to stop these experiments. Understand?" A wisp of steam curled out of a washer along the row, insinuating itself between them. Loudon heard other agents pounding down the rows behind him. He held up his hand for them to stop.

"Loudon?" said Arthur, still no expression on the pudgy little face. The bow lips pursed slightly. Beads of sweat oozed through the makeup on Lupo's forehead.

"Yes, Bobby Loudon. I'm not going to hurt you, Arthur."

"That's good. That's very good, Mr. Loudon." They were fifteen feet apart. Loudon edged forward.

Shinohara came up beside Loudon. "We understand why you're

doing this. We know about your pain. We just don't understand what you're doing. Tell us. What is it you want?"

Lupo had a large bicycle lock in his hand. He smiled, his little bow mouth curling upward at the ends. Loudon thought it was a psychopathic smile. A smile with the lips only, not echoed in the cold eyes. Loudon stopped. They were ten feet apart. Not taking his eyes from Loudon and Shinohara, Lupo calmly reached forward, and swung the chain-link gate shut. He deftly brought up the bicycle lock and clicked it shut on the gate. He backed up three steps, placing himself in a position to duck behind a stack of laundry detergent drums. He smiled again.

"Arthur, you planned this, didn't you?"

Arthur nodded twice slowly, still smiling eerily. Loudon considered drawing his pistol. But he knew the moment he reached for it, Lupo would duck behind the drums. Instead, he slowly clicked on his radio. He walked up next to the chain-link gate. Lupo and he were only a few feet apart, staring at one another. A few tantalizing feet.

"There's a way out back there, isn't there?"

Again, Lupo nodded slowly, smiling his little smile. Loudon knew the agents who heard him on the radio would immediately begin trying to discover Lupo's escape route. So Loudon took time to study Lupo's face and the way he stood with his arms held slightly out because of his roundness. He memorized his enemy.

A clang echoed behind Loudon. An agent had collided with an open dryer door, slamming it shut. Startled, Lupo ducked behind the drums and was gone.

"GET THIS GATE OPEN!" shouted Loudon. "GET BOLT CUTTERS DOWN HERE . . . NOW!" After about ten minutes, a set of bolt cutters arrived from the hospital machine shop. A burly workman sliced enough links to make a hole in the gate. The agents squeezed through, fanning out inside the small enclosure. Behind the first row of drums, they found a small, high window out of the basement, with a drum beneath it. Loudon and two other agents squeezed through the window to find themselves in a bare courtyard that held a few doctor's cars. An alley from the courtyard led to the main street, where the traffic and afternoon crowds were constant. The dress lay crumpled beside one of the cars, but Lupo was nowhere to be found.

CHAPTER 16

T hree hours later, after having cleaned themselves up, they all met at the busy main entrance to the hospital as planned. Shinohara and Doc stood among the people streaming in and out, comparing notes from the afternoon's work. She had on a fresh blue cotton blouse and wheat-colored jeans that accentuated her slim figure. As usual, Doc wore a red plaid flannel shirt and khaki work pants. Loudon sauntered up in his coat and tie, a slightly smug smile on his face. His plan was working.

"Anything?" asked Doc.

Loudon's smile faded. "Nothing. So, you ready for the expedition?"

"Sure," said Shinohara, looking around. "Where's Walter?"

"He's bringing the car around." As he spoke, a gleaming white stretch limousine rolled up to the curb, drawing admiring glances from the assorted people standing on the sidewalk. Walter was driving, and he lowered the window.

"Sorry, this was the only Bucar I could get."

Loudon's smile returned, and he swept open the back door. Inside was a plush interior with a spacious divan seat and a small table set with linen and a small candle, whose flame flickered in the breeze.

"What is this?" demanded Shinohara. "I thought we were going to Caltech. Robert, what *is* this?"

"We are," said Loudon. "But we're going to have a little dinner on the way. We've got plenty of time."

Shinohara looked at Walter, who shrugged. "Hey, hon, I'm just the driver." A grin animated his jowly face.

Shinohara turned to Doc, exasperated. "Doc, we've got work to do."

"Well, we gotta get there somehow," Doc grumped, eyeing the car suspiciously. "And we gotta eat. You should see yourself. As usual, you're going to work yourself to a frazzle. Remember Minnesota?" He gestured for Shinohara to get into the back. "Walter and I will ride up front and have a fine old time watchin' the city go by."

Shinohara raised her chin slightly and looked sideways at Doc, then at Loudon. She clicked her tongue disapprovingly against her white teeth, but climbed in. Loudon slipped in beside her and made himself comfortable.

Doc leaned into the window, speaking quietly but emphatically, so Shinohara wouldn't hear. "Remember our talk? You're not good enough for her." He backed up and stared pointedly at Loudon before climbing in the front seat.

"Right," said Loudon smiling slightly. Maybe he wasn't. But it was up to her to decide. He leaned forward to talk to Walter through the partition between the front and back seats. "You know the way, right?"

"Not at all," said Walter cheerily. "But I'll figure it out eventually. Remember our deal?"

"Yeah, you get the weekend off."

"Fine, then," Walter said and slipped the big car into gear. Loudon raised the opaque partition, and he and Shinohara were alone. The limousine eased away from the curb, and they watched the vibrant night life of LA slide past the window. Rolling in parade down the broad avenue were a shiny red Lotus driven by a smooth-looking middle-aged man; a turquoise low-riding Chevy with a furry back window ledge; a large family sedan filled with giggling girls.

"How long does it take to get to Caltech?"

"About a good dinner's worth, maybe a little dessert," said Loudon. He pulled a chilled bottle out of the limousine's built-in cooler. "Champagne?"

"You just don't give up, do you?"

"Look, tell me just one thing. Do you like when we're together? I do."

"You don't nauseate me."

"See there, we've known each other . . . what . . . a couple of weeks? And I still don't nauseate you."

"All right. You're pleasant company."

"Even better. Have some champagne."

She took a deep breath, let it out, and after a moment, managed what he took to be the faint beginning of a smile.

"All right, maybe I've been tough on you."

"Well, you have. I just want us to be friends."

"Yeah, right." She did smile this time, only slightly sarcastically, showing the little gap in her teeth. It was the first real smile he'd seen in a week, and he felt more rewarded than he did when other women smiled at him. The feeling puzzled him. "Where did you get this car? FBI doesn't pay for these things, does it?"

"Well, actually, it was confiscated from a drug dealer. Selling lots of coke paid for this car. But the Bureau keeps it on hand for undercover work. Sometimes we have to put up a fancy front. Especially in LA." He poured a gentle effervescent stream of champagne into a crystal glass and offered it to her. She accepted it with a nod, her dark eyes showing a slight twinkle. Loudon poured himself a measure, and they gently clinked glasses and sipped the icy sparkling liquid, which sloshed slightly with the gentle sway of the car. He reached over and switched on the radio and adjusted the sound. It was a Debussy piano arabesque, and the music filled the richly padded interior of the car like liquid moonlight.

"Well, I guess as long as we've got it, we might as well use it," said Shinohara, fluffing back her shiny curls and seeming to sink into the seat, relaxing and sipping her champagne. She crossed her long legs, the jeans tightening around her shapely hips and thighs. He took off his tie and unbuttoned his top button. She began to talk about the case, but he managed to steer the conversation away, to talk about themselves.

"So, do you do this for all the women you're after?" she finally asked.

"Oh no, this is a particularly important liaison."

"Really?"

176

"Sure, with the CDC and all."

"I see. Of course. Strictly business," she said a bit self-mockingly.

"Absolutely."

"So, where do we go from here, Robert?" she asked, glancing out the window. A big old rattly convertible zoomed past, crowded with teenagers out for a night of celebration.

"Wherever you want."

"I mean to get to Caltech."

"Oh. That's Walter's business."

She turned back from the window and found their faces close together.

"Robert . . ." Again he heard the low reproving tone in her voice.

"You're in control, right?"

"Yes, I am."

"And you can do what you want . . . *when* you want."

"Yes, I can."

His voice softened to a tone of gentle, practiced persuasion. He smiled. "So, why don't you try me? Just once. For yourself. Maybe for curiosity. You'll still be in control, right?"

"Yes, I will."

Three yesses, thought Loudon. Now for a big one.

He asked for a kiss and got one.

Suddenly the car stopped.

"Oh . . . uh . . . dinner," said Loudon, trying to recover. "We're getting takeout."

"Yes . . . well . . . good."

Loudon lowered the window, and the chef beamed in at them.

"Ah, yes, Monsieur Loudon. You are just on time," he said with a lilting French accent. "I have so nice a meal for you. Here we are, my dear friend." He rolled a serving cart up next to the car window, and handed in two plates with silver covers. Loudon lifted the covers and handed them back out. Each china plate displayed a steaming casserole of lobster with white truffle sauce on angel hair pasta with fresh asparagus and Hollandaise sauce. Also through the window came silverware, a basket of hot baguettes and two Grand Marnier souffles for dessert. Finally came a carafe of iced mineral water and a bottle of 1992 Henri

Boilleau Pouilly-Fuisse. The luscious, delicate fragrance of the dishes added to the music to enfold them even more in a vividly sensual present.

"And Jean, see what the boys in the front seat will have."

"Of course. I have the same for the gentlemen," said the chef. Loudon shook hands with him and pressed the switch to raise the window.

"You know him?" asked Shinohara picking up her fork. She hadn't realized how hungry she was.

"I met him when I was in LA. I helped him get out of a nasty situation. He happens to be one of the top chefs around."

She took her first bite and almost reflexively rolled her eyes at the sensation of deliciously layered tastes. He also took a bite and nodded in appreciative agreement. At one point, Shinohara glanced out the window.

"I don't think this is the direct way to Caltech."

"Well, Walter's just giving us a bit of a tour," Loudon grinned. "Look, don't worry about business for a while. Caltech students don't really get rolling until after midnight. We couldn't do anything until then, anyway. We've got plenty of time."

"Well . . . yes, we do," she admitted, opening her mouth and taking a luxuriant bite of tender, white lobster. After the meal and the accompanying wine, they dug into the crusty warm soufflés. They finished just as the limousine wound its ponderous way up into the hills, giving them a panoramic view of the glittering city. Loudon reached into the bar, brought out brandy snifters and poured two generous dollops of the golden liquid. They silently sipped their brandy for a long moment and looked out the window.

"So, you relaxed now?" asked Loudon.

"Yes. Thanks. Maybe I don't realize what I need sometimes." Shinohara looked a bit embarrassed, an expression Loudon had never seen in her before.

"Well, neither do I."

"I hope you'll stay on the case. You should for your sake, you know."

"I will. You're right. I feel different . . . well . . . now that I know you." The admission brought a catch in his stomach.

"C'mon. You want this case. You know you do."

"Well, I know I sure want to get Lupo. When I stood on the other side of that gate from him and looked at him—"

"We better get on now," she said. "Let's check Caltech, then we'll see what else happens." He lowered the glass partition and told Walter to head for Caltech. Then he closed the opaque glass, and they were alone again.

CHAPTER 17

The Pasadena Freeway dwindled to a routine surface artery, and the limousine slowed and turned right to glide smoothly down California Boulevard. After many tree-lined blocks, it passed a large sign that announced the California Institute of Technology. The limousine turned left onto Hill Avenue and smoothly u-turned to park on the broad, quiet street in front of the Athenaeum, the elegant old Mediterranean-style villa that was the Caltech faculty club. Walter pulled himself laboriously out of the driver's seat, hitching his pants up over his belly. Doc jumped out the other side, spry and ready for the hunt.

"We're here, guys," said Walter, opening the back door.

Loudon sat next to Shinohara, a distracted look on his face. Shinohara sat smiling, with her hands folded in her lap, looking crisp in her unwrinkled blouse and jeans.

"You're a terrific driver, Walter," said Shinohara sweetly.

"Why thanks." Walter was slightly taken aback at the change in tone. "I'll be happy to drive back when we're done."

"Thank you, Walter, that would be very, *very* nice," she said enthusiastically.

On either side of the tree-lined brick walk were the Caltech dorms. Even long past midnight, many lights shone, and music and voices wafted out of the windows. Walter found a sign marking Dabney House, a plain stucco building constructed sturdily to withstand the onslaughts of some of the world's most brilliant students.

They entered, walking along a corridor alive with students. Its walls and doors were festooned with cartoons, drawings, equation-filled sheets, and letters from corporations. Loudon glanced at a few; they were all rejections, posted with the sardonic wit Caltech students were known for. The dormitory's aroma was a rich, organic mix of food, sweat, and adolescent hormones, overlain with the metallic tang of hot electronics. They passed a paper-strewn room where students argued over a four-foot-high molecular model. In another room, a student fiddled with a computer, which projected intricate geometric patterns onto a large screen. A student passed with a welding mask cocked up on his head. Loudon stopped a barefoot girl with long auburn hair.

"I'm FBI, and I'm—"

"You want Sarkisian."

"How do you know?"

"Well, he deals with the FBI when they come."

"And do they come often?"

"Well, whenever something weird happens, you guys generally show up here." She smiled a dimpled smile and motioned for them to follow, padding down the darkened hall. She reached a doorway with a sheet draped across it and a sign that said "seniors only." Loudon swept the sheet aside and peered in. A skinny dark-haired young man sat cross-legged on the floor amidst a confusion of wires and electronic parts. He was up to his elbows in a large metal box covered with dials, switches, and buttons.

"Sarkisian?"

"Yeah. FBI? Lupo again?"

"Yes on both counts." Loudon and Walter entered and introduced themselves, as well as Shinohara and Doc, who remained in the hall looking in. The girl squeezed between them and sat cross-legged on the bed, flipping back her hair and watching silently.

"We told the other guy everything we know," said Sarkisian.

"We'll see. These people are from the CDC. They know lots of stuff I don't."

"Say what's all this stuff?" asked Walter, bending over to inspect the electronic console.

"We're gettin' ready for Ditch Day. It's a kind of contest, where seniors lock their doors with all sorts of chemical, electronic, computer locks and puzzles—we call 'em stacks. The underclassmen try to figure them out and get in."

"Hmmm, and this is a lock?"

"Yeah, it's based on digital phase conjugate loop theory, in which the solution of an integrated circuit array—"

"Tell me about Lupo . . . again," interrupted Loudon.

"We're not real happy about him," said Sarkisian setting down a soldering iron and twiddling a computer chip in his fingers.

"Why?"

"He broke the Caltech honor code. We do tricks, pranks. But there are rules. They have to be clever, but they can't hurt anybody. We're afraid he's dangerous. We know what the stuff he's doing is capable of."

"How dangerous?"

"Listen, techies could be the most dangerous people on earth if they wanted to. And Lupo was one of the smartest."

"Like, remember with paintball?" asked the girl.

"Yeah, *tournament* paintball," said Sarkisian, inserting the computer chip into a socket in a circuit board.

"That's the hunting game?" asked Loudon.

"Yeah, where you go out in the woods with these guns that shoot capsules of paint. Lupo was really excellent. He could sneak up on you, and once he did, he was a dead solid aim."

"Got seven guys from Fleming House, remember?" The girl bobbed her head excitedly, her eyes bright, her hair bouncing.

"Yeah, yeah, he did," said Sarkisian. "And, like, take this Ditch Day." He swept the hand holding the circuit board around the room. "Nobody ever broke Lupo's stack—figured out his puzzle. We all tried when I was an underclassman and he was a senior. We took the problem to a couple of the Nobels. They couldn't figure it out. It had to do with solving the structures of fruit fly genes that controlled thorax development and the relative contribution—"

"So you'll help us?"

"Nope."

"Why not?"

"Because we require some considerations first." Sarkisian picked up the soldering iron, clicked it on, and deftly soldered a connection, a thin curl of smoke rising from the circuit board.

"How about we *consider* your butt right on down to headquarters?" said Walter, leaning against the doorway.

"Now, Walter, let's just hear what the kid has to say." Loudon cleared a pile of papers off the desk chair and sat down. "Go ahead."

"Well, you've got a massively parallel supercomputer."

"Yeah, I guess. At headquarters."

"Give us time on it."

"That computer holds all our confidential records. No deal."

"We promise not to mess around with the records. We've got a project we want to do. Needs some supercomputer time, and we got kicked off Tech's machines."

Loudon looked resignedly at Walter. "I got a friend," said Walter, nodding reluctantly.

"Well, we'll see what we can do. We can probably do that."

"And you've got a battering ram. You use it for drug raids."

"You mean that armored car with the big shaft on the front?"

"Yeah. We want it for two hours. No questions asked. Nothing illegal . . . not exactly, in the strict sense of the word."

"C'mon, kid."

"We won't break it," said the girl seriously. "And if we do, we'll fix it."

Loudon looked at Walter again who gave an exasperated sigh and nodded his head. Another of Walter's friends would help.

"Okay, one hour. And it's your problem if you get caught." Loudon heard a muffled explosion outside the window, but Sarkisian and the girl ignored it, so he did, too."

"Hour-and-a-half." Sarkisian made another soldered connection, the burning smell of solder rising again in the small room.

"Deal." Loudon extended his hand and Sarkisian took it, with the slightest flash of a pleased smile.

"Okay, then, we'll help."

"Now, has Lupo been working here?"

"Yeah, we just found out. After the last FBI guy was here. I'll show you." He put down the soldering iron, rose to his feet and swept aside the sheet, leading them through a maze of halls. The girl followed as far as the stairs to the basement, then waved goodbye and ducked through a sheeted doorway into another room. They descended into the basement and entered a doorway that led into a long tunnel lined with pipes and wiring. A moist, dank smell, infused with the faintest odor of food, pervaded the passageway.

"We're in the Caltech steam tunnels," explained Sarkisian over his shoulder. "Subspace. Lupo used to stay down here a lot. He lived here one semester. Almost all the buildings are accessible through these tunnels." They reached a small side room, apparently an unused storage room, leading off the main tunnel. In the room, a skinny red-headed boy lounged on a cot, reading by a bare light bulb. A computer, its screen glowing, sat on a rickety table beside the bed, a wire led from the computer into one of the cables strung down the passageway. The boy looked up with the owlish expression of someone who spent most of his time in the dark. A large boa constrictor curled around the pile of books on the floor.

"This is Phil Conigliaro," said Sarkisian. "He works in the biology building that Lupo had access to. He saw Lupo in the lab late at night once."

"You live down here?" asked Walter.

" 'Course not," Conigliaro was mildly indignant. "I study down here. Sleep down here. Eat down here sometimes. But I don't live down here."

"So, you'll show us where Lupo was working?" asked Loudon.

Conigliaro looked at Sarkisian. "What'd you get?"

"Computer time. And the tank." Sarkisian raised his eyebrows in triumph.

"Awesome." Conigliaro rolled off the bed and stood, carefully avoiding the overhead pipes. "Okay, but I gotta tell you. He was my friend, even though he was weird. I think he went off the bend . . . around the deep end . . . whatever. I want you to catch him, but I don't want you to hurt him. You gotta let him come in on his own."

"Look, we only want to stop whatever he's going to do," said Shinohara. "Just help us out."

"Stay," Conigliaro instructed the large, inert snake. He motioned for the four people to follow him. Sarkisian waved goodbye and returned to the dormitory.

"You okay, Kathleen?" asked Doc as they continued down the long tunnel, lit by occasional light bulbs.

"It's not a cave, Doc. It's not a cave," she said, marching along determined. She seemed to be trying to convince herself. After walking about a quarter mile, taking a series of turns and side tunnels, they arrived at another door. Conigliaro pushed it open, and they passed through a utility closet to find themselves in a modern fluorescent-lit hallway lined with refrigerators, freezers and scientific instruments. It was deserted, but the hum of compressors and the distant clacking of some unseen piece of apparatus gave the hall a sense that the machines were biding mechanical time, waiting for their human operators.

"In here," said Conigliaro as they passed a windowed room containing several machines covered with monitor screens, buttons and dials. Their labels said Beckman Instruments and Applied Biosystems, Inc.

"This is one of the analytical labs. It's got a DNA sequencer and a synthesizer. One analyzes the structure of DNA molecules, the other automatically builds DNA. And there's a protein sequencer and a polymerase chain reaction machine. We found out Lupo worked in here a lot until recently. He'd come in through the steam tunnels at night and run samples until morning."

"How'd you find out?"

"Well, of course, I saw him that once. But people who were running samples overnight would also find them all done and recorded in the morning. Somebody had been finishing up the work and starting on their own. After a while we figured it was Arthur."

"Like a shoemaker's elf," said Walter. "Whoa. Some elf."

Conigliaro looked puzzled, but he continued. "So, he took most of his results with him every night. On thumb drives. But we found some data he hadn't erased from the machines. We copied it." He took a thumb drive out of his pocket and handed it to Doc.

Doc pocketed the drive, then bent to inspect the equipment.

"Yeah, this'll help. If we can figure out some of the stuff he's been analyzing, it might help us understand where he's goin'. Kathleen, what do you think?"

Shinohara was already walking down the rows of instruments. She stopped at a small beige box with a few buttons on the front. "These are high-end machines. If he needs things like this to do his work, then we have a handle on how to catch him. He needs major equipment, and he sure can't come back here. And the FBI can shut him down by making sure all the labs that have this kind of equipment are under heavy security."

"Great," said Loudon. "It's progress, anyway."

They finished their inspection of the lab, and Conigliaro led them up to the main floor and out into the night. They emerged from the modern tile-roofed biology building onto a sidewalk that led between the new building and its old Spanish-style counterpart. Conigliaro led them along winding, intimate sidewalks past other handsome Spanish-style buildings and ponds until they were once more on the brick walk that led past the dormitories to the Athenaeum.

They reached the Athenaeum, circling the darkened building and walking around to the street side of the limousine. Conigliaro paused, peering down the boulevard.

"Just a second," he said, straining to see into the darkness beyond the street light. They could make out a single headlight approaching, and they heard the throaty sound of a motorcycle engine echoing down the street. The motorcycle pulled up about twenty yards away, under a pool of light across the street. The rider wore a red helmet. His face wasn't visible through the tinted faceplate. He sat and looked at them. His facelessness was ominous. He beckoned.

"Just wait here," said Conigliaro. He walked warily toward the rider, crossing the broad street.

"Lupo?" asked Walter.

"Maybe," said Loudon, trying to remember where he'd seen the motorcycle and rider before. It came to him. "I saw that bike, the rider, near the shooting gallery downtown."

"I could take him in a second," said Walter, slowly moving his hand to reach for his gun. Loudon stopped him.

"You do, and we won't know where those viruses are. He could've rigged them into some kind of trap. Let's just see what we can maneuver him into." He held out his hand, palm down, toward Shinohara and Doc on the other side of the car. "Just stay still."

"It's Arthur," called Conigliaro back to them from his position beside the rider. The faceless helmet aimed itself steadily toward them.

"Can we talk?" asked Loudon. "Look, I won't try anything. We'll keep it straight." Loudon felt the old itch rise within him. He had to catch this sick terrorist! He slowly moved away from the other three and toward Lupo. He was nineteen yards away.

Lupo said something to Conigliaro. "He wants your email address," said Conigliaro. "He wants to send you an email message." Loudon was seventeen yards away.

"That's too bad," whispered Walter to Doc and Shinohara. "It's harder to trace email."

"Look, I'll write it down and hand it to him." Loudon carefully removed his notebook from his coat pocket, took out a pen and jotted down his public email address on the FBI computer network. He moved closer. Fifteen yards. Maybe he could sprint it and catch Lupo before he gunned the motorcycle away.

Conigliaro walked over and took the piece of paper and took it back to Lupo. Loudon advanced to twelve yards away, across the shadowy street and down a bit. He had come into a street-lighted area, so he was clearly visible to Lupo. He'd have to make his move soon.

Conigliaro had just turned to say something when he and Lupo were lit by the headlights of a car down the street behind Loudon. It roared past Loudon, an anonymous battered Chevrolet sedan. Loudon could see through the driver-side window to the passenger side. The passenger maneuvered a black object out the window. Before he could react, the familiar, lethal burst of a MAC 10 machine pistol erupted from the car, shattering the still night. Lupo threw himself off the motorcycle and slammed into the gutter, protected by the motorcycle. The metallic clatter of bullets ricocheting off the motorcycle made it clear who the target was. The ricochets missed Lupo, but a bullet caught Conigliaro, spinning him around and shattering the bone in his upper arm. He screamed and fell backward onto the pavement, blood running onto the asphalt.

Loudon yanked his pistol from his holster, aimed and squeezed off three rounds into the back of the car. Walter appeared beside him and did the same. The car had slowed briefly, probably to back up for another salvo. But when Loudon's first bullet punched through its rear window, the driver floored the accelerator. Its tires squealing and smoking, the car sped into the darkness.

Lupo jumped up just as the car accelerated. He bent to his friend, bleeding but alive on the sidewalk. Conigliaro waved him away, and he leaped on his still-idling cycle. He kicked back the kickstand and wrenched the throttle wide open. The motorcycle leaped forward, skidding into a turn, and he roared away down a dark side street. The throaty sound of its engine echoed away into the distance, until it merged with the low drone of the city traffic.

The whole encounter had taken less than a dozen heartbeats. Loudon looked back at Shinohara and Doc, who had flattened themselves on the sidewalk. They got up and waved that they were all right. He clicked on his radio and notified headquarters, asking for an ambulance, an FBI investigative team, and for Pasadena police to be notified. Doc ran to kneel beside the groaning boy, treating his wound, as people began to stream from the nearby houses. A campus cop arrived, and they identified themselves. Soon the Pasadena police came, followed immediately by an ambulance. Loudon stood beside the stretcher bearing Conigliaro as they loaded it into the back.

"Hey!" Conigliaro gasped through his pain. Tears ran down his face. "You tried to kill him!"

"We didn't, son. I promise you, we didn't."

Loudon stood alone as the ambulance sped away, staring after it. He experienced a flashback to the night of the Columbians. He remembered the ambulance taking away the dead and wounded as he stood beside the door to the house, rage rising within him. The rage began to rise again, hot and acid.

He managed to shake off the anger when an FBI lab team arrived. He and Walter gave their stories to the team and the police and watched them investigate the crime scene—photographing tire marks, searching for shell casings and interviewing witnesses. Unfortunately, the car's rear license plate had been obscured, so they couldn't identify the owner through the DMV.

Walter leaned against the limousine, watching the investigators go through their paces. "What was wrong with that picture? I mean the car."

"Looked standard enough." Loudon tried to fathom what Walter meant.

"Yeah, well, I think when the lab boys compare the length of the rubber that car burned with the make of car, they'll find something interesting."

"Like what?"

"That car had much more juice than your average mommy and daddy sedan. That was a surveillance car. I know the sound. I know the performance. There was too much under the hood, Bobby."

"What are you saying?"

"That's the kind of cars government agencies gin up." Walter shrugged and walked toward the street to inspect the tire marks. "I'm just sayin'."

After an hour, the four of them were back in the limousine for the drive back to LA.

Shinohara was quiet during most of the trip, as she and Loudon held hands in the back seat. She silently turned his hand over in hers, memorizing its lines.

"You could have died," she said quietly. "You know, you could have died."

"Yes. That wouldn't have been very good, would it?" he teased, trying to cheer her up.

"Is nothing serious with you?" There was a note of doubt.

"Yes. My daughter . . . you."

"And your work?"

"Yeah, okay, my work."

They were interrupted by the car's radio. It was a scrambled message from the field office for Loudon. He reached into the front seat and took the microphone.

"Hunter One, this is Hunter Base," said the tinny voice on the radio. "This is a priority one message from SAC. You are to proceed at 0800 hours to the FBI terminal at LAX. You will receive further instructions there."

"Hunter Base, what is my destination?"

"No information on that. Just be there. Ten-four."

Loudon sat back in the seat, his brow wrinkled.

"Maybe I'm being fired."

"Or maybe somebody, somewhere wants to talk to you," said Walter. "Somebody important enough for you to take a plane ride."

They reached the hospital where their cars were parked. Walter waved goodbye and drove away to return the limousine, and the other three walked into the parking garage and got into their cars. They said weary goodbyes and drove out into the streets of LA, now occupied with the scruffy denizens of the late-night.

CHAPTER 18

The party had been uneventful until the richly maroon Squirrel walked into the sliding glass door with a reverberating clunk. He bounced off and stood before the door staring dimly, looking almost offended. He may have flushed with anger, but his deep color kept it from showing. He appeared to be working himself up to walk right into the door again, when the blue-blazered security guard gently took him by the shoulders and steered him through the open side. He shepherded Squirrel into the house and into a bathroom, where Squirrel would be politely patted down for drugs, as had been the other addicts bused from the hospital.

The chatter resumed at the party arranged for the newly colored to meet the colorfully influential. The guests stood around the expansive garden-encircled pool behind the massive, angular, modern house. The California night was quiet and cool, with just a slight tinge of smog fuzzing the view out over the twinkling sprawl of LA. The crowd was decidedly mixed. It included smooth, confident Hollywood producers, directors, actors, actresses, agents and businessmen, all of whom smiled with glossy purpose. Watching them were the slightly awed doctors and nurses of LA County Hospital. But the real stars were the brilliantly hued patients, who remained foggily indifferent, except for the vague awareness of opportunity presenting itself. As the guests of honor, they were surrounded by knots of less-flamboyant flesh-colored admirers, like framed, vibrant paintings. The soft liquid blue glow from the lighted pool only slightly dimmed their spectral grandeur.

Almost all the newly colored had shown up. The young burnt-umber girl chatted wide-eyed with the sleek male star of a daytime soap opera. The teal-blue woman—whose last meal had been a hospital tray of meat loaf—stood by the buffet, staring blankly in confusion at its exotic offerings. A young serving woman in a long peasant dress and sandals explained the foods to her.

". . . and these are Argentinian duck sausage with wild mustard sauce. And for vegetarians these are meatless soyballs with Chinese herbs. And this is jicama soaked in red wine—"

"You got chips?"

"Well, these are blue corn tortilla chips, with—"

"Naw, like potato chips. Like with onion dip."

The young woman curled her lip in mild disdain. She rolled her eyes at another serving woman in a peasant dress, who passed with a tray of hors d'oeuvres to circulate among the crowd.

Meanwhile, the other colored people pursued varied interests with the influential guests.

"That him?" asked Shinohara, as a slim middle-aged man with a comfortable aristocratic slouch wandered amiably through the crowd. His drink in hand, he greeted everyone, expansive and friendly in his Calvin Klein jacket, open-collar Ralph Lauren shirt, Yves Saint Laurent slacks and Salvatore Ferragamo shoes with Pierre Cardin socks.

"Yeah, I didn't see him before," said Doc, taking his glasses out of his Walmart plaid shirt and holding them folded to his eyes, peering at the man. "That's Lew Wiener." They stood at the entrance into the pool garden from the house.

"And he's what again?"

"He's a producer or something. Hot stuff. Does all those big movies with the guy with the muscles."

"And that's her? His wife?" asked Shinohara, as a sleek, blonde woman greeted new guests with a wide perfect smile and a flip of her long curls. She wore a white Giorgio Armani strapless evening dress.

"Yeah, Gloria, I think."

"She's beautiful."

"Yeah, well, I bet she never cleaned out a barn."

"Oat bran crackers with Andalusian goat cheese?" asked a serving woman, offering a tray. Doc grunted a "No thanks."

Wiener, elegantly tanned and with a steel-gray pompadour, saw them and eased toward them. "Hello, Doc, I'm so glad you came." He turned immediately to Shinohara. "And you must be the other doctor from the CDC." He stood back to admire Shinohara, who wore a black spaghetti-strap dress that showed her rich caramel skin to its best advantage. "Goodness, you are lovely," he said. "One doesn't expect scientists to be knockouts." Shinohara formed a smile that showed a slightly annoyed curl of the lip.

"Ain't I lovely, too?" asked Doc.

"Sure," laughed Wiener. "You're smashing, Doctor Smith."

"Like I said, just Doc."

"Fine, fine . . . well . . . I wanted to thank you for making this possible. These poor people deserve some help, and I'm just glad to give them an opportunity to meet people who can."

"Yeah, great."

"Listen, let me introduce you around," he said, taking Shinohara's arm cordially. They began to circulate through the crowd, stopping here and there to chat.

Meanwhile, the chartreuse Mookie was trying his best to grasp a shorthand-sentence pitch from an intense blue-jeaned young man with wildly frizzy hair and rimless glasses.

". . . reality show . . . we'd call it 'Colored Folks,'" he said eagerly. "Follow you around as you adjusted to being colored. Dealt with people. Saw their reactions. Good stuff. Lots of interest at the networks. Commentary on our times. It'd be great! If the nets took an option, and it ran five seasons, you'd be a millionaire."

"Millionaire. Yeah, yeah, that sounds good," said Mookie his attention intensifying to that of a flashlight with low batteries. "I sure can't sell nothin' no more. Nobody'll buy from somebody just because he's turned a little color."

"I'm sure that's a real bummer."

"Yeah. Y'know—"

"Organic carrot sticks with an asparagus dip?" asked a serving woman, leaning over them with a tray. Mookie took a carrot, poked it into a thick green dip, stared at it for a moment, and took a bite. He made a face and put the remains back on the tray. The woman straightened and departed in a polite huff.

"Say, can you get blow?" asked the frizzy-haired man after she had left.

"Oh, yeah, sure, good stuff."

"Say, maybe we can work together." The young man paused while a couple strolled past. He lowered his voice. "I've got friends who'd want it. Y'know they're always willing to help the . . . uh . . . differently hued."

"Yeah, yeah, we could do the TV thing and a little dealin' on the side."

"Yeah, great . . ." They continued their conversation, periodically peering about suspiciously.

Across the pool, pea-green Carl sat cozily at a table ensconced with a lush, doe-eyed starlet in a silk dress. He chewed a broiled free-range chicken morsel.

"Y'know its true," he said sadly staring balefully into her eyes. "It's true what they say. It *ain't* easy being green." She took his hand, and his droopy pea-green face rearranged itself into a wan smile, with perhaps a glimmer of hope for things to come.

Inside the house, Jimmy D. lounged comfortably on the sofa, his bulk consuming up most of its width.

"So, you're sayin' I like, just get up in the ring and play like I'm wrestlin'?"

"Exactly, my friend," said the muscular middle-aged man in the chair beside him. "You'd be a draw."

"Yeah, I could do that."

"I'd agent you. We'd call you the Blue Behemoth!"

"But I ain't blue!" Jimmy D.'s eyes narrowed menacingly in their indignation. "I'm turquoise, man. I already turned down an offer from the Crips to be their mascot. Blue's their gang color. I told those gang-bangers I wad'n no blue, and I'm tellin' you!"

"Okay, okay . . ." said the young man, leaning toward him, his elbows on his knees, his hands gesturing eagerly. "Let's see . . . then . . ." He peered at the ceiling ". . . we'll call you the Turquoise Terror!"

"Hmmm . . ." said Jimmy D. thoughtfully. "Yeah, that's good, awright."

A serving woman approached. "Peeled grapes dipped in wildflower honey and wheat germ?" she offered the tray.

In the next room, two security guards quietly closed in on Loco, grabbed his goldenrod arms and emptied his pockets of jewelry from the upstairs bedrooms. They surreptitiously hustled him out the front door for a ride back to downtown LA.

"You wouldn'a caught me if I'd been white," he complained.

Squirrel appeared again from inside the house, walked tentatively up to the glass door and felt his way carefully through the opening. He wandered along the luxuriantly landscaped paths around the pool, passing the laughing, chatting guests. He stopped to tie his brand new shoes. Looking around, he reached into his tattered sock and pulled out a small plastic baggie full of white powder, palming it. Instantly, he drew a crowd of interested, clean-cut young men. One whispered something into his ear. He nodded sleepily, and they all walked casually back inside the house.

"So, what's a greeter?" asked Randy Joe, standing by the luminescent pool, one pumpkin-colored hand wrapped around a beer possessively. The other held a wad of spinach-and-bee-pollen pastry puffs from a serving tray.

"Well, it's a guy who stands out front of a casino and says hello," said the husky man in the pinstripe suit.

"Yeah, I've done somethin' like that before. But do I have to wash windshields?"

"Naw, nothing like that. You're kind of a guide."

"Man, I look like a traffic cone already," said Randy Joe, holding up his hands. "Guess I wouldn't be run down by no cars, huh?"

Sitting at a poolside table, the lean sunbaked older woman with the grand blonde hairdo leaned over to her stooped husband, pointing toward the buffet table with a long gloss-red nail.

"I must have that one, Lenny," she hissed. "That little blue one. Lenny, you've *got* to get that one. She matches. She matches the decor perfectly!"

"Sure, bubbie, sure," croaked the skinny old man, waving his cigar magnanimously, his large, gold ring flashing in the undulating blue light from the pool.

"So go talk to her, Lenny." She held up her champagne glass like a wand. "Tell her. Tell her we want her. Bring her over."

"Of course, darling," He got up and tottered off.

"Wait! Wait! Lenny! Talk to the other one, too. The one who's kinda orange. She could work in the New York apartment. I'd just redecorate!"

Ever the investigator, Doc had wandered from patient to patient, watching them for any signs of illness. He ended up advising the wine-red man by the buffet not to try to put a bowl of chickpea dip into his pocket along with the blue corn tortilla chips.

Shinohara had spent the last fifteen minutes with an agent who was either trying to sign her as a client or get her into bed. She wasn't sure which. Maybe there was no significant difference. In any case, she was tired, so she and Doc excused themselves and found their way through the sprawling house to the front entrance. They waited there for the valet to find their car. Carl was also there, leaving with the ingenue, a twinkle animating his hound-dog bloodshot eyes.

As the night went on and more stars managed to penetrate the smog, deals were made, liaisons formed. The party would result in three abortive television shows, five jobs, one brief love affair, a newly organized drug ring, two arrests, one conviction, and a book that would be optioned for an unmade movie.

• • •

Loudon sat at the rest stop and watched the traffic speed by on the freeway between Washington and Frederick, their lights switching on to pierce the approaching gloom of the gray dusk. It had been a long flight from LA, and he slumped slightly as he sat on top of the farthest picnic table, his feet on the bench. He'd chosen a spot as close to the cover of the woods as he could get. He stared down at his new blue running shoes. He'd bought them at an athletic shoe store that had practically given him a physical before recommending them. No, he hadn't run in years. Yes, he was going to start. Yes, he was planning to work up to long distances—equal to whatever Shinohara ran.

He was also dressed in blue slacks and a sport shirt. The usual gray suit would have attracted attention, and Colonel Gaines didn't want that. The message, delivered from the AMRIID director through secure channels, had made it clear that he would meet only with Loudon and only in total secrecy. Loudon figured he was in enough trouble with Bowers as it was. Compared with pulling a pistol on the boss, a clandestine meeting with the head of the biowarfare lab was a relatively minor infraction. So, Loudon had agreed, and to ensure secrecy had kept a close watch for tails on the drive out from Washington. He'd exited from the freeway and double-backed several times, looking for other cars that did the same. He was sure nobody had followed him when he arrived. And in the thirty minutes he'd sat at the rest stop, he'd seen no evidence that anybody had caught up. It was a good time of day for the operation. He'd arrived in daylight, so he could see tails. But now night was closing in, so their meeting would be obscured by darkness.

He followed a truck roaring past on the freeway, turning to look to his right. When he turned back, Gaines sat beside him on the table.

"Jeez!" he yelped jumping up. "Where did you come from?"

"Used to be in Delta Force," said Gaines seriously. "We had to learn stealth."

"Well, tell 'em I gave you an 'A' in stealth."

"This has to be quick."

"So go ahead."

"I did some field work. Lupo was asked to come to AMRIID to do legitimate work. But once he was there, a faction contacted him."

"A 'faction'? What do you mean 'faction'? A faction in the Army?"

Gaines looked annoyed. "No, sir. We do things by the book. Maybe a few Army people, but it's a wider group who've decided to start their own show. Biological warfare research. *Offensive* work."

"No really?"

"Yes, sir." Gaines scanned the area intently as he talked. Loudon looked down at his shoes again and noticed Gaines wore an ankle holster. "They told him they wanted to use his chromophore system with offensive weapons."

"I don't understand."

"What's the biggest problem with biological weapons?" But before Loudon could answer, Gaines answered his own question. "Control. You want these germs to act fast, so they do their damage fast. Problem is, you'd also like to make them act slow enough so the enemy has time to wander around and infect other enemy." He got off the bench and stood solidly in front of Loudon. "But if you build a long-lasting bug and launch it, your men won't know who's infected when they go in. So you stick a color gene in the germ, so that anybody who's infected shows up colored, even if they don't show symptoms. So, your men go in, they can take prisoners who are flesh-colored. They can neutralize the colored ones at a distance, so they won't catch the germ. A dictator could even have hit squads to kill off soldiers in his own ranks if they get infected."

Loudon sat down on the bench. "Makes using germs controllable."

"Yes, sir, pretty much. To some, it makes them downright strategic. Also makes it more likely some lunatic will use them. They're pretty cheap."

"So, they tried to get Lupo to develop his genes for human viruses? Where?"

"New facility. Replaced Plum Island when it went hot."

It dawned on Loudon. He remembered Lupo's travel records. "Denver!"

"That's what I was told."

"How reliable is this? It sounds kinda far-fetched. Your source trustworthy?"

"About as trustworthy as a guy gets when you're crouched by his bed in the middle of the night. With a knife at his throat. And his wife asleep beside him. And his kids down the hall. And he thinks you'd kill them all in a second."

"McLaren? He worked with Lupo at AMRIID, right? Must be him."

"Maybe." Gaines was keeping Loudon at a distance, a good strategy.

"You in danger?"

"No, sir. He knows there's no way he could keep me away from his house if they try anything on me. And if not me, my buddies would visit him. We agreed he wouldn't tell his faction about our talk. So, they don't know, and you've got a chance to identify them."

Loudon took a deep breath and looked into Gaines's dead-cool gray eyes. He decided the information was reliable.

"So, Lupo refused to help them?"

"Yes, sir. And they said they'd kill him if he didn't. So he worked with them long enough to learn what he needed." Gaines walked away a few steps and turned back. Loudon saw a hint of worry in the impassive eyes. "Like you found out, he did take some germs. The bad ones. Then he told the faction he needed to go back to his company and do some experiments. He went back long enough to get ready. Then he disappeared."

"But why would he start building viruses and releasing them?"

"Because he's Section Eight . . . he's nuts. Your people must have run up a psych profile."

"Yeah, he's not a real sociable guy." Loudon suddenly felt a thirst, but he suppressed it for the moment.

"Like I said, Section Eight. I think the death threat made him flip. Now maybe he wants to prove his power."

"Well, they just tried to kill him. Now he's probably worse." Loudon began to pace, too. He turned away to watch a car pull into the rest stop. "I still don't understand about this faction business . . ." he began, but when he turned back, Gaines had vanished.

Loudon stood in the deepening twilight, illuminated by the occasional wash of headlights. He decided the next stop was back in Washington.

• • •

Henry Cleland had his pipe clenched in his mouth and his *Washington Post* in his hand when he answered the door of his Georgetown townhouse. The faint odor of tobacco rolled out from the door when he opened it.

"Ah, Bobby," he said delightedly. "I didn't know you were coming back to Washington so soon. It's a pleasure, son. Come in."

He showed Loudon into his modest, paneled study. Loudon politely refused his gracious offer of a scotch. It surprised Cleland, but it also surprised Loudon. In fact, his drinking pace had slowed considerably since he'd met Shinohara. Pondering the phenomenon, he settled into one of the large leather chairs in the study. Cleland did the same, knocking the ashes out of his pipe and refilling it from the humidor beside his chair. The clunk of the pipe, the fiddling, and the tang of tobacco were comfortingly familiar to Loudon.

He briefed Cleland on the attempted murder of Lupo and what Gaines had told him at the rest stop. As usual, Cleland asked perceptive questions. After fifteen minutes, Loudon came to the real point of his visit.

"Hank, I need some advice."

"Certainly, Bobby. What is it?" Cleland drew on the pipe with a breathy hiss and puffed a fragrant cloud from his lips.

"Hank, what do you know about these so-called factions that Gaines talked about. Could there be a faction that started its own biological warfare research? Its own research lab? Black research, with no public budget? Maybe even private money?"

Cleland took his time answering. He allowed the silence to blossom into a sign of the gravity of what he was about to say. He carefully emptied the pipe, tamped more tobacco into it, lit it, and puffed a while. He maintained a contemplative smile on his face the entire time.

"Bobby," he finally said quietly. "You're about to advance to the next stage of understanding of your government. Most people don't understand what I'm going to tell you until they're a lot further along. And they often get it by osmosis, inference, because nobody wants to talk about it. You know your alphabet agencies, right? All the official organizations of government?"

"You mean FBI, CIA, NSC, DOD, and so forth?"

"Yes, well, the boundaries between them aren't necessarily as hard and fast as the civics books say. There's a good deal of . . . let us say . . . cross-fertilization."

"You mean interagency spies? Moles?"

"Well, there are all kinds of relationships, Bobby. Of course you know we have liaison people that openly bring, say, the FBI point of view to the CIA, or vice versa. But there may also be advocates that aren't so open. Some we know; some we don't. They may be doing it for love, patriotism, or money. And these advocates may form ad hoc alliances according to what their home organizations want. Or, maybe according to what they think their target organizations should do. Or, maybe just what they personally want. Bobby, they're all over out there."

"And in this case?"

"Sounds to me like maybe some army militarists, maybe some N and B types at the Agency." Cleland fiddled with his pipe some more, took an experimental puff and was satisfied with the resulting fragrant cloud of smoke.

"N and B?"

"Nerds and buffs. Science and technical specialists. Ninety percent of the CIA are nerds and buffs, not spooks as most people believe. Anyway, there may be some folks elsewhere, maybe even Congress. They decided it was best if we kept our options going in biological warfare. So, they found a pot of secret money somewhere and started a lab."

"Like Oliver North and the arms-for-hostages deal during the Nixon administration?"

"Sure, but nobody really asked the important question there. The important question was how often do these shadow factions get put together. The answer is all the time. It's as American as the Bay of Pigs."

Loudon sat back in his chair, his mind racing. He reconsidered the scotch.

"And the FBI might even be involved?" Loudon didn't know if he wanted to hear an answer to that question.

"Yup, it might."

The next question was even dicier. Cleland grinned knowingly, anticipating it.

"And you might be involved in such shadow factions?"

"Yes, I might be."

"In this one?"

"Well, I'll tell you now I'm not. But, of course, I hope you're smart enough to know that's what I'd say, even if I was."

"Hank, now what do I do?"

"Well, son, in the end trust your own judgment. Do your job as assigned by the FBI. You catch your Mr. Lupo and you stop his virus work cold. Don't worry about the other stuff. The time will come later when you'll have to worry about it plenty."

"I don't think so, Hank."

Cleland chuckled, keeping his pipe clenched firmly between his teeth. "We'll see, Bobby, we'll see."

Loudon thanked him and left, walking out into the bustle of Georgetown at night. He was lost in thought as he drove back toward his hotel. He decided instead to take a quick run past the Bureau, to see if he had any messages.

He pulled into the underground FBI garage, took the elevator to his floor, and made his way across the almost deserted open office past the few late workers to his borrowed desk, settling in and logging onto the computer and into his email. The messages scrolling down the screen constituted the usual routine bulletins and messages from Bowers and from the assistant director. He scanned through them and answered the ones that needed answering.

However, third from the last was a message that had come in over the Internet. The computer address information at the top showed it had been routed to him through a service provider in California. The address had a name that gave him a buzz of anticipation: Lupo. But when he read the words the buzz turned to gray dread. The message made him realize that, even if it took all the resources of government, Lupo had to be stopped. The text read:

To Mr. Loudon and the government: When you threatened me, I showed you the power I had with some harmless virus releases. Now you have tried to kill me, and you have shown me the face of your evil and the face of all humans' evil. I realize now that the earth must be cleansed, and so I am going to do that.

Specifically, I will insert the tox-genes from Ebola, Dengue and mutant influenza into an airborne viral envelope. The virus will have the same coat proteins I've used before and will not be recognized by the immune system. The three tox-genes will modulate randomly as did the chromophores in the second test system. So, I will strike with three diseases in one virus. The transmission will be swift, and the earth will be clean as before humans came.

I am sorry, but your evil is forcing me to do this.

Loudon sat for ten minutes, quietly rubbing his face with one hand, letting the information sink in. He carefully typed an email message to the behavioral science unit in Quantico, forwarding Lupo's text and asking their opinion. He had to know if Lupo was capable of carrying out his threat.

But he needed some more personal support, he realized. He checked his notebook, picked up his smart phone and began to punch in Shinohara's number. Her sleepy voice on the phone would be comforting. But then he thought better of it. This was not where he wanted to be. He used the phone to search for the next flight from Reagan to LAX. It was in an hour.

CHAPTER 19

The next morning, Loudon stood in the hotel room, waiting for Shinohara to finish replacing the bandage on her back. He could see that the slash on her shoulder blade was healing nicely. It was now only a long white scar on the coffee skin. But he noticed other scars, though, below the new one. But especially striking were perhaps half a dozen small gouges out of the flesh around her shoulders.

"Kathleen, what happened there?"

"Where?"

"You know what I mean. All those other scars."

"You don't want to know," she said, pulling back her hair.

"I do. I really do."

"Okay, but it's hard."

"If it's that hard, then . . ."

"No, no, talking about it is something I just have to be able to do. I got them in Mexico three years ago."

"On vacation?"

"No, Doc and I had gone across the border looking for a source of rabies near Laredo. We had evidence that rabid bats were transmitting the disease, and there looked to be a reservoir population in a cave down there. The only thing we could do was to go down and go into the cave."

"Oh, so that's what you and Doc meant when you were talking about bats and caves."

"Yes, that was it. Anyway, we had to walk about five miles into the interior, wade through some swamp, then rappel a couple of hundred feet down a cliff to the cave entrance. There were four of us. We started down into the cave. It was a wild cave, so there was no light except from helmet lanterns and flashlights. We hiked in and got to a point where there were two passages. We agreed to split up, and the other two guys, Doug and Ray, went into one passage. Doc and I went into the other." She paused, her eyes distant. "Well, our passage opened into this chamber and there must have been half a million bats on the ceiling. The whole ceiling was solid with them. The air was warm with the heat from their bodies. If all we had to do was enjoy the sight . . . they're really incredible animals . . . it would have been okay. But we had to go in. The guano was knee deep, like a thick, wet powder. And it was alive with dung beetles and insects like roaches and scorpions that ate dead bats. Occasionally a snake would come through, looking for fallen bats. The ammonia reek was horrible, but we wore respirators so we could breathe and suits to protect us from the rain of bat dung. Every so often a bat would drop from the ceiling and into the guano, thrashing around. It was dying from rabies. But sometimes a bat would let go of the ceiling and begin to fly erratically. It was rabid, but in the early stages where it was still dangerous."

"What a horror!" whispered Loudon. She took his hand and held it tightly to her warm chest with both hands. He could feel her heart beating.

"That's not the worst. We couldn't have known it, but part of the cave floor was a false bottom. Sometimes the limestone gets eroded away underneath, leaving just a crust. We walked out onto it and Doc broke through. He hit his head on the way down and his helmet fell into the hole. It just kept falling and falling."

"Did he fall far?"

"No. We were roped together. When he fell, it dragged me right to the edge of this huge hole, and my helmet came off and fell in, too.

I stopped myself by grabbing a stalagmite. Doc was just suspended by the rope, dead weight. I called, but he didn't answer. I thought I could hear him breathing, but I couldn't be sure."

"So you were in the dark?"

"Yes, total. I had a flashlight, but I couldn't let go at first to get it. So I pulled as hard as I could and got the rope pulled around the stalagmite, but I couldn't move. That's when the bats came."

"The rabid ones?"

"Yeah. And I was in this stuff, this guano, that had these beetles in it, these arthropods. I was getting claustrophobic inside the respirator. But I couldn't take it off lying there in the bat dung. I couldn't see anything, but every so often, I could hear the flutter of wings and a bat land. It was one of the rabid bats. I could hear them squeaking in the stuff, and I had gloves on, so I'd hit at the close ones until they were dead. Or until they stopped squeaking. I could hear some of them being eaten, but I wasn't sure by what. It was dead silent, except for my breathing and the bats. But sometimes one would fly into a stalactite above me and fall down on me. And they'd grab on and bite into me. I'd feel them on my back or next to my face or in my hair. I'd slap them off, but I could feel the blood run down. Furry little monsters!" She spat the last words out as if it were the ultimate curse.

"How'd you get out?"

"Well, I figured out how to brace against the rock and push a little slack in the rope with my legs, then take it up around the stalagmite. It took me about an hour, but I pulled Doc up to the edge. And I was all the time getting these bites. I finally hauled him over the edge, but the crust began to crack under us again, so I had to drag him back into the cave. And we were both under this rain of bat dung."

"So, I got him up and got out the flashlight and found out he'd gashed the back of his head and he had a concussion, but he was okay. My legs and arms were gone from pulling him up, but I managed to drag him up and out of the chamber, where Doug and Ray could find us. I was scared. For him, for me. But, you know, I got the samples. While I was dragging Doc out, I stuffed some of the dead bats in my collecting bag. I knew he'd give me grief if I didn't. But, I was scared. So scared."

The hotel had a passable coffee shop, so they went down for breakfast. Their coffee arrived and talk turned to Lupo.

"Have you tried to contact him yet?"

"Sure. Of course, the email message had a return address. But he's not answering. We've got to find Lupo, find his lab."

"How?"

"We haven't the foggiest idea, to be honest. I've had the LA cops, the Pasadena cops, our teams scouring the whole region. We've grilled the kids at Caltech; we've questioned the people at ArchiBiologics. We just can't find it."

"The psychological profile can't help?"

"Nope, remember the phone call last night? That was Quantico. All they could say so far was that he's perfectly capable of carrying out the threat he made in the email. It's very cold-blooded, they said."

"But he has to have a lab," she said, shaking her head with certainty. "He also needs access to a major facility. And Atlanta says he's probably having genes made for him commercially."

"Yeah, we're checking the companies that do that. Nothing yet."

"And so you're going back to Washington?" she asked.

The simple question hit him hard. "Yes, since there's nothing here, the ADC said I could just as well run the investigation from there. And you're going back, too?" Her somber expression told him she was just as troubled.

"Sure. We can't do anything until you find something. I might as well be back at Colorado Springs. I've got other cases."

They sat in silence for a moment.

"Look, what about going to Denver?" she finally asked. "You believe something's there, don't you? At the warfare lab?"

"Sure, but ADC says we don't move on it unless we know what's going on. That's above my pay grade. I can't—"

"You can go where the investigation leads. Look, I know Denver. Doc and I could start our own investigation—"

"I don't want you to do that. In fact . . ." He couldn't bring himself to broach the subject.

"'In fact' what?"

"I'm going to ask you for a favor. A big favor." He looked into the rich blackness of his coffee. He realized it was the color of her eyes.

"What favor?" She smiled, but there was a slightly suspicious wrinkle to her brow. Their waitress arrived to take orders, but they asked her for more time. "What favor?" Shinohara repeated.

"Look, Kathleen. Now that I know that there are people . . . professionals . . . out there with guns . . . a hit squad . . . and I know Lupo has some of the most dangerous organisms on earth in his possession. And he's perfectly capable of using them. This whole thing has gone far beyond what it was . . . and . . . well . . . I love you . . . and . . ."

"I love you, too." She paused, realizing with some surprise how deeply she meant the phrase. "But what are you saying?"

"We're going to be apart for a while. It's going to be bad enough not being with you, but worrying about you . . . on the case."

Her eyes showed that it was dawning on her. "You want me to drop this case, don't you?"

"Well, yes. It's just too dangerous."

"Again. I did it to myself again," she said, more to herself than to him.

"What? You did what?" He wrinkled his brow in puzzlement.

"Look, I take risks in my job. That's what I do. That's what you do."

"Well, I couldn't stand the thought of you in danger. The story of the cave really clenched it. And I just couldn't bear to be responsible—"

"That's it!" She sat up in the seat, her eyes flashing in indignation. "You don't want to take responsibility! Well, that's your problem, not mine. I was afraid of this!"

"Of what?"

"Well, I decided a long time ago that *nothing* comes between me and my job. It's too important." Her voice was raised so that people in a nearby table glanced over. She was as much anguished as angry. Her eyes glistened. "People die when I don't do my job."

"Well, people die when I don't do mine."

"But the difference is just about *anything* comes between you and your job! Robert, I thought I loved you. I really did. But if this is love, I guess I'm not going to do it." She looked away, scolding herself. "I should have known. This happened before, and I didn't learn."

"Well, maybe you should think about giving something to a relationship, rather than having it all your way."

"And maybe you should think the same."

Loudon could feel things slipping away, so he tried to recover. "Look, maybe we can work something out."

"Maybe *you* can work something out. I've already worked out what I need to." She stood up, barely missing a waitress with a loaded tray. "I'm leaving now, and I'm going back to Colorado Springs. I think we'd better just go back to the way it was." She turned and strode out.

Loudon sat quietly for a moment, drinking his coffee. He told the waitress he didn't want any breakfast. He'd go down to the field office. He would put in a full day. Then, he'd find a bar.

• • •

"Go ahead, dear, take it a while." Ella Smith handed Shinohara the curry brush and stepped back, while Shinohara applied the brush a bit too vigorously to the rump of the chestnut mare. Ella leaned against the post of the barn and watched for a moment. Shinohara had gotten really good with horses in the five years she and Doc had worked together. She was a good horsewoman, too. Wearing her big rubber boots, Ella clomped over to the hay pile, pulled up the pitchfork and hefted a mound of hay into the chestnut's stall. The gray stallion next door whinnied for attention, so she gave him a bunch, too.

Ella Smith was a trim, vigorous woman in her sixties, with long flowing gray hair that she kept in a careful bun. She still looked good in jeans, but she was just as proud of the lines of age on her face. She'd earned them all, she told Doc. She often pointed out the ones he had given her. Doc, in turn, pointed out that all those were smile lines.

"I got eight more due a good curry when you're finished," she teased Shinohara.

"Ella, you forget. Doc and I are in the bug business. We don't work with anything larger than a bacterium."

Doc shuffled in from the hot, dry Colorado summer day carrying three Coors beers. So they sat down on the fragrant bales of hay, away from the stronger smell of the horses, and took a break.

"Good to have you out here, Kathleen," said Doc, sipping his. "We haven't been together in weeks."

"Yeah, paperwork and footwork. And, Doc, I can't believe it's been two months since LA and nothing from Lupo."

"The word is he could be dead. Walter said the murder attempt was a professional job. They'd keep looking for him."

"Considering the viruses he has, that could be disastrous," said Shinohara shaking her head. "I'd hate to think of those cultures sitting somewhere for anybody to pick up."

"And nothing from Loudon?"

"Well . . . sure . . . he's left voice messages, emails."

"And you didn't call him back?" asked Doc, taking out a handkerchief and wiping his brow.

"Nothing to talk about. Nothing going on with the case. And you know he asked me to drop it."

"Yeah, well, I can't say I blame you for ignoring him. And he's got his problems. Drinking and so forth."

"He does. I don't need that."

"Uh, well, it seems you do." Doc screwed up his face, as if he'd said something distasteful.

"What does that mean?"

"I hate to say it, but you've got that *look* Kathleen. Had it for a while."

"What look?"

"The one that says there's something you want to do, but won't."

"That's enough, Doc."

Doc gave her an it's-not-my-problem shrug and took a healthy swig of his beer, letting loose a polite burp. "You hear the latest from LA?"

"No, what?" asked Shinohara, secretly hoping it would involve Loudon; that it would warrant a call to him.

"I got a report from the LA County Health Department. Looks like the junkies have gone health conscious. All of a sudden all the diseases they got from sharing needles have gone way down. Like hepatitis."

"You're kidding! Why?"

"Well, they think the junkies are afraid if they share needles and such, they'll turn colors. The junkies couldn't see the hepatitis bugs; didn't really think about gettin' infected. But turnin' color, that's another thing!"

Shinohara laughed and stretched her legs out and crossed them at the ankles, taking a drink of beer.

210

"Yeah," Doc continued. "The junkies figured if they were colored, they'd be marked. No more heroin, no more coke. Nobody'd want to be seen with 'em. Nobody'd buy from them. It was easier to be careful. So, the health people expect if this keeps up, AIDS among the junkies will drop, too. But that's not the real funny part." Doc finished his beer and leaned toward her conspiratorially. "The other state health departments are considering spreading the rumor in their states. They figure if they could keep it going, disease transmission would drop all over! Good idea, I think! Fool them all into stayin' healthy." A loud bell rang in the barn and he chuckled and got to his feet.

"Go get the phone, you sneaky old buzzard." Ella took a swipe at his baggy-pantsed rear as he shuffled off. But when she turned back to Shinohara, her smile was one of concern, her blue eyes twinkling.

"You have deep feelings for this Loudon fellow?"

Shinohara seemed to deflate.

"Ella, I never thought I'd say this, but I did. I think I still do. When we got together . . . there was just something about us . . . I think we need each other. But I can't . . . I can't even articulate it."

She was interrupted by a shout from Doc at the phone box outside the barn.

"Well, let's go see what the old man wants," said Ella, helping Shinohara up. They went outside into the bright sunlight to find Doc sitting on a small barrel with the portable phone in his hand, a strange look on his face. Shinohara had never seen anything like it. It was a mixture of awe and fright.

"Doc, what is it?" she asked.

He squinted up at her. "That was the lab. Lupo's at it again. Another outbreak of colored people.

"Where?"

"Denver."

"Really? Right here?"

"Yup."

"How many this time?"

Doc shook his head in wonder.

"Whole danged city."

CHAPTER 20

The six Huey helicopters skimmed in from the south, moving low and fast over the dry rolling hills, roaring toward Denver. They drifted very little in relation to one another as they sped, homing on their target like giant, purposeful metal hornets. Sitting next to the pilot, Loudon peered toward the horizon for the first glimpse of the city. Not yet. They'd passed over Colorado Springs, a wayward collection of sunbaked buildings, and he'd thought of Shinohara. But she was probably somewhere ahead. Near Denver, perhaps even in Denver. For that reason, too, all his thoughts now focused on the infected city. Was this an endgame for Lupo? Was this the killer virus he'd threatened to create? Was the epidemic meant to begin here? The worldwide pandemic Shinohara had warned about.

He scanned the landscape. The broad expanse of sky seemed to have been stretched tight behind the low Colorado mountains to hold it in place against the dry gusting winds that ruffled the grassland below. The sky was a God's-honest blue at the top, shading into a washed-out sand-blue farther down and finally a dull gray at the horizon. The shading was the first sign of the smog of Denver. In the distance to either side, he could see the wide horizontal mesas. Above them, as if echoing the horizontal theme, were flat frothy clouds, their bottoms so perfectly flat that they might have been resting on an invisible membrane. They were a dark gray-blue on the bottom, their tops a cotton-white reaching toward the sun.

Below the speeding Army helicopters, he could see the vegetation change from soft tan grass as they swooped into a valley to harsh scrub as they topped a mountain. There, the grass barely held its own amidst the jutting brown rocks. He saw cattle ranches pass beneath the helicopter, and in the distance, huge tan circles marking where center-post irrigation systems were used for farming.

The pilot nudged him in the shoulder and pointed ahead. Denver had come into view. Loudon shook his head in amazement. The whole city. How had Lupo done it? Denver was a huge urban sprawl, beginning with the flat expanse of houses ringing the city and working up to the skyscrapers of distant downtown—ghostly shimmering towers jutting through the gray smog. He spoke into the microphone over the engine noise.

"Tell the other units to land at the command post. Keep going. I want a look at Denver." The pilot nodded and spoke into the radio. They were following Highway 25, and at one of the main exits sat several large warehouses surrounded by a mass of camouflage-painted vehicles, tents, trailers and tankers. It was the command headquarters for the quarantine operation. The five other helicopters, carrying the newest contingent of FBI agents peeled away to land. They'd get a briefing on the situation from the agents already there.

The helicopter zoomed low over the roadblock, still clogged with lines of vehicles trying to enter or leave Denver. Even three days after the quarantine, with the media covering it to saturation, some people still hadn't gotten the word. Or maybe they had panicked into believing they could overcome the President's executive order. Nobody in or out.

The pilot yanked back on the collective and adjusted the cyclic in his other hand to launch the craft into a swooping climb. They wouldn't risk going low enough so that a random rising current might carry any airborne virus up to them.

Loudon made a circling motion with his finger.

"Let's come in from the east," he said into the microphone. The pilot obligingly banked right and brought the helicopter on a wide loop around the city. There were a couple of things out that way Loudon wanted to scout.

Shortly, the aircraft crossed an east-west freeway, and Loudon could see beyond it the mammoth complex of Denver International Airport. The gleaming white spires of the tent-like terminal jutted into the sky, reflecting the shapes of the Rocky Mountains to the west. Hundreds of airplanes crowded around the terminal like strange gleaming metal birds nestled against the structure for protection. The airport had been shut down cold since the quarantine.

The helicopter pilot nodded at the grounded aircraft.

"Screwed up air traffic all over the country," he said. "Talked to some of my buddies down there. It's a mess."

Loudon nodded as the pilot turned again and settled in for a straight run into the city. Out his window, Loudon could see the flat expanse of the former Rocky Mountain Arsenal, now largely a wildlife refuge, where once had stood rows of buildings for making and storing chemical weapons. They passed over the old Stapleton Airport, now a sprawling housing development.

Just ahead, having emerged from the smog, were the proud shimmering skyscrapers of downtown Denver. The pilot slowed the helicopter, easing it forward over the busy streets. Loudon took a pair of binoculars out of their case put them to his eyes and adjusted the focus.

"Find me some crowds," he said into the microphone, and the pilot nodded. Sure enough, as they came in over the gleaming gold dome of the capitol, through the clear window at his feet, he could see thick crowds covering its grounds. Here and there the flashing lights of squad cars added urgent punctuation to the scene. Loudon made a signal to circle, and the pilot neatly tweaked the controls to bring the craft into a tight sweep.

Loudon flipped his hand, and the pilot banked the craft sharply onto its side. Loudon was literally lying against the metal door, held in by his harness. He peered through the window of the Huey's door straight down to the ground a thousand feet below. He shifted his body and brought up the glasses. It was an amazing sight.

Below, thousands of people stood, sat and lay on the broad lawns of the statehouse. They wore the minimal clothing of a hot summer, exposing seeming acres of flesh of an amazing range of colors. He could make out myriad shades of red, orange, yellow, green, blue and purple. The colors seemed infinitely varied. Loudon imagined that if the citizenry of Denver were lined up in order of color, they would display a spectrum of imperceptibly changing shades running through the entire range of hues. The people milled around, apparently talking, holding up their arms to compare colors or listening to a speaker on the statehouse steps. Some saw the helicopter and waved. The pilot circled for a few minutes and at a sign from Loudon, started off down one of the avenues. Colored people gathered everywhere, as if the population had decided that they should display their amazing transformation to the world. Some wore bathing suits and sleeveless shirts and shorts. But there were also some trudging the hot streets in long robes and floppy hats—those who had decided that their new color was something to be ashamed of.

They continued to tour the city, and Loudon saw no sign of serious civil disorder or medical catastrophe—so far. Just more remarkably tinted people. He asked the pilot to head back to the command headquarters, and he complied, soaring above the sun-drenched city. After another ten minutes, the helicopter flared out and came in for a soft, dusty landing amidst another two dozen or so craft. Loudon climbed onto the skid and walked out into the crackling-dry desert wind. The other five agents who'd been in the passenger compartment climbed out with him, talking excitedly about the amazing sight. Walter was with them, and he looked worried.

"I didn't see any golf courses on the way in. Did you?" he asked, a bead of sweat rolling off his jowl. He insisted on wearing a long-sleeved shirt and suit.

"You've got an incredible one-track mind, Walter," Loudon teased.

"Well, this'll be over eventually, right? And we do need rest and recreation of some sort." Walter was unrepentant.

They started toward the warehouse, talking over what they had seen. Loudon breathed in the air and felt his nose and lungs desiccate. The unforgiving sun mercilessly heated the body and the dusty breeze thieved moisture from every inch of exposed skin. In the helicopter, he'd had his elbows bent, his arms becoming sticky with sweat. And when he unbent them, they began to dry, producing thin, brief crescents of cool on his arms.

They strode into the sprawling warehouse, where the air turned somewhat cooler, but more humid with the vapor of human occupation. An expanse of desks and equipment occupied roped-off areas that delineated the headquarters of the various agencies. Men and women in suits, uniforms of various shades and cool summer wear sat at the desks and crowded in knots, making plans, discussing, debating, watching large-screen map displays, talking on telephones. The echoing mix of voices, ringing telephones, radio transmissions, and humming office machines rose into the cavernous volume and blended into an undifferentiated amalgam of urgent sound that was swallowed up by the space above.

Loudon, Walter, and the newly arrived agents joined a small crowd watching a large bank of video screens, whose images competed for attention. The local stations had gone to twenty-four-hour coverage of the unbelievable transformation in their citizens. Colored anchors talked to colored reporters who interviewed colored police, government officials and ordinary citizens. And they all showed a mixture of awe, fear and a childish delight at this strange transformation. Other screens showed the network feeds, the anchors a more prosaic mix of flesh tones.

". . . and I'd like to emphasize that I've always represented all our voters, black, white, red and brown," a local ruby-red politician proclaimed dramatically on one channel. "Just because some of my constituents happen now to be blue, yellow, and green, doesn't mean they should be left out of the political process."

On another channel, a massive football player stood defiantly in a locker room, his eyes glowing as the microphone was held in his face. "Man, I'm Pepto pink and it just ticks me off!" he growled. "I go out there on the field, people gonna laugh. How'm I gonna do my commercials?"

Another channel: ". . . well, it'll make perpetrators easier to identify, I guess," said a beefy, plum-colored man into a bank of microphones. He wore a detective's badge on his pocket. "I mean, now we've got another point of distinction. But we still need to get a standard color description of some kind. Like, I think I'm some kind of purple, but I don't know what."

Another screen showed a delicate young man standing beside a beauty salon chair. "I'm just freaked, y'know. I mean really, really freaked," he said breathlessly, his eyes wide, waving a comb. "But I'm jazzed, too, y'know? Goodness, I mean it's just such a challenge now for a colorist to take all these people of hue . . . I mean there are soooo many . . . and come up with color-coordinated makeup and hair ensembles. I just feel absolutely faint, I must say." He fanned himself, but recovered, though, and added perkily, "But at least I'm gorgeous!" He waved his hands in flamboyant delight. "I mean look at me . . . goodness . . . sunflower yellow! I'm stunning!"

Yet another channel: A clearly unhappy emerald-colored man stared balefully into the camera. "Don't mean a thing to me," he said morosely. "Everybody still looks the same gray to me. I been color blind all my life, I ain't cared. But this is the one time I really miss it. Yeah, I really miss it."

Sitting before the monitors in the cavernous warehouse, watching and taking notes, were representatives of all the government agencies. They would report any significant developments to their supervisors. Two of the people taking notes wore gold FBI badges.

Walter looked troubled as he stared at the screens. "Lorna told me not to come home if I turn color." He looked over at Loudon, remembering. "Actually, she said maybe a dark green would be nice. She likes dark green."

"You're a lucky man to have a wife so understanding, Walter," said Loudon. The televised stories were fascinating, but he decided they'd better get on with his business. He motioned to the others to follow, and they found their way to the roped-off section that marked the FBI command post. The other agents who had arrived from California a day before were already at desks, hard at their assignments. Walter took the group that had come in his helicopter to join them. Over a thousand agents had flown in from all over the country, and they were spread out in smaller command posts ringing the city. The AD in Washington, Lucas White, had flown out to manage the command posts, although Loudon had been assured he was still lead case agent. He found White bent over a red secure phone to the director's office.

"I understand. Yessir. I understand absolutely. We are on it, sir. Goodbye." He hung up, looked up at Loudon without the usual greeting smile. Loudon wondered whether Bowers had warned White about him; that he was a goof-off, not a by-the-book Bureau man. That he had pulled a gun on Bowers.

"You're late." The edge in White's voice hinted that such a warning had been made.

"We had air traffic getting out of Albuquerque. And I wanted to scout the city."

"The Bureau has people to do that. Anyway, sit down. Let me brief you. We have our marching orders."

Loudon sat, and the same young lady he'd seen in Washington brought White a cup of coffee. She took a seat behind him, waiting for instructions.

White sipped the coffee and nodded at the assistant that it had passed muster. "The director agrees you'll remain on the field investigation. I'll organize the headquarters investigative system here."

"But you'll make sure everybody understands I have authority for the field investigation?"

"For now, you do." said White tersely, avoiding his gaze and concentrating on precisely stacking color-coded folders into a pile.

"What does that mean."

"It means what I said."

Loudon decided to let the matter ride, let the tension take a back seat to the investigation. "So, tell me what the status is."

White seemed to go along with their unspoken truce. "Well, at the moment, we can't actually go into the city . . . the virus and all . . . but of course, we're represented. The Denver office was infected, so they're shouldering the burden until we get in. They're working with the Denver police to check hotels, motels, and so forth for somebody fitting Lupo's description." He waved a large, bony hand at a bank of twenty or so desks with agents hunched over telephones. Loudon smiled to himself, as he realized that the hawknosed White reminded him of Ichabod Crane. "We're also going through credit card slips, phone records, and so forth, to see if he left any tracks."

"Anything yet?"

"No, nothing of note. Not yet. These other agents . . ." He waved his other hand at another array of agents bent over their desks. ". . . are checking airline records for about the last two weeks. They're trying to track down everybody who's gone out of Denver International. They're calling the people and local medical authorities to try to get them into quarantine, or at least under medical care."

"Good Lord, that's impossible. There must be hundreds of thousands of people!"

"Well, it's our duty. So it will be done." White's Adam's apple bobbed in agitation, as if it was trying to force words from him that he wanted to keep down. "The director has ordered us to help the CDC try and stop the spread. Or at least track it, so we can understand it. We've got all the other field offices around the country on it, too. We're handling mainly international through our legal attaches. We get the names and addresses to the foreign police, and they work with their health departments."

Loudon shook his head in undisguised irritation. "And what does the CDC say about the virus itself? Does it say all that's going to do any good?"

"Well, you'll have to ask their liaison, once the data have been made official." White loved official channels, thought Loudon, loved relying on them so that his butt was safely protected. "It's only been a couple of days. They're still not sure whether it's airborne or maybe in the water. And they're not even sure if it's benign. The color change could be followed by illness or death. That's what your source says, isn't it?"

"Yes." Loudon remembered the strange meeting with Gaines. Was Gaines reliable? Probably. "He said that was the aim of the people who wanted to use Lupo's work."

"Anyway, the CDC teams are in the field now. We're planning a combined briefing when they get back."

"Fine," said Loudon. "Until then, I'll call the Denver office and get situated here. After the briefing, I'll need a strategy meeting with all the field agents who will go into Denver when we can get in."

White called over his shoulder to the assistant, "See whether that's possible." He turned back to Loudon. "We'll check the schedules and get back to you."

Loudon let the petty display of authority slide again. He asked for a desk, and White had his assistant show him to one with a phone. He called the Denver field office on a private line. The public lines were swamped.

"Agent Scalisi," said a voice with a New York accent. Loudon had talked to Jack Scalisi before, when the infection was first discovered.

"Jack, this is Bobby Loudon. I'm at the main command post now. How're things going?"

"Well, fine, considering that I turned since we last talked. Scared me. Just over a few hours. Sue turned, too. And the kids."

"But you're all okay?"

"Sure, yeah. So's the family. Sue just sat there in front of the mirror and cried for a while. But it doesn't feel like you're different, except when you look in the mirror or suddenly see your hand. After they got used to it, the kids went all over the neighborhood, seeing what everybody else looked like. They think it's some kind of Halloween."

"What colors are you?" Loudon wasn't sure about the etiquette of asking, but he did anyway.

"Well, Sue got out one of her decorating books. She wanted to know exactly. She says I'm mint green. She's aquamarine. One of the kids is apricot, the other is midnight blue. She says we color-match okay. Actually, we're lucky. One of our neighbors came out kind of mud-colored."

"Poor guy. But you're holding up?"

"Well, they're doing better than me. Of course, I know about Lupo's message . . . the possible, uh, endpoint. Didn't tell them, of course."

"Yeah, well, there's no sign of that at all," said Loudon reassuringly. "Anything on Lupo?"

"Not a trace. I'm the only one here. Everybody else is out checking leads. His face is all over town . . . on TV . . . the papers . . . we'll find out if he was here. You think he still might be?"

"Well, our theory is that he's close by, but I'm sure he wouldn't expose himself to the virus, even to gather data. I don't think he's actually in the city."

"Good, 'cause if some of these people caught him, they'd whip him good."

"I'll be here for a while. There's a briefing later today of all the agencies. I'll have one of the agents make sure you're tapped in."

He wished Scalisi good luck and hung up. He decided to take a look at the roadblock and used one of the Bureau cars to drive down the side road to the freeway interchange. He maneuvered around large tanks baking in the sun and passed trucks shuttling soldiers to and from the checkpoint. Donning his sunglasses against the glare, he parked the car along a frontage road and hiked across the dry grass to the checkpoint. Long lines of cars and trucks stretched to the shimmering horizons in both directions, with drivers standing outside their vehicles, their smoldering anger made worse by the desert heat.

He introduced himself to the army sergeant in charge of the road-block. The sergeant stood in a large canopy shelter just off the side of the freeway leading into the city, a clipboard in his hand. The canopy stood next to a larger tent back from the road, where soldiers sat cooling off from their duties on the roadblock. The sergeant consulted the clipboard and bellowed a list of last names. Young soldiers appeared from the larger tent, pulling on heavy anti-chemical warfare suits and carrying their hoods with them.

"How's it going?" he asked, showing his credentials.

The sergeant looked them over and went back to his clipboard. "It's slow, and it's a twenty-four-hour-a-day job, but we're keeping the city supplied." He slapped the clipboard on a folding table. "You FBI guys got any idea how long this is gonna go on?"

"Depends on the CDC," said Loudon, thinking again of Shinohara. "They've got to tell us how the disease is transmitted—"

"And whether it's a killer, right?"

"Well, we don't know that."

"Don't lie to me, agent. We all know these people might start droppin' dead any minute. It's all over the unit."

"Well, keep it in the unit. If it gets back to the city, there'll be panic."

"Yeah, I know. But you better move fast. There's media all over out here. A reporter was here not fifteen minutes ago."

They stood for a while and watched the roadblock procedure. An incoming tractor trailer inched into position by the roadblock, and the driver slid out of the seat, talking briefly to a soldier in a bulky isolation suit. The soldier pulled his man-from-Mars rubberized canvas hood over his head and sealed himself into the suit. Peering through the bug-eyed goggles of the hood, he climbed awkwardly into the truck cab and slipped the vehicle into gear. The truck accelerated ponderously down the highway toward Denver. Loudon took the sergeant's field glasses to watch the exchange. The soldier pulled up to a stretch of empty road and got out of the truck. He crossed the freeway to the other side and immediately climbed into another one leaving Denver. Meanwhile, a driver from Denver, colored a shade of green as far as Loudon could make out, came out of a distant shelter and climbed into the inbound truck. The truck quickly accelerated down the highway toward the distant city.

"My men are getting tired in this heat," said the sergeant, wiping his brow and looking at the traffic. "I sure hope the science types settle this soon."

"Yeah, I'm sure they will," said Loudon, as the truck from Denver pulled up to the disinfecting station. The soldier climbed wearily out and was doused with disinfectant, as was the interior of the cab. Three soldiers in isolation suits then began to inspect the truck. As they raised the rear door, a stowaway, a panicked young man in dirty jeans and a torn shirt, suddenly leaped out of the back. He sprinted across the highway and tumbled into a drainage ditch. He quickly hauled himself up and ran for a distant clump of trees waving gently in the hot breeze.

"RUNNER!" shouted several of the soldiers, their hoods muffling the cry.

"Stop or we'll shoot!" yelled another, but the young man kept running, his tattered shirt flapping around his waist.

The sergeant calmly raised a walkie talkie to his mouth.

"This is Checkpoint Alpha to Bird Tango. Runner just west of Highway twenty five, Checkpoint Alpha. Please intercept." A burst of static and a garbled voice told him the message had been received. After a minute, a Huey helicopter roared over the position. Using the glasses, Loudon could see the helicopter swoop in low over the man, who zigzagged vainly to escape. A marksman leaned out of the side of the helicopter, aiming his rifle. There was the distant pop of a gun heard over the helicopter, and the man collapsed in a dusty heap. A Humvee with three isolation-garbed soldiers sped away to collect the fallen fugitive.

"You're not shooting them, are you?" asked Loudon.

"Not bullets. Tranquilizer darts. He'll be out a few hours. We'll turn him over to the Denver medical people at the check point. He'll be fine." The sergeant leaned over and took a pack of cigarettes out of his jacket draped over a chair in the shelter. He offered Loudon one, which Loudon declined. He lit up and sat heavily down on the chair.

"We get about a couple of dozen runners a day," said the sergeant, drawing deeply on the cigarette and blowing the smoke out the shelter. "A lot are whiteys."

"Whiteys?"

"Yeah, people who haven't turned color. Guess they're tryin' to escape. But some of them are coloreds. Can't figure out where they think *they're* goin'. They're already colored."

Loudon wiped his brow with his sleeve. "Believe me, there's a lot we don't understand here."

Chapter 21

"This is stunning . . . just amazing," said Shinohara in quiet wonder. Assenting murmurs came from the other three passengers. But their eyes remained glued to the bulletproof slitted ports, as the armored personnel carrier rumbled through the streets of Denver.

For the past hour the CDC epidemiologists had cruised through downtown, scanning the crowds, searching for clues to the virus's behavior. The incredible variety of colors made it seem as if a thousand new human species had suddenly arrived on the planet. The people displayed a vast range of subtle blues, from the lightest most delicate blue tinge, to the richest blue-black. They also showed a multitude of flamboyant oranges and glorious reds. And cool, lush greens and bright sunny yellows. The milling crowds presented a fleshy kaleidoscope of colored legs, arms, feet, calves, hands, necks, toes, faces, ankles, backs, knees.

A golden-amber toddler waddled along, oblivious to his color, beside his gawking parents. A pod of awkward teenagers hung out in the shade of a tree, eyeing each other timidly. Handsome body-proud young men and women strolled and lounged, basking in the vigorous luster of newly colored youth. Old men and women who thought they'd seen everything watched the brilliant procession in delighted amazement.

And the CDC team almost voyeuristically scrutinized the people on parade.

"Look how different the shades are over the body, from the darker areas of the arms, to the paler hues of the legs." Doc bent to his clipboard, recording data on the patterns of color on people and the distribution of colors among them. He was trying to discern some pattern. It was a frustrating task.

"Look at that blue on the right," Shinohara exclaimed.

Lou Martinez, another CDC investigator, pressed his face close to the slit. "See that sort of bright red. Is that cherry? Wow!" The burly man grinned, his Zapata moustache curling up at the ends.

"I didn't know there were so many greens," said the fourth CDC investigator, Lisa Klinger.

Doc made another note in his book. "Seems like their colors are affecting their behavior." He noted that a man whose tint was especially handsome might strut down the street, flaunting his hue. Another, more drably colored, might walk hugging the wall in embarrassment.

Both sexes were acutely interested in women's colors. Women would stop one another to comment on their skin, to compare, and to discuss clothes and makeup. Their brows would wrinkle in concentration as they intently discussed whether their clothes matched their skin. It was the dawn of a new era of fashion, and they were the vanguard.

And groups of men lounged in the parks watching the passing parade of women, clearly debating the aesthetic allure of one color or another.

Some of the more outgoing people showed little shyness about contact. It seemed important, not just to witness the colored flesh, but to pat it, rub it, feel its warmth—as if the color was a tactile experience. Strangers would stop one another to admiringly touch an arm or grasp a hand.

Still others made it clear they were there only to look, shrinking away when approached, unsure of the effect of touching a strangely colored skin or being touched by it.

As the armored carrier moved along the traffic-clogged streets, the four passengers felt like submariners confined in their steel vessel witnessing a gaudy parade of tropical fish outside. They longed to jump out of the confining vehicle, to mingle with the crowds, to touch for themselves the fascinating newly colored skin. But they also knew that touch might be deadly. That exquisitely hued skin might represent the beautiful prelude to a gruesome death triggered by some genetic timing mechanism crafted by Arthur Lupo for his virus.

The passage of the personnel carrier would inevitably bring stares, some merely curious, some hostile.

"Wish we didn't have to go through town like this . . ." complained Shinohara. ". . . in this ugly war machine."

"I know," said Doc. "I feel like an invading army. But unfortunately Chevy doesn't build any nice vans with anti-biowarfare features. At least we nixed the idea of a bunch of soldiers going along."

"Yeah, that would have really given the wrong impression."

Now they were cruising ponderously down Colfax Avenue. It was a long sunbaked boulevard lined with a tacky hodge-podge of nondescript pizza parlors, bars, ethnic restaurants, gas stations, and pawn shops. Strollers and loungers-in-the-shade dotted its length.

"I just hope we don't freak people out, when we come out of this thing in our suits," said Martinez.

"Hold up! Hold up!" exclaimed Lisa, peering out one of the ports. "Asymptomatic! We got an asymptomatic!" Doc radioed the driver, sealed inside his cab, to stop the carrier. Lisa unfolded her lanky frame, flipping back her long brown hair and moved so that Doc could peer out.

"Yup, we got one! Seal up." They checked their Racal isolation suits, pulled the fabric helmets over their heads and sealed themselves in. The whine of four air filter motors arose serially like the voices of an electric choir, filling the interior of the vehicle. Martinez unlatched the large steel doors in the back, swung them open and pulled himself out. Shinohara followed, but Doc and Lisa stayed inside, not wanting to overwhelm their quarry. The heated air of the Denver summer flowed into the air conditioned interior of the vehicle, immediately heating the suits. The suit filters immediately sucked the sunbaked air into the suits, transforming them into stifling furnaces. The sweating wearers wanted to tear them off, to run free and cool from the suits' hot claustrophobia.

A knot of people stood on the sidewalk, curiously eyeing the formidable army-green vehicle. A pot-bellied burgundy-colored man stood with one arm around a brick-red middle-aged woman. Beside them stood a robin's-egg-blue boy, a mandarin-orange girl and a cranberry boy. But what really attracted the investigators was a young woman standing slightly apart from the group. She was slim with fine features, and long reddish brown hair. She was flesh-colored.

At the sight of the isolation suits, the people backed away a step, curious but intimidated. Shinohara took the lead, but Martinez was available if protection was needed.

"Don't be frightened," she said, holding out her gloved hands. "We're doctors from the government. We're here trying to figure out what's causing the colors."

"Are we going to be sick?" said the middle-aged woman, her lip trembling.

"No, no, not at all." She turned to the young woman. "But we see that you haven't turned color. Could we talk to you, interview you, test you, to find out why?"

The young woman looked at the people around her for advice. She shook her head shyly. "No, no, I don't want to. I'm freaked enough as it is. I don't want to get poked at."

"Please." Shinohara smiled and raised her eyebrows. A drop of perspiration rolled down her temple. "You could help a lot of people."

"Hey, listen," said the burgundy man, stepping in front of the young woman. "If my sister says she doesn't want to be poked at, she doesn't have to. Word is, you government people had something to do with this in the first place. You're doin' some kinda experiment."

Martinez moved to protect Shinohara, but she motioned for him to stay back. "We didn't, I promise. We don't know what it is. But I understand what you're going through. I've seen it in California. I was there. I can help you understand it. Just help us."

The young woman looked confused. She tugged at the burgundy man's sleeve and whispered something to him.

The burgundy man was slightly less hostile. "How long you want her for?"

"Just a few hours," said Shinohara. "Look, tell you what. She doesn't have to come with us. If she wants, she can just come down to the hospital. You can all come. There'll be other people like her."

"Sure, okay, we'll come down," the young woman nodded at the others, signifying her cooperation. "I'll help."

"Great! We really appreciate it." Shinohara took the woman's name and gave her directions to Denver General, where uninfected people were being tested. Martinez opened the door to the APC and he and Shinohara climbed back in, doused themselves with disinfectant and turned on the exhaust fans until the air was free of the smell. Then they cranked the air conditioning up full blast, unzipped their helmets and let the cool air play on their sweat-drenched faces.

The personnel carrier gunned its huge diesel engine and accelerated down Colfax toward the capitol.

Doc consulted his notebook. "That's six asymptomatics so far today. Total of twenty-three around the city. I think we've got a start." They were updating their notes when a loud clang reverberated against the side of the vehicle.

"What's this mess?" Doc moved to peer out of the front periscope. "We're coming to a crowd," he said without looking away. "Nasty crowd." He radioed the driver and listened for a moment on the headphones. "He says we're at the federal building. It's an anti-government demonstration. Nasty. They think the feds released the virus, or it was a biowarfare disaster at Rocky Flats. He says he can get through it, though."

Out the ports, they could see the vehicle surrounded by a multicolored sea of people, their faces distorted with anger and fear. Their white teeth contrasted with the colored skins as they shouted and launched obscenities at the carrier. Many waved placards and some carried baseball bats and rocks. A fusillade of clunks and clangs resounded against the carrier's steel walls, as the crowd pounded on it in rage. The carrier moved slowly through the crowd.

"We're just fine in here," said Martinez, patting Klinger's shoulder.

"Wait a minute!" said Shinohara looking out the left-side port. "There's a person down. On the sidewalk. Collapsed."

"Any visible injuries?" asked Doc. "Wounds from rocks?" Shinohara strained to see through the crowd.

"No. Somebody's with her. They're holding her head. No blood. She's a blue color, so I can't tell whether she's pale."

"Endpoint?" asked Lisa, her eyes showing her fear.

"We've got to find out," said Doc. "Maybe its the beginning of the virus endpoint."

Martinez said, "I'm not real pleased about going out there."

"Well, we've got to," said Doc grimly. "Seal up. We'll go in force. Maybe we'll intimidate them."

Lisa looked dubious. "I don't feel intimidating."

"Sure you are," said Doc, patting her reassuringly. "You're scary." She smiled and sealed her helmet.

They switched on their filters, and Martinez opened the doors and jumped out. The crowd shrank back, but there were shouts of protest. The other three followed and stood beside him.

"You . . . !" shouted a tomato-red man. "You caused this!" He brandished a baseball bat. An aqua woman screamed an epithet and waved a sign.

"We're not army. We're doctors!" shouted Doc. "We're from the Centers for Disease Control. We're here to figure this out."

"My purple butt!" shouted a royal-purple man, moving toward Doc menacingly. "You're tryin' to kill us. Why don't you come out of those suits and catch it like us!" The mob surged forward, two men reaching for Doc, and Martinez stepped in front of him. They backed up against the carrier. A rock ricocheted off its side near Doc's head. Abruptly, the carrier turret whined to life, rotating to bring its 7.62-mm machine gun and 25-mm cannon to bear on the crowd. Staring down the two guns' barrels, the crowd paused in its advance. The gunner in the turret had decided enough was enough.

"We want to help that woman!" shouted Shinohara, pointing to the sidewalk. The people turned their attention to the royal-blue woman lying on the sidewalk, another forest-green woman holding her head. "Will you let us help her? Or do you want to just let her remain sick?"

"Is it the virus? Is she dying from the virus?" screamed the forest green woman. "Is she dying? Please help her!"

"Let us help her. Then we'll know."

The crowd backed off slightly, none of them wanting to face the guns or be responsible for a woman's death. Shinohara seized the moment and waded into the crowd. Doc followed, while Martinez guarded their back and Lisa made sure the doors were ready to be shut.

Shinohara bent down and peered through her faceplate at the woman. She reported to Doc, standing over her: "Her breathing is shallow, but clear. Her pulse is racing. And her skin is warm, but dry. There's no bleeding anywhere. No mucus."

"Let's take her in for observation," said Doc. Shinohara stood up and motioned for Martinez to carry the woman, and he bent down and easily lifted her up. Shinohara leaned her helmet against Doc's. "We'd better nip any rumors in the bud."

She turned to the crowd. "This woman has heat prostration," she said loudly to penetrate the helmet and the noise of her air pump.

"Lies!" shouted an azure man, but the rest of the crowd was listening.

"Look," said Shinohara motioning for Martinez to come forward with the unconscious woman. "She has no fever. She has no signs of a virus, like blood or sputum. She just collapsed from the heat. Do you all understand? From the heat. We're going to take her into the hospital for observation. Her friend can come, too. She'll be back soon." Shinohara and Martinez moved toward the carrier, followed by the forest-green woman. But Doc stayed behind.

"Listen, instead of going off half cocked, you can help us find Arthur Lupo," he said. "You've all seen his picture on TV, in the papers. He's the one who did this, not the government. Go find him." A few in the crowd protested, but the events had clearly taken the fight out of them. Doc made his way through them to the carrier and climbed in. Lisa followed and swung the doors shut, latching them. They heard the whine of the gun turret swinging back into place, and the carrier eased off toward the hospital. The four were sweating profusely, but because of the two passengers, they had to keep their helmets on inside the carrier. Shinohara applied wet cloths to the unconscious woman's blue face, arms and legs. The woman moaned softly. She seemed to be coming around. She took sips of water and began to revive.

Soon they reached the hospital, a modern glass and concrete building that was alive with activity. Television crews and newspaper reporters haunted the halls, interviewing doctors, nurses and patients. Two of the television reporters compared skin tones while they waited.

"Well, I'm thinking of adding a little light makeup, so it comes across better on camera," said a young man, holding up a slate-blue arm.

"Jeez, I don't know what I'm going to do," said a worried, well-groomed lemon-yellow woman, examining her own arm. "In the studio, when they light me right, the anchors are too dark. One's purple. I might get canned because of my skin. Can they do that?"

Along both sides of one hall sat rows of flesh-colored asymptomatics, nervously waiting to be interviewed about their strange "affliction," or rather lack thereof. They held the key to the virus.

The CDC team helped the woman into the emergency room. There, doctors and nurses coped with the usual collection of wounds, illnesses and complaints, except that the patients were many-colored. Doc talked to the resident in charge, who said that the only real medical indication of the change had been a few cases of hysteria.

He reported one related trauma case, though, pointing to a lavender man sitting on a gurney, his broken nose bandaged. His son had turned nearly the orange color of the next door neighbor, and he'd accused his wife of being unfaithful. The neighbor, a much larger man, had explained calmly that the colors seemed to be totally random. But when the irate husband had taken a garden rake after him, he'd settled the matter with a solid punch to the face. The husband sat nursing his nose, convinced now that the colors were random.

Several other CDC teams arrived dressed in isolation suits, bringing in asymptomatics or dropping off blood and tissue samples. A Denver CDC epidemiologist, who had herself turned rose red, gathered them at a nurses' station for a briefing. The group resembled a convention of aliens standing about in their isolation garb, their filter motors humming in dissonant unison.

"I want to show you our experiment," said the rose epidemiologist. She appeared to be in her thirties with short brown hair, although with the colored face, age was difficult to tell. She led them to two large wards that held people who had become infected late. Wearing short hospital gowns, they were filing one by one into a side room, where flashes of light marked the taking of photographs.

"This is probably the most incredible sight you'll ever see as epidemiologists," said the rose-red doctor. "We're on a schedule of taking pictures of each patient from all sides."

"So you can watch the change?" asked one of the CDC epidemiologists, his voice muffled by his helmet.

"Yes. These folks volunteered to let us watch them change. For the first time in history, we can follow how a virus infects the body. Watch this." She stepped to a computer terminal and pressed a few keys. On a large-screen monitor appeared a succession of images of men and women, young and old, boys and girls and babies. Frontal, side and back views revealed them to be in various stages of coloration. Their bodies were variously mottled—some almost entirely colored, others with large areas of flesh tones. They were like exotic birds exhibiting intricate patterns of subtly shaded plumage.

"Here's a live shot," said the doctor, tapping a key. A video image appeared of the photography room, where a white-coated Bordeaux-red doctor was taking pictures of a middle-aged man standing against a white sheet, which showed off the sea-green blotches on his body. The doctor directed him to position his body within an outline painted on the sheet.

"Ready?" asked the Bordeaux-red doctor. She pressed a button, unleashing a brilliant flash of strobe light. "Thank, you," she said to the man. "Now left side, remember your position." The patient turned obligingly to show his left side, his plump belly in full relief. The doctor pressed the button again, and repeated the procedure for the patient's right side and back. The man's back showed an almost pure sea-green.

"You do this how often?" asked Shinohara.

"Every fifteen minutes for each patient," said the rose-red doctor, tapping a key to turn off the video feed. "They're very cooperative. We can actually see what parts of the body turn first, and the evolution to the final color. It's really stunning. Watch." She tapped in a few commands. A frozen image of a young man came on the screen, every part of his body brightly lit by the flash.

"Watch this," she said. "Here's many hours of change compressed down to about a minute." She hit the Enter key and the young man's form seemed to blur and vibrate as the frames sped by. His arms jiggled about slightly, and his positions at various times were slightly different. His body at first showed the usual flesh color, but a blue tint quickly crept into his arms and legs, traveling to his trunk, as if he were made of blotting paper, soaking up the color from his extremities. Separate shadings of other colors also spread over his skin, blending with the original blue, until his whole body finally settled into a rich amethyst.

The isolation-suited epidemiologists shook their heads in amazement as the rose-red doctor proceeded to show the change in other patients. They watched in awe as the myriad shades of red, green, blue and yellow extended over the bodies of the patients like dawn over an early-morning landscape. She ended with a view of eight patients, each in a separate window of the screen.

"We've got twenty-three so far, and there are more coming. With luck, this may give us some clues about how to fight this virus. In fact, we might even learn something about viruses in general."

"How about the newborns? Are the newborn babies changing?" asked a muffled voice.

"Good question. We've had about five births. The babies are normal colored, and we've taken blood samples to see if the virus crossed the placental barrier."

"So it's not inherited?"

"Didn't say that. These babies were conceived before the virus came, so it wouldn't be inherited in their genes. But they might catch it from their mother and turn later."

Shinohara peered at the video screen, deep in thought. "It's a DNA virus. It could insinuate itself into the sperm and egg DNA. Then it would be inherited. But we don't know that yet. We don't know whether Arthur Lupo engineered it that way."

The group excitedly discussed the possibilities, and Doc and Shinohara took notes for the briefing later. Then Doc collected several large cases with blood and tissue samples to be sent back to Atlanta.

The CDC crew stuffed themselves back into the APC and took a last run through Larimer Square, where brightly colored singles lounged in the sidewalk cafes, no doubt pondering how this new development would affect their social lives. The personnel carrier then lumbered along the quiet streets of large, old mansions near the Denver Country Club. Only multihued gardeners were to be seen. The residents, as always, were keeping their lives private from one another.

Finally, the massive six-wheeled vehicle roared onto the freeway toward the command headquarters. There, the group would contribute its discoveries to the mass of data that might solve the mystery.

CHAPTER 22

L oudon stood in the shade, leaning against the hot metal of an armored personnel carrier, waiting for her. He'd checked with the CDC officials in the warehouse, and they said she and Doc would be coming in soon. So he waited patiently where the vehicles were parked. Two other CDC teams came in before the one he was interested in. So he knew the arrival procedure to expect. And even amidst the dusty traffic of waves of cars, trucks and personnel carriers, he could sense when the vehicle carrying Shinohara finally rumbled into view.

First the carrier stopped at a disinfecting station a distance from the warehouse, and four CDC epidemiologists climbed out. A pit crew doused the vehicle inside and out with disinfectant, including the occupants. The spray of greenish liquid sent a mist into the air that floated out into the desert before evaporating. The scientists then stripped out of their suits. Even at a distance, Loudon enjoyed the familiar thrill when he saw her emerge from the suit, her slim body shedding the bulky covering. He recalled the day he had first seen her, a butterfly emerging from a cocoon. The four then stepped into portable showers and washed and shampooed, putting on white coveralls. He watched Doc head off for a waiting helicopter, to drop off cases of blood and tissue samples. She walked toward him in her coveralls and sneakers, her hair still shiny and wet, thirstily drinking from a bottle of water. A few drops fell from her chin or made their way down her brown throat.

He stepped out of the shade to greet her, trying to look nonchalant. When she saw him, she tried to look nonchalant. Neither really succeeded.

"Hello, Kathleen, it's good to see you."

"Robert." She avoided his gaze. He just knew it was because she had missed him terribly.

"Can we talk? Please?"

"Well . . . we can't now. We have the briefing."

"When?"

"There's just too much now. Too much."

He touched her arm and she slowed slightly in her stride. "Kathleen, I love you." She stopped.

"Too much now," she mumbled. "I can't . . ."

He saw she was uncomfortable and backed off. "Okay, later. But sometime."

"Sure." He decided just to let the fact of his presence sink in. So they simply walked together into the huge warehouse and into a walled-off section guarded by soldiers. Television cameras and reporters were kept away, directed to another building for their news briefing immediately after the restricted one for the government teams.

There was an awkward moment as Loudon and Shinohara entered, when they were deciding whether to separate and sit with their respective organizations.

Loudon overcame it in his usual way. "Sit with me or I'll go berserk," he whispered. "Right here. I swear. I've got a gun. I'll whip it out and shoot the place up."

Shinohara shook her head in annoyance, but still unable to hide the touch of amusement. She sat down next to him. They both felt vestiges of the familiar bond between them, but they said little as the room filled with people, mostly uniformed. Loudon recognized representatives of the Army, National Guard, CDC, FBI, state police, state health department, the Federal Emergency Management Agency, and Homeland Security. A row of stone-faced men in dark suits sat quietly in the back. Loudon knew they represented organizations that would rather not be identified. Over the phones, the Denver police were listening in, as was the Denver FBI field office. Loudon scanned the group again. One of these people was also probably a mole from the faction that had triggered it all—the people who had tried to turn Lupo to their use and then tried to kill him to keep him quiet. But where?

He took out his tablet computer and began to record his observations. Bowers would want a thorough report. The LA ADC had insisted that he was still to be thoroughly briefed on the case, given that he'd contributed Loudon and dozens of his own agents to it. So, Loudon had resigned himself to calling Bowers daily with reports.

He was distracted from his typing by a pat on his back and looked over his shoulder to see Doc settle into a seat behind him. They shook hands warmly. A voice boomed over the speaker system.

"I'm John Craig, the CDC AD from DC," said the deep voice. Craig chuckled at himself. He stood comfortably at the lectern, his white shirt contrasting with his rich dark brown face and arms. He took out a large white handkerchief, which he ran over his balding head. "I expect with all us Feds you'll hear a lot of this acronym nonsense." There were laughs from the audience. "I'm running the CDC field headquarters here. The chief field epidemiologists are also with us. They're the ones who've followed the case from the beginning." He introduced Shinohara and Doc, who stood up. "They and the other field people have spent a lot of time in the city, and they're the best source of information about what's going on in there. You'll be able to ask them questions later." Craig paused, scanning the audience.

"Okay, let's take the big questions first," he continued. "Is it contagious? Is it dangerous? The answer so far to both questions is no. We've been monitoring the FBI Orion crisis management system. Our people around the country have fed information into it. They're tracking what happens to the infected people who left Denver and contacted other people. We see no evidence of secondary infections so far. And we see no mortality. Your teams didn't see any, right, Dr. Shinohara? Dr. Smith?" Shinohara and Doc both shook their heads.

A relieved murmur went through the audience. Craig waved his hands. "Now we can hope it holds, but we don't know what the incubation time is for this bug. It's brand new, thanks to Mr. Arthur Lupo. Next question," he said, scanning the sea of expectant faces. "How's it transmitted? Right now, we're leaning toward ingestion. Airborne would mean a whole squadron of planes or helicopters would have flown over the city. That didn't happen. So, maybe food or the water supply. Water supply is the most obvious, but it would be real hard to accomplish. We're looking into that now, as best we can."

In the audience, the beefy colonel in charge of the army detachments stood up. "Look, my men are standin' out there in the heat, sweatin' in those CBW suits. And they're havin' to drive trucks back and forth and chase down runners and dart them. As far as I'm concerned 'as best we can' ain't good enough."

"Look, colonel, we've got to do this very carefully. We don't—"

"Fine, sir, that's just fine," interrupted the colonel leaning back his head and looking down his nose at Craig. "But you boys had better be real quick about bein' careful. I want to get my men out of those suits. And I want to set up in the city where we can do our jobs."

"Colonel, you'll be there soon, but not one bit sooner than we say you can," shot back Craig. "This bug turns deadly, and your men will have the biggest health disaster ever to deal with. We get a pandemic and we're done for. Sitting outside of town here on road blocks will seem like a picnic. We want to protect them, too." He stared pointedly at the colonel for a moment, then proceeded with his briefing, explaining the current status of the CDC's investigation. After he'd finished, he asked for questions.

"Why Denver?" came a voice from the back.

"Good question," said Craig. "We think we've got some answers. Looks to us like he wanted to test a new virus that he could make to express three tox-genes. Sorry . . . let me explain tox-genes. They're the genes in deadly viruses that make them deadly. In the last briefing, I told you about what the combined symptoms of Ebola, Dengue, and influenza are. Fever, chills, strangulation, skin ulcers, pneumonia, bleeding, vomiting, death. Imagine all three viruses in one. It would be the meanest . . . microbe that ever hit the human race. Anyway, looks like he's using his chromophore system to test it."

"Tell 'em about the difference in the bug," prompted Doc.

"Right. This is a new virus. Atlanta's just told me Lupo's gone from vaccinia to an adenovirus as the carrier. It's a virus that could be made to be airborne, although this one doesn't appear to be. Adenoviruses are pretty benign viruses normally. About the most they cause is mild respiratory infection. A lot of them live permanently in the body, we don't even know it. They're pretty sophisticated viruses, though, so they're perfect for his use."

"Yeah, so why Denver?" asked the voice again.

"Right . . . anyway, Denver's a good place," continued Craig. "It's big and it's isolated. He could see how his new virus infected people, and he could also see how people leaving the city took it with them."

"You get a lot of spread?" asked one of the dark-suited men at the back of the room.

"Yeah, real big," said Craig, shaking his head slowly. "We've had a good look at the spread around the country, around the world. It's all over. It's pretty clear that even a geographically isolated city like Denver has so much air traffic that a virus would spread worldwide almost instantly. We'd always suspected it, now we know it. Now Lupo knows it. It means he can pick a few cities, release a highly infectious airborne virus, and watch it spread worldwide. The human race is basically doomed if he does what he says he's going to do."

White, who had been sitting in the front row, stood up.

"I'm White, FBI." He was unaware of the inadvertent joke he had made, given that Craig was black. "I think we can add to the question of why he chose Denver. Special Agent Loudon is the case agent. He and I have been talking about it. Bob, can you shed some light?"

"Sure," said Loudon, making his way to the front. He stood easily, glancing periodically back at Shinohara. "We've got his psych profile, and I've talked to him very briefly. From what I can tell, besides experimenting, he's showing off his power, too. Denver's a major federal center. In effect, he's taken on the government. We're also aware there are people here who he feels are his enemies." Loudon scanned the faces in the room for a reaction. He saw none. Not even from the anonymous men in the back. "We can't divulge our information just yet, but we know he wants especially for those people to be impressed with his abilities."

Loudon sat down in the front row, anticipating further questions. Craig finished his talk. Then White began his. His Adam's apple bobbing, waving a sheaf of notes, he detailed the FBI's findings. The Bureau had tracked thousands of infected people around the world, turning information over to the local health authorities. And they'd combed records for any sign of Lupo's travels, but found nothing.

"He's very clever," concluded White. "He's used cash, hidden his source of funds under assumed names, and he's established new identities. He's a tough nut to crack."

Loudon stood up again. "I'd like to point out that he can make himself look like anybody he wants to. The Bureau's hair and fibers lab has traced the wig he wore when he entered LA County Hospital. It came from a professional theatrical house in Hollywood. The people there said they thought it had gone out with a very large phone order for makeup, disguise appliances, and makeup instruction books." He glanced at Shinohara's chair, but it was empty.

A disembodied voice over the phone speaker interrupted his distraction. "Okay, so when we go out, we have to look at everybody?" It was one of the Denver FBI agents over the phone line from the infected city.

"Well, I don't think he's in Denver," said Loudon. "He wouldn't risk catching his own bug. And we don't see how he could have moved his lab all the way to Denver. He's probably sitting somewhere else in the country, kicking back, watching TV, reading the newspapers . . . gathering his results that way. I can say we're *sure* he's not in Denver." Loudon shook his head with certainty.

CHAPTER 23

Loudon's certainty was belied by the lobster-red Old Woman who tottered through the door into the laboratory and set down the shopping bag, clicking on the small television on the table next to the desk. The local Denver station continued its round-the-clock coverage of the color change. A talk show was on now, the screen cutting from one brightly colored talking face to another. The Old Woman left the sound low while she took off her glasses and moved a lighted makeup mirror into place on the desk.

"Please identify yourself," said the stilted feminine voice over the sound from the television set.

"Hello, computer," said the old woman, sitting down at the desk.

"Hello, Arthur," said the computer.

"Any intrusions?" asked Lupo, looking around his lab at the research bench, the isolation chamber, the sleeping lobster.

"No, there have been no intrusions."

"Good. Thank you."

"You're welcome, Arthur."

Lupo plucked out the yellow-stained false teeth and carefully lifted off the wig and set it on a stand. He gently peeled off the gnarled rubber nose, the baggy rubber jowls and even the wrinkled, flabby fake arm skin and carefully inspected them. He needed them in good shape if he was to be the red Old Woman during the day. They were slightly worn, and he made a mental note to make new ones. The Old Woman had been busy. Over the last two months, she had become a comfortably familiar sight on her usual routes in the city. To maintain the disguise, she'd turned color along with all of Denver's citizens.

He began to scrub the red makeup off his face. Once the area around his mouth was clean, he paused to fish a Tasty Klair Blueberry Pie from the box on the shelf, open it, and take a healthy bite.

"Okay, okay, now let's get cleaned up and see what we've got here." He finished cleaning his face and stripped off the dress and bra with its foam-rubber inserts. He stayed in his Walmart t-shirt and baggy Walmart boxer shorts, enjoying the cool air inside the lab. Even in the late dusk, Denver had been stifling hot. And the air conditioning on the buses the old woman rode had never managed to keep up with the heat wafting through the open doors at each stop.

As had become his regular habit, he stepped over to the isolation chamber and minutely examined its rubber gloves and the seals around its doors. Had he found even the tiniest break, he would have simply abandoned his precious lab, walked out the door and told the computer to destroy it. There was no room for error. Now he was constructing Lupo1000, his ultimate virus, inside the box.

"He's ripped us off!" shouted the kelly-green man on the television. "This Lupo has taken away our black heritage!" The sound of Lupo's name drew his attention, and he turned up the sound. The kelly-green man wore a black armband that contrasted with the yellow dashiki. "We're proud of being African-Americans, man, and this Lupo has taken our identities!"

"Hold on now, pal," said the titian-red host, leaning in and grinning fiercely, delighted at the ruckus. "You're saying your heritage depends on your color?"

"Yeah, I'm saying that exactly!"

"Well, then what about Jews, Poles, Germans, Italians? They've got a heritage. Does it depend on color?"

"You wouldn't understand, man. You're not black!"

"Actually, neither are you," said the host, gesturing triumphantly. The kelly-green man opened his mouth to answer, but nothing came out. He couldn't think of a rejoinder. He settled for a look of glowering anger at the host.

"Hey, for once I agree with him," interrupted the dandelion-yellow man to the host's left. "We believe that God made the races different colors so we could tell them apart. This color business will just encourage mixing. Our Aryan Committee is dedicated—"

"Your Aryan Committee is dedicated to racism!" shouted the kelly-green man, finding his voice again. "You're just worried I might marry your sister, you won't find out I'm black . . . uh . . . inside."

"Whoa, wait a minute!" said the host, holding a red hand up at either guest. "We've got to break for commercial. But before we go, I'll leave you two lovebirds with a couple of questions. The NAACP . . . the National Association for the Advancement of Colored People. Can anybody in Denver join now?" The host looked back and forth, his eyebrows raised in a hammy-quizzical expression. "And whites-only country clubs. Should they . . . shall we say . . . blackball all their members? Think about it. We'll be back."

Lupo stared at the screen for a moment. He opened his lab notebook and added the color information on the two guests. Turning down the sound, he picked up the shopping bag and took out the brown cardboard box. It was from GeneSynth, Inc., and it was addressed to John Dabney, P.O. Box 4356, Denver. He opened the box, inspecting the labeled plastic bottles.

"Hi guys," he said. "How ya doin'? Did they make you like I said? Hope so. I do. We'll see." He stepped to his lab bench with the box and put on his stained lab coat. He would check the new genes by running a sequencing gel on them. It was his usual, meticulous practice. He always ran an electrophoresis gel to double-check the structure of the DNA sequences the commercial company made for him. The sequence check would tell him whether the long strings of DNA he'd had custom-made possessed the right structure to function as the genetic blueprint for his new virus Lupo1000. They were the blueprints for the enzymes that were the control switches to make Lupo1000 operate properly. Ah, but he had been too clever to simply order whole genes, which the companies would have flagged as viral genes. He had ordered mere snippets of the genes from each company, and he would assemble them into the new virus.

To make room for his new project on the bench, he hefted a steel cylinder that was on the bench into a cabinet below. It was left over from the release of Lupo500. The canister, about three feet long and a foot wide, had been the only faulty one. The other cylinders had worked well to release Lupo 500. And Lupo500 had done its job well. Now there would be Lupo1000, and it would all be finished. He paused before plunging into the work to look at the photos on the wall—the large one of his mother and father, and the smaller one of the pretty Jeany Moody. He hoped they all would understand.

Over the next two hours, he conducted the analyses that confirmed the gene segments had generally the right structure. But he wasn't satisfied. He needed a more precise check. He wanted to run the samples on an automatic DNA sequencer. He also needed to build a few DNA segments that he didn't want GeneSynth and the other companies to do. So, he'd need access to a DNA synthesizer. He'd already set up his access to the machines, but he needed some more work in his lab before he went. Besides, now it was time for the Old Man to go out and observe.

He took off his lab coat and sat back down at his desk, peering intently into the makeup mirror encircled with bright lights.

"Goodbye for a while, Arthur," he said.

"Goodbye," said the computer.

"Sorry. I was talking to myself."

"I understand," said the Jeany Moody voice sympathetically. But Lupo knew it didn't understand anything. It was just giving preprogrammed responses. But it was still Jeany's voice, so he did derive some comfort from the talk.

Over the next hour, he meticulously applied a balding hairpiece, nose, false teeth and jowls. Then ever-so-meticulously he applied an egg-plant-purple makeup to his face, neck, head, hands and arms. It was a subtle color, an anonymous color. It was a color designed to hide his features and make him blend into the background in a dark room. And he had made himself an expert at shading and blending the color so it mimicked the subtlety of the real colored skin he'd observed so closely.

Finally, he pulled on a pair of padded tan pants and a brown shirt that gave him the soft, dumpy roundness of an old man.

He took a last critical look at himself in the mirror. He had a realistic bald pate with stray wisps of gray hair. He had the pocked nose of age. He had a round, wrinkled face and slightly crooked teeth that had seen many a meal. He was perfect.

"Computer?"

"Yes, Arthur?"

"Is there any movement outside?"

"No, Arthur. No signals from the motion sensors."

"Show me the scenes." The computer obediently flashed onto its screen images from the video cameras mounted outside the laboratory. They showed no intruders.

"Thank you, computer. Activate the security mechanism. Good night."

"You're welcome, Arthur," the computer purred artificially. "Security mechanism activated. Good night, Arthur." The computer screen went blank.

He unlocked and opened the door and peered outside, left and right several times. He stood breathing lightly, listening. It was quiet. He put on his worn Denver Broncos cap and stepped outside.

It was Thursday, and he would settle into the clockwork habit of his Wednesday-through-Saturday observational evenings as the Old Man. The two-block walk to the bus, the twelve-block bus ride to Colfax, changing to the Colfax bus, and the one block walk to Steve's Bar.

As he approached the bar, he heard the familiar noise, laughter and music before he even pushed through the rattly glass door. The smell of liquor and party-sweat permeated the cavernous old saloon. A small band blared out a rock version of the "Yellow Rose of Texas." A large signboard behind them listed songs with a color in the title. Steve had inaugurated an ongoing promotional contest—a free drink to any customer who could give the band a new colored-title song. The boards listings included "Am I Blue," "Blues in the Night," "Red Roses for a Blue Lady," "Blue Hawaii," "Blue Skies," "Blue Moon," "Red Sails in the Sunset," "When the Red Robin Comes Bobbin' Along," "Purple People Eater," "Yellow Bird," "A White Sport Coat (And a Pink Carnation)," and, of course, "It Ain't Easy Being Green." The theme song from Green Acres had barely squeaked by said a note on the board.

The long oak bar was burned, stained and scratched from decades of cigarettes, spilled drinks, and slammed-down mugs. It ran the length of the room and curved around to a corner that was the Old Man's favorite spot. He pushed himself up onto the bar stool. He could see the television set above the bar at the other end, on which coverage of the change continued. He could see the people in the rest of the room. But they didn't see him. Old men, especially dark purple ones, were pretty much ignored anyway, and in the large, dark, crowded bar, he quickly became part of the decor. He would sit in the corner of the bar, sip a few beers and watch the parade of colored comings and goings. He couldn't take notes, so he would remember his observations about how his virus was working. When he got back to his lab, he would write for an hour in his gray notebook.

"Well, old buddy, what'll it be tonight?" asked Steve, a mauve middle-aged man with a balding head.

"Same old," croaked the Old Man, and Steve nodded amiably and drew the usual Coors in a large glass mug. He set it before the old man and moved off to his duties.

The Old Man did a quick scan of the room for anything especially interesting. He sipped his beer somewhat daintily, to avoid having it wash off the makeup on his lips. He'd check later and retouch if necessary. The average tint of the crowd was brighter tonight. It was yellow night. Anybody with a color approximating yellow got drinks half off.

A mustard-colored young man with a mustard-rooted moustache happily downed his discount shot, while next to him a muscular lime-green man argued with Steve. He held out his arm like a salute. "C'mon man, I've got some yellow. Don't green come from mixin' yellow and blue? Huh? Ain't that right? C'mon. The TV says we could all kick tomorrow." He looked around for support. Steve finally relented and poured the man a bourbon and Coke, half price.

The lime-green man thanked him and took a healthy drink, scanning the crowd. "Glad this guy I know at work ain't here." He took another drink. "Turned yellow. He's fightin' all the time. Real sensitive, y'know? To people callin' him a yellow belly."

"Yeah, I know this other guy," said the mustard man. "Kinda sissy powder blue, sorta color. He had to take on a couple of guys who made cracks."

Four sleek young women bustled in, to the evident appreciation of lime green and mustard, and sat at a table next to the bar. The Old Man memorized their colors—magenta, grape, peach and apple red. He strained to hear their conversation.

"You like my hair?" asked grape in a white sun dress. "I'm going for highlights to match the skin. But y'know, I'm not sure."

"Oh, it's gorgeous," said magenta, smoothing back blond hair that did not quite go with her hue. "I don't know what to do, though. Mine's so hard to match."

"Look at the red stud over there," said apple red, who wore shorts and a sleeveless blouse. "You think we match? I'm just not dating men who clash with my color. Life's too short."

"I don't think it matters," said peach, a busty woman in a tank top and shorts.

"Of course it matters," said apple red, sipping her strawberry margarita. "You know Linda and Randy?"

"Yeah, so?" Peach scanned the room as she stirred her daiquiri.

"Divorce," whispered apple red ominously.

"No!" exclaimed grape.

"Yeah," said apple red, widening her eyes knowingly. "He was army green, she was forest green. He didn't care, but she was freaked. Said they looked terrible together."

"How shallow," said peach, tossing her long brown hair in irritation.

"Yeah, but I guess the stress if you're different . . . it grows on you."

"You think anything's growing on us?" Magenta made a worried face, wrinkling her button nose. "I mean, y'know like we already got a virus. Maybe we could get fungus."

The other three women giggled boisterously, and magenta would have exhibited a blush in her original color.

Lupo took a sip of his beer, set it down and hoisted himself off the stool, making his way back through the semi-darkness toward the bathroom. The band was on break, so he could overhear snatches of conversation as he went.

". . . so he's a regular color, but he wears makeup to be blue . . ."

". . . y'know, color commentary for the Broncos, it's gonna be a real different thing now . . ."

He reached the bathroom. It was empty, except perhaps for one of the stalls, so he stayed.

The door opened and another man came in after him, a husky cherry-red man with a brush haircut in a loose print shirt and jeans.

Lupo tried to calm himself. Maybe it was just another man who hadn't turned, but used makeup to be like everybody, a color. But maybe it was somebody who'd made it into Denver past the roadblock. For a reason. Or, maybe it was somebody who'd gone through the epidemic isolated in Denver. Maybe in a lab that was protected from germs.

The cherry-red man commenced his urination, seemingly oblivious to the old man at the next urinal. Lupo took a quick look at the side of the man's face. Makeup was caked slightly behind his ear.

Lupo tried to urinate. Nothing. He'd seized up. He tried hard. Finally, there came the delicate splashing sound in the urinal, and he managed a respectable pee.

The cherry-red young man turned and went to the sink and turned on the water. Lupo watched him in the mirror over the basin. He almost thrust his hands into the stream, but caught himself when he remembered the makeup. He looked up in the mirror at Lupo, who quickly looked away, zipped up. Lupo looked back. The man pretended to wash, then took a towel, rubbed his hands lightly and stuffed it in the trash. Lupo stepped to the basin and turned on the water, also pretending to wash.

As he turned, though, he could see the man staring at him. He knew! He'd probably followed Lupo into the bathroom! The man stepped between him and the door, but then one of the stall doors clattered open, and a burly nutmeg-colored man stepped out. He stepped to the basin, scrubbed his hands and started out.

"'Scuse me, pal," he said to the cherry-red man, who stepped aside. Lupo slipped through the door with the nutmeg man and followed him down the short dim hall into the darkness of the bar. The band had returned, playing an old fifties hit, "Lavender Blue."

Lupo glanced back. The man had come out, too, his hand on his side. Lupo thought he saw the squarish shape of a pistol beneath the large shirt, in the man's belt. He hurried to the bar and pitched some money on it for his tab. He looked back again. The cherry-red man was bent over a table in the other corner, talking to a raspberry-colored man. They'd chosen a table strategically located to reveal the entire room, just as Lupo had picked his spot to see the whole bar. He hadn't seen the men in the bar before. Maybe they'd just begun their surveillance here. But clearly they'd spotted him and decided to investigate.

He waved a quick goodbye to Steve and hurried out the door onto busy Colfax Avenue. Exuberant crowds of men and women strolled along the sidewalks and hung outside the bars and fast-food restaurants. They chattered and laughed, they were still amazed at their own colors, celebrating the new color, or mourning loss of the old flesh color with the same purposeful abandon.

He threaded his way through the raucous crowds and walked briskly down the street—suddenly realizing he was moving maybe a little too briskly for an old man. He caught himself, slowed and glanced behind him. Through the crowd, he saw the two men come out of the bar. The other one had his hand on his side, too. They looked the other way first, and Lupo took the chance to duck into a doorway. He peeked out, and found them looking right at him. Their gaze felt like an electric shock. He leaped out of the doorway and made no pretense of being an old man, running as hard as he could down the street. He felt sweat pouring down his face and knew the makeup was going. He looked over his shoulder. The men had guns drawn. The crowd shrank away from them like a single sensing organism. Women shrieked, and their boyfriends pulled them to safety against walls, into doorways. Men dropped to the ground, peering up to see if the guns were aimed at them.

Lupo turned and dashed into the first side street, into the relative darkness. He immediately cut left again into an alley, tripping over a box, slashing his hand, pulling himself up and continuing to run. His heart pounded, and when he looked back, the thudding became even worse. He saw the silhouettes of the two men flash past the alley. But one stopped, backed up, looked in and saw him. He beckoned to the other one, and they doubled back and raced after him.

Issuing almost a yelp, almost a grunt, Lupo ducked through the back door of a McDonalds. He wound his way through the storeroom and burst into the brightly-lit kitchen, with its thick, steamy odors of hot grease and frying meat.

"MUGGERS!" he shouted to the alarmed workers, pointing behind him. He ran past the fryer and the grill, scrambled awkwardly over the counter, scattering napkin containers and a tray of hamburgers, and lurched toward the front door. He turned to see a fat gray-green manager reach under the counter and bring out a sawed-off baseball bat with a taped handle. A young, deep-purple order-taker had yanked her purse off a peg and rummaged through it, bringing out a small aerosol can.

As he burst through the front door and back onto the street, he heard shouts and screams behind him. He also heard the explosion of a gunshot.

With relief, he recognized in the distance the familiar lighted sign of a bus, and he ran breathlessly toward it as the bus eased to a stop. The door opened and he leaped on board. His panicked look alarmed the bus driver, a large honey-gold woman.

"Man, what is your problem?"

"Muggers!" he panted, pointing behind him. He looked out the front window of the bus to see the two men burst out of the restaurant. One of them staggered against the wall, shaking his head and rubbing his eyes. The other held one arm with the other and had developed a limp. But they both still had their guns. They spied the bus and sprinted toward it. "See?" said Lupo, pointing at them. "Guns!"

"FORGET THE SCHEDULE, MAN!" shouted the bus driver, slamming the door behind Lupo and flooring the accelerator. She wrenched the steering wheel to the left, and the bus lurched out into the street, accelerating ponderously. Screeches and car horns greeted the maneuver, as cars swerved to avoid the careening metal behemoth.

Multiple cracks of gunfire resounded outside and the bus door erupted tiny shards of glass where bullet holes drilled through and slammed into the ceiling above the driver. Lupo threw himself to the floor and passengers screamed and did the same. More gunfire erupted, and slugs tore through the side windows, slamming into the metal ceiling with hollow clanks. As the bus accelerated, the bullets worked their way down toward the rear. Three rounds burst through the rear window, barely missing a citron woman and her crimson baby.

After what seemed like an eternity, the gunfire faded behind them, but the driver took no chances. She continued to thrust the old bus onward, blowing its horn as she roared down the broad avenue. After a few miles, she pulled over, peering past Lupo out the right rear-view mirror. The men were gone. She scrutinized the mirror at her left, as she reached down and radioed the dispatcher for the police. No cars followed.

"Man, that was some bad stuff," she wheezed with relief, turning back toward the door. But the Old Man was gone. He'd managed to force the door open and squeeze through. She shrugged her shoulders.

"This job just don't pay enough," she said tiredly to herself.

CHAPTER 24

Shinohara ducked her head to avoid the low door and stepped out of the small travel trailer, yawning and stretching and challenging the day. She rubbed her face, turned toward the sliver of sun peeking over the horizon and basked in the almost imperceptible warmth. The morning was deliciously cool, but soon the Colorado sun would rise high and blistering. Nobody else stirred in the cluster of several dozen trailers the CDC had brought in for their field team.

Now was the time to run. She sat down on a patch of weedy ground and carefully stretched her long brown legs and massaged her calves. As she stood and bent over at the waist, she felt her thigh muscles stretch and unlimber. She rolled around at the waist to flex the muscles in her stomach, sides and back. She took a few practice jogging steps and felt her body begin to awaken. Her muscles were ready.

She gathered her curly hair back with an elastic band and loped forward, running easily down to the long dirt road that cut through the open country outside Denver. She turned and launched her run toward the east, while the sun was low. She quickly left behind the huge collection of vehicles, tents and trailers surrounding the sprawling headquarters warehouse and the isolated CDC warehouse. She soon entered the more pastoral tracts of farms and ranches, with their rolling tan grassland. The low angle of the sunlight illuminated each stalk of grass, revealing the fine golden textures of the land.

She settled into the steady long-gaited jog that ate up the distance, rapidly adding up yards to make miles. The muffled thump of her running shoes on the soft tan earth became a rhythmic background for thought. She mulled over the incredible sights she had seen over the past months; the frightening scientific problems she and Doc had to solve. She thought of the complex, frustrating man whom she had loved. She remained deeply puzzled, deeply concerned about all of them.

Far in the distance she saw the bobbing shaved heads of a tight knot of joggers, probably soldiers. But otherwise, she had the road practically to herself. She had jogged about a quarter mile and was reminding herself to lift her head and enjoy the broad Colorado sky—as she did when she ran near her home in Colorado Springs—when she sensed somebody approaching from behind her. She could not really hear anybody following; it was more an intuition, or perhaps the subtle alteration in the air's vibrations. The person drew closer. She heard the footsteps, heavy like a man's. The stride was shorter, perhaps more labored. But it was steady, and it was gaining on her. Then she could hear the breathing, rhythmic, but on the edge of panting.

Then he was jogging beside her, seeming at first to ignore her. Then, in comic mock surprise, Loudon greeted her.

"Oh! Kathleen. You run out here, too?"

"Of course." She glanced at him impatiently. "You knew that. You followed me."

"I confess." Loudon was a little winded already, but he kept up. "I wanted to talk. You didn't have time during working hours. Thought I'd try here."

"Where's your golf cart?"

"Don't need one. I started running."

Shinohara allowed herself a sideways look of feigned surprise.

"Really!" insisted Loudon. "Look at the shoes. They're broken in."

"Well, I'm not sure what we have to talk about."

"Of course you are. Us. Do I have to keep repeating myself. I love you. You know how I can tell?"

"No."

"Because my daughter says so. She said I was acting funny. She said I was moony when I talked about you."

"You saw her?"

"Yes. She came out for a month. I want you to meet her."

"Should I?"

"Yup. Because we're going to be together. You and me and her."

"What makes you so sure." Shinohara considered increasing her pace. She was uncomfortable with the topic.

"Because I've figured you out." Loudon stumbled over a stone in the road and caught himself.

"What do you mean?"

"Well . . . uh . . . how long do you usually run?"

"About five miles."

"Oh, well, I usually do ten. Sometimes twenty on the weekends. All uphill. But I think we've got time. I've figured out why you went nuts when I asked you to give up the case."

"I reacted that way because it was an outrageous request."

"Well, I know that now. I appreciate that . . . how many miles have we run so far?"

"About one."

"Oh, then we have four more."

"Good math." They passed the marines returning to their base. The soldiers clumped by in unison, in perfect formation, all eyes left, admiring Shinohara.

"Anyway, any other woman would have just told me to bug off. And then forgiven me." They ran a while in silence, except for the rhythmic sound of their shoes striking ground.

"I'm not any other woman," she said with firm determination.

"Right, so you kissed me off. Or tried to. Do you know why?"

"Because nobody comes between me and my job. And because I made a mistake with you."

"Nope, wrong answers." Again, they ran in silence, Loudon struggling slightly to keep up.

She was resisting the obvious question. But her curiosity won. "Okay, then what's the right answer?"

"You left because all of a sudden you realized you'd opened up to me. You realized we were working toward something permanent. And you were getting scared." He stopped talking for a moment to pant. Sweat trickled several paths down his face, and his t-shirt was soaked. "You were scared that you'd have to let me in. That you'd lose control."

"You seem so sure."

"Well, we're the same. You use your career, your dedication to keep people at arm's length. I use my don't care attitude." She stopped and looked at him. Her face glistened with sweat, and she wiped her brow. But her expression showed more than the exertion of the run. Her eyes showed confusion, perhaps fright, and her hands made fists. She seemed about to say something. But then she doubled back on the road and headed back toward the headquarters. He followed.

"This means we've gone halfway?" he asked, his voice cracking slightly with relief.

"Yes."

"Oh, I wanted to go farther. Well, I'll shorten my run today. Anyway, like I said, we're the same deep down, and you know that. I'll bet you were always the outsider. Wherever you were. Like in Japan."

Again, they ran for a minute in silence. He knew he was getting to her.

"I remember the hair permission," she finally said.

"The what?"

"In school in Japan. They don't let girls have permanents. No curly hair. They're very strict. Every time I had a new class, my mother had to write a note. It said my hair was naturally curly. That it wasn't a permanent. I got sent home once. A teacher didn't believe me. In front of the whole class."

"Well . . . see . . . I understand about things like that." He stumbled again, but caught himself and hitched up his baggy shorts. "Well, not exactly hair. But we moved all over. I was always the new kid. I never had a friend more than a year at a time. See, we're the same. I can't really let anybody in. My first marriage was safe. It was automatic. I didn't have to let her in. You're the first. I love you. See . . . I've said it three times since we've been here. I guess I really do."

He couldn't tell whether it was a droplet of sweat running down her cheek or a tear. But he knew he'd convinced her. He continued. "You were scared, and you thought it would be easiest just to opt out. But it's not."

Now it was her turn to stumble, or at least to break stride.

"Tell you what, Miss Big-Time-Jock-Dedicated-Career-Woman. See the CDC building up there? What . . . about a mile away?"

She nodded.

"I'll race you."

"You're kidding."

"Naw. I'm a runner now, y'know? And if I win, we go out together." She looked sideways at him for six full strides. He thought he detected a bit of a smile showing on her face. "Look, I'm not saying you have to tell me everything. All your secrets. Just the juicy ones." She did smile this time, looking down at her feet. "If I win, we just go out together. Really together. And you have to tell me more about yourself. You have to let me in. I won't hurt you. I promise. And I'm so sorry about what I said before about the case. It was stupid . . . selfish."

They jogged along for twenty yards. She was staring steadily straight ahead, seeming to ignore him. But then she increased her pace, stretching her long slim legs out even farther. He matched it, his fish-belly-white legs stretching out their stride.

Now she bolted forward, pumping hard, head held high, kicking her legs far out in back, her arms reaching out in front to grab the air and pull it back.

"Hah!" he said in breathless triumph. The race was on, and he launched himself forward, too. His shoes slapped the dirt faster and faster. He pumped his arms, opening his mouth to greedily gulp in the air. He kept up.

She flew—her shoes barely touching the ground, her mouth wide open, her muscles working in perfect, furious coordination to drive her forward. Her legs became powerful, efficient pistons, their taut muscles standing out in glowing, sweaty relief with each pounding stride. She ran at top form, up in the rarefied mental and physical regions where runners exist when they feel like they're flying.

But he was determined, too. His face contorted with the ferocious effort, and he drove himself. He made it to his own top form, seeming to sprint on the very uppermost dust layer of the road. He stretched his legs beyond anything he'd ever thought possible. His chest heaved viciously, ready to burst. The desert air dried his mouth to cotton.

They pounded past the jogging soldiers, who hooted and cheered. He managed a thumbs-up, thrust his head forward and bellowed a hoarse grunt of new effort.

They were neck and neck. Through the haze of vicious exertion, he could see the warehouse approaching, as if in slow motion. He could only hear the chunking sounds of their feet striking the earth as they ran.

Loosing a string of guttural determined grunts, he abandoned any thought of preserving his body. He discarded any constraints, any caution. He decided deep in the most primitive reptilian recesses of his brain that even if he killed himself reaching the building, so be it. He drove his rhythm, drove his legs, ignored his screaming muscles, leaped forward. His thundering heart felt ready to erupt from his chest. He wondered fleetingly if that pumping organ would leave his body behind, reach the building first; if it would go splat against the metal wall and fall to the ground still pounding furiously.

He glanced over at Shinohara. She flew beside him, a strange look of both supreme effort and exhilaration on her face. She was a picture of perfect form, ultimate exertion. Her hair flying, her lips back in a wide grimace, almost a smile, the muscles on her neck straining.

But he'd gained on her! He'd drawn a little ahead! He raised his head for the last sprint and blew hard to inflate his lungs to their maximum. He would not slow one bit. The building seemed to come at him suddenly, and he hurled himself into the thin sheet metal with a loud reverberating clang, bouncing off and staggering back.

And with immense satisfaction, he heard the twin of that sound, a signal that she had reached the building the merest instant afterward. There were startled exclamations from the people standing outside with their morning coffee and smokes.

He staggered backward, threw back his head and sucked in the warming air, feeling it parch his throat and lungs. He wobbled blindly about, trying not to fall. But he did, folding onto the ground and collapsing onto his back in the cool dirt, his chest heaving, his heart jackhammering in his ears. A wave of nausea overtook him, but he fought it back. He smiled a beatific smile. Through the fog, he became aware of a shadow and drops of perspiration, maybe tears, falling on his face. He opened his eyes to see Shinohara standing above him in the sunlight, her chest heaving, her hands on her knees. But she was looking him straight in the eyes, smiling.

"Won," was all he could manage to croak.

"Yes, Robert," she said.

"Didn't let me . . . did you?"

"No, Robert."

"Am I gonna die?" he gasped.

"No, Robert, I don't think so." She sat down beside him, carefully shielding his face from the sun with her body. She wiped the sweat from his brow and ran her fingers gently through his sweat-plastered hair. They stayed there in the warming dirt together for a long time, silently, with him lying flat on his back. Then she got to her feet and helped him up. They brushed each other off and walked with their arms around each other's waists, sweaty bodies close together, as much in support as in affection. He stumbled a couple of times. He thought about looking back at the ground where he'd collapsed to see if he'd left any muscles or organs there. He seemed to have lost some.

"Where are you staying?" she asked solicitously.

"I don't remember."

"Let's rest in my trailer first. We'll find it."

"I hope so."

"I'm going home tonight. To my house in Colorado Springs. Will you come there?"

"Do you have a long sidewalk to get to the door?"

"No."

"Then I'll be there."

CHAPTER 25

The massive oak door opened slowly, and the two men stood looking at one another in the dim light from the shadowy house. As the visitor had requested, no entry lights or landscape lighting lit the stone mansion in the wealthy Denver suburb. The owner of the house saw a rather small man with a dead-sallow complexion, and with long fine hair combed into place with exquisite care. He had a high forehead, wide cheekbones and a narrow jaw, making his head somewhat triangular in shape. And he had a wide thin-lipped mouth, giving his face a vaguely reptilian look. Indeed, his eyes were as cold as a snake's, as fathomless as the bottom of a dark well. He wore a conservative gray suit, white shirt and striped tie.

The sallow-faced visitor saw a barrel-chested middle-aged man standing inside the house, his great shaved barium-yellow head looking as if some sulfurous substance had extruded up from his collar. He wore a suede jacket with expensive beige slacks, a striped shirt and a dark ascot. His coarse features belied the elegant clothing. He had a broken nose and a large mouth and pendulous ears that looked like misshapen yellow mushrooms growing from his head.

"Winston Cahill?" asked the visitor.

"Yeah. You're the guy who called about the business?"

"Yes." The visitor did not move to enter.

"You sure we have to handle this here? In my house?"

"Yes, we do. Where else? In a public place? Somewhere you might be followed? No, your house is best."

Cahill looked suspicious. "You're not colored. You come from outside?"

"Yes."

"How'd you get through the quarantine, the soldiers, the helicopter?"

"You don't need to know. Have you had the house checked by the company I recommended?"

"Yeah, sure."

"May I see the report?"

Cahill stood for a moment deciding whether to comply. Then he turned and strode back into the house, leaving the door open. The visitor remained on the threshold. Shortly, Cahill returned and handed him a sheet of paper, his yellow hands seeming to glow in the dim illumination from the house. The visitor held it up to the light and perused it. He wore white cotton gloves.

"Fine. No listening devices." He folded the paper once and handed it back.

"I didn't expect any. I've got an excellent security system."

"I'm sure you do. Is your family gone? The household staff?"

"Sure, nobody here, like you asked."

"Good." He stepped across the threshold. He did not offer a hand, nor was one expected. Cahill closed the door and threw a large bolt to lock it.

"The cook left us dinner in the trophy room." He motioned for the visitor to accompany him. He walked through the huge central hall of the mansion, taking care to keep the visitor in his field of view. A massive brass chandelier hung from the two-story ceiling, and a large curved dark oak staircase reached toward the darkened upper floors. The walls of the entry hall were decorated with oversized nineteenth-century American paintings, mostly of dramatic hunting scenes. In the paintings, dogs triumphantly crested hills with partridges in their mouths. Mounted riders jumped their steeds over rock walls. Heroic hunters raised their rifles against charging buffalo, lion, elk.

Cahill approached a rather modest-looking door and opened it, flicking on a bank of light switches. The effect was dramatic. In a gigantic dark-paneled trophy room, spotlights shone on the mounted heads and preserved bodies of scores of animals.

Guarding the four corners of the room were the massive snarling presences of rearing bears—a Kodiak, a grizzly, a polar bear, and a brown bear. From the right wall jutted dozens of elaborately spiral-horned sheep heads, and from the left, African antelope and North American caribou. Standing on a waist-high ledge circling the room were numerous wolves, cougars, lions, and a tiger, frozen forever in poses of attack, of stalking, of alert.

The effect was of a myriad of witnesses to the room's events. Faithful, attentive, validating . . . dead.

"A few of my favorites," said Cahill, stepping to the center of the room, where his gesture would have a full sweep. "Marco Polo sheep," he said pointing to a silky-furred full-body specimen with massive elegantly spiraling horns. "Sneaked into China for that one. Lives above fifteen thousand feet." He pointed to a small antelope. "Yellow-backed duiker from the Sudan." He moved on to others. "Asian wild ox. White rhino. Mongolian elk . . . that's a world record. Five-foot rack. On the far wall is my Super Slam," he said pointing to an isolated collection of ram heads, all with fantastically ornate horns. "To get that, you had to hunt twelve species of the world's sheep. I'm in a lot of places in the book," he said, laying his hand on a large leather-bound book resting on an ornate oak book stand. Its title was *Safari Club International Record Book of Trophy Animals*. Plastic index tabs stuck out of the book in many places. "Two hundred and eighty five trophies here, and another few dozen in the house in Canada."

The visitor had inspected the display impassively as Cahill spoke. He did not feel it necessary to react to the trophies, nor did he feel any inclination. He hunted more challenging game.

Cahill showed his annoyance by abruptly changing the subject. "You want to eat?" he asked curtly, motioning to a dining table in the middle of the room. "Do you mind eating in here? Some folks do?"

For the first time, the visitor smiled slightly, a smile that involved only the mouth. "Not at all. I find it interesting. Perhaps ironic."

They sat down at the table, covered with white linen and set with heavy silver and massive crystal goblets. Cahill opened a tureen and steam rose curling from it, bringing the rich meaty aroma of stew.

"I'm a vegetarian," said the visitor. Cahill tried to hide his second round of annoyance.

"Sure," he said replacing the cover. "What do you want? A salad?"

"That would be nice."

"Nice. Sure. I'll get something from the kitchen." Cahill rose, pitching down his napkin.

"I'd also like a bottled water, sealed. I'll open it. And wash the salad in bottled water. And the silverware should be boiled."

"Why?" asked Cahill.

"Well, it's my habit," said the visitor. "And in this case, the rumor is that the color change came from a virus in the water. I don't want to end up like you."

Cahill muttered an obscenity and left for the kitchen, slamming the door a bit too hard. The visitor spent the time wandering the room, stroking the silky fur of the dead sheep. He walked along near the walls, examining the predators with special interest. After a while, Cahill returned with a tray carrying a messily assembled salad, bottled water, and utensils. They sat down again, and Cahill pointedly ladled a generous helping of stew onto his plate, pouring himself a glass of wine from a bottle on the table. He sopped up stew with bread from a large basket and ate heartily. The visitor held up the fork to examine it.

"You sure don't look like a killer," said Cahill abruptly between mouthfuls, as he watched the visitor eat his salad.

"That's one reason I'm sitting here tonight," said the visitor, pouring himself a splash of water, swirling it in the glass and discarding it into his empty wine glass. He refilled the water glass and took a sip.

"All right. I'll accept that. You were highly recommended by this . . . associate . . . of mine. But how're you going to convince me you're worth two hundred thousand bucks?"

"I could kill you," said the visitor, looking seriously at Cahill.

Cahill let out a raucous laugh. Food showed in his mouth. The visitor continued.

"I can see at least eight ways to kill you right now. I carry fast-acting, undetectable poisons that I could slip into your wine or food or just spray on your skin. I carry a carbon dioxide knife that injects a bolus of compressed gas that would explode into your internal organs, giving a bloodless kill." He held up the fork, contemplating its four sharp tines with cold satisfaction. "If I don't care about blood dispersal, this fork can open your jugular if stuck into your neck with just the right twist. I have with me a garrote that could be around your neck before you could move. With a snap of my wrist, I can slice very easily all the way to the vertebral column, just about taking your head off. I know just the way to hit your nose with the palm of my hand that will drive your nasal cartilage straight into your brain. My left hand is under the table on the handle of a small pistol with bullets that explode nicely when they pass through the body. It would tear your backbone out after it passed through your belly. In my sleeve is a poisoned flechette that I can send straight into your chest with one move."

Cahill had stopped laughing. He stared at the visitor for a moment, saying nothing. He wavered between continuing the discussion and fetching his Luger from the drawer under the bookstand.

"That's only seven," he finally said.

"I may need the eighth."

"For what?"

"Contingency."

Cahill rejected the pistol idea. "All right, so you've got lots of toys. Who've you killed?"

"I never discuss previous targets or clients."

"Then how do I know you'll do what you say?"

The visitor showed an expression of mild impatience. "Look, here's my usual arrangement." He waved his gloved hands expressively. "You tell me who you want done and how. If I decide it's feasible, you deposit half the money into an account in my bank on Grand Cayman. If I carry out the job precisely as we discussed, you deposit the other half. If I do the job, but not to your liking, you still deposit the other half. I will give you a rebate of my choosing."

"Rebate. Huh. Like buyin' a car. And what if I don't deposit the other half?"

"Simple. If I feel I've been cheated, or if I feel that you are planning me harm, I will come back here and kill you. I will also kill anyone who may try to retaliate. I've done it before."

Cahill snorted, but eyed the visitor with some apprehension. He tried to think back to massacres of wealthy people in which the killer hadn't been found. He vaguely remembered six people killed in California a few years ago. Maybe a family in New York.

"So what do I call you?"

"Whatever you like."

"You don't have a name?"

"Not to my clients. It makes identification by the authorities harder."

"All right, I'll call you . . . Lucifer."

"Fine."

"Look, Lucifer, like I said, two hundred thousand is a lot of money."

"Then get someone else. Get one of your associates."

"You mean on the Aryan Committee? I support 'em, but most of them couldn't shoot their foot. I want this done right."

"What exactly do you want done?"

Suddenly uneasy, Cahill got up and walked over to a snarling lion, contemplating its massive silent head, its gaping jaws.

"You get to the point, don't you?"

"It's my business."

"This is something different here. I mean hunting humans. I never had anything to do with anything like this." Cahill reached up and stroked the lion's mane.

"Are you backing out?"

"No, no, not at all. But I mean humans. A white man."

"Who?"

"That Lupo guy. The one with the virus. But I mean, this is a big step. He's a white guy and all."

"But it's self-defense, isn't it?" The visitor knew all the rationales to supply to reluctant clients, and he pulled out a convenient one for this overstuffed rich man. He toyed briefly with the idea of simply killing the man and leaving. Of enjoying seeing the life flicker out of those brown eyes set in that grotesque bald yellow head. But he wouldn't, because the Businessman was in control now. The Businessman didn't kill; he set the deals, smoothly and professionally. The Killer carried them out, coolly, efficiently. The Killer wouldn't have done it, anyway, had he been in control. The Killer liked the ritual of the hunt.

"Self defense," said Cahill, mulling over the idea. "Yeah, you're right, of course. Self defense. Yeah. I want you to take out the little jerk before he does this to all the white race."

"The white race?"

"Yeah. Lupo has made it possible for the coloreds to hide their true colors. I'm doin' this to preserve truth. I don't know what the guy's doin' with those viruses. But I do know that he's made it almost impossible for the Caucasian race to keep ourselves separate . . . pure." More confident, he stepped away from the lion, returning to stand beside the table.

"You just want to preserve the truth," said the visitor, almost bored with the litany.

"Yeah, even though we can still tell mostly. By the faces." He curled his lip in an expression of pure venom. "But he's opening the way for the mongrelization of the white race. He's got to be stopped before he goes beyond Denver." He smiled with satisfaction at the reasoning. He took a gulp of wine and wiped his mouth with his hand.

The wine warmed him and he continued. "And, it's revenge, too, but that's not the main reason. No, but it's justifiable revenge. I want him killed for doing this to me." He held out his yellow hands, sloshing the wine. "He turned me yellow, like some Chinaman. Okay, maybe it's not one of those darker colors. Not like I'm dark green or somethin'. But he took away my white pride!"

The visitor regarded Cahill with the cool detachment one would apply to an interesting insect.

"How do you want it done?" he asked.

"Whatever way you usually do it."

"Depends on the effect you want. For example, do you want him whole?"

"Whole?"

"In one piece."

The idea jarred Cahill. He lowered his wine glass, almost spilling the wine. He brought it up and took a large drink. "Uh . . . yeah."

"Recognizable?"

"Sure, of course." Cahill remembered carcasses he'd seen after scavengers had been at them. The thought of a human so butchered brought a tinge of nausea. The thought also arose of backing out.

"Fast or slow death?"

"Uh . . . whatever." Cahill wondered whether backing out would cost him his life.

"Public or private?"

The question helped rekindle Cahill's enthusiasm. "Yeah, public. Yeah. Yeah, I want him on display. Yeah, I want this to be a warning to anybody else who tries to hide the races' natural differences . . . to open the way for mongrelization."

"Do you have any information on his whereabouts?" the visitor interrupted. He sensed another rant coming on, and it would not have advanced the business at hand.

"I will pretty soon. I've got friends in the police. I'll keep you posted. But for two hundred, I expect you to be pretty active yourself, Lucifer." Cahill was proud of himself for the name.

"I will be. One more thing you have to understand. There may be collateral damage."

"What's that?"

"My practice is, anybody comes between me and the target, or me and pullout, is fair game." He paused a beat, looking steadily at Cahill. "Anybody."

"Fair game." Cahill said the words with a touch of cold irony. Hunting fair game had been his life. But the term took on a new meaning here. He sighed an annoyed sigh. "Yeah, well it better be absolutely necessary. I don't want a lot of white people killed for no good reason." Cahill watched the visitor warily to see whether he had been offended.

Finally, the visitor nodded, and their business done, Cahill sat back down at the table. He composed himself. He didn't want to appear weak in front of this man. He lifted the cover off another dish, revealing a pie.

"You like some apple pie?"

"Yes, thank you."

Cahill sliced a generous hunk, put it on a plate and handed it to the visitor. He gathered himself to speak. "Y'know, I was just wondering. If you're willin' to talk about it, tell me how's it feel to hunt humans."

266

"Probably about the same as it feels for you to hunt animals."

"That good, huh? But I could never hunt humans. 'Specially white people."

"It's what I do." The visitor took another sip of water.

"Look, I don't want to insult you or anything. I sure don't want to insult you. But it sounds a little nuts to me. You're not . . . uh . . . off the deep end or anything? You won't go . . . well . . . psycho?" Again, he studied the visitor's face to see whether he might have incited some dangerous reaction. He calculated how quickly he could get his pistol from the drawer.

"I have been diagnosed as a pure, high-functioning sociopath, if that's what you mean." The visitor put down his fork after having eaten only a few bites of pie. His eyes seemed to look right through Cahill, right through the chair, right through the walls of the house. "I really have no emotional problems that interfere with the conduct of my business. That's why I have been so successful." He made the statement as a matter of fact, with no discernible pride. "I have no feelings for people. I find the hunt interesting . . . yes, and actually fulfilling. I suspect it's more of an intellectual challenge than your hunting. But maybe less of a physical challenge."

"Yeah, but white people . . ." said Cahill, with some trepidation. "Well, I guess it's a profession, right? It's a business." He abruptly rose to his feet. "My wife is due home soon. The stores are about all closed. You got everything you need?"

The visitor patted his lips with his napkin and stood, buttoning his jacket.

"Yes. When I learn the money is deposited, I'll begin." He took a blank sealed envelope from his pocket and handed it to Cahill. "Here's my bank account number and a disposable cell phone. When I want to talk to you, I'll call you. There's one number in the phone list. That's my disposable cell. Only call if it's absolutely necessary. If I think you're trying to locate me, I will kill you."

The visitor stared at Cahill for a moment, a cold stare. Cahill stared back, but glanced away quickly. He recalled once when he'd turned around in the bush to find himself looking into the eyes of a tiger stalking him. The eyes had been the same. The visitor moved toward the door to the entry hall and pushed through it. Cahill followed him to the front door. Cahill opened the front door, but the visitor did not go through.

"Walk outside, please," he said. Cahill shrugged and did so. "Do you see anything?" asked the visitor. Cahill shook his head. The visitor stepped out and turned around.

"You'll receive progress reports." He turned and walked into the night. Cahill closed the door and shook his head.

"Weird," he breathed to himself and went back to gather the dishes so his wife wouldn't know anybody else had been there. He'd pitch them in the sink for the maid. He'd also roust the little Jew banker he used and get the money transfer made. He didn't want to keep Lucifer waiting.

Outside, the visitor stepped carefully down the long dark entry road and to the large wrought iron gates. One side had been left open, the alarm turned off. He turned back and took off the lapel camera he'd used to surreptitiously photograph the entire interior of Cahill's mansion. He snapped a series of shots he'd stitch into a panoramic view of the exterior. That night, he would enter the photos and all the other recollections of the evening into his data files, in case he needed to return. He'd learned the practice as a Marine sniper. He'd had one hundred and twenty-eight kills in Iraq and Afghanistan before they shipped him home and asked him to leave the service. His commanding officers couldn't Section Eight him. He had too many medals. And they were actually frightened of angering him. So, they gave him an honorable discharge and felt well rid of the soldier who found that he deeply enjoyed killing.

His photography finished, he peered through the gate to the quiet winding road, then stepped through, shutting the gate behind him. His car was parked on a side road several blocks away. He walked a block in the darkness. Lights appeared from down the road, as a car approached. He stopped, backing off the road and into a cover of bushes. The car pulled up to another gate across the road, and the driver spoke into an intercom. After a moment, the gate swung open and the car eased through. The gates closed.

Clear of the house, the Killer now reached into his jacket pocket and pulled out a digital recorder, carefully unhooking the wire that ran through a hole in the pocket and up the jacket lining to a tiny microphone in his other lapel. He pressed the play button.

"How will you know where I am?" he heard Cahill's voice say.

"I'll know . . . walk outside," he heard himself say. *"You'll receive progress reports."* Satisfied, the visitor clicked off the recorder. The audio file would go into his data file as well.

He leaned out of the cover of the bushes. It was quiet again, and he prepared to leave. Ferocious barking suddenly erupted behind him, and a massive black form hurled itself forward. Startled, he leaped out into the road as the snarling Doberman pinscher slammed into the metal fence. Its chain collar jangled against the bars as it thrust its sleek head between them, continuing to bark, its white fangs bared, its eyes like shiny black marbles. Almost on instinct, the visitor took a step back toward the dog and abruptly whipped his right arm around and aimed at the surging black form. From his sleeve erupted a faint explosive pop, and the dog yelped and tried to withdraw its head from between the bars. But before it could succeed, its jaw went slack and it slowly collapsed, its pink tongue lolling out and froth dribbling from its mouth. The marble eyes, still open, went dull.

The visitor knelt beside the fence and reached through, feeling the furry neck for a pulse. None. He plucked a small dart with red fins from the dog's hide. He stood up and carefully placed the dart in a case from his pocket—red darts on one side, blue on the other. The faintest smile of satisfaction played on his thin lips. He turned and walked away into the night.

CHAPTER 26

The sidewalk to Shinohara's house was longer than Loudon thought it would be. He sat in the car for a while, with the door open, contemplating his immediate future with dread. Every muscle in his body had begun to hurt, and he knew it was the harbinger of worse to come. But he was determined. He reached down and used his arms to painfully lift his left leg out of the car and plop it onto the sandy roadside in front of the small house. He reached down and hoisted the right leg, twisting so that he was ready to stand. He took two breaths and with a whining groan like a creaking door, lurched to his feet. His eyes shot open with the pain. The leg muscles felt like hot coals had been surgically embedded in them. He stood uncertainly in the cool desert night, trying to ignore the screams from his legs telling him he was an idiot for even trying to move.

Shinohara's house was a neat adobe set back amidst large, handsome cottonwood trees. Its yard was carefully tended, with beds of cactuses and other plants that didn't need watering. It was a traveler's garden, meant to require little care.

Loudon rocked to his left and swung his right leg forward, keeping it stiff. He brought it down. Okay, one step. He did the same with the left leg. He walked like Frankenstein, clumping awkwardly straight-legged around the car and toward the house. But, hey, he thought, I'm moving. Earlier, when he'd tried to stand to give the field teams a briefing, he'd needed two other agents to help him up.

The veranda ahead gave forth a warm glow. Inviting. It drew him forward on his clumsy, painful stilts. Small kerosene lanterns marked the step up to the veranda. The step up intimidated him. Which leg first? Right leg first, he decided and swung it up onto the veranda. He teetered, leaned forward and vaulted on the right leg to bring the left one up.

"Hah," he whispered triumphantly to himself.

Two more lanterns flanked the front door, glowing with their welcoming golden light. He advanced to the screen door.

"Kathleen?"

"Come in," he heard faintly from the back of the house. He successfully negotiated the screen door and the step up into the house. He moved through the handsome living room, with its Japanese prints and white overstuffed sofa, and through the small dining room down a hall toward a large room in the back, beyond the kitchen. He smelled the sweet fragrance of incense and heard a low harmonious chanting voice. He followed the sound into the room and saw Shinohara. He stopped, fascinated by the scene.

She wore a white kimono with large blue flowers and had her rich tangle of hair gathered in a bun. She knelt primly, head bowed, before an altar built into the wall, her back straight, her white-stockinged feet tucked beneath her and crossed demurely, soles up. She held her palms together in an attitude of prayer. Her eyes were closed. She murmured quietly to herself, syllables of Japanese that rose delicately into the room like the incense curling from the thin sticks inserted into a small pot in the altar.

She was no longer the Shinohara who ran through deserts, plunged into caves, intimidated army scientists. She was serene, contemplative, thoroughly Japanese.

She continued to pray at the altar, which was decorated with flowers and lit candles, and upon which rested small bowls of vegetables, fruit, rice, and candies.

He stood quietly, not wanting to interrupt. Also not wanting to move his damaged muscles. After a moment, she finished and looked up, smiling graciously. With a single lithe motion she rose from her knees. He envied her that ability.

"Hello. I'm sorry I was busy. I thought you would be late." Her voice was softer, more relaxed than he'd heard before.

"Is that a religious . . . uh . . . ceremony?" He gestured toward the altar. "Are you Buddhist?"

"No, not really." She busied herself rearranging mats and a low table on the floor. "I'm celebrating a Japanese holiday. It's called *Bon*. I told you I was traditional."

"*Bon*?"

"It's a welcoming back of the spirits of my ancestors. I'm remembering them and inviting them into my home. It was originally Buddhist, but it's not really so much now. Like Christmas isn't so much Christian."

"Spirits? Like ghosts?"

"Sort of, but nicer. They're my ghosts. My father's ghosts. The lanterns out front are to guide them all back." She lit several more candles around the room, bringing the room to a soft incandescence that seemed to surround and follow her as she moved. Or, perhaps it was just the light of his rapt attention.

He didn't know whether humor was appropriate here, so he just stood awkwardly. But it was she who made the joke.

"Except for my Uncle Hiroo. I'm not sure I'd like him to come back. He drank too much saki and had bad breath." She moved a clay pot filled with glowing charcoal into place beside the table.

A desert breeze insinuated itself through the window, curling the incense smoke and spreading the delicate ashen odor of the charcoal. He found himself smiling stupidly at her. She smiled back and gestured at the mat on the floor.

"Can you sit down?"

He blanched. "You mean *really* down? On-the-floor down?"

"Oh, I'm sorry . . . you're hurting. I've got something very special planned that will help you forget the ache."

He brightened. Special! No doubt it would be worth the pain. He approached the mat and embarked on the excruciating process of bending his legs to sit down. Fortunately, she left the room and didn't hear the groans and grunts as his torn muscles were forced into unnatural contortions. But soon he was in place, and with some effort erased the residual anguish from his face, replacing it with some semblance of eagerness.

She returned, advancing slowly into the room with a tray. Her face was tranquil, her eyes bright, and on her lips was a beatific smile. She lowered effortlessly into the kneeling position and laid the tray beside the mat. It seemed to float to the floor, so smooth was her movement.

"I am going to do for you the tea ceremony . . . chanoyu. It is a very special thing, done for a very special person. It is about six hundred years old."

He was transfixed. "Uh, what do I do?" He shifted and managed to hide the twinge of pain.

"Just enjoy." She drew from the folds of her kimono a small object bundled in paper and carefully unwrapped it and offered it to him.

"Kashi . . . a sweet to begin." It was a small candy shaped like a maple leaf. He placed it on his tongue and felt the delectable sweetness fill his mouth.

"We can only talk of pleasant things now."

He tried to think of something pleasant. "I won the race."

"Yes, you did."

"And I'm with you."

"Yes, you are," She smiled. "The day was very beautiful."

"Yes. It's a beautiful night, too."

"You're doing well for your first tea ceremony." As she talked, she began to prepare the tea. He had never seen such fluid movement. Her fingers, her hands, her eyes, her body, her head . . . every part of her seemed involved in a graceful, practiced ballet of motion. Her movements were flowing paths through space and time that created a sense of tranquility. Watching her, he forgot his legs, the hardness of the floor.

"You've done this many times?"

"I practiced for years," she said quietly. "My grandmother taught me." She had placed the teakettle onto the glowing charcoal to heat. And while it was heating, she took up a small canister. It seemed to rest weightlessly in her hands. "The aim is to achieve the essence of wabi. It's an aesthetic of simple beauty, of calm."

"I could use a bunch of wabi."

She held up the cannister.

"Natsume. The container is very old. From my grandmother." She slowly, precisely spooned a small amount of tea into a ceramic bowl. The movement was slow, elegant. "You're supposed to admire the picture . . . the kakejiku," she whispered as she carried out the ceremony. He looked to his left and saw for the first time a hand-painted Japanese summer scene on a scroll nestled into an alcove in the wall.

"It's very nice. Did you do it?"

She laughed. "An ancestor did."

"Cool." He decided he could relax. In fact, he was feeling more and more relaxed. Serenity wasn't a bad deal, he decided. "You know, the only ceremony we had at my house was cutting the turkey on Thanksgiving." She held up the ceramic tea bowl.

"Chawan. It is probably two hundred years old." She picked up the teakettle, and poured a smooth stream of hot water into the bowl. She delicately swished a small bamboo whisk around in the bowl and replaced the whisk on the mat, brush up.

She placed the bowl on the mat, and with a nod, indicated he was to pick it up. Now he was a little nervous. He didn't want to bobble this ancient tea bowl. And after her elegant grace, he didn't want to handle the ceremony wrong. But she instructed him.

"Take it. Hold it up. Admire the design." On one side of the bowl toward him was an elegantly wrought flower.

"It's beautiful. As beautiful as you."

"Not bad, Robert. Now turn the bowl three small turns, so the design is facing away from you." He did so. "Now drink it . . . all." He did so, and the warm, tart liquid tasted good.

"Great tea, Kathleen."

"You're not done yet. Admire the marking on the bottom." He looked at the bottom and saw Japanese writing.

"Nice marking."

"Now, say kekko na otemae deshta."

"It means 'thank you?'"

"Close. It means that this was a very nice tea ceremony."

With coaching, he managed a reasonable approximation of the phrase. They talked some more.

"Are we having a Japanese dinner?" He realized the tea had whetted his appetite.

"Pizza. I ordered out. It's warming in the oven." She slid the warm pizza box from the oven and opened two beers. They began to eat.

"You'd better take it easy tomorrow," she said. "Those legs are really going to start aching."

"Wish I could take it easy. I didn't tell you before. There was another email message today."

"From Lupo?"

"Yeah. He was going on about another attempt to kill him. Accused us. I sent him one back, but he just doesn't respond. We've got to find him."

"He's in Denver?"

"Nah, couldn't be."

"Well, in any case, we'll get your guys in there soon. We're sure it's the water. None of the asymptomatics drank tap water. Just bottled. So, it's got to be the water. But until we find the source, we won't know how to stop new infections."

"I'd like to see the colors close up."

"They're incredible. Makes you think. About skin color. About all the racism based on it."

"We've had it in the Bureau. There's some throwbacks there."

"Oh, it's not just them. It's everybody. I mean everybody. I grew up with it."

"You mean your skin?"

"Yes. Mom's not the usual light-skinned Irish. She's what's known as black Irish. It's a mixed-race heritage. That's where I got my skin. I think people react to it. I grew up going back and forth, one culture to the other. And I learned the Japanese sensitivity to other people. Maybe the racism's built in; maybe people learned it."

"I can't believe that." He held up her hand, and stroked her arm, his whiter skin next to her rich brown.

"Everybody's racist that way," she said with a touch of sadness. "Even you. Deep down."

"Okay, I'll prove it. But you have to be absolutely dead honest with me. With yourself. Can you be?"

"Sure. Of course." He sensed a test. He was on guard. He laced his hands behind his head in a show of confidence.

"How about when I meet your parents? Think about it. Think hard. You're going to be worried about their reaction. A little bit. Mainly to my skin."

"Don't be ridiculous."

"They'll react."

He remembered his promise and considered. "Okay, okay, you're . . . exotic. Sure, they might react a little. They're sort of conservative."

"To my hair? My eyes? My nose? My hands? No. To my *skin*. And so did you."

"Come on—" He was prepared to protest. He looked her in the face. He thought. He looked into himself. His hands unlaced and rested on his chest.

"So did you," she insisted quietly.

"Well," he said, confused, staring at the ceiling for a while. "You're right. Even a shade makes a difference. Even a shade." He looked back at her.

She kissed him on the lips. "It's surprising isn't it?"

"Yeah, well, it's unsettling."

"Well, you were honest. I knew you'd be. That's why I love you. My folks will love you when they meet you."

"Your folks are coming here?"

"Sure. Next month if we get the case finished. For the wedding."

"Whose?"

"Ours."

"What?" He sat up, thinking he must not have heard her right.

"Our wedding. Probably September thirtieth. I'll let you know. I'll give you a map where it's going to be."

"What?!" Now he stared at her in disbelief.

"Well, I thought about it. Anybody who's willing to kill himself like you did today is really in love."

"What?!" he repeated.

"And anybody who can beat me is better than he thinks he is. You need me if you're going to be director of the FBI."

"What?!" He felt his senses overloading.

"And also, anybody who's stupid enough to do what you did today needs me."

"What?!" His brain was simply not functioning sufficiently to think of another word.

"And . . . I need you, too."

"What?!"

"So, we're getting married."

"What?!"

• • •

The lavender-skinned treatment plant engineer paced back and forth beside the huge roiling pool of clear water, turning the problem over in his mind. He knew his plant like the back of his now-colored hand. He'd been at the Moffat water purification plant for twelve years. So when the police had told him they thought that this Lupo guy might have infected people by contaminating the water flowing through his plant, he was sure he could find out how. But it had been a week, and he still couldn't find any evidence of tampering.

He watched the rippling water flowing through the sprawling sand filter. He decided he might walk around and think, so he took his second cup of coffee and left the giant plant, hiking out on the little dirt trail that led along one of the main outfall pipelines. He followed the big forty-eight-inch pipe as it ran for a little way from the plant then plunged underground at the tall chain-link fence. He let himself through the gate and walked along the narrow trail that crossed a rolling field. The trail soon disappeared into a grove of trees and led toward the suburb where the pipeline fed faucets and showers and toilets.

The morning was warming quickly and he had an operations meeting, so just when his cup was still half full and he reached the grove of trees, he turned to go back. He didn't know what made him glance over to the pipe right-of-way. He didn't know what made him notice the disturbed earth. He walked off the pathway and nudged the pile of dirt with the toe of his rubber-soled work shoe. Maybe a prairie dog burrow. But there were no other piles, and the dirt around was packed hard. He scratched his bald head and nudged the pile some more. It was a freshly dug squarish area. No prairie dog dug *square* burrow entrances. Since there had been no rain, the soil was still loose. He knelt his lanky frame down and nestled his Broncos coffee cup carefully into the dirt next to him so it wouldn't tip over. Then he thrust his work-hardened fingers into the dry earth, finding the digging easy even down a few inches. His fingers struck something hard, metallic, but it wasn't the dull metal of the big outfall pipe, even though the pipe ran near the surface here. He brushed away the dirt to find the top of a shiny stainless steel cylinder nestled right beside the big pipe.

"Whoa, man!" he breathed to himself excitedly and took up his precious Broncos cup, flipped the coffee out, and began to dig with it. Soon, he had uncovered almost the entire cylinder. Concentrating on the side toward the water pipe, he dug vigorously, flipping the soft tan earth far out of the hole. The cup struck another metal part, and with his fingers, he gently unearthed a small steel tube running from a black box on the side of the cylinder to the shallow water pipe. Where the tube ran into the big outfall pipe was a pressure fitting that attached it to the water pipe.

The engineer stood up suddenly and backed away.

The guy was nuts; maybe there was a bomb here! He hurried off to call the police, but returned and grabbed his cup before loping away again.

"Got it! Got it! Got it!" he exclaimed as he loped toward the plant, the heavy chain of keys on his belt jangling in accompaniment. He'd found out how Lupo had contaminated his water plant!

CHAPTER 27

Walter blew gently on his steaming coffee, took a tentative sip and tried to see through the wall of translucent plastic sheeting. Despite the shimmering distortion, he could make out the three Racal-suited figures bending over the steel cylinder on the operating table. The tiniest breezes wafting through the warm warehouse made the plastic billow, spoiling his view. The three vague figures rolled the cylinder this way and that as they examined it. One seemed to have a tool, maybe a screwdriver in his hand. He seemed to be applying it to a black box on the side of the cylinder.

Walter decided to walk around to the other side of the tentlike chamber to get a better view. The darkness of the warehouse and the bright operating-room lights within the chamber made him feel like a voyeur spying on some mysterious secret rite.

He passed the airlock—a large plastic cylinder attached to one wall of the chamber. And he stepped carefully over the yellow ropes that stretched out to tie into eyebolts in the walls of the warehouse, pulling the chamber into its cubic shape. Carefully holding his hot coffee steady, he laboriously bent his rotund body to duck under waist-high ropes that held the walls in tension. Above him, still more ropes ran to the roof girders of the warehouse.

He reached the small, whining electric pump that constantly exhausted air from the chamber, creating a negative pressure, filtering and disinfecting the air of every living thing. Walter bent and inspected the device. No bacterium, no fungus spore, no mold, no virus escaped this efficient gadget, Walter was sure. Satisfied, he straightened, sipped his coffee and remembered the fact of doughnuts in the other warehouse, the one that housed the busy headquarters of the government agencies.

He had just decided to investigate the doughnuts' current status, when movement within the chamber caught his eye. One of the figures held up the cylinder, while another sprayed it with liquid. The third figure still labored over the small box that appeared to have been removed from the cylinder. The figure that had been doing the spraying approached the airlock, unzipped its doorway and stepped in. The figure clutching the cylinder followed. Crowded in the small airlock, they proceeded to spray one another with a series of hoses—one red, one yellow, one green. They emerged from the airlock dripping. They both shook and slapped their suits and Walter backed away so his coffee wouldn't catch any of the flying droplets. The figures removed their helmets, revealing Doc and Shinohara.

"Mornin', Doc. That the thing that released the virus into the water supply?"

"Yessir. Interesting gadget." Doc set the dripping cylinder on a workbench.

"Has it got viruses in it?" Walter covered his coffee.

"Not any more," said Shinohara. "Here, take a look."

Walter had stepped up warily to peer at the cylinder, when the sheeting of the isolation chamber billowed and snapped, as a door from the outside opened. White and Loudon entered, silhouetted in the bright sunlight that streamed through the door. The FBI AD White strode briskly forward, while Loudon slammed the door and hobbled along to catch up. The hobbling Loudon gestured angrily.

"White, the army faction started the whole thing!" exclaimed

Loudon. "They're the ones who set Lupo off! We ought to take the lead on finding the faction's lab."

"The director said no."

"Forget what he said!"

"He's the director. You don't like it, too bad."

"Maybe there's information in that lab—"

"Stop it! Just stop it, now!" Lucas White halted in his stride, his gangly frame stiff with indignation. He pronounced his words with an emphasis that bordered on sputtering. A sunbeam streaming into the warehouse backlit the faint spray that spat from his mouth with his s's, p's and t's. "The director instructed you to postpone any action to find that lab! The director has more information than you. Maybe it's an Army lab; maybe not; maybe CIA . . . whatever. But there are situations that neither of us understands."

"But . . . ," said Loudon morosely.

"It will be, agent, you keep this up. Now, let's see what these people have."

They allowed their rancor to cool and approached the group surrounding the cylinder. The third Racal-suited person, technician Jerry Sievers, had emerged from the isolation chamber, unsuited, and placed the small black box on the workbench. He had just begun showing it off to the group.

"Yeah, here's a little micro-pump . . . battery operated . . . electronic controls," he recited as he pointed at the welter of components stuffed into the little box. He teased out the wires with his screwdriver and pulled out a circuit board and battery holder.

"Hmm, yeah," he mumbled. "This here . . . this here . . . it's the relay . . . and looks like you set . . . you set the flow rate . . . uh . . . here."

"Jerry, these are the two heads of the FBI investigation," said Doc, turning to White and Loudon. "This is Jerry Sievers. He's an Army electronics engineer."

"Yeah, hi, sirs," said Sievers, a slim young man with a short haircut. He eagerly shook hands and turned quickly back to his work, inserting his nimble fingers into the device to pull out more components. "Nope, no detonator . . . nothing like that. Just a flow control system."

"Detonator?" asked Loudon.

"Yeah, Jerry's also with the Army bomb squad," said Doc. "They looked it over before we brought it in. After they decided it was safe, Jerry figured out what the box was for."

"Wasn't easy figuring this puppy out," said Sievers brightly. "It coulda' been a bomb; it coulda' been full of germs. We didn't know what. But we got 'er checked and opened up!"

"It still had a little liquid in it," said Shinohara. "We sent off a sample to Atlanta."

"So how's it work?" asked Loudon.

"Oh, neat," said Sievers, showing the end of the metal tube. "The guy had an epoxied clamp system, so he could tap right into the pipe." He ran his fingers back along the tube to the attached black box. "Once he'd tapped the pipe, he opened this little door, and used a screwdriver to adjust the flow rate, and flipped this little switch. Then he closed her up, and as long as the batteries lasted . . . or the liquid lasted . . . it metered out maybe a milliliter an hour."

"That's not much," said Loudon.

"It's enough," said Shinohara. "We figure he had a nice thick culture of the virus in each cylinder. He was releasing billions of virus particles an hour over a weeklong period into each pipe. He was very clever. It's summertime; people drink a lot of water. Over a week, everybody would get at least one virus particle, and that was enough."

"I thought the water was chlorinated," said Walter. "Wouldn't they die?"

"We're betting he used a version of the envelope AMRIID developed for the enveloped HIV. He altered it so the chlorine couldn't reach the virus particles until they got into the stomach. The stomach acid released the virus." Shinohara's face showed the same disgusted look as when she first learned about the army's EHIV project.

"Any clues where the apparatus came from?" asked Loudon.

"Yeah," said Sievers. "The pump's not standard. Had to be bought somewhere special. You can trace that. But maybe not the cylinder. It's a medical gas cylinder. Real standard."

"Well, let's get on it," said White. "Any more been found?"

"We found two more of these at the Moffat plant outfalls," said

Doc. "All the plants, including Marston and Foothills, are swarming with people looking for more. But they're being told not to touch them."

"It's a good idea," said Sievers. "Y'know, Lupo might have made some of them into bombs. You never know."

"Three people," said Loudon, stepping in front of White. "I want three people on each team that removes one of these things from the pipe. CDC, FBI, and an Army demolition person." They agreed. Doc cradled the cylinder in his arms and Sievers picked up the box with the tube attached. They all filed out of the warehouse into the sunlight, past the guards ringing the isolated CDC warehouse.

Loudon motioned for White to hang back. "Look, Lucas, let's just call a truce for now, okay? I'll handle the field work in Denver; you handle tracing the apparatus, looking for Lupo."

"Fine, just fine. But you remember what the director said."

They parted as White walked ahead to the warehouse where the FBI briefing was planned. As they drew closer to the warehouse, the traffic noise on the nearby freeway increased. Denver was once more open to the outside world. Loudon was running over in his mind all the things he had to tell Bowers in his daily phone call. It was a pain, but at least the report helped Loudon get things in order.

"Congratulations," said Doc, with only a hint of sarcasm, as he dropped back to walk with Loudon.

"For what?"

"You and Kathleen gettin' married. She told me."

"Look, Doc, I am not marrying Kathleen! I told her that last night."

"Well, first of all, you don't tell her anything. And second, you're not good enough for her." Doc said the last sentence with a slight twinkle that told Loudon he might be kidding.

"Yeah, I know. You made that clear."

"I've been watching you two, though. It's possible you just *might* be getting good enough for her. In any case, she said the wedding is September thirtieth. Her father's giving her away."

Walter came up beside Loudon on the other side. "You looking for a best man? I know it's maybe not polite, but I want to put my bid in."

"I am *not* marrying Kathleen!" Loudon repeated, almost plaintively.

He looked ahead to see Shinohara striding alongside Sievers, discussing the control box in his hand.

"Kathleen gave me a map," continued Walter. "If we're still out here then, Lorna will fly out with our youngest. They can help with the plans. I've never seen a Shinto ceremony."

"Shinto! *I'm not getting married!*" His voice was nearly drowned out by the roar of a jet overhead. "Why won't you listen to me?"

"She said not to. She said you'd say that."

Loudon closed his mouth tight and stalked on. He caught up with Shinohara as they entered the headquarters warehouse. It was packed with hundreds of FBI agents and assorted liaison representatives of other groups.

"Kathleen, I told you I can't marry you. Look, I have a daughter to think of."

"I know. She's going to be maid of honor."

"What?"

"I called her this morning and introduced myself. We talked a long time. She's such a lovely young lady. She's very happy for you."

Shinohara continued walking toward the front of the room, and from Loudon's mouth came a small, inarticulate, frustrated grunt. After a moment, he recovered himself and followed her.

The marriage receded in his mind as he met Jack Scalisi, the mint-green SAC of the Denver FBI field office. Scalisi, a compact, athletic middle-aged man with curly black hair, looked extremely out of place with his tinted skin. So did the other Denver agents, ranging from chrome yellow to olive green, who sat in the crowd looking self-conscious. But Loudon knew having them there was useful. They reminded the other agents of what would happen if they were contaminated. Loudon whispered something into Scalisi's ear, and after a moment, Scalisi nodded in agreement. They badly needed to find the lab of the faction that had given Lupo the tools for his attacks.

White opened the briefing, and Doc and Sievers showed off the cylinder. Sievers enthusiastically explained the mechanism and demonstrated how to remove the device from a water pipe.

Shinohara explained the theory of how Lupo had disseminated the virus release and outlined precautions.

When it was Loudon's turn to talk, he asked White's assistant to pass out the FBI assignment sheets and went over them. One group would join with the CDC and Army specialists to search for the other cylinders. The teams would also interview residents in the vicinity of the water plants.

Another FBI team would work with the state police to find Lupo's lab, assuming it was somewhere nearby. A third group would interview laboratory workers at local universities and companies. Maybe Lupo was trying to use a molecular biology laboratory somewhere in the city.

After answering questions, he concluded the briefing, and the agents crowded through the door to their assignments.

Loudon took Doc aside, once he was sure White was occupied elsewhere.

"Doc, they've got me hemmed in and I need your help."

"Sure, for what, son?"

"We've got to find that BSL-4 lab. The faction lab. There may be something there that will give us a clue to Lupo. But the director has shut down that part of the investigation. And I'd *bet* White influenced that decision. Can you help Jack Scalisi? He's the green guy. He's the Denver SAC, and he said he'd give us some men to work on it."

"Well, I agree with you. I want that lab, too." Doc casually wandered over to Scalisi and conferred with him and soon left with two of Scalisi's men.

Shinohara arrived and announced that she needed agents to help her trace some shipments of synthesized genes that had come into Denver from gene-making companies. One might have gone to Lupo. Loudon collared White and they agreed, the tension still evident in the elaborate politeness of their conversation. Shinohara strode out with three agents in tow.

Finally, the briefing area was empty, except for White, Walter, Loudon, and Scalisi.

"Well, if it's okay with you, Lucas, we're going to check out some sources in Denver. Jack thinks some of his snitches might know something," said Loudon.

"Sure, of course," said White curtly. "But you remember what we discussed."

"Hey, Lucas, I'm not going near any secret lab, all right?" said Loudon, raising his hands in mock surrender.

• • •

The Businessman was gone; the Killer was active, and Lupo was his target. That afternoon, the Businessman had accessed his account in the bank on Grand Cayman Island and confirmed that Cahill had deposited the hundred thousand dollars. So, now the Killer coldly prepared for the hunt. He walked slowly down the darkened sidewalk from shadow into light and back into shadow. He liked the night. It made his work so much easier. And he knew that his blood-red makeup looked gray in the dark. Although he hated the feel of the greasy substance on his skin, he liked the color. It brought back memories of combat. The skin color, and dark blue slacks and a dark shirt made him almost invisible in the night.

He knew who he was looking for. Cahill had called with a tip from his contact at the Denver police station. A few nights before, there had been a disturbance, gunfire, a chase. An old blue man who could have been the disguised target had been involved. And a bus. The tip had included the bus driver's name.

That evening, the Killer drove up and down Colfax for two hours, carefully observing the laws, carefully noting the people on the sidewalk and the arrangement of buildings. As a sniper, the practice had been known as "ranging the kill zone." Then he parked and rode the buses along that route, sitting in the back and watching among the passengers for the old blue man. It would almost certainly be Lupo his hunter's instinct told him. Maybe Lupo had been frightened away, and the search would be fruitless. On the other hand, maybe he figured his pursuers would abandon their hunt after being chased away by the police, who were now looking for the cherry-red and raspberry-colored assailants.

After changing buses several times, he found the honey-gold bus driver. She'd been only too willing to talk about the incident to the quiet, blood-red man who rode her bus nearly the whole length of her route.

"That little old blue man was sure runnin'!" she had said, keeping her eyes glued to the road. "Faster than I thought any little old man could ever run. And jumpin'! My, how he did jump on my bus! And then the two other men started shootin', and I found out how fast this old bus could go!" She had laughed heartily, but because she was watching the road, she hadn't noticed that the blood-red man did not laugh with her.

Now he knew it had been Lupo. So he got off and walked a particularly promising stretch of Colfax that was lined with bars. As people of many colors entered and left the bars, spilling from the doorways were flowing eddies of cool air smelling of booze and smoke and carrying the noise of revelry. The Killer walked slowly, acutely scanning the street. Even though he remained intent on the people in the crowds, he became instantly aware of the car following him. A hunter knew when he was being hunted.

He walked on, not looking back. A siren whooped almost comically for an instant, and a loudspeaker-voice filled the street.

"You on the sidewalk. Red man. Stop and show identification." He turned to see two burly cops haul themselves from the police cruiser. One was lilac, the other sapphire. The lilac one stood by the car.

"Let's see it," said the sapphire one, remaining well back from him.

The Killer assessed his chances. He could kill both in an instant if he had to. He brought up his hand slowly and reached into his pants pocket. He pulled out a thin calfskin wallet and took out a driver's license. He handed it to the sapphire cop.

"Did I do anything wrong, officers?"

"We're looking for somebody your color," said the sapphire cop, examining the license under his large black flashlight.

"Maybe not your color," said the lilac cop, approaching his subject, taking out a thick sheaf of color-sample rectangular cards striped with shades of the same color, each with a different code. The cards were fastened by a rivet at one end, and the cop fanned them out, searching through the reds.

"Yeah, here it is. PMS 207C. That's the color the witnesses picked. Definitely a 207C. But look." He riffled through the cards to find another, holding it next to the subject's skin and motioned for the sapphire cop to shine his flashlight on the sample. The Killer tensed slightly. If any makeup rubbed off, he would have to kill the cops. But none did. "This guy's a 199c shade at least. And he's shorter than the one we want." The sapphire cop took the samples and held up another card to the Killer's skin.

"Maybe a . . . No, definitely a 199c," he said.

"What are those samples, if I may ask?"

"Oh, they're colors that printers use to decide on inks. Pantone Matching System," said the lilac cop. "Our department publications guy figured out it was a good way to ID perp colors. So we started usin' them. Really good idea. Now, we got another point of ID."

"Well, fascinating."

The sapphire cop handed him back his license, and they climbed back into their car and sped away. The Killer coolly resumed his stalk.

After an hour of slowly walking the length of Colfax, he saw a target. An old, blue squat man wobbled out of a bar and crossed the street to a Dunkin' Donuts. The Killer leaned against a signpost outside the shop as he watched the old man buy coffee and a donut and sit with his back to the window, sipping and eating. The Killer ran down his mental list of assassination techniques, discarding some, accepting others, preparing himself.

The old man finished and shuffled out of the shop and slowly down the sidewalk. The Killer followed. Still too many people. The sense of coming satisfaction began to rise in the Killer. This was his calling. His blood-red reptilian-thin lips widened in what might have been described a smile, but there was no touch of joviality. It was predatory.

The old man turned down a dark side street. The Killer followed. Halfway down the block, passing a stretch of rundown apartments, the Killer quickened his pace. He drew closer behind the old man. He could hear the wheezing breath, the laborious scrape of shoes on pavement. A good imitation, thought the Killer.

The Killer glanced back. They had walked well down the darkened block, well beyond where they would be noticed from the busy main street.

The old man came to a driveway that led into impenetrable shadow between two apartment houses. At that instant, the Killer chose his method and sprang noiselessly forward. He whipped out the piano-wire garrote and inserted his hands into the small wooden handles.

With practiced expertise, he flipped the wire over the old man's head and around his neck, zinging it tight before the old man could get his fingers under it. With a grunt, the Killer yanked the wire taut, and the old man gagged and stumbled back against him, gurgling wetly and clawing at the wire slicing a line of dark red in his blue neck.

The Killer looked left and right. No notice of the commotion. He hauled the old man backward into the dark driveway and laid him down, still keeping the wire taut around his neck. They were both on the ground. The old man flopped and struggled, his hands flailing at his throat and his attacker. His struggles were becoming weaker. The Killer breathed in, smelling the organic perfume of approaching death.

With a practiced motion, the Killer slipped one foot in a handle of the garrote, freeing a hand. A kick of that foot and a two-handed pull on the other handle, would slice the neck cleanly through. Maybe even lop off the head, if he caught a neck vertebra just right.

The Killer sweated the lovely sweat of a person hard at doing what he was born to do. He wanted the finish so badly, but he remembered his business. He pulled a penlight out of his pocket and pushed the button to light the old man's face. It was beautiful. The old eyes bugged out, the jaw worked uselessly, the tongue lolled in a helpless, silent scream.

The Killer rubbed the wrinkled gasping face with his finger, but no makeup came off. He yanked at the nose, but it was real. He picked at the scalp with his finger, but it was no bald wig.

The Killer sat there breathing hard for a long moment. He had to bring himself down. The old man was still struggling, but more feebly.

No kill. No kill. He could not kill now. It would alert the police. Newspaper stories, television stories about an old blue man killed. That would alert his target.

Reluctantly, the Killer loosened the wire and slipped it off. The old man gasped and heaved, rolling away and gagging. The Killer debated whether to rob him, but decided not. That way, the report of the attack would be even less interesting to the police. Somebody had just attacked an old man, then let him go. No harm. Just an old man. Nothing taken. Nothing to alarm people who worried more about thefts than old men getting choked a little bit.

The old man still lay on the ground, crawling slowly away, retching in fear.

The Killer rose to his feet, still breathing hard, bringing himself down. He looked down at the old man, who had not glimpsed his face. He scanned the area for possible witnesses, saw none, and walked swiftly toward the lights of the main street. He would lose himself in the dark streets and the anonymous crowds, and continue his hunt.

CHAPTER 28

Lupo felt dizzy with exhaustion by the time he finished constructing Lupo1000. He prepared the growth chamber that would mass-produce the virus and peeled his arms out of the shoulder-length rubber gloves attached to his isolation chamber. His arms dripped with sweat and smelled dankly of the rubber. He let them dangle at his sides, rotating his head around and around to work the kinks from his neck.

He'd lost track of time, as often happened in the lab. He had to quit for a while. He'd been at it for six hours, and he realized he had to go to the bathroom; he had to eat; he had to sleep. But he was driven by the urgency. They were closing in, he could feel it. They had tried to kill him twice, and he knew they were closing in.

"Okay, guys, you just grow and be happy," he said in a low voice to the single glass flask inside the small chamber.

He used the toilet and turned on the faucet in the wash basin, splashing cold water on his face. As he dried his face, he peered at it over the towel in the mirror. He breathed a tired sigh. The glow that was normally there was gone. The person staring back was haggard. But there was still the anger; still the soul-deep anger that had made a burning knot in his belly for the past year. It had powered his obsession, his inexorable drive toward this end.

He went back into the lab, sitting down heavily in his desk chair. He began to write in his lab notebook, carefully describing the steps he had just taken. The new viral construction was elegant—a perfect, indefensible, unstoppable airborne disease. All his proven innovations were in it, and more. He had almost finished.

But before he was done, he had to check on three particular proteins Lupo1000 produced. He needed to use a protein sequencer to figure out their sequence, make sure they were perfect. And he had to build one more small gene to insert into the virus and run a sequence check on another. He wrote down all the tests he needed in his notebook, mapping them out so he would get them perfect when he went out to use the university laboratory.

He reached into the large box of Tastykakes beside the desk. He groped around and brought out only a package of vanilla sugar wafers. It was the last Tastykake. And he couldn't risk ordering another shipment. He solemnly unwrapped the little plastic-enshrined confection. From now on it would be Ding Dongs, or those cheap cupcakes. Or worse still, Twinkies. Industrial foods. No soul.

He munched somberly on a sugar wafer and finished writing in his notebook.

"Computer," he said quietly.

"Yes, Arthur."

"Show me the DNA sequence information on Lupo1000."

The computer did so, and long strings of genetic code filled the screen. Lupo leaned over the keyboard, manipulating the program, zooming on different sequences, checking, rechecking, and rechecking again the genetic blueprints for his masterpiece. Just a few more adjustments. He needed to insert just a few more control DNA sequences. They would arrive soon. Finally, he simply laid his head down on his desk and went to sleep.

• • •

The outside of the club was conservative-looking enough, thought Loudon. A blue neon sign in elegantly curved script announced "Rocco's" and beneath, the information, "A night club for gentlemen."

But as Loudon, Walter and Scalisi, pushed through the door, the deep bass pounding of the music and the appreciative, male murmurings of the crowd made a very different impression.

A beefy iron-pumper bouncer in a jacket and tie loomed over them in the darkness of the large foyer. His hair was carefully sculpted in a short razor cut. His head was so small, though, Loudon thought that if the barber had charged him by scalp area, the haircut was probably cheap. In the dim light, Loudon judged the bouncer to be a pine green.

"Do you sirs wish a table?" He eyed Loudon and Walter with unspoken curiosity about their white skin.

"No," said Scalisi. "We're here to see Rocco." Scalisi held up his credentials. The FBI credential and the use of the owner's name had an effect on the large man. He blinked twice, then said, "Come in and wait over here. Lemme see if he can see you."

"Tell him it's Scalisi, and he'd better see me." Scalisi bounced slightly like a boxer when he talked up to the big man. Loudon thought that Scalisi had probably seen his share of street fights in his native New York. "Hey," he shouted over the music to Loudon and Walter, nodding at the departing bouncer. "There goes the Jolly Green Giant!"

"Looks like your big brother, Jack," said Loudon, peering critically at Scalisi's nearly-matching mint-green face.

Laughing, they followed the bouncer into the darkened, cavernous night club, redolent with an atmosphere of heavy-duty partying. The room was crowded with small tables with plush chairs filled with men of many shades of red, green, blue, yellow. They wore shorts, slacks, sport jackets, t-shirts. They ranged from husky, young fraternity boys to solid middle-aged businessmen out for a night of diversion.

Other men of the same kind stood three deep at the long bar, milling heads silhouetted against a backlit panoply of gleaming bottles holding every liquor imaginable. Loudon's gaze lingered thirstily on the rich mahogany liquids glimmering transparently in the bottles, but he turned away. His legs still hurt. His other muscles were sore. A drink or two would help. But not tonight.

On the other side of the room, sturdy, waitresses streamed from a kitchen with plates heaped with steaming steaks, chops, chicken and potatoes, fried, baked, mashed, stuffed. Others just as continually exited with the piled remains of the dinners.

But it was the center of the room that riveted the attention of every customer, even as they drank, ate, smoked and laughed.

On a large spotlit stage, in reasonable unison, a lithe line of women danced to the thunderous music. Perfect specimens of long-legged, round-hipped, small-waisted, flat-bellied, high-breasted women whose smooth, taut skins showed off myriad shades of blue.

They danced in a fleshy blue line arranged in darkening order: powder blue, baby blue, sky blue, azure, navy blue, cobalt blue, cadet blue, and indigo. They twirled to the driving beat. When they kicked, the legs showed the colors. When they nestled against one another, their hips and waving arms showed the colors.

The three FBI agents temporarily forgot their mission. They stood by the door, inspired, and watched the show, evidently a finale with all the performers.

"Sirs," interrupted the large man, snapping them out of their reverie. "Mr. Rocco will see you now."

"You always have blue women?" asked Scalisi.

"Naw," said the man, glancing casually at the stage. "This is blues night . . . the color not the music. We have red, orange, yellow night. Yellow's interesting. But blue's the best. We got sirs who come here every blue night. We tried a purple night, but people didn't come."

"I can understand that," said Walter seriously.

"Yeah, everybody likes to get blue," the large man snorted a braying laugh.

They circled the room, threading through the crowds, and walked down a long red-carpeted hallway, entering a heavy polished wood door marked "Private."

A cardinal-red Rocco lounged on an overstuffed couch, his patent-leather shoes resting on an ottoman.

"Here they are," said the large pine-green man, stating the obvious.

Rocco looked up without moving. "Yeah, say, Scalisi, how you doin' paisan! FBI man, you wanna drink, eh? Who're these guys?" He had a thicker version of Scalisi's New York accent.

"No, Rocco, we're here on business."

"Fine, good, then. Business."

"Rocco, we want some information about the guy who caused all this," said Scalisi abruptly. "This is Agent Loudon. He's in charge of the case."

"Yeah," said Rocco. "Lupo? That his name? He did this?" He pointed at his own colored face. "Can't believe he did this, man, and he's Italian, right?"

"I don't know," said Loudon. "But Agent Scalisi says you're well connected in Denver. That you know what's happening."

"Yeah, I do. I sure do. But I don't *give* nothin' away, man." Rocco, lifted his feet off the ottoman and got up to get himself a drink from a mirrored bar set into the wall. "This Lupo thing is big. I know it. I've seen the TV. This guy could do serious damage if he wanted to. I got a brother."

"I know you've got a brother," said Scalisi, annoyance tingeing his voice. "We talked about your brother."

Rocco turned to Loudon. "I got a brother in the federal pen. We talked, Scalisi and me . . . one goombah to another. I said 'Scalisi, someday when you really need me, I'll be there. So, I want you there when I need you.'"

"Your brother's not comin' out, Rocco!" exclaimed Scalisi. "No matter how much you give us!"

Rocco turned and held up one hand in a gesture of resignation. "Yeah, well, then look, I can't remember anything. I don't know anything. So, ciao, bambino." He brushed his chin with his red fingertips in a gesture of defiance. The big green man stepped forward.

"Look, Rocco, here's the deal," said Scalisi, waving the green man back. "Your brother gets parole, maybe first try. In a year. Okay?" He looked at Loudon, who nodded agreeably.

"Yeah, but we have to get major help here," said Loudon.

Scalisi walked up to Rocco and put his mint-green face right in Rocco's cardinal-red face. "And I won't tell anybody what I found out about you . . . paisan." The last word was spat like a curse. Rocco stared insolently at Scalisi, but with a flip of his hand, dismissed the big green bouncer.

Scalisi waited until the door had shut. Without moving his gaze from Rocco, Scalisi said, "He's not Italian."

"Hey, man, just ease up," said Rocco, a note of pleading entering his voice. "They didn't have to know that, man."

"Well, now they do."

"Impersonating an Italian?" asked Walter in mock astonishment. "Isn't that a federal offense?"

"Yeah," said Loudon. "Tough rap to beat, too."

"His real name's Robert Kleinfelter—"

"Scalisi, cut it out!"

"—and he calls himself Rocco because it got him some respect in this town. They think he's a tough wop from Canarsie, but he's nothin but a Kleinfelter from Queens."

"Okay, okay . . . what do you wanna know?" Rocco sat back down in his chair, sullen, resigned.

"Where's Lupo?" asked Loudon.

"He's in town somewhere."

"What!" said Loudon. "In Denver?"

"Yeah. There was a shootin' down near Steve's a few nights ago. I had my guy nose around down there, just to see if it was anything I could use. What happened was two guys went after an old guy, a blue guy, been comin' in to Steve's for a couple of months. My people think they saw him in here sometimes, sittin' in a corner, drinkin'. Steve thought about it, realized it coulda been Lupo. In fact, he never thought about it before, but the old guy always kept in a corner, like he was hidin' somethin'."

"So where is he?" asked Loudon.

"Steve don't know. I don't know. But he better not get found."

"The two guys?"

"Naw, they was idiots. Couldn't hit nothing. They ain't been around since. But now there's a pro."

"A pro? A hit man?" asked Loudon.

"Look, that's it." Rocco got up and sat on the edge of his desk and crossed his ankles, waving both hands and sloshing his drink on the rug. "I say more, I could get juiced, man. This guy's a major."

"Okay, then we take you down for questioning," said Scalisi, with casual menace. "It gets in the paper that Rocco's been with the FBI. This pro figures it out. And bang. One less bogus Italian, eh, Kleinfelter?"

Rocco looked nervously from one agent to the other, drained his drink and poured himself another one. "All right, Scalisi. But I'm countin' on you."

"Sure, right."

"There's a bunch of whackos. The Aryan Committee. Y'know, hate group. One of them's in here drinkin', maybe last week or so. He tells my bartender we got too many black women in here. Starts this stuff about how they're hidin' behind colors, but that his bunch is gonna get Lupo, so there won't be any more colored people hidin'. He says they brought in a pro. A guy who's so secret, he don't even have a name." Rocco stopped suddenly and looked down.

"What else?" asked Loudon. "What else about the guy?"

"Well, that's it."

"Downtown?" threatened Scalisi.

"Okay, man! Lemme think! Well . . . the bartender says the guy says the pro uses all kinds of ways to kill. He heard it in a meeting. He uses guns and poisons and dart-things and wires. He can do a guy in a second. And he costs a lot. But that's all I know. Man, honest. Really!"

"All right, Kleinfelter."

"Don't call me that, okay?" said Rocco waving his hand in conciliation.

"Look, contact us if you hear anything else. You understand?"

"Yeah, sure, and don't forget my brother in the joint."

"Joint? C'mon, Kleinfelter, stop tryin' to make him out to be some big-time crook," said Scalisi. "He's in a country club prison in California for white-collar crime. He embezzled money from an underwear factory."

"Man, you never give an inch do ya?"

"Not with you . . . goombah."

CHAPTER 29

Scalisi leaned tiredly back in the chair, sighed and tapped the remote control's channel button. He sat alone in the sterile, shopworn conference room of the Denver FBI field office, his first chance to rest in hours. The unyielding glare of the blue-white fluorescent lights emphasized the lines and the blotchy tiredness on his mint-green face. The light seemed like some oppressing ether that wrapped the fatigue tight around him. The contrast between the brightly lit room and the onyx blackness outside the windows, pierced by only a few lonely street lights, emphasized that the rest of Denver was asleep.

Scalisi flipped through the channels. Typical late-night shows. *Law & Order* rerun. Weather channel. Shopping channel. Late night local news. Despite his tiredness, he was looking for clues. Any little thing that might help find Lupo. Or the killer who was after him.

Loudon came in, nodded and settled heavily into a chair and watched the procession of channels.

"Get Bowers?" asked Scalisi.

"Yeah. He was just going out to a party. But he insisted on a full briefing."

"Hey, he's your boss. Gotta keep your boss happy."

"You SACS all stick together. Yeah, well, it's true, I'll have to go back there someday, and I'd just as soon not have to take abuse from him."

"More important, how about the pro? Anything on him?"

"Well, I tried NCIC. I fed in everything Rocco told us into the computer, but no match. Thought I'd get one. I asked Walter to start running his traps around headquarters and at field offices. He knows somebody in about every field office. Somebody's bound to remember something."

Scalisi had channel-surfed all the way around the dial and started over. He came back to the local news.

"Stop there," suggested Loudon, and Scalisi did. The newscaster looked poised, well-groomed and aloe green. He reported with wry amusement that the nation's braver tourists were flocking to Denver to see its amazing colored citizens.

The scene cut to a henna-colored street-corner hot dog vendor speaking into a reporter's microphone: "Yeah, the neuts are comin' in by the zillions," he said.

"Neuts?" asked the reporter.

"Yeah, neuts . . . neutrals," the vendor said with disdain, adjusting his baseball cap. "That's what we call 'em . . . yer beige, yer brown . . . no real color like us . . . neuts." He gestured contemptuously at a group of neuts wandering past him along the downtown streets, cameras at the ready, gawking at the array of coloreds. The camera cut to crowds of neuts streaming eagerly from airplane ramps into the airport.

The newscaster also reported that Denver's coloreds had taken to traveling the country, taking advantage of the demand for "people of hue." The scene cut to a grinning scarlet man snipping an opening-day ribbon at a Red, Hot and Blue barbecue restaurant in California. It cut to a moss-green woman beside a lectern telling her story at a garden show. It cut to a banana-yellow man clowning at a fruit-importers' convention.

The news show itself cut to a commercial featuring a slinky fire-engine-red woman hawking a "red-hot" sales event at a local car dealer. Loudon glanced curiously at Scalisi, slouching and rocking gently in his chair. Loudon stretched his still-aching legs and yawned.

"So, Jack, how is it, really? Being colors?" he asked. "The family okay with it?"

"Yeah, it's okay," said Scalisi sipping his coffee and regarding his mint-green hand with cool detachment. "We went down to the school. The school psychologist held a meeting. She said the older kids, the teenagers, were kind of confused. She said some were making color clubs. Y'know, Sandy, my daughter? In her junior high, the yellows formed a club. And the greens. She's apricot, so she joined the yellows. But the psychologist said it's not necessarily bad. It's more a teenage bonding thing, she said she thought."

"Your boy's younger?"

"Yeah, Anthony's nine. He thinks it's cool, like out of some comic book. He plays with the other kids, he's the Blue Avenger."

"Thing is, I think she suspects what the real danger is. Lupo's . . . uh . . . final virus. She knows me. She sees how I'm acting nervous."

"Jack, don't worry. We'll get him. He's around here somewhere. And he hasn't finished the virus, or he would've let it loose by now."

"Yeah," said Scalisi almost in a whisper, staring down at the floor. Loudon could tell he was thinking of what would happen to his family.

Just as a talk show host had launched into jokes about Denver's "yellow journalists" and "blue-nosed church ladies," Lucas White bustled into the conference room. The other agents who had been working at their desks followed him in. White folded himself into a chair opposite Loudon, and the other agents settled in around the table, quickly covering its scarred formica wood-grain surface with papers, files, and half-filled coffee cups. The team leaders readied themselves for the briefing, their forced activity and the coffee barely holding their weariness at bay. Most of the field agents were already in bed asleep; the leaders had hours more of analyzing the raw information before their heads would find rest on pillows.

As they settled in, Doc arrived to represent the CDC, his hair perhaps more awry than usual and plaid shirt and khaki trousers looking more rumpled than usual. A frustrated silent glance at Loudon said that he hadn't found anything.

He scanned the room as he sat down. "Where's Kathleen?"

"She should be here," said Loudon. "I haven't heard from her. I'm a little worried. She went to trace those gene shipments."

Doc looked annoyed "Yeah, well, I hope she kept those agents with her, so she—"

"We should get started," interrupted White, flipping open his notebook. Loudon and the others did the same. He began to ask each of the team leaders for their results.

The cylinders had all been found and removed, reported one agent, a neut. The water system had been flushed, he said, and the water was considered safe to drink.

Doc volunteered that the CDC's laboratory had confirmed that the virus was microencapsulated. "Yeah, he encased the bug in lipid so it was protected," he said, leafing through his own notes. "The bugs made it all the way into people's stomachs before the acids dissolved the capsule and released the bug. Nice job."

Another neut agent shuffled through his pile of reports and said that a motorcyclist with a large backpack had been seen on several occasions near the water purification plants.

A violet agent said that a canvass of commercial real estate agents found only a few rentals that could be used for laboratories. Teams had checked them and found nothing unusual. However, they had called in the Denver police to make a drug raid on one laboratory.

"Well, at least we accomplished one useful thing today," said White derisively, as he scribbled notes for his report to the director.

The head of the field teams checking university labs reported promising results. An ocher young agent fiddled with a pencil as he scanned his notes. He said that one university reported that the previous week an unidentified young male in a white lab coat had been using a University of Denver molecular biology instrument lab. The instruments were shared by the entire building, and the man signed up to use the equipment as a visiting colleague of a professor who was on sabbatical. But when contacted, the professor said he hadn't heard of the man.

At the news, Loudon came alert.

"Did he fit Lupo's description?"

"Generally. He was kind of mauve. Had different hair, nose. The people at the lab didn't recognize his picture. But it could have been him."

"Let's put a stakeout on it immediately. I wanna get out there myself."

"Not a particularly useful step," said White, tapping his pencil impatiently. "We've got more important things to do than to stake out a lab that the target probably knows is watched now. We're stretched pretty thin, anyway."

"Okay, so at least send the Denver police. C'mon, Lucas, this is a prime chance!"

White shrugged and nodded reluctantly at the FBI's Denver police liaison, who left to make arrangements.

They had just turned back to their briefing when shouts and whoops rolled in from the outer office. Shinohara rushed through the door with two large dark-suited agents—one cerise, one paprika.

"John Dabney!" Shinohara exclaimed triumphantly, waving a fist and grinning widely. The two agents echoed her.

"What?" asked Lucas, slightly annoyed at the unseemly interruption.

"That's his alias!" said the paprika agent. "Lupo's! She got it. She found it out."

Shinohara paced the room, too excited to sit down. "One of the gene company's records listed some gene sequences that were going to a post office box in downtown Denver. It looked funny. We found a postal clerk who remembered the person who rented the box and came in to get the packages. Everybody else at the post office just remembered an old man coming in. But she remembered that after the color change, she could tell he wore blue makeup. She saw some rub off on the counter. We got her to check the rental list, and the name was John Dabney!" She looked over at Loudon and widened her eyes in both greeting and provocative signal between them.

"Where've you been all this time?" asked Doc.

"We had to go out to her house, out in Littleton. We waited till she got home from a movie. Then we had to get back to the post office and look in the records."

"Okay, well then, good work, Kathleen," said Doc.

"Gentlemen, you know what to do," said White, and the agents gathered their papers and rushed for the door. Over the next hour, they would launch a nationwide search of credit card records, bank records, phone records, and car rental records. Before the night was over, four unfortunate John Dabneys in various parts of the country would be rousted from their sleep by FBI agents pounding on their doors. None would be Arthur Lupo.

White snapped his notebook shut with finality. "I guess that's about it. I'll call the director in the morning. Let's see about getting some sleep." He stood and stretched and left.

Shinohara plumped into a chair, still pleased with her discovery. She looked around expectantly at Doc, Loudon, and Scalisi, who had remained.

Loudon waited for the last agent to leave before leaning over to Doc. "Anything on the faction lab?"

"Nah. I went with your boys all over the area. We flew in the helicopter, we drove in the car. Anywhere there was enough isolated land to keep a BSL-4 lab secret. But we didn't find anything."

"Anyplace you missed?"

"Sure, of course. There are still some big private lands that we couldn't get to that could hold labs disguised as warehouses. We couldn't do them all."

"Well, you want to keep looking?"

"I do. I sent the boys home, but I'm gonna get a few hours sleep, then get their butts out and look some more."

"Great! Thanks, Doc!"

"Anything on Lupo?" asked Shinohara. Loudon told her about the university laboratory. "What do you think, Doc?" she asked.

"Same thing you probably think." They looked at each other significantly.

"So could you two maybe share what you both think, then?" asked Loudon.

"We think he needs instruments badly," said Shinohara. "DNA sequencers, DNA synthesizers. He may be in the last stages of putting together the virus. He's got to have instruments he can't possibly have in his own lab. And he might be more willing to take chances. He might have a prototype nearly done."

"He may be braver," added Doc. "I'd bet he's already made the airborne virus equivalent of a regular bomb; maybe he's going for thermonuclear."

Walter appeared at the door, saw the gathered group and came in. He looked at Loudon and made a pleased face that indicated that his information was interesting.

"So, we stake out the university lab along with the Denver police," said Scalisi.

"No question," said Loudon. "Jack, how about you go home and get some sleep? Be with your family. I'll go out to the lab. I'll contact the cops on the scene. You can take over tomorrow." Scalisi nodded gratefully at the excuse to see his family before he went back on the case.

"I'll go, too," said Shinohara. "You have to have somebody who knows labs."

Loudon turned to her and opened his mouth. He was planning to tell her he didn't want her in danger. But a subtle flash of her dark eyes was a fleeting glance of warning. He wisely closed his mouth.

When he opened it again, he declared, "Great," with a careful mix of mild enthusiasm and resignation. He saved himself further embarrassment by turning to Walter. "What's up?"

"Real interesting," said Walter, settling into a chair. "I asked all over about our pro hit man. Field offices, RAs. Nothin'. I finally got a little bird up at headquarters to tell me about DFS, Director's Files."

"What are those?"

"Well, there are some cases where the target is so expert they're afraid he might have a tap into the Bureau. They have DF files on high government types, real smart Mafia, and so forth." Walter found a half-filled coffee cup on the table, checked it for cigarette butts and took a sip. "If your average brick agent got into those files and went after one of those targets, he'd probably get taken out, and the investigation would go sour. So, DF cases have special teams, and they keep the files in the director's office. My little bird said there are a few top-level assassins in those files. Real pros, she said. She said our guy might be one of those. We need to get into those files."

Loudon sat for a moment, thinking. His old mentor Henry Cleland could get into those files. "I've got a source," he said.

"I know," said Walter. "Now's the time to use him."

"I'll make a call."

CHAPTER 30

The warm, dry night breeze brought the smell of the lush university campus greenery mixed with a faint leftover aroma of the day's smog. Loudon had all the car windows open, letting the breeze play gently through the darkened car. From his space in the parking lot, out his window, he could see one of the back entrances to the massive concrete-and-glass research building complex. The structure looked like an intricate jumble of massive gray blocks, an angular collection of buildings that was one of the university's main molecular biology labs. The entrance was lit by a small light, but the area was surrounded by deep shadow made deeper by the overhanging trees. Only a few lights shone in the large windows. Nothing had changed in the windows over the past three hours, ever since the professor who was their contact in the building had made a surreptitious search. Loudon was grateful for the professor's cooperation, because the sight of police and FBI agents in the building might have caused too much of a stir.

The trees whispered with the breeze, an occasional creak marking branch rubbing branch. The leaves danced in front of the street lights, casting ever-shifting patterns of light and dark on the pavement and the car.

Shinohara stirred in the back seat, and he couldn't resist reaching back to gently touch her warm sleeping form. He had promised to wake her in a couple of hours, so that she could take over the watch. He was tempted to let her sleep, but he'd learned his lesson. She would not be denied the right to do her job. He smiled. Faint voices on the radio marked the Denver police units checking in. He looked at his watch. Three a.m. They were doing the half-hour check.

"Four oh three DPD, no activity," said one voice.

"One oh two DPD," came the answer. "Couple of kids. Looking for a dark place to smooch. Threw 'em out. No other activity."

"Al, you have no heart," said the first voice.

"Yeah, but I got a memory. And I got a daughter."

Other units checked in, including some of the campus cops. The terse voices from the radio seemed to linger and fill the shadowy confines of the car. It was his turn.

"Fed One, no activity," he said into the microphone. He listened for signs that Shinohara had awakened at his voice, but heard none. Good. He rubbed his face and shook his head to keep awake.

He mulled over his call to Cleland earlier that night. The old man had answered sleepy, but alert. He was used to being brought from deep sleep to instant functionality. But he was still drowsy enough that Loudon's mention of the Director's Files caught him off guard. Loudon detected a slight hesitation in the voice on the phone. Cleland was deciding whether to admit to the existence of the files, admit to his knowledge of them. Finally, Cleland agreed to take Loudon's request and decide later how to handle it. Maybe he'd do something, maybe he wouldn't. He couldn't promise. Cleland wasn't normally wishy-washy. Loudon sensed that something else was going on there.

After half an hour, Loudon gave in to weariness and laid his head back, promising himself it was only for an instant. The warm fog of sleep began to envelope him. His breathing became heavy, regular. He almost woke himself with the opening snort of a snore, but he settled back.

Through the fog, he heard the radio.

"One oh two DPD, I got activity. I got lights on. Third-floor window. That's the floor, isn't it?"

"Yeah one oh two. That's the one. Fed One, you copy?"

Loudon jerked forward and grabbed the microphone. Sleep fell away in an instant.

"Yeah. How did he get in?"

Over the radio came a chorus of "I don't knows."

"Well, somebody secure this entrance. I'm going in. If you see him, follow, but do not apprehend. Repeat, do not apprehend. Subject could be hotter than anybody could handle." He swung the car door open and pushed himself out, sprinting for the doorway. Behind him, the back car door opened. He turned to see Shinohara behind him. He kept jogging, his legs still two painful sticks from his race with her.

"Robert," she said in a low accusing voice, as she caught up.

"Honest, I was going to wake you. I forgot. Honest."

"After the wedding—"

"Kathleen, I just can't—" But he didn't have time to finish the sentence as they both reached the door. He put his finger to his lips. He opened the door and stepped inside. On the first floor, the hall was brightly lit, but the nearby labs were dark. A faint noise came from a door at the end of the hall. He hurried down, and peered around the corner of the door. A small, thin cherry-red oriental woman stood at a lab bench pipetting. She jumped as he appeared, her eyes wide with apprehension.

He showed his credentials. "FBI. Anybody else come through here?"

She shook her head mutely, still clearly frightened. Shinohara appeared beside him and the woman settled down.

"Anybody else in the building?" asked Loudon.

"Maybe on two, maybe on four, I think." The voice was small, timid.

"Fine, now you're going to have to leave the building." Without questioning him, the young woman quickly capped several chemicals, picked up her knapsack and hurried past him out the door. "Kathleen, could you take the stairs and check two and four and get the others out? I'll go to three on the elevator. Watch for him." Loudon left for the elevator.

Shinohara nodded and hurried to the nearby stairs. She took the steps two at a time to the second floor. She reached the second story, striding the length of the hall past seminar-notice-cluttered bulletin boards and doors covered with cartoons, signs, and photos. She paused at the bathrooms, checking inside each one. She continually peered the length of the hall in front and behind her for anybody who might emerge from a lab. The hallways were bare, except for an emergency shower in the middle of each wing. The shower was for quick decontamination of workers and was little more than a large showerhead extending from the ceiling with a metal pull-chain and a floor drain beneath. Beside each shower was a smaller eyewash fountain, with twin spigots to flush the eyes of workers who splashed caustic chemicals in their eyes.

She hurried between the doorways, her sneakers occasionally squeaking on the slick floor, pausing at each to peer in through the window in the doors. Most were pitch black, with a few showing the faint glow of computers or instrument control panels. She reached one where the lights were on and the door was open. She peeked around the corner. It was empty. She stepped in and quickly walked through the lab before moving on. She noted that each laboratory was directly connected with its neighbor by a door, so researchers wouldn't have to carry experimental materials out into the hallway to reach the next lab. It was a standard architecture for such labs. She wished they'd been able to scout the building earlier.

The next lighted laboratory held a bearded, cypress-green young man taking apart an electrophoresis apparatus. As he looked up, she could see that the roots of his beard were beginning to turn the same color. It wasn't Lupo.

"Yeah? Can I help you?" He was blearily interested in the beautiful wild-haired young woman who had arrived slightly out of breath at his laboratory door in the middle of the night.

"I'm looking for somebody. A short man. Round."

"Well, no, haven't seen anybody. A while ago, though, I heard the elevator open."

"You working down the hall, too?"

"Yeah, in two twelve. I've got that open."

"How about the third floor?"

"No, I'm not up there."

"That's shared instruments, right?"

"Yeah, and the fourth."

"The fourth, too?"

"Yeah, just part of it. Some DNA sequencers."

The young man asked Shinohara who she was, but she only told him she was with the government. She warned him to leave the building and moved on. The hallways in that wing of the building formed a huge squared circle, and she made the full circuit without finding anyone else. Back at the stairway, she pushed open the metal fire door and bounded up the stairs. She paused at the door with the huge white 3 marked on it. She was tempted to go through it, to catch up with Loudon. To tell him that the fourth floor was a shared facility, too. But she had promised to clear out four. It was the top floor. She could do it quickly and come back down, sure that Lupo wasn't above them. If Lupo was anywhere, he would be on three.

She quickly mounted the stairs to the fourth floor and entered the hall. It was the same as the others. But maybe quieter. She moved carefully, stopping at a lab whose door was open, its inside lights on. She looked quickly around the corner into the room, prepared to draw back. Nobody there. She moved on. Almost at the end of the hall, she reached another laboratory that was dark except for a faint glow. She peeked quickly around the door, expecting to see a computer left on. She saw a flash of white fabric. Someone was working at one of the laboratory benches that was not visible from the door. Anybody outside the building wouldn't have noticed the faint light from the instruments or the small light over the lab bench. She stood quietly, watching the figure move. She heard the click of plastic vials. The indicator beep of controls being manipulated. Then, between two of the shelves, a face came into view, lit dimly by the lamp. It was round, very round, with small eyes, little bow lips. It was mauve.

She gasped in a breath and backed away from the door against the wall. It was Lupo! Her heart began to pound. She stood against the wall, trying to think what to do. She could go for Loudon, but Lupo might escape. She could try to grab him. She was probably stronger than him. If she could grab him away from any virus cultures he had with him, it would be over. She considered texting Loudon, but realized time was too short, and his approach might alert Lupo.

Then she knew what to do! He had never really seen her before. Only that once on the dark street in Pasadena, and she had been on the ground obscured behind a car. And he'd had on a motorcycle helmet, restricting his vision. She could get close now and he probably wouldn't recognize her. She moved as silently as she could away from the door down the hall, glancing back several times to see if Lupo had come out of the lab. Her shoe squeaked and she froze and looked back. The squeak had sounded like the yelp of a small dog in the deserted hall. She tried several doors until she found one open. The light from the hallway spilled into the darkened laboratory. She found what she needed hanging on a coat tree. A lab coat, luckily with a security badge still attached. She put it on. It was too big, but it would have to do. She found a rack of plastic vials and picked it up.

She stepped back into the hall, and walked toward the door. She took several large breaths and tried to still her shaking hands, which made the rack of vials rattle slightly. She would get close to him, and if he wasn't within reach of any virus cultures, she'd grab him. She'd wrestle his undoubtedly soft, doughy body out into the hall. If necessary, she'd knock him unconscious.

She tried to mimic the kind of nonchalant, noisy walk of any lab worker going up to use a research instrument in the middle of the night. She reached the doorway, steeled herself and strolled in, flipping on the overhead lights.

"Oh, gee, hi," she said as perkily as she could.

Lupo's head jerked up with the frightened look of a deer caught in a car's headlights. He blinked at the bright lights and almost dropped the sample tube in his hand. He wore a lab coat with a university photo identification tag attached. Shinohara realized that the badge on her own coat didn't match her. But she forged ahead.

"Oh, I'm sorry. I didn't mean to scare you," she chirped. "I didn't know anybody was in here. The lights were off. These labs make me nervous at night, too. I'm Kathy."

"Uh . . . hi." Lupo continued to stare at her. He licked his lips. She noticed a wild look beginning to rise in his eyes, a look that said he might do anything. She had to put him at ease.

"I see you're using the sequenator. I'll just come back later. I thought it might be free this time of night and I wouldn't have to sign up for it. I'm a night person. I guess you are, too." She smiled. It seemed to be working.

"Yeah, well—"

"When do you think you'll be done?"

He glanced nervously at the machine the size of a microwave oven. Its control screen showed that it was in the midst of an analysis. He probably badly needed that analysis.

"Maybe an hour. I'm doin' my last sample." He glanced over at a large leather satchel.

She glanced at it, too. It was probably full of samples, but what else? A long awkward pause grew between them. He clearly expected her to leave. Her plan was failing. She turned to go, then turned back.

"You know about the bad chemicals?"

"What? The *what*?"

She had him worried.

"About a week ago, they found out they had a bad batch of reagents in here. They were giving false sequences."

"*When? Where? What days?*" He reached for his lab notebook. He forgot his rising panic in the concern over his work. She moved slightly closer. If she could just get him away from the satchel.

"I think it was the fourteenth they found out."

Lupo thumbed though the notebook. She slipped past him, down the aisle. She decided to maneuver herself between him and the satchel, to push him away from it.

A movement at the door caught her eye and she looked up. Loudon stood in the doorway, an expression of surprise frozen on his face. Lupo looked up and shocked recognition rose on his face. The instant seemed to last forever.

"I . . . I heard your voice . . ." stammered Loudon.

Shinohara looked from Loudon to Lupo, transfixed for a moment, then tried to recover the situation. She knew she was the only one who could. She opened her hands to Lupo. "Arthur, we're not going to hurt you—" she started to say, but Lupo let out a desperate yelp and leaped past her for the satchel. He plunged his hand into it and pulled out a glass flask sealed at the top. He held it above his head, his eyes wild with fright and grim resolve. The swirling brown liquid glimmered in the overhead light.

"Lupo, don't do anything stupid!" exclaimed Loudon. "We're not going to hurt you!"

"Like before!? Huh!? Like before!?" Lupo's voice became a caustic shrill. "Yeah, right! Stay there! Don't come closer!" Waving the flask at them like it was some poisonous reptile, he stuffed his notebook into the satchel, grabbed it and backed past Shinohara, toward the connecting door to the next laboratory.

"Arthur, you don't know what you're doing," said Shinohara.

"Yes, I do!" Lupo turned the flask in his stubby fingers. He fumbled it, almost dropped it, and Shinohara found herself involuntarily lurching to catch it, but stopping herself. A yellow biohazard symbol rotated into view. The liquid sloshed threateningly in the flask.

"Arthur, is that a virus?" asked Shinohara. "Don't let it loose, Arthur! Don't do this!"

"What's going on here?" Another voice behind Loudon. He turned to see a uniformed blood-red Denver policeman, striding down the hall, his gun drawn.

"I told you people to stay outside!" shouted Loudon. "Get out of here!"

But the policeman, an impassive look on his face kept coming, didn't even slow. He reached Loudon, rounded the corner of the lab door and saw Lupo. He brought his gun up in a blood-red hand that contrasted with the shiny blackness of the metal.

"NO!" shouted both Shinohara and Loudon simultaneously.

With a faint whimpering sound from deep in his throat, Lupo backed through the connecting door and awkwardly flung the flask at Shinohara. It shattered against the edge of the lab bench, splattering her with the liquid.

She screamed in an agony of fear, backing hard against the opposite bench, holding her hands out helplessly and staring in shock down at the brown liquid staining the lab coat, her shirt and her pants. She uttered a deep, anguished cry, droplets of the liquid running down her cheek.

Lupo slammed the door between the labs and disappeared.

"What is it? What was that?" asked the cop.

"Virus! We don't know! Get back!"

Shinohara, recovering slightly, reached over and slammed the lab door, leaving Loudon and the cop outside, staring through the glass window.

"GET AWAY!" she cried, her hands still held wide, palms up. "GET BACK! LEAVE THE FLOOR!"

"But Kathleen—" Loudon heard a door slam at the end of the hall. Lupo leaped into the hall, after having gone through all the connecting doors to the end. Before Loudon could react, the policeman crouched, leveled his pistol at Lupo and fired three times in quick succession. The deafening explosions filled the hall, and the bullets slammed into the concrete wall and shattered the window at the end. Lupo jumped into the door to the stairwell. The policeman raced after him.

"I SAID STOP!" Loudon drew his pistol, ready to shoot the cop if necessary, but the cop was gone. He was small and very quick. Something about him didn't sit right with Loudon. Cops weren't that small. And his features —high forehead, wide cheekbones, narrow jaw—were just too delicate for the typical cop. Still nagged by his gut feeling, Loudon holstered his pistol and turned back to the door.

Shinohara had moved to the other lab bench, her hands shaking, scooping samples of the liquid into vials. She turned back to him.

"Robert, get back. Get off the floor and call the CDC team. Get Doc." Her voice was lower now, but still shaking. It carried perhaps a touch of resignation, which frightened Loudon even more.

Loudon backed away down the hall, keeping his eye on the door, all the way to the end. But he would not leave the floor. If this was the last time he would be with her, he would risk whatever she'd been infected with. He stood at the end of the hall, his hands helplessly at his side.

Muffled explosions marking more gunfire came from outside. Round after round in quick succession. The cop was emptying his gun at Lupo. Loudon's disquieting sense about the cop rose again for a moment, but he had more important things to worry about.

Far down the hall, Shinohara emerged, walking slowly, her face an impassive mask. She carried a rack of vials and a bucket. She saw him, but didn't react. She looked pale with fear, almost in shock. She stumbled a bit, then caught herself. She stepped to the emergency shower and bent slowly and deliberately to set the rack down on the floor. With deep anguish, Loudon remembered the smooth elegant movements of her tea ceremony. She pulled a bottle of bleach out of the bucket, poured some in, and reached up to pull the metal chain on the emergency shower. The water cascaded from the shower head, filling the bucket. She lifted the bucket over her head and poured it over herself, holding her breath and keeping her eyes tightly shut. The cascade of water soaked her clothes and flooded the floor, swirling into the drain. She scrubbed herself and removed the sodden lab coat, stuffing it into the bucket, pouring the rest of the bleach into it. She stepped into her shower, raising her face almost prayerfully to the stream, allowing it to wash away the bleach. Her wet hair plastered against her head and down her back. She removed her sneakers, then her shirt and pants, stuffing them into the bucket. She stood in her wet underwear for a moment, examining her arms, chest and legs, scrubbing them thoroughly, obsessively, with her hands, and let the water flow down her body in silvery rivulets against her light brown skin.

She seemed so small, her body trembling beneath the deluge of cold water. She turned and looked at him, the water flowing down her face. She wiped the dark hair from her eyes. They were wide with pleading. She mouthed the words "Go. Please." and nodded her head for him to leave.

A choking knot of despair rose in his chest, and he almost rushed toward her. He wanted to hold her so badly. But he caught himself. The best thing he could do was to get her help. He paused for an instant to look at her again, then pushed open the door to the stairwell and ran down the stairs.

CHAPTER 31

The two Denver cops lay still on the ground, half hidden in the bushes. One was sprawled on his back, the broken branches of the bush over him revealing that he had collapsed backward into them. The other lay nearby on his side, his arms stretched out above him, as if he had tried to crawl away after being hit. The paramedics had to drag the patrolmen's inert bodies out into the light before they could begin to work on them. Loudon watched the process, but he didn't really see it. His mind was riveted on what was happening in the building. His heart ached for the woman inside. Kathleen had been in there a good thirty minutes before the CDC team arrived. Alone. So alone. What agony must she have suffered? Had she begun showing symptoms? Was she in there dying?

"Look at this, willya?" One of the paramedics held up to his flashlight a small dart with blue fins. "It was stuck in his neck."

"Yeah, here, too," said the paramedic examining the other cop. "In the chest." He held up an identical dart.

Loudon forced himself to concentrate.

"Are they dead?" he asked. Three other Denver cops stood beside him looking down, their colored faces shades of gray in the shadows, grim with anger at the attack on their comrades.

The first paramedic began his examination. "Naw, looks like just unconscious," he said looking up, his rust-red face also looking dark gray in the dim light. "Breathing's okay."

"Here, too." The other paramedic, a lighter ultramarine color, was listening intently to his patient's heart with his stethoscope. "Heart's fine. Just out like a light. Let's get 'em in." With the help of the other cops, they loaded the burly unconscious men onto stretchers and began to move them into a waiting rescue van.

Walter appeared beside him.

"They're coming out," he said. Loudon forgot the cops and moved toward the building. The multiple whirling lights of the gathered emergency vehicles played a colored kaleidoscope across its darkened concrete face. Police held back a growing crowd of sleepy onlookers, including many students dressed in night clothes, behind a string of yellow plastic tape far back from the activity. A large white truck, with no markings save a small US government sticker on its door, backed up to the entrance. The door opened. Loudon moved so he could better view the small group of Racal-isolation-suited figures emerging from the building that he and Shinohara had entered only an hour before. Their suits glistened wetly with the disinfectant they were using to kill whatever had been loosed inside the building.

The suited, anonymous CDC technicians surrounded another of their kind, dressed just like them. The person in their center was clearly being escorted. It was Shinohara. Loudon knew how she moved. They had put her into an isolation suit as well, but it was designed to contain, not to protect.

"That's her," he said to Walter beside him.

"Yeah, she's not moving good."

He stood so she could see him, but he wasn't sure she did. They quickly hustled her into the back of the truck and slammed the doors. A police car in front revved up its whooping siren, and the two vehicles accelerated away, speeding into the night.

One of the suited figures approached Loudon and Walter, unzipping his helmet. It was Doc. He looked grim.

"Is she okay?" asked Loudon.

"Yeah, so far. Scared. But we don't see any symptoms. Most of these bugs take anywhere from a day to a week to develop. Whatever it is, though, we've got to try to catch it early. We've got to know right now what he threw at her."

"Could you do anything for her?"

"Maybe, if we knew. We could start vaccines, countermeasures, antivirals. Don't know."

They watched another truck back up to the building, and isolation-suited figures emerged from the building entrance to begin carrying boxes inside.

"Did you tell the CDC people what we want out of there?" Loudon asked Walter.

"Yeah, I'll stay around, make sure they get what we want. And I'll make sure we get the information from the Denver cops."

"Be careful, Walt. Something's wrong here. Something about the cops. That cop. The shooter."

"Yeah." Walter moved off, his bulky frame looking somehow more imposing than it usually did. Walter seemed to change personas when he was on a hunt.

Loudon turned to Doc. "But you've got samples?" His voice was almost pleading.

"Yeah, we've got samples. Thanks to her. She got fresh samples before the stuff evaporated or got flushed away. But we need a BSL-4 lab to test them. The portable won't do. We need a full lab, with an electron microscope, testing facilities . . ." Doc trailed off. He went over and leaned against a police car, staring at the building.

"Will it spread?" asked Loudon, gesturing at the building.

"Don't know. Don't know what it is. Y'know, it could be nothing. But we can't chance it."

"So what's going to happen?"

"Well, they'll seal it up tight. The whole building. Tape the windows, the doors. Then they'll put electric frying pans inside, fill 'em with paraformaldehyde. Turn 'em on and get out. The stuff heats up, the fumes are pure formaldehyde. Kills everything."

"She needs a lab?" asked Loudon.

"Yeah."

"Why not Atlanta CDC?"

"Takes hours to get the samples there. We don't know if we have hours."

"How about the secret lab? The faction's lab? It's here somewhere."

"Well, yeah, it's probably got everything we need. And Lupo was there. They know what he was doing. Maybe they've got information that pertains. But we don't know where it is." Doc lowered his head tiredly and flipped the helmet of his suit onto the hood of the car. For the first time since Loudon had known him, he really looked like an old man. Loudon took a deep breath.

"Then we'll find it."

. . .

Lupo burst wildly through the door of his laboratory, slamming it behind him. He dropped his satchel on his desk and sank into the chair, his chest heaving. He sat glaring at the floor, a slightly mad look on his face.

"Please identify yourself," said the computer.

Lupo didn't answer.

"Please identify yourself, or I will begin the destruct sequence."

"It's me, computer," croaked Lupo.

"Please identify yourself again. Your voice does not match Arthur's."

Lupo cleared his throat, sat up in his chair and repeated the sentence. The computer identified and greeted him. Its cool efficiency bucked him up. He had to finish his work. But first, he vaguely felt around his body again, still wondering that he hadn't been hit by the hail of bullets. He found a nick in his shirt just below the armpit. A bullet had passed through, just missing his side. He shuddered, and a wave of nausea enveloped him.

He remembered again how the cop had chased him, firing and firing and firing. He remembered the explosions behind him, and expecting each time to die. He remembered the bullets slamming into the wall of the alleyway as he ran. How the cop was far behind him at first, but began to catch up as he made it to his motorcycle.

He remembered the frightening impact of the bullet careening off the helmet as he put it on. How the bullet almost knocked the helmet out of his hand. The cop had given him no chance. He would *never* be caught defenseless like that again. Nobody had given him a chance.

Now, he would show the FBI, the CDC and everybody else what he was capable of!

He reached over and pulled his notebook from the satchel. The act helped calm him. He meticulously recorded the final tests from the university lab that night. The sample that he'd run was only a backup. He'd already run one, and the DNA sequence had checked out. He was satisfied that the virus would do its job. His thoughts then turned to weapons. He needed inspiration. He looked over at the lobster nestled quietly in the corner of its aquarium, its antenna waving back and forth with fluid grace.

"What do you think?" he asked the lobster.

As if in answer, the lobster twitched, turned around and rearranged itself in the corner.

Inspiration came and Lupo smiled puckishly. He knew the perfect weapon; one that he had long ago mastered! He bent to his notebook and began to sketch out initial plans.

But after a moment, the smile faded into the familiar look of brooding intensity. He closed the notebook and stepped to the isolation chamber, thrust his arms into the black rubber gloves and began the final molecular assembly of his virus. As he worked, the muscles on his jaw rippled as he clenched and unclenched his teeth. His time had come.

● ● ●

Shinohara lay on the bed in a white hospital gown. She looked so vulnerable, her small form surrounded by the examiners, looking like aliens in their bulky, anonymous isolation suits. Her own Racal suit lay crumpled over a chair in the corner. Loudon couldn't see her face, but he suspected that she had the same grimly stoic expression he'd seen in the lab building. He could see her feet, so small and still, shod in paper hospital slippers. A doctor moved, and he could see her hand gripping the side of the examining table. He couldn't make out what their voices were saying, given that they were muffled by suits and plastic walls and the whine of the air pump.

The wrinkled plastic wall of the portable isolation chamber distorted the scene into a kind of glistening impressionistic painting. He moved his head this way and that to avoid the distortions, to try to see clearly what they were doing.

One of the figures turned and stepped into the airlock, going through the laborious procedure of decontaminating himself. He emerged and took off his helmet to reveal a coral-red face.

"No symptoms," said the doctor. "Doesn't mean much, though, but it's a baseline."

Baseline. The word seemed coldly impersonal to Loudon. Shinohara's ordeal had been reduced to a baseline, to data . . . perhaps to an endpoint.

The doctors began emerging from the chamber, taking off their helmets and breathing in the cooler night air that filtered into the warehouse. They smiled at him, but the smiles were mere kind reassurance, offering no solid hope. One remained briefly in the isolation chamber, helping Shinohara cover herself with a sheet. He came out, and she lay there for a while, staring at the ceiling, her chest rising and falling beneath the sheet. He moved to the plastic wall, waiting patiently.

She turned her head and saw him. Without expression, she folded back the sheet, sat up and swung her bare legs over the side and pushed herself off the bed. She walked over to him, her steps seeming slow, leaden. They stood on either side of the shimmering plastic wall, nevertheless seeing each other so clearly, their memories clarifying the distortion. Her eyes glistened, but she held her composure. He almost didn't. He felt the massive lump in his chest grow, his eyes fill. He raised his hand and placed his palm flat against the cool, slick plastic, and she did the same. Each felt the warmth come into the plastic, the topography of the other's flesh beyond the intervening film of the sterile material. Each did the same with the other hand.

"You'll be fine," he managed to say, inwardly cursing his inarticulateness.

"Sure, of course." She looked up at him, and he was touched to his soul by the look of need in those dark, fathomless eyes.

"I love you." He felt the tickle of a tear running down his face.

"I love you, too."

"I'm going to do something. I'll fix it. Don't worry. Go back and lie down. Get some rest."

She smiled at him, a calm smile that gave him strength. She drew on the serenity of her heritage. He remembered the same smile when she was kneeling before the shrine in her home. She was drawing on the strength of her ancestors.

Still smiling, she turned her face and put her cheek against the plastic. He bent and did the same, and felt softness and warmth beneath the plastic. After a moment, she turned and went back to the bed, walking slowly. He realized that they had given her a tranquilizer. She lay back down and drew the sheet up beneath her chin. He took a deep breath and turned away to see the doctors and other agents actively pretending not to notice them.

Scalisi had come in. "She okay?"

"Far as they can tell. Jack, we need that lab. The faction's lab. Can I count on you?"

"Anything, Bobby."

"I may need more than you can give."

"You'd be surprised what I can give, pal."

The door to the warehouse opened, letting in the bright dawn, and White entered followed by a group of headquarters agents.

"Can you brief us?" he asked Loudon. Loudon explained what had happened.

"That's too bad," he said looking curiously over at the white form in the chamber. "Look, we need to meet and work out a report for the director."

"Well, it'll have to wait. I've got some calls first."

Before White could answer, Loudon stepped away into a corner of the warehouse that held a phone and a desk. He sat down and took out his notebook, flipping backward through its pages. He found the number and punched it into the phone. It rang, and an aide answered. Loudon negotiated past him. Finally, the voice of his quarry came on the line.

"Gaines," was the terse answer from the AMRIID director.

"This is Robert Loudon. Colonel, I need your help."

"Yessir?"

"I want you to find out from McLaren where the lab down here is. It's a matter of life and death."

"Can't do that. He's gone. Disappeared about a week ago."

Loudon pounded the desk. The red-headed Army scientist was his only firm link with the faction. "Do you know where he is? Do you know where the lab is?"

"This is Army business, Agent Loudon. We're going to take care of it."

"Colonel, you remember Shinohara?"

"Of course."

"She was exposed to something . . . maybe a virus . . . we don't know what. Lupo attacked her with it. She could die. Colonel, the only way we can find out what it was is to get into a BSL-4 lab fast. That means the one here."

There was a long pause.

"This is Army business."

"Colonel, you could be killing her!"

"We have to take care of this in our own way."

Loudon's mind worked furiously, casting for some approach to the soldier. He gripped the phone, looking blindly around the room. There was one possibility. A remote one. As he talked, he stared absent-mindedly at the dusty, scarred surface of the desk.

"You were in Delta Force?"

"Yessir."

"I hear you had a rule. A rule that was never broken. You never left a fallen comrade. Never."

"No, we didn't."

"Colonel, Dr. Shinohara is one of us. She was working for the same things you and I were. To stop this epidemic. If you don't help save her life, you're leaving her."

There was another long pause. It grew, and Loudon didn't know what it meant. It seemed to fill the room.

"Take down these GPS coordinates," said Gaines finally. At first Loudon was confused. Then he realized and threw his head back in relief.

"The lab?"

"Yessir. It's an abandoned ranch outside the city . . . or so it looks like. We traced the ownership. It's government. Off the books. It was a secret arm of the Rocky Mountain Arsenal. There are bunkers where they kept a black ops supply of chemical weapons in case Rocky Mountain was compromised. Bunker forty two. They've made it a BSL-4 lab." He recited the coordinates, and Loudon scribbled them down.

"I don't understand. How could the Army not know?"

"Officially it was sold to a civilian contractor working on detoxification chemistry. Company called Malfus, Inc."

"So, how can we get in?"

"That's your problem. You can't go through channels. There are Army brass who are part of the faction. They know about Malfus. We still don't know everybody who's involved. They'll tip them off and Malfus will blow the place."

"Do you have any suggestions?"

"Like I said, that's your problem." Gaines hung up the phone.

Loudon sat for a moment, striking the desk absentmindedly with his fist. There was no other way. He stood up and walked over to White and Scalisi.

"Lucas, Jack, we need to talk," he said, and without waiting, moved back to the corner with the desk. They followed and he turned and stood face to face with White.

"Lucas, the only way we're going to save her is to get into the faction lab. I know where it is. I want the HRT. I want to go in and take him."

"No, Bobby, absolutely not." White's face grew red. He was a head taller than Loudon and peered down at him with all the authority he could muster. "You've countermanded my explicit orders. The director—"

"Lucas, I want the HR—"

"The director—"

"Give me the Hostage Rescue Team, Lucas, or I will hold you personally responsible for her death!" He stepped forward, his face inches from White's. His voice lowered to a vicious whisper. "And I will never, ever let you rest from it as long as you live. And who knows how long that will be?"

White stepped back in shock, and three of his agents stepped between them.

Scalisi moved toward White. "Wait a minute. Look, Lucas, think about it," said Scalisi.

"I have, and I'm ordering Agent Loudon's arrest for threats against my life!" He flipped his bony hand, motioning for his agents to step forward. They grabbed Loudon by the arms.

"Well," said Scalisi, suddenly smiling wryly, his white teeth contrasting with his mint-green face. "That's just too bad you did that, Assistant Director White." He reached down to his belt and clicked on his radio. "This is Green Hornet to all personnel. Converge on the CDC unit. Now. Wait for instructions." He turned back to White. "Let's see, now. You've got one, two, three, four, five guys. I've got fifteen coming over from the other building right now. They look silly, being all different colors. But they're good agents, and I'm going to tell them to stop this business."

White began to sputter. "You can't countermand me. I'm—"

"In Denver, you're just another headquarters geek. Look, Lucas, let's reason a little here. I know you can't go against headquarters. Well, you won't have to. As a SAC, I can call out the HRT. All you have to do is walk away. Wash your lily-white hands, pal." White looked back and forth between Scalisi and Loudon. It was a standoff.

The warehouse door opened, letting in the light. Loudon recognized Doc and Walter. They first noticed the CDC doctors, who had been standing by the isolation chamber anxiously watching the argument. Doc followed their gaze to the large knot of FBI agents across the warehouse. He and Walter came over.

"So what's going on here?" asked Doc, eyeing the agents holding Loudon.

"We're going for the lab," said Scalisi. "Bobby found out where it is."

"Great!" said Doc. He motioned for the CDC doctors to come over. The warehouse door opened again, and a crowd of variously colored agents burst in. Scalisi held up a hand to hold them at bay, smiling expectantly at White.

Disgusted, White made a curt gesture, and his agents released Loudon. Without a word, he strode toward the door, followed by his agents, slammed it open and was gone.

Scalisi and Doc gathered the CDC doctors and FBI agents to discuss the upcoming mission, while Walter took Loudon aside. Once again,

Loudon peered longingly across the warehouse at the figure lying still on the bed.

"Bobby, you gotta look at these," said Walter, pulling several small plastic bags out of his pocket. "CDC got this one out of the wall in the university lab building." He sorted through the bags. "And the Denver police got these from an alley where the shooting took place."

Loudon took the bags and examined their contents, misshapen slugs of lead. He looked closer. Tiny prongs protruded from some of the slugs making them into vicious-looking metal flowers. He handled them carefully, to avoid being cut through the plastic.

He whispered turning the lethal chunks of metal over in his fingers. "Forty caliber Smith and Wesson PDX1. Hollow point."

"What're those?" asked Doc, joining them, looking down his nose through his spectacles at the bullets.

"It's what that fake cop was shootin' at Lupo," said Walter.

"Are they unusual?" asked Doc

"They're nasty bullets. They burst open on impact, making sharp spines that rip out of your insides. Even the best surgeon can't put somebody's guts back together when one of these hits. Denver cops don't use them. But they are legally sold only to law enforcement. Illegally, they're hard to get, but possible for somebody with connections."

"So, he wasn't a Denver cop?" asked Doc.

"He was the pro," said Walter. "He was the hit man."

CHAPTER 32

The armored personnel carrier shifted smoothly through the gears as it accelerated its sixteen tons to top speed. Loudon crouched in his seat, still marveling at the results of Scalisi's efforts. Within thirty minutes, the FBI's Hostage Rescue Team, which had been headquartered nearby, had procured from the army three of its vehicles. At least White had done something right, thought Loudon. He'd established a cooperative agreement with the army early in the Denver operation. But if the army had known its APCs would be used to assault one of its own bases, it undoubtedly would have refused. But the HRT had only told the Army that the FBI was going after a secret laboratory.

Loudon scanned the faces of the HRT's members. They were determined, alert, and with the tautness of disciplined training. Each was dressed in desert fatigues and body armor with FBI in large letters on his back. Each carried the Bureau's official-issue automatic MP5 assault rifles and an assortment of grenades—smoke, concussion, tear gas, fragmentation. Their training had served the FBI well. They had rescued school children safely out of hostage situations. And they had stormed fortified terrorists' houses. He hoped they would be willing to face deadly viruses.

He turned to look out one of the slits in the side of the APC. Although the view was limited, he recognized the freeway that was taking them to the GPS coordinates programmed into the navigator held in his hand.

He was thinking again of Shinohara when his radio crackled and a faint voice came over it. It was Walter in the APC behind him. Doc rode in the third, with his team of CDC scientists and their equipment.

"How far?" asked Walter.

"Ten minutes out," said Loudon, nodding to Scalisi, who rode beside him and Charlie Acree, the HRT leader. He was a wiry, sharp-featured man in his late thirties. He was a neut, beige-skinned with short brown hair and gray eyes that darted about, acutely examining his team, assessing their readiness.

"We should try and negotiate our way in first," said Loudon.

"Hey, negotiate is my middle name," said Acree with only a faint smile. Loudon didn't doubt it. The HRT was willing to negotiate, but their philosophy was that once negotiations were impossible, overwhelm the target.

After a few minutes, the APC downshifted, slowed and rolled to a ponderous stop. Acree handed his weapon to another agent, and Loudon and Acree opened the metal doors in the rear and stepped out into the blinding summer sun.

They went around to the front to find a very curious, slightly nervous pair of private sentries standing stiffly in the roadway behind a ten-foot chain-link fence topped by razor wire. The fence held a small green sign that said "Private." The sentries obviously lived in Denver, for one was orchid, the other port-wine red.

"Please state your business," said the orchid sentry crisply.

"Yeah, sure," said Loudon. "We're with Malfus. We're bringing some people out to inspect their lab."

The sentry scanned the convoy of three APCs. "Malfus never used APCs before," he said. "They used vans. Show me some identification." Loudon and Acree showed their FBI credentials through the fence. The guards stiffened and backed away.

"This is a private—" began the orchid sentry, but Acree had raised his hand, and a team member appeared through the APCs roof hatch and clutched the vehicle's machine gun. The APCs turret rotated around to bring its guns to bear on the sentries.

"Sorry, gentlemen, but we've got to go in."

The port-wine-red sentry's hand twitched. He was considering going for his pistol. "We will not open the gate . . . under any circumstances," he said.

"OK, I understand. Then just take your sidearms out slowly and pitch them over the fence. Then step away." After staring for a moment at the machine gun, the two sentries complied. Acree gave a forward signal to the lead APC, and he and Loudon stepped clear. With a deep roar of its engine, the mammoth vehicle leaped forward, slamming into the steel fence. It began to climb the chain link, and with the twanging pop of wires snapping and the groan of yielding metal, the fence gate gave and crashed downward beneath the weight, raising a cloud of dust. The APC eased forward, and two more team members leaped out of its back, gathering the sentries' weapons and standing beside Acree. Acree pointed to the guardhouse.

"Anybody in there?"

The orchid sentry shook his head, as did the port-wine-red sentry.

The turret whined to life, bringing its 25-mm cannon to bear on the guardhouse. The gun erupted with a thundering series of blasts, ripping massive holes in the structure, tearing into its supports. The withering fire blew splinters and whole chunks of wood away into the desert scrub. With a cracking sound, the guardhouse slumped tiredly and finally collapsed into a pile of rubble.

"Sorry," said Acree amiably. "But we didn't want you using the phone or getting to your equipment for a while."

At Acree's signal, the HRT agents handcuffed the sentries to a section of the fence that was still standing, and took their cell phones. The agents climbed back into the APC, and the column accelerated ponderously down the road. They approached a collection of huge weatherbeaten concrete block warehouses flanking the road. Each was perhaps a hundred feet long and forty feet wide, plenty of room for a BSL-4 lab.

"Any of these could be the one we want," said Acree into the APC's intercom. "Keep an eye out."

Loudon peered out the slits on one side, then the other as they slowly rolled past. They came to one with three vans parked outside." "Stop here," he commanded. "We've got activity."

The APC slowed and stopped. Acree spoke into the radio. "Deploy as planned," he said calmly. "Number three, remain in the rear."

One of the men clanged open the metal doors of the APC, and Loudon, Scalisi, Acree and his HRT team members leaped out, staying close to the vehicle. The second APC accelerated beyond the warehouse, looping around to come up on the other side of the entrance. It disgorged Walter and the other HRT agents, who took up positions, aiming their weapons at the entrance. The third backed into the space between the opposite warehouses, waiting.

Loudon, Scalisi, and Acree peered around the side of the APC at the massive windowless warehouse.

"We use cannons on that, we'd destroy the labs," said Loudon.

"Not to worry," said Scalisi, peering shrewdly at the warehouse. "I've got a bit of an idea. Take off your gear and follow me." Loudon and Scalisi removed their jackets with the large FBI emblems and their bulletproof vests. Dressed now in a khaki short-sleeved shirt and khaki pants, Scalisi turned his FBI baseball cap around backward and strode confidently away from the APC toward the warehouse door. Loudon, now in a white dress shirt and tie, followed. Acree and the other agents moved quickly to take up positions on either side of the door, flat against its wall.

They passed the vans, and the two strode up to the door. Above it was a small video camera aimed downward to image visitors.

"This has worked before," said Scalisi. "See, they don't know what is going on out here. They think they're in a secure facility. We take advantage of that." He turned and knocked loudly. The welded steel door was so thick that his knocking made only a faint metallic clunk. He looked around, saw what he needed and stepped over to pick up a large rock near the door. He returned and pounded on the door with it. The loud clang was far more satisfying. His mint-green face serious, he winked at Loudon.

From an intercom beside the door came a tinny voice.

"What do you want?"

Scalisi made a series of unintelligible noises, doing an excellent imitation of a static-prone intercom.

"What?" asked the intercom voice.

Scalisi stood back, looking into the camera and gesturing in annoyance, repeating the unintelligible noises.

After a moment, metallic rattling sounds of locks being opened filtered through the door. It opened an inch and an eye peered suspiciously out.

"What do you want?" asked lips below the eye that peered through the crack.

Scalisi flashed his credentials in a quick blur. "You can't park here."

"What?"

"Didn't they tell you? Alternate side parking." He gestured at the long row of warehouses and the vast desert beyond.

"What do you mean?"

"Look, come out and let me show you. Road maintenance. You've got to move these vehicles."

There was a long pause, and the faint sound of voices issued from the crack. The people inside seemed to be discussing the matter. Finally, the massive door slid open and a middle-aged sport-shirted man stood in front of them. The white vans blocked his view of the APC across the road.

"So, what's this about parking?"

"Look here," said Scalisi, backing away from the door. He pointed down the road at a place the man couldn't see unless he stepped out of the door. Loudon followed suit and peered convincingly down the road.

The man stepped out and two agents jumped him from both sides and wrestled him to the ground. One held a gun at his head, while the other efficiently bound his hands behind him with plastic-strap handcuffs. Simultaneously, Acree and six HRT agents burst into the warehouse, and others ran full tilt from the other APC to crowd in behind them. Still others moved to establish a protective perimeter around the entrance.

"Good fake-out," said Loudon to Scalisi, who gave a mint-green thumbs-up. "Let's go in." Loudon and Scalisi strode out of the sunlight and into the fluorescent-lit entrance room. They found a lounge with comfortable couches and a dining table, a coffeemaker, stove and refrigerator. They ran with the HRT agents down a long corridor. The first rooms were offices, the ones farther on were chemical laboratories. In the laboratories, metal racks supported wall-sized interconnected networks of glass tubing and stopcocks, flasks, spherical reaction chambers, gas cylinders, vacuum pumps and electric heaters. Boiling liquids sent vapors curling from one flask to another. White plastic magnetic stirrers whirled busily in the liquid-filled flasks. Each room held white-coated scientists, who turned in shock, as an armed HRT agent took up a post at the doorway, leveling his assault rifle at them.

"We need Doc and the CDC people," said Loudon, and Acree spoke into his radio. Loudon sprinted the length of the corridor and returned to the entrance to the warehouse just as Doc came in.

"Whatcha got?" asked Doc, gesturing for the CDC scientists to stay at the door.

"Well, Doc, I don't know about labs, but these look like chemistry labs to me. I don't see a BSL-4."

Doc hurried back to see for himself. Acree followed to begin the process of moving the captives out of the warehouse.

"Who's the head here?" Loudon asked the intimidated balding man in the first office.

"What is the meaning of this?" demanded a voice behind him. Loudon turned to see an old man with a thinning bush of combed-back gray-black hair. He had thick eyebrows that jutted above black-rimmed glasses. The earpieces of the glasses disappeared into the thick hair cascading over the large ears. He wore a stained white shirt with a thin blue tie, a perfunctory badge of authority. As were all the other scientists, he was a flesh-colored neut.

"You the head?"

"Yes. Stadler. What do you mean doing this? We're Army subcontractors. You've got no right to—"

"What are you subcontracting?"

"Chemical weapons detoxification chemistry. You should know that."

"And biological warfare research?"

Stadler's answer was well-practiced. "No, we're sampling the stored chemical weapons and determining their chemical status in order to—"

Emerging from the back Doc said, "You're doing work on biologicals here. And I'm sure you've got a BSL-4 lab here somewhere." The two old men faced each other, each summoning decades of wile in dealing with people.

"Yes, there are some biological assays of chemical weapons. But these are *chemistry* labs," said Stadler.

"Look, I know bad bugs when I see 'em. Show us the BSL-4 lab."

"No." The answer was said with finality.

"Pace off the warehouse outside," said Doc to a CDC doctor. "I'll pace off inside here. We find a difference, we just blow the back wall of the last room to get in." He looked back at Stadler.

Stadler was too clever to believe him. He knew that nobody would set off explosives anywhere near a biosafety laboratory. He stood his ground. There was a tense silence. The invaders' advantage was slipping away.

"DON'T BE A HERO, YOU TELL HIM!" bellowed Loudon, ripping his pistol from its holster, slamming Stadler against the wall, backing up and firing twice, the explosions echoed deafeningly through the sealed warehouse. Each round punched large holes into the concrete block wall, narrowly missing on either side of the old man. Wild-eyed, Loudon backed away another step and took aim at Stadler's head. He fired again, and the bullet barely missed again, shattering a picture behind Stadler. "WE NEED THAT LABORATORY. SOMEBODY MAY BE DYING. SO IF YOU DON'T TELL HIM, THE NEXT SHOT, AND YOUR BRAINS, ARE GOING TO BE PAINTING THAT WALL." He glared defiantly around the room, challenging anyone to stop him.

Scalisi and Doc backed away, stunned. Agents appeared at both doors to the room, weapons ready. Acree stood among those at the front door, with Walter behind him.

Stadler cowered against the wall, an involuntary whimper gurgling from his throat, and sank to the floor. Loudon stepped forward over the old man, planted his feet apart and thrust his gun hard against Stadler's forehead, holding it in both hands. He cocked it. He took a breath. Stadler shrank back, and the gun followed, still jammed against his forehead.

"ONE . . . TWO . . . "

"No! No! Don't! The back wall! The back wall! I'll show you!" Stadler waved one hand in front of himself in feeble defense, supporting himself with the other. A stain spread on his pants at the crotch.

The group stood transfixed.

"GO!" commanded Loudon, lifting Stadler and throwing him toward the door into the hallway. He followed, pistol stuck hard against Stadler's back, Doc pushed his way past the guns after him, and the others followed. They passed down the long hall, Loudon periodically shoving his pistol into Stadler's back to keep him moving.

They reached the last laboratory, and Stadler went to the back wall, which held one of the intricate arrays of glass apparatus. He flipped open a plastic cover, revealing a keypad, and punched in a number code. The wall swung open to reveal another corridor, bare except for several doorways and a ceiling of bright fluorescent lights. A flashing red light lit the other end of the corridor.

"Very clever," said Doc, peering down the hallway. "They get inspected, nobody's going to poke around behind a lab setup that's testing chemical warfare agents." A delicate breeze pulled air into the open door, indicating that the area was under negative pressure. It was a sign of a biocontainment facility.

Loudon shoved Stadler forward down the hall. "By the way, I don't think I mentioned how high I would've counted before I shot you," he said calmly to the terrified man. "About a million."

He popped the clip out of his pistol, releasing the faint odor of burned gunpowder. He clicked a full one into place. They moved carefully down the corridor toward the flashing light.

"Yeah . . . yeah . . . good," mumbled Doc as they went, looking left and right into the offices and laboratories. "These are all support labs for a BSL-4, all right." They passed a small darkened room containing the console and beige metal cylinder of an electron microscope. As they inspected room after room, some of the occupants looked up, startled, while others failed to notice the intruders, intent on their work. They hadn't heard the gunfire. The back section was obviously well-insulated against sound.

Stadler led them toward a sealed door at the end of the hall beneath the flashing red light. Loudon glanced back to see Acree and his men following behind, moving swiftly into the labs, rousting out the occupants. Stadler pushed through the door, and they moved into what Loudon recognized as a large BSL-4 staging room, like the one at AMRIID, with showers and changing cubicles. Dragging Stadler back into the arms of one of the HRT agents, he opened the door beyond and peered in to see the bulky blue isolation suits hanging from walls. The room also had an airlock, and beside it a glass window. He moved to the window. A lone isolation-suited figure bent over a large cryogenic storage freezer, packing vials into an insulated case. Vapors of liquid nitrogen swirled out of the vessel and the case and snaked onto the floor before evaporating. Other cases stood stacked in the corner. The lab's contents were being moved.

The figure turned to open another case, and his faceplate came into view. He looked up and saw Loudon, and even in the bulky suit, Loudon could see the shock of recognition run through his body like a lightning bolt. He stood straight up, stunned for a moment.

Suddenly Loudon recognized him. He saw the familiar reddish hair, the pale skin. It was McLaren!

CHAPTER 33

Loudon motioned crisply with the barrel of his pistol for McLaren to come out. A flush of desperation rose on McLaren's face as he realized the meaning of Loudon's presence. This didn't just mean a blown operation, but life in prison, maybe even the death penalty.

Doc moved up beside Loudon. "We've got to get in there! And the whole place has to stay intact. We need what's in those vials. There's virus cultures, maybe vaccines, maybe test antibodies."

As if he had heard Doc's words, McLaren twisted quickly and pulled a sample from the case. He held the vial up and shouted something, but Loudon couldn't hear through the suit and the glass. He gestured for Loudon to leave, then held up the sample again. Loudon didn't move, and McLaren clumped over to a sink, pulling his air hose along, uncapped the sample and pitched it into the drain.

"We've got to stop him!" shouted Doc. "He can't do that!" Doc moved toward the isolation suits, but Loudon put a hand on his shoulder.

"I'm stronger, and I've done this." Doc stepped aside and they hauled an isolation suit off its peg. Loudon handed Doc his gun, stripped down to his underwear and quickly began to put on the suit. He stepped into the suit's legs and pulled on the feet. He thrust his hands into the arms and into the thick rubber gloves. Doc helped him zip up and seal himself in. His faceplate had just begun to fog as he motioned for Doc to hand him his pistol. He tried to thrust his finger into the trigger guard.

"Oh, no!" he exclaimed peering through the fogging faceplate at his blue-gloved hand. "It doesn't go!" He poked the large gloved finger into the finger guard, but it wouldn't fit, at least not without pulling the trigger. For a moment, he was flummoxed. The gun had always been such a natural extension of his hand that he'd never thought about it. He'd never dreamed something as mundane as a glove would deprive him of the weapon.

"Don't force it," warned Doc. "You tear that glove, you're dead."

Again, Loudon saw the image of Kathleen beneath the white sheet. He handed the gun back to Doc. "I've got to go in now. Find some way for me to use the trigger and put it through the little airlock." He pointed to the chamber beside the door through which scientists passed smaller objects. "Then go back and get your people ready."

His faceplate was badly fogged, so he pushed it against his face, wiping the inside with his nose and cheek. The faceplate was now a smear of moisture, but he could see better. It immediately began to fog again. He fumbled with the airlock door and stepped into the larger chamber.

Until then, McLaren hadn't been able to see what Loudon was doing. When he did glimpse Loudon through the windowed inner door, he slammed himself against the door to block it. But before he could brace himself, Loudon managed to pry the door open a crack. He used the leverage to shove it all the way open, falling clumsily into the lab. He jumped up, expecting McLaren to attack. But through the fogged faceplate, he could see that McLaren had retreated to the other side of the room, doing something at one of the lab tables. But he couldn't tell what. McLaren was only a vague moving blur through the faceplate. Loudon found an air hose and plugged it into his helmet. The familiar hiss filled his ears. The cool, dry air began to clear the helmet and cool the length of his body.

Clumsily pulling the hose along, Loudon moved to the other end of the long laboratory table, opposite McLaren. He stumbled on a large bucket by the table and caught himself. McLaren's faceplate bent down;

he was fumbling in a drawer of the metal examining table. As Loudon moved around the table toward him, he pulled out a plastic box, opened it, and Loudon caught the glint of metal. McLaren held the object up so Loudon wouldn't miss it. Loudon stopped in his tracks. It was a scalpel. Its razor-sharp tip glinted dangerously as McLaren pointed it at him, making sure that Loudon wouldn't mistake his intention. He took out another one, putting it in the same hand. Holding both scalpels toward Loudon, he reached over to the faucet and filled a large beaker with water, setting it before him on the stainless steel table. Then he stepped back to the cases and lifted out a rack of samples, the liquid nitrogen vapor swirling around his gloved hand. He set the rack on the examining table, and began uncapping the plastic vials.

He looked up at Loudon. His face was paler than Loudon had remembered. His eyes were mad with desperation. One by one, he dropped the uncapped vials into the water. He swirled the beaker a few times, to let the cultures thaw and mix with the water. Loudon could see small globs of tissue and reddish swirls of blood floating in the water, along with the plastic vials. McLaren lifted the beaker and poured its contents over himself, the vials falling to the floor and some of the tissue clinging to the suit.

"McLaren, what are you doing!" Loudon's voice echoed inside his helmet.

"I'm hot now!" came the muffled reply. "Anthrax, influenza, hantavirus, Ebola! I'm going out! All the way. Anybody comes near me dies! I'm walking out in this suit! And you're going to let me go."

He took a scalpel in each hand, held the points at Loudon and moved toward him. He slashed the scalpels back and forth. Loudon backed away, trying to keep the table between him and McLaren. The tiniest nick, the tiniest pinhole and he was dead. He heard a thump behind him and knew that Doc had inserted the gun into the small airlock. But if he turned to get it, McLaren would lunge, and he'd be dead. He looked desperately around the room. There was no weapon. He looked down at the bucket he'd almost fallen over. He'd knocked the cover off.

It was full of monkey carcasses. The scientists had done a last round of experiments. They'd just sacrificed the animals, and the carcasses hadn't been disposed of yet. Several small bloody heads and torsoes floated in a thick brown and red slime of disinfectant and internal organs liquefied by the viral infections. The eyes of some of the heads were open, the mouths wide, tiny teeth bared, in death rictus. The tops of the heads had been sliced off, revealing the brains. A small paw and what might have been a foot stuck up above the surface of the muck.

McLaren was almost on him, the points of the scalpels only a foot from his suit. He jabbed one of the scalpels viciously at Loudon. Hindered by the suit, Loudon jerked violently to the left in a clumsy attempt to avoid the hit. Did he feel it catch a sleeve? He couldn't tell. McLaren thrust the other scalpel forward and Loudon feinted right. Then McLaren held both scalpels wide apart, like a toreador going in for the kill. Loudon felt trapped between the gleaming points. He saw no way out. Maybe the cover as a shield. But it wouldn't stop both scalpels, and only one nick could kill him. McLaren stepped forward, bringing the scalpels up toward Loudon's throat, poised for the last thrust. A desperate idea struck Loudon. He reached down and thrust his hand into the bucket, feeling for something solid. He came up with a carcass, the head lolling back, held only by the ligaments of the spine. It was splayed open, the rib cage holding the remains of the glistening organs, the arms and legs dangling. The carcass dripped with brown pus.

Loudon flung the carcass directly at McLaren's faceplate. It hit with a slap and the carcass draped itself over his helmet. McLaren gasped and involuntarily recoiled in disgust, reaching up to claw at the carcass. Loudon had counted on that reaction.

He leaped forward, grabbing McLaren's wrists. The carcass fell away, leaving a bloody brown scum on the helmet, but McLaren could still see. He struggled to bend his wrists to bring the scalpel points into contact with Loudon's suit. With a heave, Loudon wrenched McLaren to him and brought his knee up viciously between McLaren's legs. Loudon hoped the thick suits and padded knees wouldn't reduce the impact. He felt McLaren sag slightly and heard a grunt. He immediately repeated the motion, slamming his knee up again and again.

"Drop the scalpels!" he shouted.

McLaren was determined, but the first blow had weakened him, and the subsequent ones bent him over and buckled his legs. But Loudon took no chances. As McLaren went down, Loudon's knee smashed into his stomach again and again, raising his body off the floor.

"Drop them!" Finally, the gloves opened, and the scalpels clattered to the concrete floor. Loudon backed up, dragging the groaning McLaren forward away from the scalpels and flinging him to the floor. His air hose followed him down. Loudon kneeled on his chest and reached down to yank the air hose out of McLaren's helmet. That would slow him down further.

Abruptly, a shower of liquid cascaded over his suit and onto the floor. Loudon twisted around to see Doc in a space suit, spraying both of them with disinfectant. Another CDC doctor was coming through the airlock. Doc motioned Loudon to stand up, and he did so, yanking McLaren up with him. Doc sprayed them both thoroughly and he began to inspect Loudon's suit for tears, while the other doctor examined McLaren's. Loudon held his breath as Doc ran his fingers over the suit, holding his faceplate close to Loudon's body. One pinhole and he was dead. McLaren sagged and Loudon jerked him up so the other doctor could do his inspection. Doc took one of Loudon's hands and turned it over in front of his faceplate, inspecting it minutely. Then he took the other and did the same. After what seemed like forever, he stood up and looked into Loudon's eyes.

He nodded and gave a thumbs-up, and Loudon blew a relieved breath that left a temporary fog on his faceplate. He unhitched his air hose and shoved an unresisting McLaren into the airlock, following him in. He could hear the man gasping, both because his air supply had been cut off and because he'd been kneed as brutally as Loudon knew how.

Once the airlock decontamination procedure completed itself, he pulled McLaren into the dressing room and they stripped off the suits. McLaren's eyes were rolled back in his sweat-soaked head in a near faint. The room was crowded with three more CDC researchers, two of whom took the suits for themselves. Loudon pulled his pistol out of the small airlock. Doc had taped a stick to the trigger. It was a good idea; too bad he hadn't had a chance to try it. Loudon shoved McLaren into a shower, removed the stick from the gun's trigger and held it on him as he groggily scrubbed down. An HRT agent had come into the staging room, and Loudon turned the wet, battered McLaren over to him. He showered and put his clothes back on.

"You'd better go back out front," said the HRT agent. "There's a situation."

Loudon hurried through the long corridors, past the biology labs where CDC doctors had settled in. He first heard the noise of machines and voices outside as he moved past the organic chemistry labs. The foyer was crowded with HRT agents, all standing at the ready. Walter stood at the door, peering out.

"The Army figured out we were here, and they sent a delegation," said Walter. Loudon walked out the door into the sunlight to be greeted by the roar of vehicles and the deep throaty rattle of helicopters circling overhead. The smell of diesel fumes mixed with the rising desert dust. He squinted against the light and put on his sunglasses.

The four APCs had been drawn into a tight defensive semicircle around the bunker entrance, with the knot of prisoners huddled in the middle. HRT agents crowded behind the APCs, guns pointed outward. Beyond was an invasion force.

Hundreds of troops ringed the warehouse, with more behind them arriving by truck and Chinook helicopter. Bradley fighting vehicles churned up a small dust storm as they careened into place, bringing their guns to bear.

A broad open space lay between the two forces. Loudon spotted Scalisi and Acree behind one of the APCs and made his way around the huddled prisoners to reach him.

"What's happening?" Loudon shouted.

"Well, the Army figured out why we borrowed their APCs," said Scalisi, leaning against the hot metal of the APC and watching the mass of troops form itself into position. "Probably tracked us. Maybe they even know this is their black ops base. Maybe they're even . . . faction,"

"In the bunker," came an amplified voice from one of the Bradleys. "Identify yourself, or we will open fire."

"So, what do you think, Charlie?" asked Scalisi. "Fight to the death?"

"I'd rather not," said Acree.

"Okay, then. My lead?" asked Scalisi.

"Sure, you're the SAC. We're just tourists here."

Scalisi reached over and picked up a bullhorn that had been placed on the APC for him. He clicked its trigger and raised it to his mouth.

"Hello, Army. We're FBI. We've just completed an operation on an illegal facility that appears to be military. We need to talk to your commanding officer. We're coming out." There was a long pause of a minute. The last of the army soldiers settled into position, leveling their weapons at the APCs. Atop the Bradley fighting vehicles, the soldiers threw the bolts on their machine guns and aimed. The HRT agents tensed.

"Very well, FBI," came the amplified answer. "Commander's landing now."

Scalisi, Acree, and Loudon moved into the open space and squinted into the sky as a Huey helicopter swooped in for a landing. Before it had even settled, a thin, wiry colonel leaped onto its skid, stepped onto the desert and stormed toward them. A platoon of troops and three officers hurried forward from the line to back him up. He had a gray brush haircut and a leathery hawklike face, and his garnet-red color marked him as a Denver resident. His color was perhaps made ruddier by his fuming anger. He thrust his face to within inches of Scalisi's.

"WHAT DO YOU THINK YOU'RE DOING HERE! I SHOULD HAVE JUST HAD YOU BLOWN TO LITTLE PIECES!" He almost rooster-danced with outrage.

"You had a problem, and we solved it for you, that's all," said Scalisi.

"I DIDN'T HAVE A PROBLEM! NO, YOU'VE GOT A PROBLEM!"

"You had a black ops Army biowarfare lab right in your city."

"Yeah, I know, and I didn't find out from you! I had to find out from Gaines up at AMRIID! Why didn't you have the good grace to tell me about it?"

"Because we didn't know who in your command we could trust," said Scalisi calmly. "These guys are rogue . . . a faction that's researching biowarfare agents. Maybe you were part of them. It's in your area. You might have alerted these people," Scalisi said, gesturing back at the prisoners.

"What ever made you think I might have been part of this?"

"Because you cheat at golf," said Scalisi instantly. Loudon and Acree both looked curiously at him. "He does," said Scalisi earnestly to them.

"You keep score, and that's beside the point!"

"Look, Phil, these guys . . . these Malfus guys . . . were masquerading all along. They were really part of a group that included . . . we don't really know who. But they were running a biowarfare lab. We had a woman maybe dying who needed that lab. We had to go in."

"Had to go in, did you?" shouted the colonel. He stomped off a few yards and paced back and forth in front of them for a long while, muttering darkly and occasionally glaring at them. He consulted his officers briefly, thought a moment and went back to Scalisi's face.

"This was a *joint* operation, right?"

Scalisi instantly caught his meaning and grinned. "Sure, Phil, sure. We planned it together all along."

"And we get the prisoners and all the evidence you have?"

"Sure, of course."

"And you pay for my next golf round?"

"All right."

"And you buy dinner for me and Alice. A nice dinner. And Sue, of course. I like her better than you."

"Well, okay."

"Well, then . . ." The colonel harrumphed and motioned to a lieutenant who stepped forward smartly. The colonel informed him of the joint operation and the prisoners, and the lieutenant looked puzzled, saluted and took a squad to appropriate the prisoners.

"Come to my office when you're done. We've got to get to the bottom of this." The colonel turned to leave.

"And we're still on for Sunday?"

"Yeah, yeah," said the colonel over his shoulder, climbing into his helicopter, whose blades raised a thick cloud of sunbaked dust before lifting the machine swiftly into the sky.

"He's like that on the golf course, too," said Scalisi.

They walked back through the line of APCs as the army squad herded the prisoners into trucks. Walter emerged from the bunker.

"We got a call from the front gate . . . or what's left of it," he said. "There's a CDC truck coming in." He pointed past the line of troops, now loading back into the trucks and helicopters. A white truck sped through the troops along the narrow road and threaded its way between two APCs. It came to a halt near the bunker and the back door swung open. Two CDC doctors stepped out and helped a third person in a

Racal suit down from the truck. Loudon could tell instantly that it was Shinohara. He sprinted toward her, taking her shoulder. He turned her around and saw a determined, tired face through the faceplate.

"What are you doing here?"

"I couldn't just stay there in that bed like some Camille. This is my life, and I wanted to know what was going on. Where's Doc? You get into the lab? What're the results?"

He showed her into the warehouse and through its featureless corridors past the offices and laboratories toward the BSL-4 lab. On the way, they passed a groaning McLaren being half-carried out.

"We had a discussion," explained Loudon.

They reached the BSL-4 lab and peered through its window. One of the space-suited CDC doctors was bent over the rack of samples that Shinohara had scooped up, while Doc and another doctor sorted through the vials the faction had left. She peered through the glass until she caught Doc's eye. He waved and came up next to the glass.

"You okay?" he shouted. The words were unintelligible through the suits and the glass and over the whine of the air pump on Shinohara's suit, but they could read his lips.

Shinohara nodded and shrugged. Doc motioned vigorously for her to wait outside. "I want to help!" she shouted, but Doc was insistent.

"You go wait!" he mouthed. Loudon took her arm and she reluctantly agreed. They made their way back through the lab to the front room and sat on a sofa. Loudon held her gloved hand. Walter wandered in and sat with them, as did Scalisi. Acree was out organizing his agents to return to their base.

"Anything on the killer?" asked Shinohara.

"Oh, yeah, I forgot," said Loudon. "I called Cleland before we came out here. Told him what happened with Lupo. Told him that I needed the file on the guy."

"And he said?" asked Walter.

"He said he'd try. I've got to find out who that guy is."

"Well, they traced John Dabney," said Shinohara. "They've got credit cards slips and bank accounts. He's been in Denver a long time. But there's nothing in California. No trace. And no lab space rentals under that name."

"He's probably got other names, other bank accounts," said Walter. "Clever little genius."

For an hour, they waited, discussing the case, with Shinohara sitting determinedly on the couch in the Racal suit. Abruptly Doc emerged, disheveled and distracted. They leaped up expectantly.

"We're working on it, Kathleen," he said waving her off. "You just stay out here." He opened a refrigerator in the office and scanned its contents. He gathered an armload of canned sodas and disappeared. They sat back down, puzzled at the behavior.

Loudon took the time to call Bowers, briefing him on the raid and its status. He also checked in with the local headquarters to find out whether Cleland had sent material on the killer. But it was busy work, meant to distract him from the analysis that was going on in the laboratories.

Finally, a tired-looking Doc emerged, flanked by two of the CDC doctors. Were they there to treat Shinohara? To help brace her against the bad news? Shinohara stood up awkwardly in the baggy suit, looking so very vulnerable, thought Loudon. Doc stood in front of her, a yellow sheet of paper in his hand.

"Take that thing off," he said, pointing to the helmet.

It took the briefest instant for them to realize the import of what he had said. When they did, they all whooped in delight, and in a few seconds, the helmet was off and Shinohara was breathing deeply, deliciously of the fresh air. Doc handed the sheet of paper to Loudon. "You read this; you got us in here."

Loudon studied the paper, then smiled broadly. "Well, says here they looked at the samples under an electron microscope. Nothing. Not a thing."

Shinohara looked at him expectantly. "Yes? Well, that isn't all."

"No," said Loudon. "They could've just missed the virus particles. So they did some antibody tests. The lab here had antibodies for all kinds of viruses. Didn't get any reactions. No virus; no bacteria, either."

"So? So?" demanded Shinohara impatiently.

"So, they decided to use the organic chemistry lab. It was an organic solution of some kind. Could've been a poison. So, they used gas chromatography, infrared spec . . . spec . . ."

"Spectrometry," corrected Shinohara.

"Yeah, and mass spec-whatever. Well, they did some comparisons with some known samples."

"We had a devil of a time," said Doc, smiling. "We found the comparison samples right here in the refrigerator."

"Will you two get to the point!"

"Coke," said Loudon. "He threw Coke on you."

"Coulda been Pepsi, though," cautioned Doc.

Shinohara threw back her head, her eyes closed, smiling in relief. She said nothing for a while. They all crowded around, hugging her.

But Doc made sure the respite was short-lived. There was work to be done.

"Look, this just means he didn't want to spoil his fun later," warned Doc. "He's out there. His lab's out there." His words brought them abruptly back to their task. They moved quickly out into the sunlight to the APCs to return to headquarters.

CHAPTER 34

"Y ou awake?" asked Loudon. He pounded on the door to Shinohara's tailer to wake her.

"My head finally feels clear. I don't think I could've even stood up much longer," he said. Shinohara made a sleepy hmph of agreement. "Come on in," she said.

He rummaged around for the makings of coffee and stood dimly for a moment, trying to sort out how to make it. He managed to find a pan, boil the water, and produce a dark, rich brew, adding cream from the refrigerator.

"Coffee," he said. Shinohara opened her eyes wide, as if the act would prop them open. A light brown arm extended unsteadily, the hand searching for the steaming cup and grasping it. She held it in both hands and took a sip. The sips of coffee began to bring him awake.

"Today . . ." said Loudon. "Today we're going to find him. We've got to."

Shinohara nodded sleepily and hmphed again.

"His lab is somewhere in Denver. Some . . . where." He took a sip of coffee. He recited the information they'd gathered so far. As he talked, Shinohara hmphed, nodded again, and sipped her coffee.

"Would it be like his lab at the company? About as big?" he asked. Shinohara shook her head.

"Then not big. Not like the one at the university?"

Again, Shinohara shook her head in puzzlement. They were still at a dead end. They sipped their coffee.

"You use this trailer on all your field trips? It yours?"

"No." Her voice was husky with sleep. She cleared her throat and repeated the word. "CDC has a whole bunch it uses."

"Brings them all in, then, when something happens?"

"Yes, for field emergencies. Sleep trailers, equipment trailers, lab trailers."

Loudon sipped his coffee. As the caffeine level rose in his brain, and his mind crystallized to wakefulness, two ideas came together, like two electrodes. They sparked. He jumped as if the spark had shocked him.

"Whoa! His lab!"

"What about it?"

"It's in a trailer! It's in a trailer! It's in a *big trailer*!"

Now Shinohara came awake. She knotted her brow. "Sure, of course! That's how he got it around!"

"Yeah, he could just get a trucking company to . . . *trucking company*! The ones in San Diego! We had it all wrong!"

"What wrong?"

"He wasn't shipping boxes from a company! He bought a trailer there! We've got to go see Walter. He knows those companies."

Loudon and Shinohara leaped from the trailer, they ran across the dry, grassy field to the isolated CDC headquarters warehouse, circled it, and sprinted down the road to the main warehouse headquarters of the FBI and other agencies. Loudon's legs twinged slightly, reminding him of their previous sprint down that road.

They found Walter beside the warehouse, his coat and tie off, with a golf club in his hand. He expertly chipped a ball out into the field beyond the warehouse, and absentmindedly scratched his belly as he watched it bounce to its resting place.

"Walter, his lab's in a trailer!" shouted Loudon. "It's in a trailer!"

Walter considered the news. He raised his jowls in a broad smile. "The little punk! Now, we've got him!"

"Call California."

"Yeah, I'll call the trucking companies."

"He bought it from them."

"Yeah, and I'll bet they hauled it for him, too!"

Walter hurried into the FBI headquarters, carrying his golf club, and they followed. Inside, White was at his desk conferring with several of his lieutenants. Walter sat down at a nearby desk, took out his notebook and began calling. Loudon told White his theory. Forgetting his pique, White waved his bony hands vigorously, sending the agents off to call real estate companies about rental spaces in downtown Denver that could harbor a trailer.

"Look for garages, small warehouses, anything like that. Understand? Understand?" he said to the scattering agents. "Oh," he said, turning to Loudon. "I forgot. Bureau messenger brought this." He went through a pile on his desk and handed Loudon a sealed manila envelope. Shinohara squeezed Loudon's arm in triumph and left for the CDC building to find Doc and organize a field team.

Loudon sat at an empty desk and opened the envelope, pulling out a file. The file was not thick, but as he studied it, its importance began to sink in. True, the evidence was extremely fragmentary. The cases described were a dozen or so seemingly unrelated deaths over a decade. They included a knifing, a garroting, a bullet from a high-powered rifle, an automobile accident, a cardiac arrest, and food poisoning. The incidents had been reported as random muggings, acts of deranged gunmen, natural deaths. They didn't seem connected. But a detailed report in the file tied all the deaths together, however tenuously. In each death, someone had an obvious motive. One person in each case had something very considerable to gain—presidency of a private corporation, victory in an election, inheritance of a fortune. But there was absolutely no shred of evidence linking that person to the crime.

The report was written by an anonymous, obsessed agent in the Bureau who had obviously spent countless weeks sifting through computer records searching for the subtle threads of evidence that linked one case to another. Each case involved considerable wealth, a California connection, and an especially expert use of weapons. In two cases, an autopsy found unexplained injection marks. In one case, a small dart was discovered at the scene. A dart, maybe like the ones that got the two cops, thought Loudon.

And when all the threads connecting the cases were woven together, like the threads in a tapestry, a picture seemed to form. It was vague, but it seemed to reveal a single person behind the murders. An adept, vicious killer. One who commanded many instruments of death. That was who the Aryan Committee had hired.

Loudon continued to pore over the file, grimly fascinated. His life might depend on knowing every detail. He was aware of Walter standing beside the desk holding his notebook. Walter was still grinning.

"File on the hit man?" Walter leaned over the desk, resting his hands on his golf club.

"Yeah. He's tough."

"Y'know, they still haven't found those cops' car. The ones he darted. He disabled the GPS, so he's out there with a police uniform and an untraceable car."

"Yeah, and maybe somebody in the department helping him. That's why he didn't kill the cops, you know. Didn't want to tick off an information source. What've you got?"

Walter added a raised eyebrow to his grin. "I got gold. A guy by the name of Ralph Fleming bought a used fifty-foot trailer from this San Diego outfit. Before Lupo started all this. They never saw him. He did it over the phone. I asked them why they didn't tell me. They said I didn't ask."

"And where's the trailer?"

"They moved it to an empty lot outside San Diego for the guy. Then a few weeks later, they moved it to LA . . . to a garage a mile from the hospital!"

"How about to Denver?"

"Not them. Maybe some other company. I called Bowers. He put some agents on it. They're going to trace the owner of the LA garage."

Loudon made a victory fist, slapped the folder shut and stood up.

"You update him on the whole thing?"

"Yeah, the guy is happy for once. He's going full speed on the warehouse."

"Well, we can do something at this end, too!" He found White on the other side of the warehouse and asked him to look for warehouse rentals by a Ralph Fleming. White immediately instructed the agents at the telephones.

"Let's get Kathleen and the CDC people and go downtown," said Loudon. "That's where this is going to break." He told White to reach him by radio with any information on the lab's location.

"Look, don't tell the Denver cops, okay?" he added. "I think one of them's dirty, maybe more." White agreed, and within thirty minutes, a caravan of cars and vans sped away from the headquarters and onto the freeway leading into the city. In the lead car, Loudon would periodically consult his radio. Doc and Shinohara rode in the rear van with the CDC doctors.

"Anything yet?" he would ask, receiving a negative reply. The caravan reached downtown and parked on Grant, beside the ornate, gold-domed state capitol. The group got out and stood beside the vehicles, drawing curious stares from a crowd of flesh-colored neut tourists and multi-hued Denverites. A Denver cop stopped to ask their business. Loudon showed him his credentials, but was careful to give him no more information.

After half an hour, a call came. A real estate agent had remembered the rental and found the record.

"A garage!" shouted Loudon down the line of cars and vans to Doc and Shinohara. "Down Bannock!" He slid into the lead car with Walter driving. They maneuvered through traffic, heading south to the site. "CDC, stay back until we figure out what's going on," he said into the radio. "I don't want a big invasion. I just want Walter and me going in. This guy is spooky. Maybe we can calm him down, get him to surrender."

Immediately, Shinohara's voice came back over the radio. "You need somebody in there who knows him, knows his lab. I'm going in."

"You sure?" asked Loudon. He wondered if she could take the stress; whether animosity toward Lupo would cloud her judgment.

"Yes, I'm sure," was the succinct radioed reply.

They reached the stretch of Bannock, a nondescript area of small businesses. Loudon instructed the rest of the convoy to stop a block before they reached the garage's address, and directed Walter to drive slowly through it. They passed an auto repair shop, a paint store, an upholstery shop, and a plumbing supply company. As the rising summer sun began to eat away at the shade on the street's east side, the shops were coming to life. A truck rumbled down the street, backing up to the paint store to unload a shipment. Two mechanics slouched against the cool wall of an auto repair shop having smokes. The activity made even more obvious the lack of activity in the anonymous-looking garage in the middle of the block. Its tall overhead steel door was shut tight.

Loudon noted that the door was large enough to take a tractor trailer. Beside the larger door was a battered gray steel entrance door, also shut tight. Walter pulled the car over to the curb across the street, and three other FBI cars cruised slowly past and circled the block to cover the rear of the garage. The last van eased up to let Shinohara out and continued on.

Loudon, Shinohara, and Walter stood on the east side of the street still in shadow, looking across to the sunlit entrance. Loudon raised his hand to launch the operation. FBI cars pulled across either end of the block, diverting traffic. Agents emerged from the cars to sprint down the street, flashing their credentials and warning the shopkeepers to close up. They persuaded the auto mechanics to crush their cigarettes on the sidewalk and move inside, shutting the overhead door and peering out its narrow slit window. A few pedestrians began to gather nearby—a homeless man, an old woman, a couple of workmen—and they were hustled away.

"You really sure about this? You okay?" Loudon asked Shinohara.

"Robert," she said reprovingly. The one word reminded him that it was her job. "I just went through this with Doc. I had to convince him that I could move faster than him."

Loudon nodded his head reluctantly, and the three of them ran across the street, Loudon and Walter drawing their pistols. FBI agents on either side crossed with them, guns drawn, staying well down the street.

They reached the building and flattened themselves against its front. Loudon took a quick look through the small, dirty window in the steel door and drew back. He nodded to Walter, indicating that there was no activity, then took a longer look. Sitting in the garage, taking up almost all its length, was a fifty-foot trailer. It was not new, its surface scarred and dented from years of use. It rested on its wheels and front brace. There was no truck in sight.

Loudon tried the door. It was locked. He waved down the street, and an agent hurried forward with a crowbar, thrust it into the door jamb, and with an efficiency borne of experience, popped the steel door open with a loud clank. The agent flattened himself against the wall as Loudon, Shinohara, and Walter ducked inside the garage.

The odor of decades of grease and oil permeated the darkened garage. Two service bays held hydraulic lifts and a random assortment of old tires and rusty car parts. The main doors to the trailer faced the rear of the garage, no doubt just as the trailer had been backed in when it had arrived.

Loudon held his pistol pointed upward and motioned for Shinohara and Walter to stay back. He made his way silently down the length of the trailer to the end, while Walter began to explore the rest of the garage. Loudon peered under the trailer, noting the power and water lines leading to it. But nobody was under the trailer, nobody on the other side. He peered around the back end. The trailer had the two usual large doors, but there was a long metal ramp leading down from them. He stepped quietly up the ramp and tried the latch on the door. It opened. Shinohara had moved to the trailer's rear, peering around the corner at him. He motioned her forward. She hurried around and up the ramp.

Loudon swung open the door, and they ducked inside. Before them, lit efficiently by fluorescent lights, lay a fully equipped genetic engineering laboratory. Loudon moved quickly past a littered desk, pausing curiously at an empty aquarium, and continued down the long lab bench to a large Plexiglass isolation chamber. The chamber's black rubber gloves protruded plumply into it, inflated by the negative pressure inside. Shinohara followed behind him, quickly inspecting the desk, the aquarium, and the neat lab bench, and peering into the isolation chamber.

Loudon moved to a door at the other end, threw it open and looked inside. He saw a small disheveled bed, and a plastic all-in-one bathroom cubicle, the kind found in motor homes. The room was empty.

"Please identify yourself." The stilted female voice startled both of them, and Loudon leveled his gun at the sound. The voice came from speakers beside a computer screen on the desk. He moved to the computer. Its screen showed a swirling DNA molecule.

"Please identify yourself, or I will begin a destruct sequence," said the young female voice again. It was familiar, but Loudon couldn't quite place it.

"This is Special Agent Robert Loudon."

"Loudon?" asked the computer. Loudon startled at the sound of his name from the computer, but Shinohara nodded for him to answer.

"Yes."

"I have a message for you."

The computer's voice changed from the female's to Lupo's. His face appeared on the screen, his expression madly intense.

"Mr. Loudon, this is Arthur Lupo. All the times you tried to kill me didn't work. You're too late. I've finished my work, and now everybody will know the consequences. Goodbye."

A large number twenty appeared on the screen, and the female voice returned. "Automatic destruct sequence initiated . . . twenty . . . nineteen . . . eighteen . . ." Large red numbers on the screen mirrored the countdown.

"He's going to blow the place up!" shouted Loudon. "Get out!" He kicked open the back door and grabbed Shinohara's hand, but she wriggled free.

"Seventeen . . . sixteen . . . fifteen . . ."

Shinohara leaped to the desk. "He might have left his notebooks!" She reached up and yanked open the cabinets to reveal a row of gray laboratory notebooks. She began grabbing them by twos and threes off the shelves, piling them onto one arm.

"C'MON!" shouted Loudon. Exasperated, he grabbed a pile of notebooks from her and moved toward the door, but she kept pulling more off.

"Fourteen . . . thirteen . . . twelve . . ." recited the computer voice.

"KATHLEEN!" he bellowed.

"Eleven . . . ten . . . nine . . ."

She finished, and they plunged out the door.

"Eight . . . seven . . . six . . ." They ran down the ramp. Shinohara dropped a notebook and bent to pick it up.

"WALTER!" shouted Loudon and Walter appeared from the depths of a repair bay. "BOMB!" Walter ran toward the side of the building, beckoning to them. Loudon figured he had found a closer side exit and followed, making sure Shinohara was with him. She ran awkwardly, hindered by the notebooks.

They reached a back door, and Walter burst through. They followed him into a garbage-strewn back alley, turning and running at full tilt away from the building. FBI agents stood up from behind a garbage dumpster ahead of them. Loudon shouted into his radio for all the agents to evacuate, and they, too, sprinted away down the alley.

They had run only thirty feet from the building when a massive thump shuddered the ground beneath them, followed instantly by an eruption of flame that blew the door off behind them, sending it with a massive clang against the opposite wall. A hammer-blow of a blast slammed Shinohara and Loudon to the ground, scattering the notebooks before them. Shinohara scrambled forward on her knees, and Loudon followed. Flames erupted toward them from the garage's shattered walls, like a blinding orange-red fluid, splattering against the building across the alley with a deep crackling sound.

As they ran down the narrow alley, Loudon saw that Shinohara's back and hair had begun to smolder. He slapped at the smoking cloth with his hands. She turned toward him, and an alarmed look rose on her face. She tore off his coat, throwing it away as it began to burn.

Finally, they made it far enough away from the flames to safely turn and look back. The building was engulfed by fire, its roof popping and crackling as the flames ate their way through it, curling toward the blue sky. A wall of thick smoke advanced toward them down the alley, enveloping them and penetrating their lungs with an acrid stench of burning oil.

Beside them, people emerged from the back door of an upholstery shop, saw the flaming building and ran.

"The notebooks!" said Shinohara. She stood for an instant thinking, then disappeared into the open door to the upholstery shop. She emerged with a large swath of dripping fabric draped over her head. She ran back toward the fire before Loudon could stop her, disappearing into the opaque swirl of black smoke.

Walter returned from up the alley.

"What the . . ." he asked.

"Notebooks!" shouted Loudon, entering the upholstery shop himself. He found a large piece of cloth and a bathroom where he ran water over it.

He came out, covered himself with the cloth and plunged into the smoke. He ran forward twenty feet, almost tripping over Shinohara, who was on her knees, coughing and gathering notebooks into her arms. The searing heat transformed the cloths covering them into steamy, smothering shrouds. He gathered the rest of the notebooks, and they staggered, retching, out of the swirling smoke toward the end of the alley. Behind them the garage roof collapsed with a roar.

They reached Walter and threw off the fabric, its surface scorched and steaming. Walter helped them to the street, where they dumped the notebooks into their car.

They leaned against the car, examining each other for injuries and coughing the smoke from their lungs. Shinohara had a few burns on her arms, and Loudon's shirt was sooty and scorched, but they were all right.

Across the street and well down from the fire, the crowd had grown larger. The workers and street people excitedly traded stories about the raid and the explosion. A plump lobster-red old woman stood quietly at the front of the crowd, watching the smoke roll out of the building, her face impassive. Incongruously, she carried a leather backpack. She turned and threaded her way back to the rear of the crowd and down the street into an alley. After several minutes, the roar of a motorcycle erupted from the alley, and the machine zoomed out onto the street carrying a round figure in jeans and a jacket, wearing a red helmet with a vicious gash in the side. The leather backpack was strapped on the motorcycle's carrier. The black motorcycle accelerated quickly away down the street.

From another side street, a siren whined to life and a Denver police car leaped forward, its tires smoking, its lights whirling, and fishtailed onto the street, giving chase.

CHAPTER 35

"Walter, something's wrong!" Loudon wiped the soot from his eyes with his sleeve and leaped into the front seat of the car, grabbing the microphone. "Hear that siren? What's a Denver police car doing here?" The police siren still whined in the distance, its sound rapidly receding.

"You think White alerted them?" Walter wedged into the front seat, starting the engine and revving it to a deep roar.

Oblivious to her burns and scorched clothes, Shinohara had crawled into the back seat and began sorting through the pile of a dozen gray notebooks, stacking them in chronological order. She chose the last and began to flip through it, scanning it quickly, her head bowed. She swept her mane of sooty hair back from her face, her brow furrowed, her eyes intent on the intricate hieroglyphics of technical jargon, abbreviations, diagrams, chemical formulas, graphs, photos, and drawings.

"That might be him!" Loudon flipped the radio to the Denver Police frequency. "DPD Central, this is Fed One. What've you got near Bannock? You got a car?" he asked.

"It's all here," mumbled Shinohara. "Everything. Everything he did."

The radio crackled with the police dispatcher's voice. The answer was negative. Loudon instructed the dispatcher to call in a helicopter, to locate the car.

Shinohara continued to pore over the notebooks. "He wrote summaries of each experiment. It's clear. I think here's where he started on the second virus. Here's where he put the modulation in . . . the coding sequences for the immune suppressor. . . But it's really hard to tell for sure." Shinohara flipped through the pages with rapt fascination, scanning them as quickly as she could.

A report came in from the police helicopter. The police car had been spotted. It was chasing a motorcycle. "That's him, Walter! Stick the bubble on, and let's go!" Loudon clicked his seat belt into place and drew his pistol. Simultaneously, Walter slapped the magnetized red light onto the car's roof, slammed the door and wrenched the car into gear.

"Incredible—" Shinohara started to say when the car plunged forward, throwing her back against the seat. She looked around absent-mindedly, her thoughts still on the notebook. "Where are we going?"

"The shooter," said Loudon over the siren Walter had switched on. "He's after Lupo. In a squad car. Put on your seat belt!"

Shinohara wrestled the seat belt around her body and chose the next notebook, studying it with even greater concentration.

Walter drove with a ferocity that surprised even Loudon. He roared past car after car, vaulting through intersections, tires squealing, swerving sharply and precisely from lane to lane. Loudon worked the radio, gleaning information from the helicopter about the path of the rogue squad car.

"Got him!" Walter finally shouted after five minutes, swerving expertly around a brown Honda and cresting a small hill. Ahead, they could see the flashing red lights of the squad car.

Loudon clicked on the radio. "Fed One to all units. We're in pursuit of DPD squad car. Instruct DPD to stay clear. This is ours. Suspect may be extremely dangerous. Do not apprehend, do not approach. Track and report."

• • •

Ahead, the Killer took aim with his left hand and fired twice at the motorcyclist as he steered the squad car with his right. Soon it would be over, he was sure. He felt the familiar thrill deep in his gut. Soon a large hole would blossom on the motorcyclist's back. The explosive bullet would burst into a deadly razor-sharp metallic flower and ricochet through the cyclist's body, shredding vital organs. A larger hole would mark the exit, and the motorcyclist would careen out of control, slide and tumble down the street, dead. Then his client would be happy. The Killer would be happy—as happy as a sociopath could be. The Businessman would appreciate the job completed, payment received.

But the motorcyclist zigged and zagged through traffic, crouching low on the machine. The Killer was annoyed. The motorcyclist was not like the bicyclist the Killer had targeted the year before, a straight-line rider who took only one bullet that ripped out his spine. Fortunately, the motorcyclist wasn't expert, and the machine was a small one, or the Killer would have lost it immediately. But the motorcyclist was good enough to stay ahead of the Killer, weaving among the downtown traffic, ducking behind cars and trucks and turning down an alley.

The Killer managed to follow, smashing garbage cans and boxes, as he pursued the motorcyclist. He considered turning off the siren and the lights. They were clearing his path, but they were also clearing the motorcyclist's.

They zoomed back onto a main street. He aimed and fired again and the errant bullet tore a thumb-sized hole in the trunk of a green Ford, just as the motorcyclist swerved out of the way. As the two vehicles roared along the street, the Killer caught blurry images of pedestrians diving for cover, some standing dumbstruck. His clip was empty. Still trying to maintain speed and manage the steering wheel, he ejected the clip and loaded another from a canvas bag beside him. He had lost ground, so he sped up, driving with both hands, the gun still in his left. His bag had plenty of ammunition, plenty of weapons, his folded business suit, some simple disguises. He had it all planned. Now, if he could only target one lethal slug of metal into the body of one fleeing target.

Ahead, the motorcyclist abruptly careened onto Route 70 heading east, and the Killer followed, accelerating to eighty miles an hour, then ninety. The motorcycle's lead was shrinking. The rider was cautious, and that caution would kill him. The Killer was almost within shooting range again, when the motorcyclist swerved off the freeway onto an exit ramp to Peña Boulevard.

The Killer exited, too, and he smiled his dead smile. It was a straight surface road, perfect for taking out a target. The cyclist was just ahead in a clear stretch of road, with no cars to duck behind. The Killer aimed.

But before he could shoot, he heard his siren joined by another, whining in dissonant unison, as they sped past rows of sunbaked shopping malls. He glanced in the rear-view mirror. A dark green car with a single whirling red light grew larger behind him. FBI!

He set his jaw and gripped his pistol harder. His client wouldn't be happy; there would be collateral damage.

• • •

In the green car, Loudon shouted, "Come on, Walt, get around it! Get around!" He rolled his window down, bringing the roar of the wind and the smell of hot engine exhaust swirling into the car. Walter yanked the steering wheel left and right, trying to overtake the squad car, which swerved wildly in front of them. Other cars swerved onto the shoulder to get out of the way. Walter leaned forward, seeming to urge the car on with his large body, trying to pull even with the squad car.

Finally, the squad car quit its wild gyrations and settled into the left lane of the boulevard, just as they took a right curve. Walter saw the chance and slammed down the accelerator, slowly, slowly, pulling nearer.

"I'm going to have to shoot across you!" Loudon aimed his pistol past Walter, who leaned back, his hands gripping the wheel hard, preparing himself for the explosions of gunfire.

Suddenly, the squad car decelerated, drawing even. Loudon aimed his gun, but before he could fire, from the shadows of the squad car's front seat emerged the barrel of a gun held by a red hand. For an instant, Loudon's vision riveted on the lethal hole in the end of the barrel. What followed seemed to happen in slow motion: Explosions erupting from the barrel, one after another. The gun kicking back but returning unerringly to its deadly aim. Silvery cracks spreading across their car's windshield as the first bullet struck. The terrible relentless blasts seeming never to end, the vicious chunking sounds of bullets impacting inside the car. On plastic? On flesh? Loudon could not tell. All in slow motion. Walter tearing the steering wheel to the right and throwing his body over Loudon. The car swerving, leaping skyward, slamming down, plunging forward, smashing against a building. The explosion of white fabric obscuring all vision, as the air bags blossomed then shrank. The tortured shriek of tearing metal and the glimmering splinter of shattering glass.

Then quiet, except for distant screaming of a frightened woman. Or maybe the siren of the squad car speeding into the distance.

Walter was a suffocating inert form on top of him. He almost dared not to move, to find that Walter was dead. But then the bearish body stirred ponderously.

"What!" it said.

"You okay?"

"Walter heaved himself upright, a droopy, dazed expression on his large face.

They pushed the limp air bags out of the way and looked at each other. No blood. Loudon twisted in his seat. He couldn't see Shinohara behind him. But he could see two large holes in the left rear window. His breath deserted him as if he had been punched in the stomach. He clawed frantically at his seat belt, managed to release it and slammed his shoulder against the car door, forcing it open. He rolled out of the car, shaking off hands that reached to help him.

He saw only one bullet hole in the right rear window. Only one bullet left the car! He yanked at the back car door, ripping a finger open on the twisted metal.

"Locked! Locked!" His fingers bleeding, Loudon yanked again with all the force he could muster. Walter reached to his left, and there was the click of unlocking doors. He pulled yet again and the door gave, creaked open on sprung hinges.

Shinohara's hair cascaded out, her face hidden beneath it. Her head lolled out of the car, and he caught it. He bent to cradle it in his hands, feeling wetness. Sticky wetness. He held up a hand and saw it was red. He gasped. He swept the mass of curls from her face. The eyes were closed, the face in repose. The beautiful face did not move. He put his fingers to the side of her neck. His own blood stained her neck.

"Oh, no. Oh, no. Oh . . ." He stopped, not even breathing. He felt the throbbing of life. A pulse. Then he felt more. His heightened sense of touch felt the vibration of a groan deep in her throat. She opened her mouth and breathed, the sweet warmth on his hand. She opened her eyes.

"What—?" She stopped, groggy, confused.

"He shot at us. We crashed." Loudon helped her up to a sitting position and unfastened her seat belt. He became aware of Walter standing behind him. Of Bureau cars screeching to a stop nearby. She groaned again and sat up, her expression blank, as if she had just awakened from a deep sleep.

"She okay?" asked Walter, but Shinohara answered for Loudon by nodding her head.

"Did you get hit?" asked Loudon.

Again, she nodded.

"Walter, get an ambulance, we—"

But Shinohara waved at him not to. She clumsily reached down, groping for something on the floorboard. Loudon craned forward. She came up with a stack of notebooks.

"I saw him. He shot at me. I held up the . . ."

She showed him the stack of notebooks. The first had a thumb-sized hole ripped in its cover. She peeled it from the second notebook beneath, torn pieces of the cardboard cover falling away to reveal a larger more jagged hole. She pulled away another notebook and another, each looking as if a grinder had been thrust through its center. Her lap became littered with shredded paper. The fifth notebook held a large chunk of viciously twisted metal. Loudon plucked it out and turned it over in his fingers. It was a PDXI, its grotesque razor-sharp claws spread open. When the bullet had slammed through the car window, it had opened, so that the deadly metal flower could be stopped by a mere five notebooks.

"The last notebook. I had one left." She looked at him with groggy triumph and lovingly patted the cover of the last notebook, its surface dented but unbroken.

"But the blood?"

"The bullet threw me against the door. I got a head knock." Her eyes focused, her face became more alert. "You okay? Where'd he go?"

"Toward the airport."

She pushed her way out of the car, standing and leaning on him for support. She rubbed her hands with her face. When the face reappeared, its expression was one of fierce determination.

"Then let's do it!"

Loudon knew better than to argue. He wrapped his bleeding fingers in a rag from the wrecked car, dug his pistol out of the front seat and signaled to a driver of one of the Bureau cars, who started his engine. The other agents opened the doors, standing aside. Walter fell into the front passenger seat, issuing instructions, and Loudon and Shinohara climbed into the back.

The car careened onto Peña Boulevard, its siren rising to a whining scream, its light flashing.

They immediately accelerated to high speed, dodging cars and barreling through intersections. After a few minutes, ahead of them rose the airport's towering tent-like roof. So that was Lupo's destination! The perfect site from which to launch an epidemic. Loudon peered intently out the window.

"There!" he said, pointing to one of the airport entrances. Walter spied the commotion and directed the driver to pull to the curb. A motorcycle lay on its side next to the entrance, where it had apparently jumped the curb and skidded to a halt. The squad car had also leaped the curb and smashed through the door, perhaps in an attempt to ram the fleeing rider. Its lights still whirled, its siren warbled deafeningly. A pedestrian lay on the ground nearby, baggage handlers crouched beside her. She moved and moaned and clutched her leg.

Loudon leaped out of the car and Shinohara followed. Other FBI cars arrived behind them, and the agents leaped out, guns drawn.

"Where?" demanded Loudon, and one of the baggage handlers pointed inside the building. Loudon, Shinohara and Walter climbed around the squad car and forced their way through the smashed door into the sprawling interior of the airport. The cavernous building rose above them, criss-crossed with girders supporting the many levels. Crowds of passengers streamed through the terminal, with many stopping to gawk at the motorcycle and the smashed police car.

An airport security guard pushed his way through the crowd, his gun drawn. Loudon pulled out his credential wallet and slipped it into his pocket, so the badge hung outside.

"There's a likely biohazard. Keep your people clear and shut down the exits. Where are they?" he asked the security guard.

"I think up the escalator."

They ran across the broad sun-brightened expanse of the main terminal and bounded up the escalator, shouting for the people on it to step aside. The other agents crowded behind, Walter in the lead. Their voices seemed to be swallowed up in the immense space. They reached the top. Nothing unusual. Loudon felt a sinking in his stomach. Had he lost them?

A faint scream and a quick succession of two gunshots echoed from the floor above, and a woman stumbled down the escalator from the upper floor. The terror on her face told them what they needed to know. She pointed up the escalator and managed to say, "A man with a gun!"

"Walter, clear this area," said Loudon. "Keep everybody down here. I mean everybody! But don't evacuate the airport. If we do, it might trigger Lupo. And with the virus airborne, it wouldn't make any difference, anyway."

Loudon and Shinohara stepped on the escalator, and allowed it to bear them upward. He crouched low and motioned for Shinohara to stay several steps behind him.

"What did you find out," he whispered as the escalator carried them upward.

"Maybe he had all the pieces," she said. "Maybe he developed an airborne virus with the tox-genes. But the last notebook is missing, and I just didn't have enough time to study them."

"But you can tell something?"

"Maybe. He wrote summaries."

They reached the top and crawled low off the escalator. They had reached an upper-level lounge area, where visitors could watch the planes take off, or stand at the balcony and look out over the expanse of the main terminal. Above them spread a latticework of metal struts that braced the soaring cable-tension roof. Behind them lay a small snack bar, with tables and a cafeteria-style serving counter.

A group cowered beneath overturned tables nearest them—a portly businessman clutching a briefcase for protection, a woman and her child, and three teen-aged girls. Loudon looked at them questioningly. One of the girls saw his badge and pointed urgently toward the serving counter.

Another gunshot exploded, and a third large hole joined two others in the stainless steel front of the counter. Loudon scrambled to the right and glimpsed a Denver cop aiming his pistol at the counter. His blood-red face and arms marked him as the assassin! The Killer crouched behind a table, waiting coolly for a sign of movement, his pistol aimed at the cafeteria counter. He chose a spot and fired another round, shattering the glass in the counter. He was attempting to flush somebody from behind the counter, almost certainly Lupo.

Loudon joined the businessman behind a table, and keeping his eye on the Killer, motioned for the people to leave. The Killer hadn't noticed him yet. One by one, the people followed suit, ducking past Shinohara to the down escalator. Loudon still didn't have a good shot at the Killer.

He leaped toward another table, and the Killer saw him. Glancing quickly back and forth between the counter and a running Loudon, he switched his pistol to his left hand and held his right arm directly toward Loudon. He leaped for the safety of the table, and just as he slammed into its back, he saw a faint puff of vapor erupt from the Killer's sleeve. A thump on the table told him that a dart had impacted just inches from his head.

He swung both arms over the table and leveled his pistol at the Killer, just ten feet away. The Killer's arm was still aimed at him, like some sorcerer waving an incantation.

"Try it again, and you're dead!" shouted Loudon.

The Killer ducked behind a steel table. Shinohara sprinted into place beside Loudon. The Killer's eyes darted coldly back and forth between Loudon and the counter.

"You thought you got us, didn't you?" asked Loudon tauntingly.

"We seem to have a quandary of sorts," said the Killer. His voice was emotionless, its sound seeming to fill the space between them with a cold resonance.

"Arthur, are you there?" asked Shinohara. "Is that you?"

A hand appeared above the counter. It held a flask containing a brownish liquid.

"Anybody shoots again, and I drop it. Everybody dies!" He flipped the flask, holding it by its long fragile neck. His head appeared above the counter, behind the shattered glass. The remains of his rubber disguise clung to his face. The makeup on his lobster-red face was smeared, with white blotches of skin showing beneath. His eyes were wild with fright and anger.

"That's it!" Shinohara grabbed Loudon's arm in warning, pointing at the flask. "That's it!"

CHAPTER 36

"You heard him," said Loudon to the Killer. "He drops that, we all die."

"Unless it's a soft drink," said the Killer sarcastically. "Then, it'll be just another mess for the janitors."

It took a moment for Loudon to realize it. The Killer apparently knew something he wasn't supposed to.

"What! How did you know about that?"

Lupo shifted his round body, holding the flask farther above his head, looking from Loudon to the Killer and back. He took care to stay behind the cash register so the Killer didn't have a clear shot at him. "Just leave!" he demanded. "Just leave, or I'll drop this!"

"*Is* it Coke?" asked Loudon, still baffled by the Killer's knowledge.

"No," said Lupo, a strange edge to his voice. Somehow, it was a convincing answer.

Shinohara moved forward, crouching behind an overturned table so she could see Lupo better. "Arthur, believe me, we're not trying to hurt you. We're trying to save you. Please!"

Lupo stared at Shinohara curiously. The little bow mouth pursed. He was considering something. Behind the black-plastic-rimmed glasses, his eyes hinted that he was making a decision.

"Arthur, please?" said Shinohara to Lupo again.

"You're afraid he'll drop a soft drink?" The Killer allowed himself another faint sarcastic smile, as he raised the gun slightly. He was looking for a shot.

"It's the virus," said Lupo simply. "It is." He nodded. Loudon had seen the nod before. It was the slow, unequivocal nod Lupo gave when he was expressing absolute certainty. Still holding the flask above his head, he moved down the counter and reached beneath it, probably into a bag or knapsack there, and held up a gray notebook. He stepped back to the cash register, reached around it and pitched the notebook over the counter toward Shinohara. It landed and slid with a hiss across the tile floor, coming to rest beside her. She picked it up and began to scrutinize the pages.

"Read the summary," said Lupo, ducking back behind the cash register. "Last three pages. It's all there."

Lupo and Loudon both watched her expectantly, Loudon taking his eyes off the Killer only for an instant to glance aside at the formulas and scientific notations inscribed precisely on the pages. After a moment, Shinohara had read the summary and was flipping quickly back through the pages to confirm that it reflected the experiments in the notebook. The Killer glanced at Shinohara, but was clearly concentrating on looking for a clear shot. But he still couldn't move in on Lupo without exposing himself to Loudon's fire.

Shinohara's brow knitted in concentration. She closed the book slowly and looked up at Lupo, a stoic expression on her face. They stared at each other for a long moment. Lupo peered owlishly through his glasses over the counter.

"It is," she said, still staring significantly at Lupo and pronouncing her words slowly and emphatically. "It's the virus. I know his notation now. It's got tox-genes for Ebola, untreatable H5N1 influenza, Dengue fever. It's airborne. It's deadly."

"Well, that really complicates things, doesn't it?" The sudden voice from behind Loudon made him whirl around and look up from his position behind the table.

It was White, standing behind him, a pistol in his hand.

"Lucas, how'd you get up here? What do you think you're doing!

Get down!" Loudon shot a glance back at the Killer, then at White, who looked totally out of character with a gun in his hand.

"Came up on the elevator." White motioned behind him. "Thought you'd like some help."

"Then get down!" Loudon turned back toward the Killer behind the table. But when he did, he felt the cold metal of a gun barrel pressed against the base of his skull. Shinohara gasped, but she could do nothing.

"No, you stand up."

"What? What are you—"

"I came to straighten some things out." White looked up and called across to the Killer, his Adam's apple bobbing nervously. "You the one they hired?"

"Yes," said the Killer standing up. He smiled his cold smile and turned his attention toward the counter and his target. Lupo had disappeared beneath it. But there was nowhere he could go without being seen. There would be plenty of time to carry out the assignment.

"The one *who* hired?" demanded Loudon. "White, what's this all about?"

"Pitch the gun away." As Loudon complied, White backed away to cover Shinohara as well. "You dimwit. Haven't you figured it out? You've been had."

"You're with him?"

"No, he's with me . . . us."

"You're with the faction."

"Bright boy. And who else would you guess? I'll give you a hint. Who got you into this whole thing?"

"Bowers?"

"Of course. He knew you would . . . cooperate . . . when we needed you to."

Loudon felt a chill like a ball of ice was growing in his stomach.

"But he works for the Aryan Committee." Loudon gestured at the Killer.

"That's what the police will think," said the Killer, popping the clip out of his pistol and replacing it with a fresh one. He stared at Loudon with dark, cold lizard eyes. "Especially when they anonymously receive the tape of me and my supposed client. But I don't work for them. It was a setup. I was recommended to him by an FBI plant . . . White's plant . . . on the Aryan Committee." His thin lips curled in a mirthless smile.

"Do I have to explain it all to you," said White, as if he were talking to a child. "Bowers was working with the Columbians. The faction found out. So, when Lupo went sour, they blackmailed Bowers, told him to put somebody on the case who would go along in the end. You."

"What on earth made you—"

"Because you did it before. You let Bowers alone after you linked him with the Columbians. Bowers knew you were . . . persuadable. So, now just walk away, both of you. Look, let's quit messing around here," said White. He lowered his voice to a whisper. "Bobby, you and the woman have two choices. You can go along, and there'll be one dead body up here. Or you can refuse and there'll be three. It'll be harder to explain, but I think this gentleman and I can work it out."

"What about that virus? It could kill everybody."

"We'll persuade him that we'll let him go," White whispered, glancing at the counter. Lupo was still nowhere to be seen. "He'll give us the virus, and we'll be better off than before."

Loudon concentrated on calculating which gun would kill him first if he leaped for White. Despite his words, the icy fear rolled up from his gut to envelop his body. He *was* going to walk away. He and Kathleen. They would leave this to White and the Killer. The Killer would stop Lupo. It would be his responsibility. That was his job. Why did he, Bobby Loudon, have to do it? He needed a drink for the first time in a month. He felt Shinohara move closer beside him. She said nothing, but the tension of her body told him what he needed to know. If he took her by the hand, if they walked away, he would abandon his job and his newly restored self respect.

White raised the gun. "Very well, then."

Suddenly a dozen faint pops erupted from behind the counter. Loudon started to glance toward it, but White's agonized scream brought him back. Splatters of bright blue liquid covered his face and dribbled down his chest. He screamed again and clawed at his face, reeling backward. Dozens of bright blue balls continued impacting him as he fell to the ground. Paintballs!

The rattle of pops continued, and Loudon heard another yelp from the direction of the Killer. Leaping forward, Loudon punched White square in the face, sending the man staggering. Red blood spurted from his nose, mixing with the blue paint. Loudon swung again, catching White on the side of the jaw, spinning him to the floor.

Explosions of gunfire sent Loudon and Shinohara for the cover of a table. Another succession of pops answered from the direction of the counter.

Loudon grabbed White's gun from the moaning man and scrambled back to the table, peering over it.

From behind the counter, Lupo coolly leveled a futuristic-looking, automatic large-bore pistol at the Killer, whose blood-red face was almost completely covered with blue. He staggered about in blind agony firing wildly in the direction of the counter. Blue splatters also began to appear on his uniform, as the rain of balls splattered against it.

Loudon turned to see Lupo dodging from one end of the counter to the other, his finger on the gun's trigger, sending dozens of spheres into the Killer's body. He ignored the bullet-struck bottles shattering around him, and the coffee urn behind him squirting brown liquid from bullet holes from the Killer's wild shooting.

"Arthur, what is that?" shouted Shinohara. "What are you doing?"

"Paintball gun . . . tournament-level Dye NT gun," said Lupo, pulling up a large plastic cylinder, flipping it open, and dumping a new load of paintballs into the gun's hopper. He launched one last burst of paintballs at the disoriented Killer, hitting him in the temple. The Killer swerved blindly toward the sound and aimed, but his pistol bore clicked open indicating the gun was empty. Loudon leaped toward him, slamming his pistol down across the Killer's skull, knocking him cold. He stood looking down at the dye-splattered Killer, whose eyes were clogged with the thin paint.

"Don't touch him," said Lupo, still aiming his paintball pistol at the Killer. "Wash your hands."

"Why?" asked Shinohara.

"Paint's got pepper juice in it." From behind the counter, a plastic water bottle lofted toward Loudon. "Paint's full of virus, too."

Loudon caught the plastic bottle and backed away from the Killer, opening the bottle and dousing his knuckles where he had struck White. The smell of antiseptic filled his nostrils. He washed White's gun for good measure.

"Arthur, you're not killing them, are you?" Shinohara moved slowly toward Lupo, gesturing at White and the Killer.

"Naw, it's just the gut virus. They swallowed it, they'll turn colors. But that's all. Made the paintballs after I got shot at."

Lupo moved from behind the counter, the paintball gun in one hand the flask in the other, toward the railing.

"You're not going to . . ." Shinohara moved with him. Loudon calculated whether he could shoot Lupo without breaking the flask. Instead, he decided to try persuasion.

"C'mon, Lupo, you don't want to kill everybody. Just give it up."

Lupo smiled that inscrutable smile.

"Nobody'll die," said Shinohara, her eyes riveted on Lupo. A faint smile rose on her lips, too.

"What do you mean?" Loudon shifted his eyes back and forth between Lupo and Shinohara.

"It's not deadly. I lied," said Lupo.

Loudon gave Shinohara a puzzled look.

"I lied, too, just now." She continued to look steadily at Lupo. "We both did it to fool them. Right, Arthur? So they wouldn't shoot at you. So you could save us."

Lupo nodded slowly.

"You knew he had the paintball gun?" asked Loudon.

"Well, I thought he had something up his sleeve. He's been too smart all along not to."

"Then what is it? What's in the flask?"

"Tell him," said Shinohara.

Lupo glanced at the flask, the brown liquid glimmering inside it. "It's got the same color genes. But it's airborne. That's what's new."

"This would spread worldwide, wouldn't it, Arthur?" Shinohara walked to the railing and looked over, staying far enough away from Lupo so he wouldn't be nervous. "It would infect the world."

"Yes. It would make us into a rainbow. It would be a rainbow virus.

And I just sent packages of it all over the world. They're rigged to release the virus when they're opened."

"And you lied earlier to scare everybody. To make them think you made deadly viruses."

"Yes."

Loudon glanced back at the Killer and White. They had not stirred. He turned his attention back to Lupo, holstering his pistol and staying well back from him. "Look, we'll settle this, we'll talk. You're doing this in memory of your mom, right? That's why you want to release that virus?" He had to keep Lupo talking.

Lupo took a deep, determined breath, a sorrowful expression on his face, and extended the flask out over the railing. Now if Loudon did anything, the flask was sure to fall and break. Lupo looked out at the flask in his pudgy red-smeared hand. He had never had to articulate his feelings before. He had just acted.

"Yes. Mom wouldn't want me to hurt people. But I had to do something."

"So you decided—" began Shinohara.

"I didn't decide then. I just knew I had to do something. There was something I had to do, whatever it was."

"And what about the faction?"

"Yeah, then they tried to recruit me. They wanted to make warfare agents. Even first-strike weapons. Controllable. To use against people. That made another reason. And there was another friend, my friend. You probably don't even know who he is. He died of AIDS. I knew it could've been stopped early. But you didn't pay enough attention." His voice was low, tired. "You could have stopped it. And you could stop the viruses that will come after AIDS."

"You're right," said Shinohara, her face grim. "The governments aren't paying attention. Just like AIDS, not to other viruses—"

"So, you think this will change everything?" said Loudon reproachfully, but measuring his words carefully. "You think by releasing this virus, by changing everybody in the world to different colors, you'll scare everybody into stopping germ warfare? You'll make everybody pay attention to the other viruses out there, the ones that could kill everybody?"

"Yes. All that," said Lupo.

"Arthur, you saved our lives," said Shinohara gently. "And we saved yours. If you just bring the flask in, everything will be fine. You've made your point. People will always remember what you did here. They'll think about biological warfare differently from now on. And if you just bring the flask in, they'll listen to you."

For a long moment, Lupo looked back and forth from the flask to Shinohara. He peered over the railing. On the concourse far below, people craned their necks upward from the safety of cover. Police dashed across the broad expanse of the terminal.

"They'll listen?"

"Yes," said Loudon, extending his palms and moving up beside Shinohara. "They'll know you were just trying to protect yourself from people who were trying to kill you."

"Will I go to jail?"

"Probably."

"What for?"

"I don't know. Maybe for practicing cosmetology without a license. But you'll testify against the faction. And they'll listen. They won't listen if you do this."

"Arthur, please?" At Shinohara's plea, Lupo sighed. His hand drooped slightly. He slowly brought the flask in and held it with both hands. They all stood for a moment looking at each other in relief. Loudon heard a pitiful moan from White's direction.

"Good," said Loudon. "Tell you what. You go down the escalator with that, you'll see a big guy down there. Name's Walter. Tell him everything's okay. Surrender to him in front of everybody. Give him the flask and give him all the information on those packages of virus you sent out. And tell him we've got another couple of presents for him up here."

"And tell him to call Doc to bring in a decontamination team," said Shinohara.

"I need a Coke," said Lupo.

"He'll get you a Coke." Loudon felt odd talking to Lupo like he was a child, the brilliant scientist who had stunned the world.

Lupo nodded his head and started off.

"Oh, yeah, can I ask you one question?"

"Sure."

"The aquarium in your lab. Was there a lobster in there?"

"Yeah."

"What happened to him?"

"Gave him to an aquarium shop. They said they'd take care of him. That's where I'd gone when you went into my lab."

"So, if it hadn't been for that lobster, we'd have gotten you then?"

"He was a nice lobster." The round little man curled his bow mouth into a smile, set the paintball gun on a table and walked away with the flask, stepping on the escalator and sinking from sight.

Loudon glanced over at the Killer, who had also begun to stir, groaning and pawing pitifully at his face. He stepped over and efficiently handcuffed the man, and did the same with White using White's own handcuffs, then rinsed his hands thoroughly in the antiseptic. He returned to Shinohara.

They put their arms around one another, and he smelled the smoki-ness in her hair. He stroked it gently.

"How's your head?" he asked.

"Woozy. I could use a rest." She rubbed his back and hugged him tightly.

They righted two chairs and sat tiredly together, amidst the bullet-riddled ruin of the snack bar and the bright sunlight filtering through the fabric ceiling, and the distant noise of travelers returning to their business, and aircraft roaring into the sky.

"If that flask had broken, if those packages had been opened, we'd all have turned colors?"

"Sure. Within six months the whole world would have been colored. Arthur did his work brilliantly." She examined his shirt, which was sooty and torn, and attempted to dust it off.

"What if we clashed? What if our colors didn't go together?" He looked into her eyes.

"Why would you have cared?" She gave him a wry look, a touch of sarcasm in her voice.

"Well . . . we'd have looked kind of strange at the wedding."

"Oh?" Then she realized what he had said. "Oh!" Shinohara

smiled broadly, showing the little gap in her teeth. He really loved that little gap.

Read on for an exciting sneak preview
of Dennis Meredith's new science fiction novel,
Wormholes.

Visit *www.DennisMeredith.com*
for more information

CHAPTER 1

"Ed? *Ed?*" The husband opened his eyes and squinted up at his wife. "We're going to the store," she announced. She stood over him with the sun at her back, her curly hair highlighted like a frizzy halo, so he couldn't fathom the expression on her shadowed face. The commanding edge in her voice, however, told him what was coming next. "Now you remember the barbecue's tomorrow, so if you don't mow the lawn today it won't get done in time for all the grass to dry—"

"Okay, sweetie."

"—and I don't want everybody tramping wet grass through the house."

"Absolutely, dear." He strove to prove his commitment by making a dramatic effort to rise from the chaise, achieving a sitting position on its side. The cool breeze swirling beneath the trees felt good on his face. He looked beyond her out into the large sunny lawn where it was hot. The lawnmower still sat there in red grass-stained patience where he had trundled it earlier that morning.

"Okay, then," she said with the curt exasperation of a woman at the

1

top of her daily energy curve, whose husband was indolently wallowing around at the bottom of his.

A soft, small form barreled lovingly into him, wrapping its arms around his neck, and he laughed and fell back onto the chaise. The little girl sat up imperiously on his chest, her sweet big dark eyes staring seriously into his.

"Daddy, you got to mow the lawn. Mommy says."

He laughed again and looked up at his wife, still silhouetted against the sun.

"*My* daughter," she declared with mock haughtiness. He couldn't see her face, but he knew she was smiling with womanly triumph at their daughter's sassiness. She gathered the giggling girl into her arms, kissing her loudly on the neck and padded off through the tall grass to corral her older brother from the yard next door.

Ed resumed his prone position, hearing the garage door open with a whine. There was a pause. He tensed slightly. The car started and backed out, the door rattled shut, and the sound of the car faded. Home free! After a few vague plans wafted through his heat-soaked brain, one cool image crystallized itself. A *beer*.

He heaved himself to a standing position, felt around in the grass with one foot to find his comfortably ratty deck shoes, slipping his feet in, and letting a full-fledged plan slowly accrete around the concept of a beer, like a pearl around a grain of sand. It was near noon. Hottest part of the day. She'd be back in an hour, maybe two. The sun would have begun to go down beyond the tall oaks in the Matthews' back yard. He would have plenty of time for a leisurely beer or three. Then maybe a nap.

He went into the quiet house, pulled a cold can of Coors from the refrigerator and relished the fizzy whoosh when he opened it. He took a healthy sip of the cold malty liquid to help him face the return trip. He shuffled back outside and cagily estimated where the shade of his own more modest stand of trees would be in an hour. He moved the chaise to ensure that he would be safely situated in shade the entire period of her absence. He kicked off his shoes and curled his toes in the lush grass, congratulating himself for having fertilized it well that spring. Finally, he eased himself back down onto the creaking chaise, felt around on

2

the grass beside him for the *Sports Illustrated* and placed it on his chest, closing his eyes.

Enough activity for a while. He lay there trying for perfect, blissful immobility, save for an occasional smooth move of his arm, raising the beer to his lips.

Zen, he thought as the cold liquid tingled his mouth and washed down his throat. Perfect Coors Zen. He blanked his mind. He would send all the bad stuff into Coors Zenland. He sent away into Zenland that memo from his boss about excess inventory. Away went the big mistake that Shipping made Friday on the Baker order. Away went the business trip to St. Louis next week. His mind thus cleared, he made significant progress on the beer and hazily considered getting another. But the breeze played over his body and he began to doze.

In his dim torpor, at first he thought the annoying sound was the guy down the street starting up his chainsaw. The noise was kind of a chainsaw sound, but deeper, with more . . . rumbling. He sleepily lifted his head as the sound grew louder and cocked his ears one way then the other, the better to pinpoint the direction. The muffled sound originated toward the yard. A lawnmower? Nope, his Lawn Boy stood silent.

With a gut-rumbling roar, the sound erupted into the open, sending him leaping with a loud startled curse off the chaise. He glimpsed a movement out of the corner of his eye, turning to see one of the big trees in the Matthews' yard—one of the really big ones—jerk over violently at an angle. Its massive branches quivered as if being shaken by an unseen giant hand, and it slumped several feet into the ground. The grinding, sucking noise rose to a deafening level, like being thrust inside a jet engine.

Unthinkingly curious, he took a few steps toward the massive, shuddering tree—the worst mistake of his life. The tree sucked down into the earth like a celery stalk chewed away into an unseen hungry mouth. For an instant, the vibrating tips of the topmost branches slashed back and forth before disappearing. The earth around the vanished tree began to collapse away, opening a great spreading maw of a crack. The smooth green fabric of the lawn slumped and tore, falling away in tattered chunks. The widening gorge revealed the hidden earth beneath, like a deep slash in the skin exposes raw flesh. The gaping hole ripped its way up to the red lawnmower sitting in the grass like innocent prey, and the lawnmower too was sucked away. The devouring of the machine produced a brief shriek of tearing metal above the subterranean roar.

With a chest-clutching horror he had never known, he realized that the rift was eating its way toward *him* at the speed of a running man, so he became one. He turned and hurdled the chaise, sprinting barefoot toward his house and, he hoped, safety. He leaped onto the back deck and glanced over his shoulder to see the gorge yawning into a great dark malignant cavity, widening to devour his yard and part of the neighbor's. Panting with fear, he slammed the door open and backed through the kitchen, watching through the screen the crater's hellish approach. Jesus, dear Jesus, it seemed like some predator coming for him!

The phone! He yanked the receiver from its cradle, checked for the dial tone and punched in 911. He gathered his wits, took a deep breath, prepared his speech. But it rang only once, then went dead.

A crunching, grinding roar enveloped him, a sound of pulverizing concrete mixed with the explosive crack of snapping foundation timbers, and his whole house dropped with a massive thud, tilting toward the inexorably approaching, invisible monster. The abrupt slanting of the floor made him slip and fall, and he scrambled desperately up its treacherous slickness toward the dining room.

"OH! OH HELP ME!" he screamed, grabbing the door jamb and hauling himself through the doorway. The oak china hutch tilted and crashed to the floor with the lethal tinkle of shattering glass. It slammed into him with a ponderous inanimate determination, smashing one hand on the jamb, crushing the bones like matchsticks. He screamed in agony, desperately tore the shredded bleeding hand from the trap, and clawed his way over the top of the hutch, cowering behind its bulk. The kitchen imploded with tortured sounds of tearing metal, splintering wood and cracking ceramic tiles, all ripped away into a darkness he could not fathom. Sobbing with gut-wrenching fear, cowering on the floor, he felt the house shake to its very foundation in its death throes. He heard the snakelike hiss of a ruptured gas pipe and smelled the sickening stench of natural gas filling the house and his lungs.

He screamed a final scream as the dining room walls collapsed over him, as moist earth smothered him in darkness.

4

• • •

Firemen, rescue workers, policemen, reporters, TV crews, and neighbors crowded around the crater . . . or sinkhole . . . or earthquake fault . . . or whatever it was. They stood and speculated, still trying to figure out the frightening chasm that had devoured a chunk of quiet residential neighborhood, an entire house, and a man some of them knew. Taking care to stay behind the yellow police tape and away from the edge, they stretched and peered down into the gaping pit as if intense scrutiny would compel the hole to give up its secrets. The crater slashed seventy-five yards through the well-tended suburban lawns. Because the low sun shone palely through the trees, its depths remained hidden in shadow, making it even more ominous. Only the periodic flash of camera strobes or the glare of video lights lit the hole. Everybody, it seemed, was taking pictures. The Internet was already rich with video and images of the pit.

An occasional car horn blast, a revved motorcycle, and other street sounds reached the crowd, but the unfathomable hole in their neighborhood, and their lives, riveted their attention. All day long their numbers had grown, attracted by television news reports. The police assertively held the crowd well back, except for the neighbors who lived nearby and asserted their property rights to examine the hole.

The rescue chief stood solidly scowling into its depths, his large tanned arms folded over a pronounced stomach. It wasn't the hole that had provoked his anger. The hole was a freak of nature to be dealt with. And it wasn't the crowds. From beneath his battered, yellow hardhat, he glowered at the idle equipment and people poised to mount a rescue effort. A full complement of ladders, ropes, climbing gear, stretchers, emergency technicians . . . all just waiting. The fire chief had ordered him to hold.

An insistent growing sound of honking made him turn away from the hole to see a battered Range Rover jump the curb, bull its way through a line of policemen and speed across the front lawn stopping smack up against the police tape.

A young woman leaped out and ducked lithely beneath the tape. She ignored the shouts of the cops, striding briskly toward the hole. She peered down into its blackness from beneath the bill of a baseball cap. Her light brown ponytail jutted impertinently out the back hole of the hat, above the adjustment strap. She wore a sleeveless work shirt, slightly baggy khaki shorts and sturdy hiking boots with rumpled white socks. She stood with her hands on her hips, her feet apart, her sturdy tanned legs braced.

The rescue chief strode toward her, a freshened anger raising the veins in his neck. But he reined himself in at the last instant, remembering the public relations class he'd had to take.

"Honey, what do you think you're doing? You just get on back there. You might fall in. I'm the rescue chief here, and—"

"What's the situation?" She turned to the scowling middle-aged man, her gaze intent from beneath the cap bill. He took note of the attractive, oval, apple-cheeked face, the full lips, the slightly bent nose and the light blue-gray eyes. She was certainly an athletically attractive young woman, but he had other things to deal with.

"Look, honey, I'm going to have the cops take you out of here."

"I asked what's the situation?"

"The situation is, honey, that my boss says we got to wait for some geologist from the university to tell us it's stable and we can go down and start a rescue operation. That's what the situation is. Now get on back."

"I'm the 'geologist,' chief."

The rescue chief blinked. He decided to hide his embarrassment with bluster. "Fine . . . well, honey—"

"And my name's not honey. Dacey Livingstone. Now, tell me what's known."